What Readers are Saying

Donna Keel Armer has written a colorfully crafted page turner that illustrates, in chilling fashion, how loyalty, devotion and naiveté can quickly propel us into the vortex of our friends' misfortunes and tragedies. Love isn't just blind. It's often deaf to the inner voice that warns us to proceed with caution.

~ Joe Palmer, Author, *A Mariner's Tale*

Born on the same day, two women forge a life-long friendship. When Cat gets Stella's desperate phone call asking for help, she doesn't hesitate to get on a plane from the Low Country of South Carolina to the Italian village of Castello del Mare. When she arrives and learns Stella is missing, she finds herself caught in a web of treachery, danger, and deceit. Can she decipher the clues Stella left her? Is there anyone she can trust? The Red Starfish is a gripping and suspenseful tale that will keep you guessing right to the end. Donna Keel Armer has crafted a superb mystery–and if you've been to Italy, you'll delight in the descriptions of the food and the countryside. If you've never been, you'll long to go.

~ Sally Handley, author of the *Holly & Ivy* cozy mystery series.

Donna Keel Armer's debut novel deserves praise. The author takes us on a journey from South Carolina to Puglia, a charming southern Italian region, following personal chef/caterer Cat Gabbiano. But what looked in the beginning as a long overdue reunion with her best friend Stella, a model/actress now living permanently in Italy, turns Cat into the role of investigator of Stella's mysterious disappearance. Armer skillfully weaves the charms and flaws of a place rich in natural beauty and history but also plagued by corruption and risky deals with the journey of transformation that a reluctant Cat finally embraces since love, at the end of the day, is stronger than fear. A powerful tribute to women's friendship.

~ Gloria Mattioni, award-winning author of *California Sister*

In The Red Starfish, Donna Keel Armer immediately sweeps her readers into the secret and dangerous undercurrents of a seaside town in Italy. I couldn't put it down. In caterer-turned-sleuth, Cat Gabbiano, Armer has created a strong hero who is as stubborn as she is resilient, as wary of the past as she is hopeful for the future. At the heart of this mystery lies the complicated friendship between Cat and her lifelong friend, Stella. Armer's storytelling is a testament to trust, loyalty, and heart-stopping suspense. As she did in her first book, the memoir Solo In Solento, Armer treats her readers to her love of place—and of food. Since Cat, like the author, loves to cook, no character in this book—despite the intrigue and imminent danger that surrounds them—is ever far from a good glass of wine and a lovingly prepared spread in all its tantalizing particulars. Donna Keel Armer has created a page-turner as intricate and as captivating as the starfish itself.

~ Karen Warner Schueler, author of *The Sudden Caregiver: A Roadmap for Resilient Caregiving* and president of the coaching firm, Tangible Group

In The Red Starfish, author Donna Keel Armer weaves a spellbinding tale of murder, intrigue, and revenge using the glorious Italian countryside as a backdrop for this exciting mystery. I can't wait for the sequel.

~Dana Ridenour, author of the award-winning *Lexie Montgomery FBI* series.

Cat Gabbiano's bond with her glamorous movie star friend Stella is literally lifelong, beginning with their shared birthday. Stella's sudden disappearance prompts Cat to travel from her home in the South Carolina Lowcountry to the Adriatic coast of Southern Italy, where she must become an amateur but nonetheless capable sleuth as she crosses the threshold into a world of unknown dangers, long-held secrets, and powerful machinations which test the bounds of her loyalty, courage, and tenacity. Donna Keel Armer's beautifully written debut novel is also a sensual immersion into Italian cultural and culinary life, truly a page-turner of an international mystery certain to appeal to those who adore tales of travel, friendship, and adventure. A gifted storyteller in all aspects of her life, Armer has already established herself as an exceptional author of travelogue and memoir; now she has proven herself to be an adroit and crafty novelist as well. In Cat Gabbiano, Armer has given us a resolute and empathetic new heroine whose further exploits I already look forward to with eager anticipation.

~Jonathan Haupt, coeditor of *Our Prince of Scribes: Writers Remember Pat Conroy*

In The Red Starfish, author Donna Keel Armer weaves a spellbinding tale of murder, intrigue, and revenge using the glorious Italian countryside as a backdrop for this exciting mystery. I can't wait for the sequel.

~Dana Ridenour, author of the award-winning *Lexie Montgomery FBI* series.

Cat Gabbiano's bond with her glamorous movie star friend Stella is literally lifelong, beginning with their shared birthday. Stella's sudden disappearance prompts Cat to travel from her home in the South Carolina Lowcountry to the Adriatic coast of Southern Italy, where she must become an amateur but nonetheless capable sleuth as she crosses the threshold into a world of unknown dangers, long-held secrets, and powerful machinations which test the bounds of her loyalty, courage, and tenacity. Donna Keel Armer's beautifully written debut novel is also a sensual immersion into Italian cultural and culinary life, truly a page-turner of an international mystery certain to appeal to those who adore tales of travel, friendship, and adventure. A gifted storyteller in all aspects of her life, Armer has already established herself as an exceptional author of travelogue and memoir; now she has proven herself to be an adroit and crafty novelist as well. In Cat Gabbiano, Armer has given us a resolute and empathetic new heroine whose further exploits I already look forward to with eager anticipation.

~Jonathan Haupt, coeditor of *Our Prince of Scribes: Writers Remember Pat Conroy*

THE RED STARFISH

CAT GABBIANO MYSTERY SERIES

BOOK 1

DONNA KEEL ARMER

Red Penguin Books

Bellerose Village, New York

ISBN

Print 978-1-63777-463-2, 978-1-63777-464-9.

Digital 978-1-63777-465-6

This is a work of fiction. Unless otherwise indicated, all the names, characters, businesses, places, events and incidents in this book are either the product of the author's imagination or used in a fictitious manner. Any resemblance to actual persons, living or dead, or actual events is purely coincidental.

to
Forever Friends
&
Sempre Ray

One BEAUTIFUL day our paths crossed
You reached across the void
with love and grace
and
welcomed me into your world

Contents

Chapter 1 1
Chapter 2 5
Chapter 3 8
Chapter 4 16
Chapter 5 24
Chapter 6 31
Chapter 7 37
Chapter 8 46
Chapter 9 53
Chapter 10 56
Chapter 11 63
Chapter 12 67
Chapter 13 72
Chapter 14 77
Chapter 15 84
Chapter 16 92
Chapter 17 97
Chapter 18 105
Chapter 19 112
Chapter 20 116
Chapter 21 122
Chapter 22 127
Chapter 23 131
Chapter 24 136
Chapter 25 140
Chapter 26 142
Chapter 27 148
Chapter 28 157
Chapter 29 163
Chapter 30 169
Chapter 31 172
Chapter 32 176
Chapter 33 187

Chapter 34 192
Chapter 35 199
Chapter 36 203
Chapter 37 208
Chapter 38 213
Chapter 39 219
Chapter 40 223
Chapter 41 232
Chapter 42 236
Chapter 43 244
Chapter 44 253
Chapter 45 256
Chapter 46 261
Chapter 47 264
Chapter 48 273
Chapter 49 280
Chapter 50 285
Chapter 51 289
Chapter 52 295
Chapter 53 299
Chapter 54 302
Chapter 55 308
Chapter 56 312
Chapter 57 316
Chapter 58 320
Chapter 59 324
Chapter 60 328
Chapter 61 333
Chapter 62 339
Chapter 63 342
Chapter 64 347
Chapter 65 349
Chapter 66 352
Chapter 67 355
Chapter 68 359
Chapter 69 366
Chapter 70 370

Author Notes	377
Acknowledgments	379
About the Author	383

We are nothing but starfish, abandoned on the beach,
waiting for the sun to rise, hoping, praying
that someone might pick us up and throw us back
into the waves where we can survive another day
Robert Steiginga —Tossing Starfish

CAT

ROME, ITALY

My skin is loosely knitted flesh full of imperfections. I ask myself what one thing would allow me to fit back into my skin, to become me? Thirty-seven years I've floundered in a body that doesn't recognize me.

It started the day I was born next to Stella. I grew up in her shadow—the shadow of perfection. From the beginning, my mother compared us and asked only one question, *why can't you be like Stella?*

As an only child, I forced myself into Stella's mold and into my mother's expectation of the person she wanted me to be, but I failed. All of my life I tried—through school, then college, my career, and even into my marriage. The angst of not living up to everyone else's idea of who I should be ate away at my flesh, loosening the skin from the bone. The truth is I'm in the process of unraveling but I'm not sure what to do about it.

The plane shimmies. I grab for the miniature sink next to the toilet to stay upright. I refuse to sit on the urine splattered seat. The distorted mirror discloses swollen eyes, smeared mascara, and out-of-control hair. I shift my feet in the wet, sticky mess on the floor.

Clearly a puddle of pee, thanks to those who visited this smelly hell hole before me—mostly men, who are good at missing the mark.

I hate planes, I hate flying, I hate being cramped into a tiny less-than-human space for endless hours next to a seat mate who snores Beethoven's 5th. But here I am.

An urgent rattling of the door handle motivates me to flush. I wash my hands using a paper towel on the faucet. I look in the mirror. Fear is written there. All I want is to be on the ground and on my way. Stella's face flashes into my thoughts. Will she be at the airport to meet me? The best possible answer is yes. If not, will she send her limo driver to pick me up? That would give me a chance to sleep on the drive to Castello del Mare instead of listening to Stella talk about *Stella*.

The rattling of the door handle escalates. It's accompanied by a forceful knock and a snarly voice, "Hey, other people need to use the john. Hurry it up!"

I open the door to a leer, whiskey breath, and a belly that protrudes into my space. There's no room to squeeze past him without our bodies touching. Taking a deep breath, I plunge into the aisle and push with my elbows until his body shifts enough for me to retreat.

I flop into my seat as the seatbelt sign flashes, not that it was ever turned off during the entire nightmarish loop-de-loop flight across the Atlantic. Although I refused the processed pre-packaged food and only sipped water, my stomach still pitched. The night played out in slow motion while I gazed at the dead blackness outside the window.

As the dense darkness dragged on, my mind never shut down. The images played and replayed—Stella swinging from a noose, or lying in a spreading puddle of blood, or sinking to the bottom of the Adriatic Sea, her body tossing in endless rotation.

Now with gray light on the horizon, I stare out the window and wait, counting the seconds until the sunlight bursts over the Alps.

Stella and I have been friends forever. She's the reason I'm on this plane. According to her ex, she's disappeared. Part of me thinks this is just another dramatic episode in her life. One that is sure to attract media attention, and goodness knows Stella thrives on the publicity. She's notorious for pulling stunts that manage to get her face splashed in the tabloids. And yet, there's a tingle up my spine that smacks of sinister—*a sinistra*—the left hand of evil.

Chapter sixteen in Andrea Camilleri's latest Inspector Montalbano novel, *A Voice in the Night,* must have prompted the grisly scenes in the book to tip over into my nightmarish thoughts of Stella's demise. My warped imagination always shifts to the dark side.

As the cabin crew make their last walk thru, I speed read to the end of the page and tuck the e-reader into my purse. The announcement to turn off and store all laptops and electronic devices is made. The landing gear deploys with a thud.

On this cool, overcast morning in January, the plane bounces on the tarmac at Fiumicino Airport. The world outside the window paints a landscape of gloom and despair. There are no sun-filled skies or riots of flowers to welcome me after the exhausting trans-Atlantic flight.

Pushing through the crowded terminal, I race to catch my flight to Brindisi. Sweat gathers in my armpits as I skid to a stop at the gate with only minutes to spare.

Why am I doing this? Why don't I stay in Rome? Just for one night. I could relax over a meal at Mamma's—my favorite trattoria hidden away in a side street of Prati. I could shop in the market for truffles. Stella loves them shaved over pasta swirled in butter. She'd be thrilled if I arrived bearing such a heavenly gift.

But each time I listen to the message Stella left on my cell, gruesome images of her demise force me to keep going. There's no time to stop in Rome. Waking and sleeping, her face contorts in a painful grimace with mascara-ladened tears flowing down her cheeks. In the ghoulish scenes, she whispers frantically. I can't understand her. Just as I can't understand the incoherent message she left on my phone. Calling and texting repeatedly brings zero results. After twenty-four hours without hearing from her, I called Antonio, her estranged husband. That conversation propelled me to drop my life into a zip lock bag and catch the next flight to Rome.

It was Antonio's lackadaisical conversation regarding Stella's disappearance that indicated there's a lot more wrong than just Stella missing. He insisted I wait until there was more information before I hopped on a plane. That really unnerved me.

What does only missing mean?

He was adamant she would return before our planned reunion, which is still several weeks away. But his words were contrived. The only thing that will put my fears to rest is to see her radiant face.

Crap, it had been such a hassle to change my plans, but three weeks seemed far too long to wait. If Stella knew I needed help, she'd drop what she was doing and fly halfway around the world for me.

The crowd pushes me toward the plane. In my mind I hold an image of Stella waiting for me at the end of the flight. Face-to-face is the only thing that will calm the anxiety churning in my stomach.

My only backup plan is a name and phone number of a man in Lecce that Antonio said I should call if Stella didn't meet my flight. In the next breath, he reassured me she would. But just in case she didn't, this Signor Rossini has a key to Stella's villa.

Why? I'd asked, but Antonio skipped over my question.

Stella—always Stella—all my life she has dumped chronic chaos into our long on-again-off-again friendship. Yes, I'd already planned to meet her in Italy but not now, not today. The trip I'd planned was supposed to be my dream, my time—not another hare-brained scheme of Stella's.

CAT

BRINDISI, ITALY

It had taken months for me to finagle my way onto the wait list with a brilliant chef in Rome—that is until I told Stella. Without my input or permission, she changed my plans. She loves freewheeling with other people's lives.

She called me, breathless with excitement, and explained that she'd removed my name off the list with the chef in Rome. She said she knew a fabulous chef in Castello del Mare and since that's where she lives, it would be so much more convenient for her if I'd spend my sabbatical in Castello. She ended the call by saying it had all been arranged and she'd see me soon. I was still stuttering when she hung up. Not only did she rearrange my job but she insisted I arrive in Castello well before my job began so I could spend time with her. I lost another piece of myself when I didn't call her on it. Stella has perfected the art of undermining me.

We were born on the same day. Our mothers were best friends. For all of our growing up years, we spent our summer vacations in Castello del Mare, a place that after all this time still clings to me and conjures up equally pleasurable and painful memories. I had buried them deep, never planning on returning. Being locked in the past isn't my idea of a quality life. Those summers are long gone, and I don't want to resurrect any part of them. But Stella has never listened to what I wanted. She was a successful actress. She made Castello her home. She assumed, as she always does, that I'd want to be where she was.

Instead of anticipating a time of joyful culinary discovery on my own, I'm going to be with Stella in Castello del Mare. The truth is no matter how mad I get when she interferes in my life, I continue to let her.

It's the same old thing. Our entire friendship has always been about her. She still calls the shots. I'm still treading water, indecisive about whether to sink or swim away. Sadly Stella's friendship, no matter how lopsided, is all I know about friendship.

As I wait for the flight to Brindisi to board, the garbled message she left on my phone whispers in my ear. I've listened to it so many times, but I still can't make out the words—frantic and fueled with a cacophony of background noise.

The intense fear in her voice left me with no choice but to call someone. Only two names from our past surfaced: Antonio or Lorenzo. There was no way I'd open up the painful past by calling Lorenzo. That left Antonio and a choice I knew would make Stella angry.

The last time Stella and I met she told me they had separated. She would abhor that I called him, but I didn't know what else to do. I finally worked up the courage to place the call, but it went to voice mail. When he didn't call back, I kept calling and leaving messages.

In desperation I changed the quiet, composed sanity of my messages to angry warnings. Finally, when I told him I'd call Lorenzo if he didn't call me back in twenty-four hours, he responded. Not that I'd ever call Lorenzo, but it worked.

We hadn't seen or talked to each other in years which led to a silted conversation. I stammered and sputtered, finally saying, "I can't reach Stella. She's not returning my calls or texts. What's going on?"

He gave a snort and answered in his vaguely familiar voice, "Don't get excited. She's just not around right now. Hasn't been for a while. But you know Stella, she comes and goes on her own terms.

She's good at disappearing when it suits her. Probably one of her publicity stunts."

Stella's not being around for a while was ludicrous. What was *a while*? Why wasn't he concerned? Even if my friendship with Stella is dysfunctional, we've always come through for each other. Questions circle in my head, swirling in irregular patterns of light and dark until I decide that Antonio's indifference to her disappearance was enough for me to rearrange my schedule and my departure date.

But if Stella is really missing, what will I do? Would I stay in Castello and wait for her return? Would I try to find her? And should I take the job she arranged for me? What if she doesn't return? Why would Antonio say she's disappeared before? Why don't I know that's a habit of hers? In our thirty-seven-year friendship, she's never once mentioned that she disappears from time to time. What else don't I know about Stella?

The crowd on the tarmac shifts. My feet are glued in place as the ungainly mass of humanity vies for position. They push and shove to get on the plane. Images stagger like wooden soldiers in my mind. They march and yell out in cadence, *I told you so, I told you so.*

In retrospect with the information I have in my pocket today, I could have changed the course of events—turned them right around and dictated a better result. But we all know retrospection won't buy us chocolate in a pizzeria.

CAT & STELLA

NEW YORK CITY, USA

Six months ago, I traveled to New York for one of our semi-annual visits. Our get-togethers are always on Stella's time and dime. New York was a stopover on her way home to Italy. It was the one time that worked for both of our busy schedules. We planned to smush as much as possible into the four days we had.

The hotel door at the Plaza had barely slammed behind me when she burst out, "Cat, thank God you're here. We have to talk. I've left Antonio for good."

I was rushing to hug her until she spoke. I stopped short and said, "What?"

She shrugged and said, "Antonio—I'm leaving him."

This is so Stella—all drama right from the first moment. No "hello, how are you?" conversations ever occurred with her. It was always something unexpected, a little shocking and sure to provoke a response from me. I'm so used to Stella's acting skills that my script was ready.

"Why don't we have a glass of wine, and you tell me all about it."

She swept across the room and embraced me, "Oh, Cat, you always understand."

My hands shook a little as I opened the bottle of Opus One, 2017

Cabernet Sauvignon that Stella had selected for her storytelling time. As I pierce the cork, memories crash into the room. It was my ex's thirtieth birthday. I mistakenly ordered a bottle of Opus One 1996 without asking for the price. I breezily said to charge it and almost choked when the extraordinary cost showed up on my credit card. Far more than we could afford. I didn't dare tell him, and I don't dare mention it to Stella now. She wouldn't understand. She's never had to be concerned about the cost of anything.

When I handed her the glass, she took a sip and declared it drinkable. She swirled to the center of the room, her stage for the next hour or so. I curled up in the corner of the plush sapphire sofa and waited for the first act.

"Cat, I haven't been honest with you, or at least I haven't shared much of what's been going on in my life for the past year. Antonio and I have separated. We can't work things out."

Now Stella is a first-class actress. She shrugged with the perfect amount of indifference. She continued her soliloquy, nodding, frowning, and tossing her thick blonde curls at all the strategic moments. I waited for the pause which meant it was my time to rush onto stage, say my lines, and rush off again.

"Stella, why would you want to leave Antonio? He's your rock, your security, and what about his family connections—the ones you love to gloat about? What aren't you telling me, Stella?"

She inhaled and continued in a petulant voice, "Oh, Cat. He's having an affair with that tacky nurse in his office. I wouldn't have cared about the affair except he did it right under my nose. He didn't have the decency to go out of town or even be discreet. In Castello del Mare, you know what that means. We have become everyone's business. It's humiliating. It might hurt my career."

"Or it could put you in the spotlight. You know the old saying, *there's no such thing as bad publicity*?"

She hesitated and smiled at me, "You're right about the publicity. I can massage it to my advantage."

"What do you plan to do about your marriage?"

The petulant frown returned to her face, "It's over, Cat. Antonio stopped loving me years ago. His education and medical practice have always been what's important to him. What makes me furious is he never had time for me. Yet now he has time for his disgusting little bitch."

She paced back and forth while I carefully constructed words that wouldn't send her off the rails.

"Stella, what else is going on? It's not just Antonio who's having an affair, is it? Are you involved with someone?"

"What do you mean?" She sputtered, staring at me with intense anger in the wide-eyed innocent way she had perfected.

"You're not telling me everything, are you?"

Words hovered on her pouting lips, waiting to spill. Her mouth opened, but she clamped it shut and turned away from me. But just as quickly she swung around, rushed to the sofa, and knelt down in front of me.

She reached for my hands and said, "Oh, Cat. You know me too well. I can't hide anything from you."

"What's going on, Stella?"

She responded differently than I expected.

"I need time to work through everything before I tell you. There are some heavy-duty things going on in my life, Cat. I lost my way for a bit."

"Stella, we've always shared our secrets. Is someone harassing you?"

She responded too quickly, "No, no, nothing like that. It's just a little problem. It'll be worked out by the time you arrive in Italy. I promise. You're finally coming to stay. It's been too long, Cat."

Before I could respond, she jumped to her feet and switched subjects the way she always does.

"Tonight we're staying in. I arranged for room service so we can talk about your trip. You do realize the job I found for you is at the best restaurant in Castello del Mare? The owner, Giorgione, is a dear friend, as is the chef, Sebastian. You won't find a more creative chef, plus he's one of the best in Italy. You'll love working with him. But more importantly, you and I will have plenty of time to catch up."

In her mind, the conversation was over. She picked up the phone and requested that dinner be sent up right away.

It perplexed me that Stella wouldn't talk and her edgy attitude left me wondering about our friendship. We had always shared secrets, even those about lovers and recreational drug use. Now I'm wondering if she'd ever been totally truthful? A flip in my stomach reminded me that our friendship had always been lopsided. She'd had the upper hand since childhood. Of course, my need to be accepted meant I had allowed it to happen.

We finished the week with Broadway shows, shopping, a spa day, and fabulous lunches at all the best restaurants. On our final evening, a grand gala had been scheduled in Stella's honor at the Metropolitan Museum of Art.

The day of the gala, our suite was invaded. First, there were make-up and hair specialists. Then racks of evening dresses were ushered in. Stella looked me over with her usual scrutiny and selected a Versace black silk dress with plunging neckline. She pulled it off the rack and handed it to me along with a pair of Manolo Blahnik black satin heels decorated with leaf-shaped gems on the straps and across the toes. I went for the price tags but she slapped my hand away and with her usual exuberance and said it was her gift to me.

We stood side-by-side facing the mirror. Stella admired her reflection. She was a beauty in a shimmering red dress which perfectly matched the signature red starfish she clasped around her neck. Beside her, I squirmed and pulled at the gapping v-neck of my dress.

She looked up and said, "Quit, Cat."

"What?"

"Quit squirming. The dress looks perfect on you."

As she spoke, she removed her necklace and placed it around my neck.

"Look, Cat. It's perfect with your dress."

She playfully punched my arm and said, "Stand up straight, relax, smile, and imagine you are the guest of honor. If it wasn't my signature piece, I'd insist you wear it. It suits you so much better than it does me."

"Oh, Stella. That's not true. The necklace was made for you."

We stood with our arms entwined, not speaking until I said, "Take it off. We need to finish dressing or we're going to be late."

Stella laughed as she removed the necklace and secured it around her neck.

"One day it will be yours, Cat."

"What? No, Stella. It will never be mine. It's totally you. I could never pull it off."

She smiled, gave me a hug, and said, "One day I hope you'll wear it with this little black dress. Promise me you will."

My mouth dropped open. "What are you saying? You know I won't ever wear your necklace."

She grasped my arm tightly.

"Cat, I want to know that you'll wear this dress again. I want to know that you'll think of me when you wear it. And, there's always the possibility I'll loan you the necklace as long as we're not going to the same function."

The air lightened. We laughed like we used to when we were kids. But something lingered in the air between us—something she hadn't told me. Her mouth was curved in a smile but her eyes were flat and without joy. They were laden with sadness, defeat, and finality.

She did everything to make our time together spectacular yet I hovered between perplexity and annoyance. We separated without discussing what was going on in her life—a first, since the day we became forever best friends thirty-seven years ago.

The only thing we had agreed on was that in two years on our fortieth birthdays we'd meet in Tuscany. Stella had made all the arrangements. We would attend an Andrea Bocelli concert on his family farm in Tuscany. Of course, we could go to any of his concerts whenever we wanted, but we had agreed that our fortieth birthday would be the start of a huge celebration with Maestro Bocelli at the top of our list.

When we parted, Stella gave me a small hug and said, "I'm sorry, Cat. I need some time to work on a few things before I can tell you what's going on. Everything has been arranged for you at the restaurant. Cat, I want you to stay with me. The restaurant's within walking distance of the villa. Please say you will."

I didn't respond. I didn't want to spend a year in the town of my childhood memories. I certainly didn't want to live with Stella for a year. It had been seven years since my divorce. Living alone has changed me for the better. It has forced me to become independent and courageous. Something I'd never accomplished with Stella in my life. As her closest friend I've always been second best. Even now when I'm in her presence, feelings of assumed inadequacy flail away at my hard-earned confidence. It would be hell to endure that for a solid year.

I stuttered about early morning and late night restaurant schedules being disruptive to her *dolce vita* lifestyle. She didn't back down.

What worried me the most I wasn't able to tell her. I knew if I stayed with Stella she would continue to arrange my life. I felt peevish, and Stella was trying to placate me—our usual roles. But what if I told her how I really felt? Would that be the beginning of a more balanced friendship? Maybe things would change.

After a long pause, I said, "La Ristorante Canzone sounds good. I've heard great things about the chef's culinary skills. He was written up in *La Cucina Italiana*."

Stella clapped her hands and embraced me.

"Oh, Cat. It will be perfect. As soon as I get back to Castello, I'll stop by the restaurant and tell Giorgione to call you. Please say you'll stay with me?"

"Stella, I can't promise."

That's where we left it.

Just before I left she handed me a large envelope and said, "These are the arrangements for the Bocelli concert. The itinerary, the limo, the tickets to the pre-cocktail party, front row seats, and a backstage event to meet the Maestro at the end of the concert. And I've picked the most divine place for us to stay. A friend of mine owns Casali di Casole. We'll be staying in one of his luxury villas. For a week."

"Why are you giving this to me?"

"These concerts are sold out more than a year in advance. You know how often I misplace things. You're the reliable one. You'll make sure we show up on the right date and with everything we need. My assistant put the packet together. Her phone number is in the envelope. If after checking it over you have questions, give her a call. She'll arrange the flights when it's closer to the date. All we have to do is show up."

I grumbled a bit about the responsibility. But Stella hugged me so tightly and thanked me so profusely that I let it go.

A couple of months later, Stella called and asked if I had heard from Giorgione. She squealed with delight when I told her he had confirmed the job. Once again, she insisted I stay with her.

When I didn't respond, she said, "Things are better now. No, not with Antonio but with my life. I've found some solutions that might work. We'll have a long talk once you're here. I promise to tell you everything."

She hesitated and then said so softly I almost didn't catch the words, "Cat, I really need you to stay with me. At least give it a try. If it doesn't work out, I promise I'll find you another place. Please?"

Stella has never needed me for anything other than to boost her ego. In a moment of weakness I said yes.

The last thing she said before the call ended was, "I'll be waiting for you at the airport."

There were a few more back and forth conversations and then nothing until the garbled message she left on my phone a few weeks before my departure.

STELLA

She wove life from the threads and fate of dreams and she was and wasn't a dream herself...

CASTELLO DEL MARE, ITALY

The whole thing could have been avoided, if she had turned a blind eye to what she saw. But she hadn't. Her mind wrapped around it like a python. Could it be the answer? The one that would extract her from the mess she was in?

The surveillance began as an accident. It was by chance she stumbled across the clandestine activities. She had watched, not sure what was happening or what she was seeing. She had almost dismissed it. But the movements had been furtive. Something was going on besides the simple task of unloading fish.

For a long time, she had managed her addiction. She had kept her distance from the murkier side of the *Sacra Corona Unita* (SCU - The United Sacred Crown). But she had been naive to think the drugs weren't dangerous or that she could stop whenever she wanted. Her initial intent had been to use them as a means to cope when she was feeling anxious. But that turned out to be most of the time.

Once the SCU had her in their clutches, they threatened to expose her unless she played along. This meant she had to help them out—just a little they'd said. She had refused.

When she didn't cooperate a black rose was left on the terrace table. *Omertà* was painted on the front gate—demanding her silence. She knew it was the mandatory code of honor for the mafia. She ignored it all. They continued. The most recent was a note, nailed to the gate. It had been accompanied by a tiny sparrow. Its wings quivered in the evening breeze as she parked in front of the villa. For a second she thought it was still alive, but in her heart she knew it wasn't. Destruction and death were treading on her path. She needed a way out.

For nights thereafter, sleep had been impossible. She had wanted to confide in Cat when they met in New York. But Lorenzo, the commissario of the *Guardia di Finanza* in Puglia, warned her not to. The time with Cat had ended without repairing the damage Stella knew she brought to their friendship. She just hoped it wasn't too late for her to patch things up with Cat once they were together in Castello.

If only she'd gone to bed that fateful night. Instead, her sleeplessness had her pacing through the villa. She tried to distract her tumultuous thoughts by admiring the local art and pottery crammed onto the shelves. Cat would flip when she saw it. Before moving into Villa dei Fiori, Stella collected only clothes and jewelry. Fiori was her new home—the very first place she had lived alone. The old trappings of her life with Antonio had fallen away when she moved in.

She picked up a large starfish book from the hand-tooled coffee table and flipped through the pages. Books usually bored her enough to bring sleep but nothing was working tonight—not books, not alcohol, not even drugs.

She poured another brandy and lifted a cashmere throw off of the back of the sofa. The cool blue-green fabric reminded her of the sea. With brandy in hand, she opened the door. Goosebumps rolled up and down her spine as the damp night air coiled around her feet and drifted up her body. She dropped the throw on the lounge chair and pushed it close to the stone banister.

On nights when she couldn't sleep, she frequently sought out the familiar sounds of the sea and the fishermen returning home. The rhythmic cadence and the steady hum of activity in the marina from her perch on the terrace often lulled her to sleep. She loved the low throaty voices of the fishermen calling to each other as they unloaded the night's catch. Sometimes they sang songs about life at sea and lost loves.

Stella leaned into the cushions and took a long, full sip of brandy before wrapping the throw around her shoulders. Night after night the fishermen left their homes and families. The wives waited on the sidelines and reassured the children their papa would return. But often the sea laid claim and there was no returning. What a dreadful life, she thought, but then her own wasn't ideal either.

After she'd moved into the villa, she began to visit the tiny chapel on the hill overlooking the harbor—*Chiesa della Madonna dell'Altro Mare.* The wives of the fishermen gathered for prayer as they had in ancient times. It had been off-putting when she had first listened to their chants, the click of their rosary beads, and the ancient melodies rising and falling like waves. They never looked up when she came in although there would be a subtle hesitation in tempo before the rhythm began again. She was the intruder in their midst. Yet she returned again and again. She felt the timeless draw of the sea, a calmness in the midst of her tumultuous life.

It was during one of her visits to the chapel that the idea of a movie took shape. She increased her visits, not because it was a sacred place but because she wanted to visualize how the age-old story could be turned into a story fit for the big screen. During her sleepless nights, she outlined a screenplay and presented it to her agent. He was already selling the idea to some of the top Italian producers.

The setting would be the fifteenth century. Of course, she would play the lead role of the youngest wife in the group of women. Her character would be a beautiful, sassy, young woman. Her hair would be plaited with silk ribbons. She would sashay barefoot through the streets when her loathsome husband was at sea. The husband was a smelly old fisherman who pawed at her body. She had been forced to marry him at fifteen when her parents arranged the match. While her husband was sailing the high seas, her character Idrusa would fall in love with the captain of the Spanish invaders. Stella was sure, even at thirty-seven, she could play the role. She placed the brandy on the railing and lifted her hair, coiling it high on her head.

She closed her eyes as scene after scene played out in her mind. Her body grew still and her eyes heavy as sleep danced on the perimeter of her daydreaming. She visualized the applause as she walked the red carpet in a stunning fifteenth century costume—fans calling her name.

The night faded as sleep joined her on the terrace.

Loud voices rose and fell on the still air—angry voices, startling Stella out of her dream world and rousing her from sleep. She sat up, slid to the end of the lounge, and peeked through the railings.

A shoving match was playing out on the dock. Jabs were thrown and expletives exchanged. For an instant, the real, live fight entered her dream-like state. It would be a perfect scene for the movie—the miserable old husband and the dashing soldier—fighting over the beautiful young girl. Stella lingered in her movie role until a shout broke the spell.

The group of fishermen surrounding the fighters stepped back as a man dressed in dark clothing strode onto the dock. He pushed between the two men in the midst of their punches. His movements were swift, powerful, and full of authority. He positioned himself between the two fighters and placed a hand on each chest. His voice rang out as he demanded the fishermen return to their work. They scurried to their boats and began to unload their catch. He grabbed the two men by their arms and escorted them off the dock.

Stella contemplated the man's actions. In her semi-dream state of mind she envisioned his role in the scene. When he returned to the dock, she studied his movements until it dawned on her that this was not some scene from a movie. Instead she had witnessed something ominous playing out in the early morning hours—something that was very real and terrifying.

She changed positions to get a better view. The man who broke up the fight was clearly in charge. He inspected every tray of fish that came off the boats. He probed and pushed the fish aside as he moved his hands through the ice. It made no sense until gradually Stella let the idea of the movie slip away. A tiny flicker of hope lodged in her mind. Something was going on at the marina, something illegal. Maybe the missing link—the one that would tie all the other pieces together—the one that might save her. Although her back and knees screamed from the cramped position against the stone railing, she didn't move until everyone left and the first rays of sun penetrated the black horizon.

After that first night, she set her alarm and watched every night until she discovered Sunday nights were the link. Italians were notorious for large family gatherings and sublime meals on Sundays which left everyone exhausted. It was the one night that sleep came early to the citizens of the ancient fishing village. It was also the only night the man in black who had broken up the fight was often visible.

Weeks had passed since that first night. She was sure it was drugs. She only had to prove it. Once she did, she had two choices:

she could threaten the SCU with the evidence or she could simply give it all to Lorenzo.

Of course giving it to Lorenzo would be the safest choice, but it would take time for Lorenzo to act and the Guardia di Finanza to follow protocol. She didn't have time. The Grim Reaper was already hovering on her doorstep. Confrontation would be dangerous and possibly the most stupid choice, but it might work.

It took more sleepless Sunday nights to determine the fishing boats were involved in drug smuggling. She waited dispassionately, observing every movement through the high-powered binoculars she had purchased in another town along with a top-of-the-line camera. She took photographs of the wooden ice trays, the fish, and the number of men on the boats and number of vans until they created a story.

Every fifth tray contained only one large fish. Ten trays were put in each van—eight trays crammed with a variety of fish and two trays with one large fish. She now understood why the man had plunged his hand into the ice. He had been checking to ensure the drugs were there and that there had been no breaches.

Two weeks ago she had followed the last van. The first eight trays had been offloaded at the local fishmonger. The two remaining trays had stayed in the van. Without using headlights, she could only follow the van to the edge of town. She wasn't familiar with the back roads and couldn't risk being seen. If she was caught, the consequences would be brutal. She wasn't ready to risk her life.

She needed help to collect evidence, but who could she trust? Gino and Maria were the only two she considered. But taking anyone into her confidence was a huge risk, and they had a sick grandson to raise. The price was too high for them.

She'd first met the caretaker couple when she rented Casa Fiori from Carlo Rossini. She had made a point of befriending them. After she realized her marriage couldn't be repaired, she'd first rented the villa and later bought it. She had asked the couple to stay on. They had agreed with the understanding that they would still work for Carlo as caretakers for his other rental properties in the area.

The relationship had evolved until Stella was able to share more of her life with them than she had with Cat. They were always there, always willing to listen without judgment. They were the stable force in her otherwise unpredictable life. Yet, it didn't seem fair to ask them to risk their lives.

Stella had wrestled all night with the question. She was taking a big chance to include anyone else. As loyal as the couple were to her, they might be more loyal to Carlo. And Carlo, like so many of the men she thought she could trust, turned out to be a jerk.

Men like Carlo were drawn to her for one reason only. Once she had realized the power of her looks and sexuality, she had used them to get what she wanted. Carlo had been useful for only a short time. He was more suspicious than most men and hadn't fallen into her information gathering trap.

As dawn broke, she tallied up the positives and negatives of asking only Gino to help her. As the sun crept over the horizon, she pounded on their door. It opened a crack.

"I'm so sorry to wake you this early, but there's a leak at the house. Gino can you help me?"

He nodded in his dark surly manner and closed the door. Hushed voices whispered. The door opened again and Gino emerged with this tool box.

The conversation that followed was long and awkward. Stella asked him numerous questions before she was willing to explain what she needed from him. She showed him photographs and diagrams and sketches. She told him she couldn't track the vans alone, and she couldn't think of anyone else who knew as much about the area and the mafia as Gino did.

Gino's unease had hung in the air. He questioned her motives and reminded her of the danger before he agreed. They worked out an alibi that would hold up in case he was stopped.

"You understand the consequences if you're caught, *vero*?"

He didn't flinch, just nodded and said he was ready.

"Can I keep one of the photos? This man seems like the leader and someone I've seen before but I need a closer look."

Stella gave him the photo of the man and a photo of the location where the vans turned off. Last week he had driven into the countryside and waited. She now had another missing piece of the puzzle—the location of the distribution center. But Gino said he still wasn't sure about the man in the photo. It was crucial that she identify him.

CAT

SOUTH CAROLINA LOWCOUNTRY

My cell phone shrills. I ignore it and sink deeper under the fleecy, lightweight duvet. It had been after midnight when the event I catered ended. By the time I cleaned up, repacked the equipment, loaded the van, and drove home, it was after two. Exhausted, I crawled into bed without checking my messages.

The ringing continues, but my eyes refuse to open. It's my own fault that my schedule is overloaded. To justify my Italian sabbatical, I've crammed in way too many events. Now the debt collector is here, and I'm out of cash.

My mind drifts ahead to Italian days with Stella—sleeping late, reliving our summers in Castello (her idea), and sharing our current lives while eating our fill of Italian food. Stella promised me that she would tell me every sordid detail of her life during the three months we have before I start my job as the sous chef at La Canzone and before Stella's next assignment. The sheer pleasure of lazy days without commitments is so close.

The insistent shrill blasts through my thoughts. I check the time. Oh, I moan, it's not even six yet. Who would be mean enough to call at this hour? Of course, my better self decides it might be an emergency. I fumble for the phone.

"Lo," I mumble.

Inwardly, a sigh escapes when the little-girl voice of Charlotte reaches my ear. Of course, she's acting on behalf of Mrs. Harrington but calling this early is spiteful.

"Oh gracious, Caterina. I was about to give up. You know I wouldn't think of calling you so early, but you didn't answer my message. It's urgent. Mrs. H insisted that I keep trying, and you know how she is."

That I do. There's no wrath that equals Mrs. Harrington's.

Charlotte blathers on as I rub my eyes open, "Something unexpected has happened, and Mrs. H insists on planning a special celebration on short notice. She said I had to call you first because she knows you're pushed for time. You're the only caterer she trusts to prepare the food for this important event. Please say it's possible to add one more small function to your schedule before flying off to Italy?"

Shuck a duck is the only phrase that comes to mind as Charlotte pleads and rambles on about this grand soirée and how grateful Mrs. H would be if I would please, please, please squeeze in one more event. A low groan lodges in my throat as Charlotte keeps up her non-stop chatter.

When my patience runs thin, I break into her long-winded speech, "Okay, Charlotte, give me the date? If it's open, I'll do it."

Later, I wished those words had never left my mouth. If I had known the party was for my ex-fiancé and his soon-to-be bride, Mrs. Harrington's daughter, I would have said no. All I knew at the time was Mrs. Harrington isn't the kind of person you turn down. She sets the social pace in the South Carolina Lowcountry. Her first-rate endorsement has made me the number one caterer in the area.

While Charlotte drones on, I check my schedule and with a few changes, I can handle one more event. Charlotte squeals with happiness when I tell her the date is available. Her high-pitched voice buzzes on and on like a saturated bee about cocktails and hors d'oeuvres. But the strange thing is she never mentions the occasion or the guest of honor. She doesn't even hint. When I ask, she refuses to say, telling me it's a surprise party. Even when I protest, she doesn't relent.

"Oh child," she says, "Mrs. H knows you are pushed for time with your trip right around the corner. She wants to make sure you are not overworked. She's hired a decorator to prepare the house and flower arrangements. And she hired that cute bartender Kyle from the club. Your only job is the food. I have the menu right here. Tell me when you're ready."

I clicked on my iPad and said, "Go ahead."

"Here we go," Charlotte gushed. "She wants those delectable crawfish tartlets, your marvelous BLT pimento cheese biscuits, Pat Conroy's recipe for pickled shrimp, the miniature puff pastry stars with sour cream and caviar, and the scrumptious bite-size beef tenderloin on crostini. Those little nuggets of goodness are everyone's favorite, especially when topped with those fabulous caramelized onions and Gorgonzola. You, my dear, have a magical touch.

"Oh, add that fancy fruit and cheese board—that's just about the prettiest spread I've ever seen. And, of course, your fabulous caramel chocolate truffles. La Buona Pasticceria will provide the cake; but you, my dear, make the best truffles. Those will be party favors—you decide how many per guest and use those small packages with your trademark silver and blue wrapping. We're going to put them in Mrs. H's great-grandmother's silver punch bowl in the reception area. Won't that be grand?"

I don't have time to agree or disagree as words roll off of Charlotte's tongue like sugar-coated wasps.

"As I said, it's a small party, only a hundred guests with setup at the pool. Mrs. H has already hired wait staff so you don't have to stay once you set up the food. But ask Cassie and her daughter to oversee the service. We want to make this as easy as possible for you. We're just so grateful you can work us in."

Before I could ask any more questions, Charlotte says, "Now don't worry, sweetie. Send the invoice to my email. I will personally deliver the check to you before you leave. Everybody's talking about your trip. Oh my, a year in Italy. Whatever will we do without you to cover all of our celebrations? Oh, gracious, you'll miss the wedding."

Her sentence tapers off as she changes the subject realizing she has relinquished some part of the secret celebration.

A week later in the wee hours of the morning, Charlotte's ominous voice still lingers in my ears as I garnish the last of the hors d'oeuvres for Mrs. Harrington's surprise party. It's the last event on my calendar.

I stretch my back and glance out the window to admire the advent of a Lowcountry sunrise. A winter glow appears on the horizon and begins its dramatic ascent across the marsh, weaving through threads of whispery mist that cradle the morning air. The marsh grasses push toward the sun, begging for its warmth—for those first brush strokes of red and bronze to grace their upturned faces. The grasses drift as nature dictates, tangles of undulating blades, big slabs of life-sustaining turf loosely rooted in pluff mud. They glide in their unstable foundation, capitulating to the constant shift of the tides.

My eyes skim across the familiar gray-blue water, smooth as slate in the first flush of dawn. Just below the water's surface the sea creatures wait to erupt. But at this edge of sunrise moment, there is only a peaceful stillness. I will surely miss this morning ritual of watching the seasons change, the wild creatures in their natural habitat, and the sullen water's ebbing and flowing in and out of my life.

I push away from the large expanse of windows that extend across the length of the kitchen. The calendar hangs next to the fridge. I grasp the marker and slash a bold red 'x' on today's date. Each 'x' brings me a day closer to a reunion with Stella and a much needed sabbatical. The past few years establishing my business have been grueling. I am so ready for a break.

In culinary school, I'd focused on the catering side of the hospitality business. I wanted a career where I could pick and choose my clients and events. Catering offered me the chance to create a personal signature. The added bonus is always knowing what the expenses are upfront. So far being a caterer has met all my needs and my business is booming. But for the last year or so working in a restaurant in Italy has crept into my thoughts so many times that I decided to give it a try. It has to be my nonna's voice in my ear. I finally decided to listen.

My work is my life. The hours slip away as I create food for each celebration. It's a solitary job most of the time and for that I'm thankful because I'm a solitary person. But when I need extra hands, the fabulous Cassie never fails. She's always willing to help and often brings her adorable daughter, Sam, with her.

In the five years since I relocated to the Lowcountry, I've accumulated a consistently strong and active client list. Instead of a job, I have a vocation that allows me to commemorate all the magical moments in other people's lives.

Even Mrs. Harrington, who has a reputation as a badass client, has become less difficult with each event she deems me worthy to cater. So many horror tales were circulating about her when I arrived in town that I steered away from accepting any work from her. Other caterers in the area warned me she was impossible to please. In hushed voices they told me if Mrs. H wasn't happy, her angry remarks were heard by everyone present. She had actually dismissed previous caterers on the spot when they did not meet her stringent expectations. I was petrified when she called me, yet I let her talk me into catering one of her events. That's another problem I have—doing what other people think I should do instead of doing what's best for me. Mrs. Harrington wasn't the best for me.

It took several of her events before my shakiness left and I felt confident I'd made a passing grade in her eyes. One evening when I was packing up, she pulled me aside. She said she liked my quiet personality, my organizational skills, and my non-dramatic performance. She even managed to say my food was excellent. But just so I didn't get a big head, she ended by saying if I ever did step out of line, she'd fire me on the spot. She smiled with great satisfaction after she delivered that little dribble to me.

I often ask myself why I continued to cater for her after that snarky remark. But I have a habit of getting in too deep. Now I'm in a position that if I ever turned her down, she'd make sure my business was ruined. So I continue to work for her, continue to be the good southern girl I was raised to be, and I continue using too much energy to maintain politeness in the face of all that adversity.

The peaceful marsh scene fades as I turn back to the hors d'oeuvres. They wait on a cooling rack—edible jewels ready to be popped into an open mouth. I check the time. If I don't hurry, I'll be late. If I'm late, I will become one of Mrs. H's casualties.

Before placing the last batch of hors d'oeuvres into the container, I count them again. I've had this propensity to count longer than I can remember. Whenever I find myself in stressful situations, the drone of numbers in my head centers me and brings balance to my upside-down thoughts.

After counting, I transfer the tiny bites into the plastic container and snap the airtight lid into place. I stack the remaining boxes under my chin and cautiously cross the courtyard. In my haste to deposit the food in the cargo space, I stumble. My knee slams into the trailer hitch. The boxes teeter as I grind my teeth together to prevent a string of expletives from flowing. The containers and I flounder on the edge of disaster. My elbow and shoulder crash into the van. I howl with pain.

Damn, damn, damn, I mutter. It would be the horse's butt—if hundreds of hors d'oeuvres cascade into the dirt. Somehow I managed to regain my balance without dropping a single container while depositing them in the van.

Tossing back my unruly red curls, I examine my throbbing knee. Shit, it's already swelling, and I don't have time for an ice pack. Mrs. Harrington will not be pleased if the food does not arrive intact and on time.

STELLA

...She had filled the first hourglass with the sand of the deserts of the time before and upon flipping it over set the hands and gears of the first clock in motion...

CASTELLO DEL MARE, ITALY

Stella slipped through the French doors, not sure why she was treading so cautiously. No one could hear her this high up on the expansive terrace overlooking the sea. She was only another shadow. Her long, blonde curls were tucked securely under a black knit cap. Binoculars hung around her neck and a small flashlight was secured in the waistband of her dark jeans. The camera was positioned on the tripod with the shutter release cable attached. It had cost her a small fortune but the range and capability for shooting in low light without flash was necessary to collect the evidence she needed. The photos the camera had produced so far were worth the cost.

She pivoted into place and aligned her silhouette with the contour of the pergola. Her eyes adjusted to the dark then swept across the terrace until she was satisfied nothing was out of place. Prickles danced along her spine when her eyes passed over Gino concealed between the low wall and the staircase. She was both relieved and dismayed he was part of this craziness.

He had proven to be loyal and steadfast. He moved easily and silently through the town and countryside. He was born here and knew every backroad, every dealer, every mule, and probably some of the bosses. His family had stayed clear of the SCU but it had cost them dearly. Gino was not one to forget or forgive which is why he agreed to help her.

The wind stirred the vines. Stella shifted her gaze from the marina to the sea. After weeks of surveillance, this was her last night. She had enough information to tie up the loose ends. The only question left was who would receive the information. The Guardia di Finanza or the SCU? She hadn't answered the question yet, but she had to move quickly before Cat arrived.

The air hung heavy on the terrace as the old tower clock struck three. The moon in its last quarter waned in its elliptical journey around the earth. It skimmed across the Adriatic—dancing to some ethereal music. Stella didn't notice the moonlight. Her only focus was to save herself and anyone else her drug habit had dragged into this black abyss.

From hours of watching, she knew the vans were already lined up to transport the early morning catch into town. She had taken countless photographs of the activity on the dock, but tonight she wanted a close up of the man who only appeared infrequently on Sundays. So far he had been elusive. The new camera would do the trick but only if he showed up. With Gino's additional photos of the drop-off point and other pertinent information she had been collecting, it could be enough to bring down a large portion of the drug ring. If that happened, there was a strong possibility she would be free from the threats and could resume her life. If that didn't happen? She shrugged and let the thought trail off.

She scanned the brooding horizon. Soon the small fishing boats would arrive, bringing their glistening loads of fish. Hidden among the fresh seafood would be marijuana, cocaine, hashish, and *Captagon,* better known as fentanyl—her drug of choice.

In her addictive state, she hadn't realized she was putting her life in jeopardy. She hadn't considered the drugs might be impure. Street drugs were often cut with other dangerous substances without the user's knowledge. The death statistics were high. She'd been both stupid and lucky.

It had taken the threat of extortion and destroying Antonio's medical practice to rouse her from her drug induced inertia. She hadn't thought twice about paying a king's ransom for the pleasure the drugs brought her. But once she was hooked, the SCU wanted more.Their campaign to recruit her began.

Of course, she thought, d*emanding I become a mule was a smart move on their part.*

Her career took her everywhere, on private jets with easy clearance through customs. When she didn't respond to the threats, menacing notes began to arrive on her doorstep. One said Antonio's practice would be destroyed followed by another threatening her career and her life.

When she continued to say no, they started terrorizing her. Explicit reminders—a mutilated bird—its heart pierced with a tiny arrow. A black rose with the dreaded word *Omertà* painted on the door frame. But the strangest demand had been for her starfish necklace. It was valuable, well over a quarter million euros, but the demand had confused her. The necklace was her trademark and easily recognizable. It would be difficult, if not impossible, to sell.

On most days she blamed herself, but sometimes she blamed Antonio for the mess she was in. If he had loved her enough, this wouldn't have happened. She would protect him, but she would never give them the necklace. These damn scum-of-the-earth creatures didn't know who they were dealing with.

She smiled in the dark. The accidental discovery of how the drugs were coming in had opened her eyes to the perilous game she was playing. The threats increased, but instead of scaring her, they had given her courage to seek help for her habit.

She was on the road to recovery. Without anyone's knowledge she had randomly disappeared and entered rehab. The one thing the mafia didn't want was for her to break the habit. Once she started rehab, she continued to string the mafia along by only buying small amounts of the drugs. That backfired. She was an addict and having drugs in her possession was too much temptation. The threatening notes, her stressful work schedule, and her disastrous personal life positioned her to once again take a pill or two to keep calm.

The only way she could stay clean was to expose the network. That meant risking her life, Antonio's career, and possibly his life. The surveillance that had started months ago by accident was coming to an end.

She shifted her weight and refocused the binoculars far out to sea. First one light and then another twinkled on the surface—navigational lights signaling arrival of the fishing boats. She struggled with her inner demons. She was to blame for the predicament she had forced on others against their will. She had implicated Antonio as well as Gino and Maria and Lorenzo had also been compromised by his relationship with her.

She didn't want to add Cat's name to the list of innocent bystanders. If she wrapped everything up now, Cat would be safe. She briefly wondered what Cat would think when she told her everything. She prayed their friendship would survive.

She set the binoculars on the table and zipped up her jacket against the cool breeze. She slowly scanned the cars parked at the marina. Usually, the man in charge would have already been in place. As the boats docked, she focused the lens and waited. He didn't come.

She slowly lowered the binoculars. It was more than disappointing, as she hadn't been able to get a good face shot of him. Every photo she'd taken was nondescript. His back would be turned or his cap pulled so low none of his features were visible. She had taken several videos. She hoped that his movements or clothing might be recognizable. Gino had been studying the videos. He hadn't said anything yet.

She hesitated before packing it in for the night. One last sweep might reveal something she hadn't seen before. As she adjusted the lens, a flash of light appeared from the other side of the marina. She paused, but it didn't reoccur. She repositioned the binoculars and scanned the villas dotting the hill.

She whispered, "Did you see that?"

There was a slight movement. She could just make out Gino's shape as he positioned his binoculars across the expanse of water and scanned the villas and terraces. A slight nod indicated he'd seen the light.

Stella had been careful, but the light was spooking her. She prayed someone wasn't watching. When no additional flashes occurred, she turned her attention to the marina as the first fishing boat tied up at the dock.

She smiled. It was almost over.

On the other side of the marina on the terrace of a magnificent penthouse, *il padrone* crouched under the table long enough for Stella to lose interest. He'd inadvertently hit the switch on his flashlight. But he was sure she hadn't seen him.

He duck-walked to the baluster and squatted behind a large potted plant. Slowly, he rose to his full height and positioned his binoculars across the water onto Stella's terrace. He enjoyed the cat and mouse game they were playing, particularly since she didn't know she was the mouse.

His gaze shifted to the boats as one by one they docked and offloaded the fish and drugs. Sunday's fishermen all desperately needed their jobs. It'd been easy to buy their loyalty. A few weeks ago one of the boat captains had noticed movement on Stella's terrace and reported it. Initially, he'd remained uninvolved. It was Riccardo's job to work out the daily problems. But when Riccardo confirmed the suspicious activity on Stella's terrace, he decided to take a look. At first he thought she was having a sleepless night or perhaps she was entertaining someone in the early morning hours.

Around the same time, Riccardo had told him some of the fishermen were disgruntled about their take and a few fists had been swung. For a while, they took turns being in the marina on Sunday nights. But Stella's veranda had remained dark. Riccardo had checked around and reported to *il padrone* that she was filming out of town. He continued to keep an eye on things until she returned.

He didn't get to be *il padrone* without checking out every situation. Although he usually never got involved in the daily operations, this was personal. When Stella returned, he set up counter surveillance. He'd stayed in the penthouse. He watched and waited to see what she was up to. It didn't take long for the pattern to emerge. She only showed up on the terrace on Sunday nights which meant she was onto his game. He was surprised at her quick intelligence as she seemed like every ditzy blonde he'd ever bedded.

Watching her, he realized she was getting close. After tonight, he would redirect the boats to another location. She was eager to pounce, but he was way ahead of her. She was, after all, a woman and would never be as clever as he was. In the end, he would get the money, the necklace, and revenge. She would get nothing.

CAT

S*OUTH CAROLINA LOWCOUNTRY*

After busting my knee, I limp back to the house and pick up my purse and keys. As an afterthought, I stuff one of the less-than-perfect chocolate caramel truffles into my mouth—the ones that wouldn't meet the perfection grade for Mrs. H's party. The chocolate shell explodes with the first bite. The rush of sweet, buttery caramel coats my tongue. With the first blast of sugar deposited in my bloodstream, the pain of my bruised knee lessens.

John Ashley Williams, IV would not approve. Ah crap, I've been trying to get through each day without thinking about John Ashley. It messes up my head to conjure up so many rotten memories. But the thoughts rage on as his holier-than-thou voice blasts into my consciousness, "What's so hard about self-discipline? How could you be addicted to chocolate? You're indulging yourself, that's all!"

His use of the exclamation point in his pattern of speech always made me cringe. He sounded like a judge pronouncing a long prison term as he stabbed me while I was being dragged out of the courtroom in cuffs.

John Ashley was mystified that I could eat an entire batch of chocolate brownies before they had completely cooled. But I was needy and slow to acknowledge that his fine-honed words were just plain mean. Initially, he performed so smoothly I missed his underlying meaning, the little jab at the end of a sentence that you could take more than one way.

When I met him, all I saw was this gorgeous man—so southern and charming with hair the color of burnished chestnuts. He was already a full partner at the largest law firm in Savannah, the one his daddy owned. Money and a life of ease were there for me to scoop up. My life was finally taking the right turn after an abusive first marriage and a messy divorce. Everything was lining up: my home on the marsh looked out on deep water, my catering business was profitable, and I had believed that I was in a happy, healthy relationship—okay, that last bit was a lie I was telling myself.

Meeting John Ashley had been a ray of redemption for me until it wasn't. For months he'd created the image of a perfect partner. He had been loving, compassionate, charming, and so considerate of my every wish. Early in our relationship he hadn't pontificated in those damn declarative sentences. Of course, there's no such thing as a perfect relationship. I know that, but as our relationship deepened, I allowed the door to my heart to crack open. That's when the little personal jabs at my character began.

As I was settling into a long-term commitment, he was grumbling about how much time I spent at work and how my catering hours didn't suit him. I countered with how important my job was and how hard I'd worked to be independent.

When he saw the fire in my eyes, he changed tactics and returned to his sweet, soulful self that had won my heart. It worked for a while or at least until his good intentions fell apart and he began to pick away at the scab of my soul.

Standing my ground was mandatory. I refused to back down from the hours I devoted to my work or from my plan to live in Italy for a year. That trip was etched in stone and for once I wouldn't be bullied. The trip had been planned before I met John Ashley. No man, no matter how much I loved him, was going to change those plans. I had discussed my pending trip with him on our first date.

My excitement about the trip meant I forgot to analyze his reaction or even consider that it might not have been an honest one. In my blind sightedness, I believed he was championing my independent spirit when he expressed interest and asked questions. I totally missed the small inflection in his voice when he said, *you sure are independent* and then his follow up question of, *isn't a year rather long?* The thing is, I never deceived him about my aspirations. For years I'd dreamed and saved to make this trip happen. That apparently didn't matter much to him.

Initially, his comments about the trip didn't register. I was sure he was joking. Everything else about our relationship was ideal. It was only after he presented me with a splendid engagement ring that his words took on a disparaging slant. He stopped pretending to be supportive and came at me with a frontal attack. Every conversation wound up with him strategizing about all the things we could be doing together if I weren't flying off to Italy—like planning our wedding or house hunting, or picking a honeymoon destination. Finally, he stopped trying to understand and asked me to postpone the trip. After all, he said, preparation for our wedding should come first. When I stood firm, his glib remarks became more frequent and insistent.

A redness had tinged the outer edges of his cheeks when he prodded, "I could take a few weeks off and go with you. Or why don't you stay three months instead of a year?"

When I said no, he continued, "Why don't we get married first and then talk about whether it makes sense for you to go?"

And, finally, the deal-breaker words, "You know, once we're married, you'll have to give up your business. You won't have time to cater other people's events with all the entertaining that's required for my position in the firm and in the community. With your culinary skills, you'll be the perfect hostess. All the right people will be banging on my door for an invitation to one of my events."

I kept hearing the "my door and my event" conversation over and over. I was reliving my worst nightmare. I'd already survived an eight-year marriage with a sorry son—a drunken, gambling, womanizer—not to mention abusive control freak. I had worked too damn hard to attach myself to another controlling man. I would not repeat this very bitter lesson.

Growing up in Stella's shadow had provided enough angst. I built on that faulty friendship by selecting the wrong mate and then staying too long in a marriage that was doomed and a job I hated. My failed marriage, the bitter divorce, and a career change were simply a continuation of a long list of situations that had provided me with enough stress to bounce the Richter scale off the charts. I've done enough damage to myself. I certainly didn't need John Ashley or anyone else in my life to tip the scale further.

To this day, I battle bouts of anger, anxiety, and depression from my failed marriage with Richard, my parents' death, and the malfunction of my relationship with John Ashley not to mention all the childhood trauma of being Stella's best friend. As a result, I'm saddled with a permanent case of reflux which I have fondly christened acid indignation. If that isn't enough, I count everything. It doesn't matter whether or not it makes sense. What matters is that counting has become my method of maintaining balance when I'm stressed.

When my divorce from Richard was final, I left that less-than-desirable life behind. I packed my bags and resigned from the secure financial position I had at the largest accounting firm in town. To everyone's shock and dismay, I enrolled in culinary school. All my life I had loved cooking for others—that love had been nourished by my Italian Nonna. I was proud that I had finally mustered up enough courage to walk away from my sorry past and embark on a new life.

But, of course, trouble packed its own bag full of tricks and traveled with me. I had barely gotten out of my miserable marriage and enrolled in the masters program for culinary arts when my world spiraled out of control. A phone call, the kind you never want to receive—informed me that my parents had been killed by a drunk driver. Heartsick, I made the journey home. Stella had rushed to my side, abandoning the filming of her latest movie in Italy.

It had been a strange reunion. We hadn't seen each other for a couple of years. I called to tell her what had happened. I told her not to come, but she did. We hadn't spoken about our parents since that long-ago incident. Of course, Daddy didn't blame Stella. But he sure blamed Stella's Dad. The two had been best friends. They'd worked at the same company until my daddy was fired over some big account screwup. I was a kid, but I'd overheard whispered conversations. At the tender age of twelve I was prone to eavesdropping. Everything changed that year—the year Daddy lost his job.

We had to downsize while Stella and her family moved across town to a mansion. When Daddy told me we could no longer afford the summer trips to Castello del Mare, I was devastated. In my prepubescent world I thought only of myself and that trip to Italy every summer was why I existed. Lorenzo, my one and only childhood crush, was my reason to be—he was a rogue Rhett to my sassy Scarlet. In my mind, I couldn't survive without seeing him. It didn't matter that he only had eyes for Stella.

I was a self-centered little beast, but somehow my mom understood how important those summers were for me. She and Stella's mom maintained a secret relationship after our fathers quit speaking. The two moms figured out a way for me to join the Lombardi family for the next five summers. But it was never the same.

The lifelong friendship of our two families disintegrated. Stella and I tried hard to recreate the summer magic, but it was never recaptured. I was the interloper and every time her father looked at me, I could see the sneer in his eyes—heavy duty stuff for a kid to handle.

It took years for me to understand and appreciate what had happened. Seeing my daddy's pain was a huge part of the gap between Stella and me. But thankfully, my dad and I had many long conversations before his death. Daddy said Mr. Lombardi stole a big account right from under his nose by making promises that the company couldn't keep. But when Daddy finally went to the owner, it seems Mr. Lombardi had beat him to the punch and had mapped out all the reasons he deserved the big account instead of my dad. He went so far as to say that my dad had made all the impossible promises to get the account. A kind of brawl took place and Dad punched Mr. Lombardi. Broke his jaw. That ended Daddy's international career and the life-long family friendship.

After the summer we turned seventeen, Stella and I drifted apart, she to modeling and me to college. As she became more famous, she reconnected, saying there wasn't anyone in the business she trusted. She would often call to talk about how difficult her life was. I hated those calls when I was slugging my way in the corporate world and my marriage was unraveling. Her life seemed magical to me while mine was a hell hole.

When she asked me to help with her wedding, our relationship improved. After that, we tried to meet once or twice a year. When my parents were killed, she was the only person I thought to call. She came immediately. I was grateful.

When the funeral services were over, the house sold, and treasured memories put into storage, I returned to culinary school. I swept aside all emotions and worked non-stop to complete my degree. After graduating, I checked out the rambling farmhouse left to me in the will. It had been in the family for over a hundred years and when my uncle passed, it went to my daddy. It checked out to be exactly what I needed to start a new life and my catering business. I packed up my belongings and relocated to the South Carolina Lowcountry.

At one of the big political events I catered, I met John Ashley. He was the guest of honor after winning a big murder trial. He worked his magic on me. I was sure he was a different kind of man than the one I'd left behind. He was so loving, and well, I was so needy. Goes to show you that no matter your age or experience making lousy decisions happens when your emotions go rogue. My brain malfunctioned until after the damage was done.

Before John Ashley entered my life, I didn't have a therapist to shed light on some of the more inane decisions I'd made. Now, I do.

When I moved to the Lowcountry, I was one hair away from sliding off the dark edge of the earth. My family doctor recommended Dr. Virginia Hollister (Ginny). With her help, I walked away from John Ashley.

Dr. Ginny said to me, "Cat, you are approaching forty. This year-long trip is one of those lifetime chances. Your business might suffer a little the year you are in Italy, but it would suffer a heck of a lot more if you caved and married John Ashley. And Cat, if he really cherished you, he would want what's best for you. He would champion your trip."

She also reminded me that John Ashley was trying to control me with his demands. She simply asked me if that's how I wanted to spend my life. We both knew the answer to that question.

When I asked John Ashley to postpone the wedding until I returned from Italy, his only reaction had been to hold out his hand for the magnificent sapphire and diamond engagement ring. He put it in his pocket and walked away. Not once has he called to check on me or ask if I would forgive him for being such a fool. Sure, I made the right decision but his dumping me hurt like fire ants attacking my heart.

I wept for days. And even worse, I reverted to that frumpy red-headed kid with scabbed, knobby knees, glasses sliding down my nose and braces glittering. The image of my frowning, scrunched up face still echoes after all these years. But I was able to walk away and that's progress even if there is another crack in my heart.

I slam the lid on the tin of the less-than-perfect truffles, store them in the fridge, and exit the back door. I drag my swollen, painful knee with me. There's no time for whimpering. I back out of the driveway and slide into autopilot as I join the flow of traffic on Highway 21, a road so familiar I can dream up a new recipe while traversing it.

This morning I roll through green light after green light, wishing just one would turn red. My proclivity for counting even covers the seconds required when waiting at a stop light. Without that calming effect, I'm left with my jittery thoughts—the ones that play over and over in my brain about how I've screwed up again.

Shit, slides out of my mouth as I almost miss the Old Sheldon Church Road. With a squeal of brakes and a sharp right turn, I maneuver the curve. The view instantly changes from barren highway into lush hideaway. Shivers march down my arms as my eyes skim the ghostly Spanish moss, dangling like giant chandeliers from ancient oaks. Spiraling branches stretch across the road in saber-sword fashion in perpetual preparation for a military wedding. After last night's ferocious storm, the moss sways in luminous lime. The sunlight shimmers, skating across the lingering rain drops. Those glittering droplets remind me that I'm leaving for a new life in Italy far away from Mr. John Ashley Williams IV.

My heart leaps into joyful overdrive until I remember that Stella will be the ghost traveling with me. Stella, after all these years, is the one person still dictating my next move. Her message has baffled me. There was so much background noise that I couldn't hear much, but I heard her frantically whisper, *Help me!* I played it over and over but simply can't make heads or tails out of it. Her low, rapid, garbled message conveyed something is wrong—really wrong.

I scrunch up my face. I push away the negative images crowding my thoughts and focus on Stella's smiling face and warm embrace. She will be at the airport to greet me when I step off the plane in Brindisi. I have to keep believing she'll be there.

As I turn onto the gravel road leading to Harrington Plantation, Stella's radiant image leaves me. It's replaced with fear of what I'll find when I arrive in Italy. My brain hums off key. It plays with my tormented heart.

This is crazy. Antonio has to be wrong. Stella can't be missing. Gracious, I'm supposed to be staying with her, not looking for her.

She will be at the airport waiting for me when I arrive. Surely, she will be there.

My reverie is broken when the wrought iron gates embossed with gilded birds swing open. I steer the car down the long oak-lined driveway.

STELLA

...There is no secret buried in the endless depths of the ocean she doesn't know and she was the one that had arranged and named every twinkling orb in the night sky...

CASTELLO DEL MARE, ITALY

Stella glanced in the faded antique mirror. The silver coating on the back had oxidized leaving dark blotches, distorting her face. She sighed and heaved long, blonde curls off her damp, sticky shoulders. Humidity hummed in the air, swaying the curtains with a limp breeze. Her hand trembled as the hairbrush dragged with effort through her thick hair.

Two months had crawled by since her last hit. She was on the verge of crazy with a desire so strong she could taste the saliva building against her tongue. She nodded at the mirror and thought, *I'll beat it this time.* But the mirror knew that years of addiction were mounting a full-scale assault against her.

She needed this photo shoot to go well but what if she couldn't do it without a fix? She shifted her weight and searched for a clear spot on the mirror. Trying to work out the tension, she arched her neck and pulled her shoulders up and back.

One of the more compelling reasons to stop was her age. The calls were less frequent as more and more young ingenues clamored for roles. According to her agent, she needed to stay clean and accept whatever work came her way. Today's assignment had come suddenly and with only a few days' notice. That was worrisome. Stefano always made her booking arrangements but this time an assistant had called. And, it wasn't his usual assistant. Stella had hesitated, even thought about turning it down, but she needed the publicity.

The photoshoot was for one of the most popular magazines in Italy. It guaranteed publicity. This latest film had to be a big box-office hit. The agency had hinted at dropping her if it wasn't. Having to accept roles in B-rated movies would be the death of her. She sighed as the shadow of herself vacillated. The craving grew stronger as the desire to fight it grew weaker. The feel of the euphoric glow rushing through her body when the pill dissolved in her system was powerful.

She adjusted the thin, white gauzy gown and repositioned the jewel-laden starfish necklace nestled in the hollow of her throat. Earlier she had removed the complimentary bracelet, the gift Antonio had given her at seventeen.

There were times she didn't wear the elaborate necklace, but she always wore the bracelet. She felt naked without it. But this morning when she slid it onto her wrist, a sharp pain had pierced her heart. Her breath had come in short gasps as she studied the design. The starfish pulsated as she clutched it between her fingers. Was it her imagination or had the pain retreated when she unclasped the bracelet and returned it to the faded blue velvet box?

Before placing the box in the secret drawer, she picked up one of her gold embossed cards and wrote a message. She tucked it inside before she closed the box and positioned it in the ceramic container. Her fingers caressed the intricate mosaic pattern on the gilded container. She remembered the shop window in Rome where she bought it. The gold leaf edging, the brilliant colors, and the two doves resting on the water-filled urn had catapulted her into the store.

She studied the design one more time before tapping the tiny indentation on the back on her desk. The lock on the secret drawer sprang open. It was only after she placed the container in its hiding place and closed the drawer that the pain fully subsided. She shuddered, forcing the strange thoughts to go away.

Several nights ago as a precaution, she had shown Maria the secret drawer in the antique roll-top desk. She had sworn Maria to secrecy.

When Maria questioned why Stella was doing this, she said, "Goodness, Maria, you know how chaotic bank hours are and I never know when I might have an event. The most important thing to remember is if anything happens to me, please make sure Cat gets the box and all its contents. Can you do that for me?"

Maria nodded and whispered, "But nothing's going to happen to you. Promise me?"

Stella had laughed and tossed her head, "Of course nothing is going to happen to me. It's a precaution. Since I'm separated from Antonio I worry that when I'm out of town, he might snoop. No one knows about this but you and Cat. It's really important, Maria."

It wasn't the best solution, but it was the only thing she could think to do. After everything settled down, she'd rethink her plan.

Stella glanced in the mirror. The sunlight flickered across her face. Warm memories flooded into the room. Twenty years ago she had opened the small blue velvet box and gazed in astonishment at the magical bracelet with the ruby starfish in the center. Antonio was almost jumping with excitement when he told her it had been designed by the well-known jeweler Aldo Cipullo. She'd been too naive and embarrassed to admit she wasn't familiar with the designer or any designer for that matter. She only knew it was the most beautiful piece of jewelry she'd ever seen.

A small ruby starfish glowed within a circle of twinkling diamonds.

One side of the bracelet was covered in diamonds molded into leaf clusters while the other side spiraled into white-gold bands that gave the illusion of floating with each movement of her wrist. She had trembled from head to toe as she held the bracelet close to her heart and listened while Antonio told her the story about the first time he had seen her.

As he spoke, she recalled that long ago summer morning and her horror when she had discovered hundreds of beached starfish, the little red bodies washed up on the shore as they struggled to live. Without thinking, she'd flung them back into the sea. She certainly hadn't been aware that Antonio was watching her or that he had fallen in love with her that day. To her, he was just one of the Italian summer boys that she and Cat had giggled over during late night conversations.

Five years later, he had given her the bracelet before he left for medical school. He'd held her in his arms before placing it around her wrist. He whispered into her hair, "*Sei la mia stella rossa dal mare* —You are my red star from the sea. Please wait for me."

And later, right before their marriage, he had presented her with a second much larger blue velvet box. When she opened it, a spectacular starfish necklace lay nestled in the silk.

It was a few years later before she read an article in one of her fashion magazines about Aldo Cipullo. She had no idea that the designer of her jewelry had been so famous. His fame began in Naples before he had been enticed to Rome. As his prominence grew, he left his homeland and crossed the ocean to design jewelry first for Tiffany's and then Cartier. During his time with Cartier, he had created the iconic love bracelet. He had become one of the most prominent jewelers of his time. Because of Antonio's family connections and considerate wealth, it had been easy to commission Cipullo to create the bracelet and the magnificent necklace.

Stella stared at her image in the mirror. Her fingers stroked the rows of diamonds nuzzling her slender neck. There were 17.3 carats of princess, pear and marquise hand-cut white diamond clusters.

Antonio had bought her soul with this necklace and his words of love and fidelity. What a joke!

Over time, the necklace and bracelet became her identity. She wore both pieces to all her publicity events. She was sure that the priceless gifts would guarantee her and Antonio's love forever, but of course they hadn't.

The necklace had become a heavy weight around her neck. Its original beauty had dimmed and become ordinary just as their passion had faded. A few years into their marriage she realized his medical practice took precedence over time spent with her. She was a prize for him, and his one revolt against his family's wishes. The painful awareness of his indifference followed her to every photo shoot, film set, and dinner party.

The mirror gave her no answers but it no longer mattered. It had been over between them for months, maybe years. The jewelry was the last thing that connected them. She knew he might ask for the valuable pieces back. But for now, she needed to make sure they were safe.

It didn't make sense that someone, and she assumed that someone was *il padrone*, was demanding the necklace. *Why did the creep want it?*

Initially, the demands and threats hadn't mentioned the necklace. It happened slowly with notes like *if you can't pay in cash, your necklace can be held as collateral*. Then the notes changed to *the necklace will cover all your debts*. And finally, the necklace became the central theme of each demand. It confused her that someone wanted the necklace, but why? She intended to find out. If she knew the answer, maybe she could save herself.

The surveillance had given her a lot of information. She now had photographs to identify the drug smuggling ring. But she still couldn't identify *il padrone*—that was the missing link. That and why he wanted the necklace.

She had returned the previous day to the secret hideaway she and Cat had shared as children. The opening in the rock ceiling they had used for stashing secrets was still there. She had stuffed the folder with all the SCU information into the hiding place. She had carefully sealed the rocks with wet sand, moss, and twigs. Until she could decide who would get the information, she needed a safe place—a place only Cat could find.

Next on her list was a way to reveal to Cat how to find the information. Initially, she had written the name of the hideaway on a piece of paper and placed it in the ceramic box. Several nights later she had awakened from a dream and destroyed the piece of paper. If anyone else found the box, it would lead them directly to the hiding place.

She remembered a game she and Cat had played as children—*caccia al tesoro*—treasure hunt. They loved writing clues on pieces of paper and hiding them. The trail of paper clues always led to a prize. She considered riddles that only Cat would understand. It took a while, but she came up with three. She placed those in the box and went back to bed.

After another sleepless night, she realized the ceramic box wasn't the right place to hide the clues. If anyone tore her house apart, they might find the secret compartment. She separated the three clues and scattered them throughout the house in places she knew Cat would poke around in. If anyone else randomly found one of the clues, it would be dismissed as some unimportant note she had scribbled.

Last week she changed her will. She removed Antonio and made Cat the executor and beneficiary. The wrong people were watching her every move. She was scared. If something happened and she didn't survive, then everything depended on Cat finding the incriminating folder. She hoped this part of her plan didn't become a reality.

She had done as much as she could. In a few days she would retrieve the folder. As much as she wanted to confront the SCU, it would be wiser to turn everything over to the Guardia di Finanza in Rome. She no longer trusted anyone in the local Guardia. She sniffed back a tear and pushed away thoughts of Lorenzo. He'd let her down, but she wasn't surprised. Too much time had passed for them to start over. When Cat arrived she could at least tell her Lorenzo was available, although she doubted if Cat would be interested.

All her life men had used her. Lorenzo had turned out to be no different. In a way, she was relieved that their reconnection had been brief. There were too many memories and too much pain to work through.

When this was over, she and Cat would laugh about the fears, loves lost and found again, and they would recommit to their friendship—maybe this time they wouldn't have to cut their fingers and smear blood. She smiled at the image of those two little girls, so earnest in their attempts to be forever best friends. That's all Stella wanted now—a chance to let Cat know how much she loved her and how sorry she was for being such a pain in the butt all their growing up years.

She caressed the necklace. Today's photo shoot would be the last time she would wear it until she was free from the mafia. Tomorrow it would go in the safe deposit box. Her fingers lingered lovingly on the starfish. The jewels flashed across the mirror. She closed her eyes. The memories pour over her like warm, gentle rain.

CAT

SOUTH CAROLINA LOWCOUNTRY

As the gates to Harrington Plantation swing shut behind me with a loud clang, my cell phone rings. Cassie's name pops on the screen. A smile spreads across my face. Cassie's my right-hand woman for most of the events I cater. Bumping into her at the grocery store had been one of those magical serendipity things that happens on rare occasions.

Of course, Cassie tells everyone I drove my cart right over her. She hoots with laughter describing how I offered to buy her new shoes after I left black skid marks on her new white sneakers.

"Hey, what's up?"

"Cat, are you on the way to Harrington's?"

"Yes, I just drove through the gates. Why?"

"Pull over and stop the car."

"What?"

"You heard me. Pull over! Now! There's something you need to know before you go any further. Okay?"

My heart skips a beat as I maneuver the car off the driveway and park on the grass. "Cassie, what's wrong?"

There's an incredibly long pause—so long I can feel the shit heading in my direction.

"Cat, the party tonight is for John Ashley and his new fiancé, Caroline Bailey Harrington."

"No, Cassie, don't joke with me. I was up all night preparing the food. I'm not in the mood."

"It's not a joke. I bumped into Kyle, you know Kyle, the bartender at the club? He was hired to work tonight. He told me. Cat, what are we going to do?"

Even in the midst of the storm gathering in the pit of my stomach, I hear Cassie's *we*. Unlike Stella, Cassie is a person who has my back. In the few years we've worked together, she has proven that more than once.

"How could that be?" I shriek. "He only broke off our engagement a couple of months ago. What a bastard!"

"Yep, that's exactly what he is. But we need a plan before you go in that house with the food."

When I don't speak, Cassie says, "Okay, here's one option. You can wait at the gate. I can be there in 25 minutes. You can hand off the food to me. I'll tell Mrs. Harrington that you don't feel well, and I'm taking your place."

Angry pistons fire inside my head.

"No Cassie. I'm going in. Mrs. Harrington will hear directly from me. She's paid for the food. I'll make the delivery but she won't get my services."

"Are you sure you want to face her, Cat? You know her reputation. She can ruin you."

"You know what, Cassie? I've bowed down to her for the past five years. There's a strong probability she will damage my reputation. But I have a waiting list of people who want to become clients. Surely, a few of them are not in her clutches. Maybe they won't listen to the rumors she'll spread. Besides, Cassie, it's exhausting working for her. This time her despicable actions are presenting me with an opportunity to quit. As difficult as she is, I never expected her to be deceitful. For me, that's enough."

"Oh Cat. Are you sure? You know she'll screw you over with all her friends."

"Yes, Cassie. You're right. There's a strong possibility that she'll destroy my business, but I have to stand up to her. If she tries to ruin my reputation, I'll hire a lawyer."

"Wow," is all Cassie says.

"It's time I stop jumping every time she demands it."

"Okay, I'm with you. I'll be your best witness if we go to court. But you need to get on that plane and go to Italy before there's a lawsuit to deal with. Everything will blow over while you're away."

"Maybe, but knowing Mrs. H, I doubt it. Okay, I'm going to the house. Cass, she will probably call you to take my place. That's your choice. I would understand because she does pay well."

"Not to worry. If she's smart, she won't call me. She knows I wasn't born in the South with all of those good manners in my mouth like you have. It won't bother me in the least to tell her what I think. I'm with you, Cat. Call when you leave. A glass of wine will be waiting for you."

"Thanks, Cass. I would have been the party's fool tonight if you hadn't found out and told me. You saved my butt. All I can say is I'm grateful you're my friend."

"We're a team Cat, and the Harringtons of this world cannot buy our souls. Don't forget to call me when you leave."

I disconnect and stare at the palatial mansion at the end of the drive.

STELLA

...Using nothing but a small kiss and a sprinkle of magic from the colors of her eyes she brought dead starfish back to life and taught them to dance in the palms of her hands...

CASTELLO DEL MARE, ITALY

In the throes of first love, Stella chose Antonio instead of Lorenzo. She still remembered Cat's expression when she told her—part horror and part happiness. At the time, she didn't realize Cat was in love with Lorenzo. But after that day, she saw it. Up until then, Cat kept her distance from Lorenzo. But after Stella chose Antonio, Cat dropped her guard and wore her devotion to Lorenzo all over her face.

Stella hated that. She was used to all the attention. Once she chose Antonio, she was no longer sought after by the male population. She missed the adoration, and she missed Lorenzo more than she thought possible.

Lorenzo had pursued Stella with all the eagerness of a smitten teenager. His rugged good looks and intense blue eyes that danced with fire had made it difficult to choose Antonio when she knew in her heart she loved Lorenzo more.

Antonio was handsome but cool and distant. Cat had pointed this out time after time. Stella hadn't been able to explain to Cat that Lorenzo's passion frightened her, or that she was much more comfortable with Antonio's strong commitment to his studies and his almost indifference to their romance. It had also made the pursuit of Antonio more exciting.

But Cat had been right. Antonio had kept her at arm's length throughout their relationship while Lorenzo had hounded her with exuberance. He had continued to pursue her discreetly after she was engaged to Antonio. When he'd danced with her at the wedding, she'd seen the blaze of passion in his eyes—something she'd never seen in Antonio's.

The dreamy expression on her face reflected by the mirror changed abruptly. She regretted choosing Antonio. But back then his family and financial connections were what she thought she needed to support her lavish lifestyle. Even at that young age, she wanted a life of glamor, excitement, and being the center of attention. When he presented her with the spectacular bracelet and asked her to wait for him, she was ecstatic.

What she hadn't counted on were the rules and regulations involved with a commoner marrying into a royal family—no matter how far removed. His family had not supported their engagement. They demanded he marry someone more suited to be a doctor's wife, someone who would stay home and raise children. They pointed out that Stella would not be well received by the family and her behavior would be under a microscope—no politics, no public displays of affection, no drama or opinions, and endless other infractions not to be committed were drummed into her head. The lectures from Antonio's parents were ongoing. They said he was too old for her. He was already in his fourth year of medical school with two years left and a five-year residency to complete before they could marry.

The most heated discussions centered around Stella's career. As a model and film star, they considered Stella unworthy of the only son of their well-connected family. They told her repeatedly that she would have to give up her foolish pursuit of such a career. When she said she wouldn't, the warm and welcoming embrace of his family found during the earlier summer vacations turned formal and cold.

Once before the wedding, she'd overheard a whispered conversation between Antonio's parents as she paused in the hallway outside the sitting room door. Their raised voices carried into the long, marbled corridor. Comments like Hollywood slut and a family that didn't have a pedigree flowed on the summer breeze, wrapping around her throat until she gagged and tiptoed away.

She had made it her mission to win them over, but in their eyes she was not worthy of their only son. Antonio was indifferent to her discomfort and suggested she try harder. That's when she discovered he wouldn't stand up and fight for her. He shrugged and said they'd come around.

But at seventeen, the idea of marrying Antonio was too strong and the disagreements fueled the fire of their passion until his parents reluctantly agreed to the marriage. But their consent didn't come until after Antonio's ultimatum. It was the one and only time he stood up to them. He said he would drop out of medical school, move to Australia, and never marry anyone if he couldn't marry Stella. Although Antonio's family kept their distance, the engagement stood and plans for the wedding began.

All those years ago when he had clasped the bracelet around her wrist and asked her to wait for him, she had believed in the fairytale version of love. They promised each other that the miles and the long separations wouldn't change them, but they had. Seventeen had been too young for her to know anything about love, betrayal, or fear.

Modeling had required interaction with supercilious men who believed they owned her. She protested but was told by the agency it was a necessary part of the publicity required to become a top model. If she didn't participate, there were plenty of other young girls yearning to take her place. Stella had broken into modeling with great success and soon she was tapped for films. Antonio completed his medical training and began his residency.

And that's how it started—a little weed or a pill, something that would ease the pain of unwanted hands on her body. At first, she only used drugs for the coerced sexual encounters that were, according to her handler, a necessary part of her career.

Soon she needed something to help her through the big photo shoots. When panic attacks hit, she increased her dosage. When she was selected for a small role in a film, her anxiety ratcheted up and the marijuana and pills became a part of her daily routine.

She tried telling Antonio about the pressures she was facing, but he was overwhelmed with his medical studies. Those inseparable, childhood years they had spent on the beaches of Castello del Mare dissolved into infrequent sleepovers in Milan, Rome, and London with conversations on the run.

When the wedding day finally arrived, all went as she imagined. His family connection to the last king of Italy had sensationalized the event. The venue was the Vittorio Emanuele II Monument in the center of Rome. So clever, everyone said. The edifice everyone called a wedding cake became the setting for one of the grandest weddings of the year.

They bought a home in Castello as they had always planned. The terrace and gardens overlooked the sea but rarely were the two of them there at the same time. Days had turned into years. What she thought was love had disappeared, replaced by disappointment and indifference.

His family had been devastated when they chose the town of Castello del Mare in Puglia over Milan and a small clinic over a major medical center. His parents were doctors. They had expected him to come into their practice in Milan. It was the beginning of a huge rift, and they blamed Stella.

It was as if she didn't exist. Although they were angry with Antonio, they maintained contact and said he could come to visit but they preferred he come alone. They even told him they were embarrassed he had married her. She hated it when Antonio surfaced from his work and decided to spend his time off with his family. He'd take the overnight train to Milan. Sometimes she'd tag along but they ignored her. One day she stopped going. No one noticed.

In the early years, her drug usage had been recreational. Everyone in the business accepted it as natural. She told herself that she was a responsible user, as if that wasn't a joke. She thought she could control her habit until it became uncontrollable. Marijuana quickly turned to cocaine and finally to fentanyl. It was a more expensive drug but easier to get and conceal. She stayed with Antonio longer than made sense because he had become her main supplier.

He was oblivious to her growing addiction. When she was in town, he was careless about leaving drugs available for her to steal. His attention was always directed toward his practice and his patients. As the years fled from her grasp, she required more and stronger drugs. Antonio kept those locked in a cabinet in his office. She easily found the key. When he discovered she was stealing, he'd changed the locks. She crossed the line by breaking in and stealing the opiates. After that, his office became a fortress that she wasn't allowed to enter.

She had no choice but to find other contacts. In her glamorous world it had been easy to find resources. So-called friends were eager to connect her with the shadowy underworld. Over time these sources became increasingly dark and demanding. It was only after the threats began that she became frightened enough to seek help for her addiction. She had to get clean. The cost had become too great.

She sighed remembering the last clash with Antonio. She'd stopped by the house with the intention of discussing grounds for divorce. Instead, she had found him in bed with Sylvia, his nurse practitioner. He said she was trespassing. She dangled her key in front of his face and asked how that could be. He called her a liar, a thief, a prostitute, and an addict. He threatened to call the police. She called him a traitor, an adulterer, and a faithless prick. It had been an ugly screaming match. She had stupidly come at both of them with a kitchen knife. Thankfully, she only managed to slash Antonio's hand before he had wrestled the knife away from her. That was the last time she saw him.

Ha, she laughed at the mirror and at the woman no longer a girl. *Who will win? Me or the drugs? Will I be able to give up the one thing in life that gives me courage? If I don't, what then?*

Cat was the answer. If anyone could help her out of this mess, it was Cat. Only a few more weeks and Cat would be here.

Stella shrugged, straightened her dress, and turned sideways to check the necklace. This would be her last appearance for a while. She had cleared off her calendar. Cat had agreed to come early before her job at the restaurant began. They would have three months to reconnect. It would be their time. If everything fell into place, this mess would be over before Cat arrived. But Stella was leaving nothing to chance.

She grimaced at the mirror one last time and even managed a smile but it froze across her mouth as the sunlight bounced off the necklace. It was a constant reminder of the privileged life she lived. She'd made enemies. She didn't know who. But clearly, there were people angry enough to humiliate or even kill her. The person who had demanded the necklace was someone she must have wronged along the way. She had no answers as to who or why.

She had not responded to the last note. It was only a matter of time before she was forced to comply with their demands. She told the mirror she was ahead of their game and had time to put her plan into place. The mirror reflected the hopefulness in her eyes.

She snorted thinking about all the men who thought she was some stupid female available to conquer. Soon they would know that steadily over the years in backrooms, bedrooms, and ballrooms she had overheard and recorded numerous confidential conversations. She had a lot of evidence. A lot of people would go down—not just the mafia but politicians, judges, police, and local citizens.

She only had to get through today's session. Tomorrow she would put the necklace in the safe deposit box, retrieve the information from the hideaway, and send it to the Guardia in Rome. Then, she would gladly accept the protection she knew they would force on her.

She faced the mirror. She needed answers. Something important was eluding her. She'd felt uneasy ever since the night she and Gino had watched the boats arrive with the fish and drugs. She was sure they were being watched. Although the light from the hill above the marina had only flashed once, it was enough for her to move up her plans to turn in the evidence.

She checked her makeup and hair one last time. Her hands trembled as she pushed a stray curl back in place. Without drugs she was jittery about the photo shoot. She smiled at her image but not with happiness. She smiled because the end was in sight. She was gambling with her life. She could only hope she would not have to pay the price.

CAT

SOUTH CAROLINA LOWCOUNTRY

My knuckles whitened as they knot around the steering wheel. Glancing into the mirror, I back the van into the space next to the kitchen door. The steady purr of the engine does nothing to calm the anger rising from my gut. My shoulders tense like an iron blade is holding them in place. My face flushes a deep red hue. If Mrs. Harrington opened the door, I would explode. That can't happen. I can't lose it. It's critical that I at least appear calm and in control when I confront her. Sweat rolls off my face as I consider losing my most lucrative client.

My forehead presses against the steering wheel while I hunt around for serenity. Instead of centering and finding calmness, I butt my head against the hard rubber. What am I going to do? I simply cannot face John Ashley and his bride-to-be. I cannot. I will not allow them to make a fool of me.

There's a tap on the hood. I raise my head.

"Hey, you the food lady? Mrs. Harrington sent me out to help you unload."

There's still time to put the gear in drive and haul ass out of here. Instead I open the door and smile like a storefront mannequin

Two guys bound from the porch. I line up the containers cautioning them to be careful—don't tilt, shift, or drop. They sense my foul mood and stay out of my way as they quietly and quickly remove the containers. I sigh with relief when there's no sign of anyone.

Confrontation is something I don't do well—or at all. I prefer sneaking out and not being available when someone messes with me. It's passive-aggressive behavior, something taught to every well-bred southern girl. It's why I fell into Richard's controlling, abusive clutches. I thought I'd learned that lesson—that is until John Ashley and Mrs. Harrington entered my life, and I succumbed to their manipulative hands.

My hand is on the door handle when a commanding voice calls my name.

"Cat," the forceful sound rings out—strong and clear just as I remember it.

John Ashley Williams, IV stands there tall and so proud of himself, calling to me like I'm a long, lost friend. A cheerful smile is smeared across his superior face.

A growl starts low in my throat. I slam the door and stride to the back of the van.

"Well, if it isn't the happy bridegroom," I snarl. Even as the words leave my mouth, I regret them. I don't want a confrontation with John Ashley. I don't have enough energy for two such encounters in one day. It would be a bonus if the ground opened and sucked him off the face of the earth.

He hesitates, probably wondering what I'll do next. I put his mind at ease when I say, "Well, I hear congratulations are in order."

He starts grinning—so pleased I'm not going to cause a scene. But the asshole is wrong.

"John Ashley, if I'd been informed the party was for you, I would have put rat poison in the food."

Perplexity shows in his eyes. He's caught between acting upset at what I just said or pretending I've made a joke. Of course, he chooses to laugh and say how clever I've always been with the comebacks.

Before we can continue, the screen door opens and Mrs.

Harrington joins us with a look of wild dismay on her face.

"What are you doing out here, John Ashley. I asked you to assist Roger in setting up the tent on the far side of the lawn. You weren't supposed to be here when Cat delivered the food."

"Now Mrs. H, you know I'm not mechanical. Hell, I can't even put a new blade in my razor without cutting myself. I figured you had me mixed up with someone else when you sent me on that mission. Now, I know why."

He chuckles like this little scene playing out is a big joke. I ignore him and stare down Mrs. Harrington.

"Cat, honey, I'm so sorry. I didn't mean for this to happen. That's why I wouldn't let Charlotte tell you who the party was for. It's your fault because you simply prepare the best food. I couldn't have another caterer for such a special event. I'm sure you understand."

My voice is a low growl. My legs tremble. I shift my weight and lean against the back of the van. "No, Mrs. Harrington, I don't understand."

"Well, I'm sorry that John Ashley didn't do as I asked. If he had, you'd be long gone and none the wiser. But since it's happened, I hope it won't spoil our relationship."

"Didn't it dawn on you that someone would tell me? Don't you think it's a pretty deceitful thing to do?"

"Of course, I knew you would eventually find out. Since Cassie's working tonight, she would have told you. But you're leaving for a year. You'll forget all about it by the time you return. And we'll all be waiting for you to cater our parties."

"You must really have a low opinion of me, Mrs. Harrington. You think it's okay to lie to me?"

"Oh child, I didn't lie to you. I just didn't tell you. I didn't want to upset you. Of course, I was thinking of you."

"You were not thinking of me. You were thinking of yourself and no one else. You have the food because you've paid for it. But that's it. You'll have to find someone else to serve and clean up. Cassie and Sam will not be here tonight. This is the last time I will cater for you."

Mrs. H puffs her chest out. A sharp laugh echoes across the space between us.

"Well, you're quite the little spitfire aren't you? I don't appreciate your sassy mouth. I can easily ruin you. Remember that."

I stare her down before saying, "I'm not a pushover Mrs. Harrington. You can spread any rumors you want but I won't ever work for you again."

With as much grace and dignity as I can muster, I hold my head high, climb into the van, and drive off. When I reach the end of the drive, the gates are open. I gun the engine and swerve onto the road before the tears slide—first a drop at a time, gathering speed and volume until the flow covers my face and the front of my shirt.

I pull off the road by the ruins of the historic Sheldon Church and let the tears cascade until they subside into a series of hiccuped sobs. My anger and resentment boil over as well as fear. Without a doubt, Mrs. Harrington can ruin my reputation and my business.

My two forever homes—the Lowcountry and Italy have both deserted me. The Lowcountry has ostracized me and there's a mess waiting for me in Italy. The only tape that plays in my head is I don't belong. I have never belonged.

A final sob escapes as I wipe my eyes and then my nose on my sleeve. I text Cassie that I'm on my way. Then I tap Stella's name and wait for the call to go through. Although I don't expect her to answer, I still hold my breath and pray she will. But there's only her soft voice asking me to leave a message.

I clear my throat before saying aloud, "Oh Stella, you'd be so proud of me. I stood up to Mrs. Harrington today. I can't wait to tell you all the details."

I pause then say, "Stella, please pick up. It doesn't matter if you're in trouble. I'll be there in a few days. We'll fix whatever is wrong. In my last message, I left you my new arrival date and time. Please be waiting for me in Brindisi. Oh, Stella, we'll have a grand time. Can't wait to see you. Stella, Stella, please be there.

STELLA

...And when she wasn't choreographing new ballets for the fish in her hands and the stars in the sky...

CASTELLO DEL MARE, ITALY

It was almost time for the photo shoot. The driver was waiting, yet Stella lingered, not ready to leave the safety of the villa. Her fingers hovered over the starfish necklace.

Those long ago Midas days of summer infused her with images and scents of sandy beaches, the large family villa that stayed cool in the Mediterranean heat, mounds of mouth-watering seafood, the first sighting of the Italian boys, and her forever friendship with Cat.

She could see herself and Cat skipping through the waves. She smiled, remembering the splendid summers with Cat by her side. Growing up they'd always been together. But the last time they were together in New York was awkward. The smile left her face.

Stella had never divulged to Cat the extent of her addiction. Cat knew she used recreational drugs. But she hadn't been able to tell her about the long stretches of not remembering anything, the time she overdosed, and her visits to rehab centers. Those times she disappeared for a while. And there was Antonio—he had insisted her addiction be kept a secret because of his practice.

What if Cat couldn't stomach her behavior? What if Cat deserted her? Cat had been the one person in her life who had always dropped whatever she was doing and flew to her side. But things had changed between them. The erosion had started the summer they were twelve.

Cat's father had been forced to resign or was fired. She never knew exactly what had happened. Both their dads had worked in international sales and spent most of their lives traveling. But that year something went wrong. Her dad's jaw was broken and the families who had been inseparable, no longer spoke to each other. Cat stayed out of school for a week. No one would answer Stella's questions. She eavesdropped on conversations until she pieced together a story of sorts. For months Cat wouldn't talk about it. Her eyes were always swollen and red. She shrugged off all of Stella's attempts to make things right between them.

When Cat told Stella the summer vacations were over because of her family's difficult financial situation, Stella panicked. Summers without Cat would be unbearable. She summoned her parents for a conference.

In her twelve-year old innocence, she dropped her announcement, "I won't go to Italy without Cat."

She rushed to her room and refused to come out until a solution could be found. Her parents spent days trying to persuade her otherwise. Nothing changed Stella's mind.

Finally, their mothers found a solution that would allow Cat to continue the vacations with Stella's family. Cat would have to work to pay for her airfare and food; otherwise, there would be no trip.

At the tender age of twelve, Cat found work—babysitting, pet sitting, raking and mowing yards, tutoring younger children, anything that allowed her to squirrel away money for those summer trips. Somehow, Stella and Cat patched the gap that their parents were never able to mend. But the split between the two families left them both confused and leery of what waited for them as they approached adulthood..

Of course, Stella's intervention was another secret she kept from Cat. If Cat had found out, she would have refused to go to Castello.

Stella and Cat had resumed their from-birth friendship but something had been broken and the family rift was never repaired. They tried to put it behind them, but the sweet days of innocence had blown away. The tender years of schoolgirl giggling throughout the night, staying up until the sun joined them had abruptly ended.

Stella remembered how they had lived for those summers in Castello del Mare, a place they loved fiercely. During the long, lazy days, they'd thrived and grown into stunning young women. Those days were the glue that kept their bond strong throughout the years.

Five years later in their seventeenth year, those endless summer days came to an end. Life caught up with them. University, then careers and marriage intercepted the friendship until it became a random visit or phone call a couple of times a year.

The loss they suffered at twelve increased when Stella chose a career in modeling, film, and relocating her home to Italy. Cat chose the traditional route of university, a corporate job in finance, and marriage.

When Stella announced her engagement to Antonio, Cat was the first person she called. As soon as the wedding date was set, Cat came to Italy to help her, and their friendship seemed to grow stronger.

Things changed eight years later when Cat divorced her husband, left her stable career, and embarked on a career in culinary arts. Then the catastrophic death of Cat's parents had occurred. Stella had rushed to Cat's side and stayed until Cat was strong enough to return to school. But that had brought up all the unspoken and painful memories of the schism between their families.

Stella's thoughts regressed further into the past. Their growing up years had been hell for Cat who had been shy and clumsy. In Stella's mind, Cat had been clever and had been at the top of the class, but she was never popular like Stella. The thing about Cat is she'd always forgiven Stella even when she stole her boyfriends, copied her notes and homework, and ignored her. Cat was the reason their pledge to be forever sisters had never been broken. *But would Cat forgive her now?*

The years had piled up so many secrets. When they were in New York, Stella had longed to tell Cat about her addiction. More importantly, she wanted Cat to know she was determined to break the habit. She needed to tell Cat the role Lorenzo had played in the mess she was in. But Lorenzo had warned her not to tell anyone about their affair or the drugs. He was adamant. He could easily lose his position as head of the *Guardia di Finanza* if anyone poked into her life.

Stella argued that Cat was her most trusted friend, but it didn't matter. Lorenzo made her promise not to tell Cat. He said if Cat knew, she'd not only be surprised, but she'd be angry and angry people said and did things they later regretted. He insinuated that telling Cat would also jeopardize the friendship they had. So she hadn't told Cat. But now she was stronger. She was ready.

"Cat will be here soon," she said to the mirror. "I'll call her after this evening's shoot. When she arrives, I'll tell her everything. She'll know what to do. She always does."

Stella smoothed the flowing skirt, a sad smile twisted her mouth into a smirk. The filtered sunlight revealed her long, shapely legs through the see-through material—a little erotica for the shoot. The setting sun with the backdrop of the sea would expose all of her. Of course, that's what they had always wanted, every little piece of her.

She smiled at the mirror, thankful that her long-time friend and photographer Stefano would be on location. He had discovered her all those years ago, the summer she turned sixteen. He'd convinced her parents to let him photograph her. He assured them she had a chance to make it big. And she had, thanks to him.

She sighed as the tension mounted. Instead of the memories easing her fear and pain, they exacerbated them. *What if she couldn't make it through the photo session without something to ease her anxiety?*

It had been two months—a lifetime for an addict. She had a choice to succumb or to walk away. Surely one small pill would be okay. Her fingers trembled as she opened her purse and poked around until she found the small concealed pill box hidden in the lining. Pressing the clasp, she snapped it open. Her fingers twitched as she selected a fentanyl from the mix. Before placing it on her tongue, she told the image in the mirror, *this is the last time.* She lifted the glass of lukewarm Locorotondo wine to her lips.

CAT

IRPORT BRINDISI, ITALY

Antonio called just before Cassie drove me to the airport in Savannah. He gave me the address and phone number of a property attorney in Lecce—just in case Stella didn't meet my plane. When I asked about the person, he said, "Carlo Rossini is a friend of mine. He has a set of keys to Stella's villa."

When I asked why, he changed the subject.

"Is there any news about Stella?"

"No," he snapped. "Stella hasn't returned, but you know Stella. She'll probably meet your plane."

Obviously after all these years, Stella has changed enough so that I don't know her. But surely she'll be waiting for me. I believe that right up until I grab my luggage off the carousel and walk out into the masses of waiting people. Scanning the crowd, I search for her smiling face until I realize she would be easy to spot—the one person everyone would be staring at. The information booth has no messages for me. After another thirty minutes of waiting, there's nothing left to do but rent a car, drive to Lecce, and contact this Signor Rossini.

After a long wait in the rental car line, I stop for a cappuccino. A caffeine kick always helps my travel fatigue. The aromatic Italian coffee infuses me with warmth and memories of all the trips to Italy. It's a small ritual I have of not leaving the airport until the first cup is drunk. I gaze into the white foam swirled with a triple heart. The barista smiles when I say *bello*. I drain the cup, gather my luggage, and walk through the automated doors.

Puddles stretch across the pocked asphalt. Dragging my luggage and my body, I search for the numbered space. Renting a car for a year isn't something I included in my already tight budget. I'll have to sort it out later. For now, I add it to the growing list of problems gathering in my head.

Eventually, the number on the rental form, the space, and the key fob match. I stow my luggage in the trunk, slide into the driver's side and toss my purse on the passenger seat. It spills open, dumping the contents onto the floorboard. I reach for the large envelope, the one Stella gave me in New York. The one that contains everything for the Andrea Bocelli concert. What possessed me to bring it? Maybe as sort of a talisman—to guarantee Stella is okay. I stuff it back in my purse.

My Italian passport lies open on the floorboard. A red-headed Caterina Maria Lucia Gabbiano stares back at me. The fake smile evokes an escapee from Alcatraz. My USA passport's photo isn't any better, twin terminators.

Caterina was my grandmother's, my Italian *nonna*, name. When I was a child, she came to live with us. She was a natural storyteller and a fabulous cook. Her stories saturated my mind as they came alive in our kitchen where she instructed me on the art of Italian cuisine.

She had arrived in the United States wearing all the clothes she owned. She was sixteen, married three months, and pregnant with my mother. I'm not only named after her but her passion for food transferred to my DNA along with the ease of learning another language. Nonna only spoke Italian to me from the day I was born. She easily corralled me into the love of cooking. Every dish she prepared included fascinating history about the ingredients and her life and that of her family.

All of her stories were mixed with the fragrant goodness of food.

She taught my hands to mix, blend, and pound. She leaned in close as she whispered secrets of her long-ago family in Puglia. She knew where I was destined long before I did. She said I was born to cook no matter where my journey took me. Generations of women would guide my hands and my heart until I found the way to the one skill that would sustain me.

But it was the story of my naming that I always begged her to tell me. Nonna would sigh, roll her eyes, and say my name carried with it a grand legacy. It was not bestowed lightly. Caterina had been passed from generation to generation and was always given to the oldest female. Much was expected from the child. It was a saintly name meaning pure, although Nonna would chuckle and wink at me when she told the story. Only after I was an adult and Nonna was no longer with us did my mom tell me that Nonna wasn't as pure as she had led me to believe. It seems she was pregnant with my mom before she was married.

As a child, I didn't understand the chuckle or the wink. I was in a hurry to hear the stories—to taste them as they became firmly entrenched in my memory with the flavors of southern Italy. My nonna had already mapped out my life for me. It just took me a while to discover she knew best.

My other names came from my mother. She would chime in as she worked side by side with Nonna and me.

"You must remember Caterina that all your names are significant. You are named Maria for Our Lady, the Blessed Virgin Mary. You were born in May, the month we celebrate her sainthood. And, Lucia is my chosen name for you because you are my light."

The image of seven-year-old Stella and me waiting with our parents for an appointment in Atlanta to obtain dual citizenship are still vivid. Stella and I were the only two kids in our school to have passports—not just one but two. Dual citizenship made travel easy for us. Secretly, even at that tender age, I felt a tiny bit smug with two passports.

Tears distort the passport photo as I think of Mom and Dad.

Their lives so quickly snuffed out by a drunk driver. Their deaths still haunt me. But, I can't allow myself to start this journey sobbing. I grab a tissue, toss the passport into my purse, turn on the engine, and back out of the space.

The highway out of the airport is slick with rain. Fighting the wheel, I skirt through the debris-cluttered road. The drive vacillates between heart-stopping moments of torrential downpour and staccato bursts of hail. The wind propels the car toward the steep, rocky coastline devoid of railings. Just when I think I'll be swept over the side, a brilliant sun bursts through the low-lying clouds. It spreads a spectacular rainbow that stretches from the land, heavy with olive trees, into the tossing sea.

The rain slows as I turn off the exit to Lecce. Antonio told me very little about this Signor Carlo Rossini. It makes no sense that he has the keys to Stella's house. Who is he? Why didn't Antonio meet me or at least send someone from Castello?

Before I left the US, I had checked out a few rental properties just in case Stella didn't show up. Antonio hadn't exactly made me feel welcome to stay at her place. As I was surfing rentals, I came across her villa on a website.

I called Antonio on the pretense of making sure it was okay for me to stay at the house without Stella. I nonchalantly asked him if Stella owned or rented the villa. I didn't tell him that Stella had shown me photos when we met in New York or that I knew she'd bought the villa. She'd named it *Casa dei Fiori*—House of Flowers. If Stella owns the house, it makes no sense for it to be on a rental site. But then nothing seems to make sense including Antonio when he admitted he wasn't sure if Stella owned or rented the villa.

If my memory is correct, this Rossini person was the contact on the rental website. What does that mean?

As I drive through the narrow, intertwined streets of Lecce, the GPS goes berserk and propels me in a circular pattern. Glancing up, I see a bright orange sign for a *marcelleria.* I'm sure I passed it before but the GPS insists I go by again. When I drive by the same butcher shop a third time, I surrender to my body's demand to stop. Pulling into the nearest parking area, I cut the engine and lean my head against the cool steering wheel. My body slumps. But not for long as my chaotic mind keeps feeding me images of Stella in distress, or hurt, or even dead. I hunt for a street sign before I tap in Signor Rossini's number.

"*Buongiorno, Signor Rossini*. It's Caterina Gabbiano.

"*Sì, Signora*. I was expecting your call.

"*Mi scusi,* but I'm lost.

"*Dove Lei?*"

"I'm in the last parking spot at the *Museo Fantasia* on via Spineta. Your office complex has escaped my detection. I'm sorry to bother you, but when the GPS took me past the same *marcelleria* three times, I knew I was in trouble. Is it possible for you to find me, or can you give me directions to your office?"

His low, throaty laughter eases some of the tension from my neck and shoulders,

"I know where you are. Stay right there. You are only a few minutes away. I'm leaving now."

STELLA

...She was collecting lost dreams and broken hearts
and suturing the cracks closed and finding new roads to follow
and teaching laughter to the tears they had shed...

CASTELLO DEL MARE, ITALY

Stella gagged on the warm wine. It spewed out of her mouth along with the dissolving pill. Her fingers frantically clawed, scrapping at the disintegrating bits in the sink. The mirror flashed images of her desperate attempt to salvage the fentanyl—the look of a wild, out-of-control animal.

She stopped as a vision of Cat moved into the mirror and stood by her side. Their eyes locked. Cat was wearing her long-ago neon blue Wonder Woman cape. Stella gagged again, coughing up the remains of the pill and spilling the last bit of wine. She watched in horror as the fragments slid down the drain.

But Cat's image reached out to her, pulled her back, and stopped her trembling. Cat had been the great rescuer from sewer kittens to snotty-nosed kids. She always had someone or something in tow, muttering words of comfort. She had that magical touch. Her small child's hand had patted away tears with the torn edge of her cape while offering a smashed Reese's peanut butter cup that had been tucked into the sweaty waist band of her blue tights for who knows how long. Cat had protected and rescued Stella over and over. She sighed with relief. Yes, Cat will be here soon.

She tucked a stray curl behind her ear, patted the sweat from her forehead, and touched the starfish for luck. Her ragged sigh joined the humid air. Her body trembled as the heavy puff of air escaped. It left a trail of despair tinged with hope. Dropping the pill was a signal. This was her last chance to stop, to turn her life around. She picked up the small case and dumped the rest of the pills into the toilet and flushed.

She glanced at the mirror one last time, slid her cell phone in her pocket, opened the door, and stepped out on the terrace. She stopped briefly to seek guidance from the lone tree perched on the small edge of land jutting into the sea. Soon she and Cat would be sitting on the terrace drinking wine and catching up. Cat would understand her relationship with the tree and the strength she found there.

Buying this house had been a shrewd move but paying cash had not been smart. She'd missed several payments for the drugs. Then, she had opened a line of credit—such a stupid move and now she was trapped. She hadn't seriously considered she was being watched until the pressure had intensified right after the night she and Gino had seen the flicker of light. Her line of credit had been pulled. She was frightened.

She stroked the starfish once more and whispered to the lone tree. She closed her eyes and wished for the day this would be over and only a sordid memory.

She lifted her dress and moved like a gazelle down the steps.

L'ape waited for her. The driver wasn't her regular.

"Where's the Mercedes?"

He grunted and gunned the gas as she reached for the strap. She hit the seat hard. Grabbing her skirt which was still billowing outside the vehicle, she cried out, "*Aspetta, Wait!*" She tapped the driver on the shoulder but he didn't turn around or slow down. She grasped at the side pole which supported the canvas top and managed to swing her body onto the seat. She pulled her skirt inside the vehicle and held on as *l'ape* bolted down the narrow street.

She formed the words—*l'ape*, smiling as her tongue curled into the *lah pay* sound bringing the bee's hum to her ears. How perfect to name this tiny cart-like structure the bee—buzzing through the tiny passageways that were too constricted for cars.

As *l'ape* made its way toward the craggy coastline, she promised herself as soon as the photo shoot was over, she'd call Cat. Tinges of happiness and excitement crawled up her arms as she imagined having an entire year for them to spend together. Twenty years after their last summer in Castello, the circle of life was bringing them together. She and Cat, forever friends. She laughed and hummed snatches of one of their favorite summer songs *Banane e Lampone* as *l'ape* buzzed its way up the coastal road.

It passed the main piazza and her favorite restaurant La Canzone, the restaurant where Cat would work. The hill crested, and *l'ape* shuddered as it lurched off the road and onto the sandy soil.

Stella leaned to the left to get a better look but the driver's burly shoulders barred her view. The path to the top was narrow, unstable. The vehicle shimmied to a stop as low-growing shrubs prevented it from going any further. She glanced at her white ballet slippers. Realizing they were useless, she slipped them off her feet and slid them under the seat. A barefoot photo had a certain appeal. When she was posing, she would remember those glorious childhood days on the beach with Cat—those days when the entire world belonged to them —when they were fearless and there had been no darkness in their lives.

Stella's thoughts slid into the murky recesses of her mind. *What happened to me? When did I give up on myself and allow others to use me?Is it too late? Can I change?*

The questions ended when the driver turned and said, *Devi camminare per il resto della strada.* "You'll have to walk the rest of the way."

She jumped from the vehicle. Her feet sunk into the warm sand, coarse as granulated sugar. The breeze lifted her heavy hair, cooling her long, slender neck. She stretched into the wind, feeling more alive than she had in a long time. Tomorrow will be a new beginning. She smiled and moved effortlessly up the slope.

A shimmering shaft of light burst into her eyes then skipped in front of her, twisting into somersaults. She glanced up and saw the source—a mirror. She shuddered at the thought as Stefano never used gimmicks. Plus, the timing wasn't right. The ambient light was not at its softest until just before sunset.

The descending sun struck the mirror again, creating a brilliance so harsh she ducked her head and looked down at the path to avoid being blinded. Her irritation grew as she reached the summit. *This can't be right. Stefano would never allow a mirror as a prop, and he would never choose this time of day.*

Stefano had been her photographer for the twenty plus years she had been in the industry. She trusted him and no one else. Early on she had put a stop to the overcrowded shoots by learning every craft herself except set design and photography. Stefano had buckets of talent in those areas.

To avoid the startling reflection of the sun bouncing off the mirror, she kept her eyes on the ground. When she arrived at the plateau, she shielded her eyes from the glare and turned to the photographer, "Ciao Stefano, do you have a pair of sunglasses for me? I forgot mine."

The luminosity of the mirrored sun impaired her vision but not her speech.

"Stefano, "Why are we using a mirror? It's not like you. Did the magazine suggest this bizarre setting?"

The large man she assumed was Stefano turned and walked toward her. The outline of his face came into view. Dark shadows, a scraggly beard, crooked yellowed teeth, and a single gold earring made her exclaim, "You're not Stefano. Who are you?"

He shrugged. "Stefano had another assignment."

"That's impossible. He arranged the shoot. I talked to his assistant a few days ago. She assured me Stefano would be here. I won't do this shoot without him. Where is he? Call him now!"

"You will do the shoot because you are under contract. You're obligated. We don't have all day. If you don't cooperate, I will call one of the other actresses. You can explain to your agent and to the magazine why there are no photographs of you. Your choice. I don't give a damn whether you stay or go, but make up your mind."

Stella shivered, mesmerized by his contorted face.

"Well?" the photographer sneered as he lit a cigarette.

"Smoking isn't allowed on the set," was all she could think of to say.

His dull eyes looked through her as they swept the landscape before returning to leer at her breasts. A bit of drool appeared at the corner of his mouth.

"On this set there's smoking," he snarled. "Like I said, we can go ahead with the shoot or not. Means nothing to me."

She flushed and lamely said, "I'm not wearing shoes. Is that a problem?"

"Who cares. Although I'd like it better if you weren't wearing clothes."

Stella wished with all her heart she had taken the fentanyl. She looked at her bare feet. She felt naked—vulnerable. There was nothing to do but get it over with.

"Where do you want me to stand?"

"In the center of the mirror. I want the full effect of the setting sun behind you."

Stella picked her way gingerly through the rocky earth and positioned herself. The sooner she finished, the sooner she could get away from this dreadful person. She flung back her hair, arched her back, and shifted her weight slightly to the right. The fading sunlight picked up the outline of her body under the sheer dress. It revealed just enough to tease the viewer.

She didn't see the photographer turn his back and walk down the hill where the driver of *l'ape* waited. She didn't see the man in black crouched among the boulders. He had been in place for a while so there would be no risk of her seeing him prematurely.

Riccardo shifted his weight and fidgeted with the gun. The distance between his hiding place and the mirror was further than he liked. The mirror complicated the situation. When he stood up, the sun would bounce back in his eyes, momentarily blinding him. If she ducked, moved or ran, or if he missed the shot, it would be his head. It was such a damn nuisance that *il padrone* wanted to witness the event from a safe distance in the penthouse. He had ordered the blasted mirror for dramatic effect.

It was absurd that he chose this highly visible location and a time just before sunset when anyone could happen by. Maybe that was it —*il padrone* loved living on the edge, loved putting others at risk while he stayed in the background.

But complaining wouldn't change the facts. Riccardo owed him everything. He would be dead if *il padrone* hadn't plucked him out of the sea. He'd been ten. His passage was paid by a relative after his parents were killed. The old fishing boat with over a hundred people crammed inside broke up as it struggled toward the rocky coastline. The cargo of Albanians, mostly children, had been swept overboard. Most of them didn't know how to swim. The weight of the sea pulled him under but the strong arms of a young mafia lieutenant rescued him. He was forever indebted. He would have followed *il padrone* into hell and back. He gladly embraced the ways of the SCU. As his rescuer rose in the ranks, he guided Riccardo, grooming him each step of the way until he became second in command to *il padrone*.

He glanced at his watch. It was almost time.

Stella stood completely still, her eyes closed to the intense sun. She listened, waiting for the photographer to move into position. When there was no movement, she glanced up but the sun was too strong, forcing her to turn away.

She tucked her head down and pulled out her phone to check the time. It was still too early for photographs, so she hit the speed dial for

Cat's number. It went directly to voicemail. She debated whether or not to leave a message but decided to when the indicator beeped.

"Hi Cat. I just wanted to hear your voice. I'm on set. Stefano's not here. He's always on set. Something seems to be wrong."

Riccardo tensed his thigh muscles and rose. She didn't see the figure in black creep from behind the outcropping of rocks. She paused as a shadow crossed the sun. She wasn't sure but there appeared to be movement in the rocks. She looked up but the cloud moved quickly away, leaving the sun to cast a sharp blazing light in her eyes.

The movement and light startled her. The phone slipped from her hand. She reached down to grab it just as a shot rang out, splintering the mirror behind her. She grappled for the phone and wept into it, "Please, Cat. Help me—someone is..."

The sun struck the mirror and Stella screamed as she saw the man in black standing among the boulders. The intensity of his dark eyes radiated across the distance. She whispered into the phone, "Please, please, Cat, help me."

She dropped to her knees as the slam of the silencer swept across the plateau. For one single moment the world was silent. Her fingers fluttered to the necklace. She yanked it off as the bullet struck her neck, pierced its way out, and shattered the remains of the mirror before ricocheting off the rocks and dropping into the weeds.

CAT

L*ECCE, ITALY*

By the time I rearrange my windblown hair and count to three hundred, Signor Rossini materializes. He's at the car door before I can open it. He reaches for my hand and clasps it tightly in his while assisting me from the car. His hand is strong and warm and holds onto mine longer than necessary. His hair is short and dark, his skin an olive glow. The exquisitely tailored suit hangs perfectly on his slim athletic body. Mid-forties, I think.

He transfers a packet of information along with a set of keys and says, "I'm so sorry I couldn't meet your plane. Antonio didn't call me until late last night. He asked me to pick you up and drive you to Castello. But the short notice didn't give me enough time to rearrange my schedule. I'm truly sorry, but Gino will meet you in the main piazza. I'll call you in a day or two and drive down as soon as I can. If anything doesn't suit you, please contact me directly."

His English is impeccable and matches his slightly sullen good looks. He does justice to the dark stubble on his chin, something Italian men do so well. He manages to simultaneously look immaculate but casual—a trait most American men can't pull off.

His smile doesn't quite reach his eyes as he continues, "Antonio didn't explain why Stella might not meet your plane or why he couldn't. Was Stella delayed at one of her publicity events?"

"Possibly," I stammer as the question startles me. I don't know what to say to him about Stella. His face doesn't reveal how well he knows her. I can't help but wonder if he's concerned about her well-being or if he's probing for information.

He takes a sharp breath and then says, "Antonio said that you might not feel comfortable staying at *Casa dei Fiori*. If that's true, I have other properties. But Fiori is beautiful. I'm sure you'll love it. Gino and Maria will do everything to make you comfortable."

I must have frowned because he continues with a question in his voice, "Gino and Maria? The caretakers? They have keys to the house, handle most situations, and are available for whatever you need— repairs, cleaning, cooking, shopping, *va bene*?"

I nod, surprised and uncomfortable with the thought of someone else having keys.

"Is that what they do for Stella?"

"Yes, of course. Maria and Gino adore Stella. They can't do enough for her. She feels the same way about them. Whenever I stop in Castello, she and Maria are usually planning some dinner party or rescuing sick children or senior citizens. Stella has a presence in the community."

He smiles that half smile again, "Once you've rested for a couple of days, I'll check on you. And please, call me Carlo."

"Of course, Carlo. My friends call me Cat."

He extends his hand again. As I reach for it, his gray eyes widen and soften.

"You are exhausted, aren't you? Do you have time for coffee?"

"No, grazie. It's another forty-five minutes to the villa. I want to beat the storm."

"Of course, maybe another time."

"*Certo*," I say, turning to leave.

He touches my arm, "I know you."

"What? What do you mean?"

My fatigue is momentarily forgotten. I search his face looking for signs of familiarity but see none.

"You're Caterina—Cat. It was the way you said your name just now. It triggered a memory. You signed the *licenza matrimonio,* the certificate at Stella and Antonio's wedding, *vero*?"

"Yes, that's true, but how did you know that?" I back up, lean against the car, and realize too late that the seat of my jeans will be saturated when I move away.

"I was there. I met you. It was just for a second. You were busy playing hostess while Stella held court with the royal branch of Antonio's family. It was a long time ago. Your surname was different—maybe Signora Andrews or Anderson. That's why I didn't make a connection when Antonio said a friend of Stella's would be picking up the keys. He gave your surname as Gabbiano. I didn't recognize the name."

"It used to be Anderson. When I divorced, I took my family name back. How did you recognize me? That was years ago."

He strokes the stubble on his chin, raises an eyebrow and chuckles, "Your hair, it was and still is amazing. You were so vibrant standing next to Stella. Please, don't get me wrong. Stella is a beautiful woman, but she was in head-to-toe white. You were such a contrast, full of energy and dazzling color against all her whiteness. Your red hair and cobalt dress were like Venus rising out of the sea."

"Hmm," is all I manage.

"I'm so sorry about Stella."

"Sorry? Why?"

He has the good grace to look confused before continuing, "I"m not privy to what's going on. Antonio didn't confide in me but there's talk in the village. A rumor that she's disappeared. Is that why you are here? Has Antonio filled you in?"

"Actually, Stella invited me to stay at the villa before she went missing. We had planned it ages ago. She's responsible for connecting me with Giorgione and Sebastian at Ristorante La Canzone. I'm going to be working there."

I hesitate a second, then blurt out, "What do you know?"

He stares at me a second too long before replying, "Why would I know anything?"

One of my other problems besides counting is I'm dogmatic and don't always know when to keep my mouth shut.

"It seems that Stella's villa is listed with your vacation rentals. Why? Stella told me she owned the villa."

His eyes turn steely. His jaw muscles tighten. Instead of answering my question he asks, "What do you know about Stella's disappearance?"

I stammer, "Well, I, I guess I don't really know anything. I didn't know Stella was missing until I talked to Antonio. I called him when I couldn't reach her."

Carlo searches my face, for what I'm not sure. I force my muscles to stay neutral. There is no way I will tell him about Stella's incoherent message. Uneasiness crawls along my spine. When he doesn't respond, I pursue the subject.

"Does Antonio know Stella's villa is on your rental list?"

"Look Cat. I'm not sure why this is a problem for you. But it has not been that long since Stella bought the villa. One of the office clerks must have forgotten to remove it from the website. Are you accusing me of doing something illegal?"

"Well, it seems strange. Stella's only been missing a short time and her villa is listed on your rental site." I let my words trail away into the sultry air.

A crease gathers on his forehead as he scowls at me. "Of course I don't plan on renting Stella's villa. That would be Antonio's decision. Besides, everyone knows Stella has a track record for disappearing. She has done it before, sometimes for a couple of months. But usually someone knows where to find her. But not this time, according to Maria and Gino."

The wind stirs the treetops. Clouds thicken and clot, obscuring the already muted sunlight. Thunder rumbles in the distance. A growing unease gathers steam. Everyone except me seems to know that Stella has a habit of disappearing. And these people Maria and

Gino seem to be feeding Carlo information about Stella. I wonder why?

Carlo glances at his watch. It's elegant. Looks like a Panerai. If it is, it costs a chunk of change. He straightens his cuff and turns to leave. My mouth opens. Words spew out before I can harness them.

"I'm worried about Stella. The last time I saw her she was unhappy."

I bite my tongue which abruptly stops my chatter. I talk too much —something I'm prone to do when I'm nervous.

He waits for me to continue. When I don't, he says, "Did she say anything that might be a clue to her disappearance? Have you heard from her? If you know anything, please tell me. I'm sure it would help the police. Of course, we're all concerned."

His words are contrived as he positions his face into a look of concern. The two don't match.

"No, sorry. During our last conversation, we talked about our upcoming plans. She was supposed to pick me up at the airport. Since my job at La Canzone doesn't start right away, Stella had cleared her schedule so we could catch up and travel a bit."

I pause, then plunge ahead, "What about you? Do you know her well? I guess you must since you were invited to the wedding."

He's quiet for a few seconds then says, "I really did not—do not know Stella. My connection is with Antonio and Lorenzo. It's pretty much a business relationship. I met Antonio a year or so before the wedding. He introduced me to Lorenzo. Our paths kept crossing, mostly through criminal investigations."

He places his hand on my arm and says, "Come back to the office with me and wait. Then I can drive you to Castello later this evening."

The touch is unexpected. I recoil.

He pulls back, "I'm sorry. I didn't mean to startle you. It's just that seeing you is such a surprise after so many years. You are as lovely now as you were then. It brings back a lot of memories about the wedding. I remember asking everyone who you were. Finally,

Antonio told me that you, Stella, Lorenzo, and he had been childhood friends."

When I ignore his comments, he pauses. I jump in.

"So you, Antonio, and Lorenzo work together? That seems unusual since you are in such different fields."

"It's not that unusual. Antonio is often involved with patients who overdose, falsify prescriptions, or forge information to get pain medications. Criminals need doctors too. Then the property management business is rife with mafia-style landlords and crooked housing deals. Antonio and I often end up testifying in court. Lorenzo saw how well we stood up against the criminal element around here and asked us to team up to assist him."

He frowns, "Antonio and I gather information and stay on the lookout for suspicious activities through our medical and legal channels. Anything we discover that might assist Lorenzo we pass on to him—names, connections, or anything that might lead to an arrest and conviction. For instance, property damage, slum landlords, illegal prescriptions, prostitution, drug smuggling, and break-ins. The information has put some of the players away for a while. It has been a good relationship for the three of us. Probably not something I am supposed to tell you, so please keep it to yourself."

"That's impressive," I say but what I really think *is who is this guy?*

He nods and glances once more at his Panerai Luminor watch, "You said you hadn't seen Antonio in a long time. Be prepared for a change. His and Stella's relationship has been on the rocks for a while. We all knew about Stella going off for long periods of time. Maybe for her job, maybe not.

"These days he keeps to himself, still practicing but not socializing. He doesn't talk to anyone unless he's forced to. Of course, that doesn't include his patients. But sometimes it does include Lorenzo or me. He's been that way for a while, even before Stella disappeared. He has no interest in anything other than his practice. When I'm in Castello, I drop by his office. Sylvia usually says he's with a patient so you can imagine my surprise when he called and asked me to meet you."

I'm still caught up in his *no interest in anything but his practice* statement about Antonio. I don't buy it since Stella told me he was having an affair. Antonio might even be glad Stella disappeared. I wonder if this Sylvia person is the one Stella said was involved with Antonio? When I tune back into the conversation, Carlo has changed the subject.

Before I can catch up, he says,"The villa has been empty since Stella's disappearance. No one is sure when she left but at least a few weeks have passed. At first Lorenzo said the villa was a crime scene but when he couldn't find any evidence there, he released it. No one mentioned you were coming to stay until Antonio called me. I'm sorry that you saw Stella's villa on my rental site. That must have been a shock but rest assured it's a mistake. When I get back to the office, the correction will be made."

"It's okay," I hear myself saying.

"If you would rather stay in another place, it will only take me a few minutes to go back to the office and get keys to several other properties. While I cannot drive you to Castello, Gino and Maria know where all the properties are, and they will show you."

A raindrop blurs the world as one plops on my head and another into my eye. My knees quiver.

"No, it's okay. I'm too tired to think clearly or make a different decision. Stella wanted me to stay at her place. That's where I want to stay. It's close enough for me to walk to La Canzone. Staying there will give me an opportunity to be part of Stella's life. That's where she expects me to be. I'll stay there unless Antonio decides differently. I'm guessing all her belongings are still there. Do you know?"

"I really don't know although it might make sense for Antonio to remove some of her personal things, like jewelry and other valuables. Legally they're still married."

"Well, Antonio has said it's okay for me to stay for now. Do I need your permission too?

"Look, the villa is Stella's. She invited you to stay so you don't need anyone's permission."

"If I need to pay rent, I can do that. Just tell me how much and who gets the money. Is it you or Antonio who is in charge of the place in Stella's absence?"

"It's Stella's house. Of course you won't pay. My only concern is that you're comfortable. If not, I can easily find you another place."

"Give me a day or two, then I'll let you know. I'm too tired to make a coherent decision at the moment."

As I open the car door, he says, "Cat, Stella must have pulled some strings to get you a job at La Canzone. Of course, Giorgione adores her. You'll like him and the food. It's the best restaurant around. When I'm next down your way, maybe we could have lunch?"

He hesitates as if to say something else, shakes his head, starts for the car, and then turns and says, "Be careful. Stella has a track record for upsetting people—dangerous people."

My knees buckle as I slide my damp butt under the steering wheel. I start the engine and turn on the windshield wipers. Carlo shouts something about Gino and Maria being reliable and to call if I need anything. But the storm intervenes, allowing only time for a quick wave as he sprints to his car.

My body trembles. My hands clutch the steering wheel. Why would he tell me to be careful, and why would he say Stella has a track record for upsetting people? He doesn't like Stella very much. His attitude toward her is as gray and stormy as the day. I close my eyes and lean back against the headrest.

My life continues to roll toward a trajectory to hell with Stella as the drum majorette.

STELLA

...And if you are ever lost between always and heartache
if you follow the roads and
The sky of the starfish ballet you will find her sitting and waiting to weave you a new day and
A new dream and a new fate under the street sign that reads
Oceans End

CASTELLO DEL MARE, ITALY...

Jagged edges of pain dug into Stella's neck and slammed through her shaking body. The agony crept like octopus tentacles—squeezing the life out of her. She grabbed at the necklace and ripped it from her throat. She flung it into the air—a silent prayer spiraling to the earth. It landed with the slightest tinkle as it hit against stone and slid into the bramble. She crumbled to the ground.

Riccardo's instructions from *il padrone* had been clear: shoot to injure, remove the necklace, reveal *il padrone's* identity, force her to divulge the place she was hiding information about the SCU, torture her if necessary, dump her body in the sea, and clean up the mess. No loose ends. *Il padrone* had made it clear. She had to understand who she had crossed and why the necklace was required.

He picked up the ejected casings, heaved a tarp and rope over his shoulder, and made some attempt to gather up the largest shards of broken glass as he worked his way toward her unmoving body. In his haste, he failed to see the necklace wedged in the soil between the boulders.

He stood over her. His entire being breathed in her beauty. But there was no time for sentiment. She wasn't moving but he knew she was alive. He was the best shot around even under the miserable conditions. Between the sun bouncing off the mirror and her movements before he pulled the trigger, he was sure the second shot had only nicked her. He glanced around the area. It was important to locate the two bullets before he left.

He nudged her shoulder with his shoe just below where the bullet grazed her neck. A low moan escaped from deep within her. The sound made him shudder. He was used to killing point blank and not hanging around to check for survivors.

For a moment his mother's face superimposed on the body at his feet—an image he had forced himself to forget—his entire family lying on the ground with bullet-riddled bodies while he hid in a tiny space under the steps of the burning house. That same animal-like moan had emitted from his mother.

He squatted next to Stella and gently shook her. Her brilliant blue eyes filled with terror stared back at him. She clutched her blood-soaked neck, but he pulled her hands away. He had to remove the necklace before it was a bloody mess. He stopped in mid-air. Then dropped her hands. There was no necklace around her throat.

The sun blasting against the mirror had blinded him. He had no idea if she had been wearing it. *Il padrone* had assured him that she wore it to all of her publicity appearances. For a moment he considered what to do. Binoculars were trained on his back.

He shook her again and growled, "Where's the necklace?"

A slight smile touched her lips. A tear slid down her cheek, "Where you will never find it."

He rocked back on his heels and pulled the black mask off his face.

She wasn't shocked and simply said, "Riccardo, why?"

The question hung in the air while he rummaged in the pocket of his vest. He removed a newspaper clipping and smoothed it across his leg before he held it in front of her face.

"You can thank *il padrone*."

Her whimper chilled him to the core as he watched her eyes take in the faded news clipping. He didn't understand why he was supposed to show it to her. It was one of those fancy society settings that used to flood the newspapers during the summer season. His eyes moved from the clipping to Stella's face. Her look of panic made his chest hurt but he knew she understood.

She struggled to sit up. He pushed her back down and said, "*Il padrone* said once you saw the clipping you would remember. He said the necklace is your gift to him—a sentimental thing that he knows you will appreciate. He also wants you to know the necklace is just a token. It is only part of the price you will pay for your interference in his business. Your activities cost him, and now it will cost you. *Il padrone* wants you to know the others will die too—even Caterina."

"Please no," she sobbed and grabbed at his sleeve. "Not Cat. She doesn't know anything. No one else is involved, only me. Please don't hurt Cat. There's money at the house—more than enough for you to start a new life. Please, Riccardo."

He pulled away, "Stella, I would be dead within two hours or less if I helped you. My only allegiance is to *Il padrone*. He saved my life. He wants the necklace, the money, and the information. Give me that, and it will be quick. If you don't, *Il padrone* said you must suffer.

Stella closed her eyes while her thoughts raced like mice in a maze. The gun was close. She began to mumble incoherently flinging out words: necklace, secret hideaway, Zinzulusa, a statue in the garden--anything that would bring him closer.

He leaned in. With all her strength, she lunged at him and cracked the bridge of his nose with her forehead. She grabbed his hand and twisted it until his grip loosened on the gun. It spun away from both of them. He flung his body after it. Her hand clutched at his leg and held on, pulling him back. His elbow slammed into her chest but she clung to him.

It was over in seconds, the gun reclaimed. The anger oozed from his eyes. She lunged again. The point-blank explosion filled her ears until she heard nothing.

For a moment, he was horrified. He had lost control of his emotions. *Il padrone* wanted her dead but not until Riccardo had extracted the information. His orders had been explicit. He straightened his body and stood. The binoculars trained on his back would pick up any hesitancy.

He yelled down to the driver to check for any traces of evidence left in the vehicle. The driver searched and found the white ballet slippers tucked under the seat. He walked to the edge of the cliff and flung them over the side.

Riccardo processed her last garbled words into some kind of cohesiveness—enough to take back to *il padrone*. He made the sign of the cross for Stella and for himself.

As he searched for the two bullets, he spied the cell phone a few meters away. He put it in his pocket and continued to poke through the scrubby landscape. *Il padrone* would be furious when he returned without the necklace.

He walked back to the area where she had been standing. With his boot he sorted through the broken glass. The bullets didn't surface which meant they'd ricocheted. He couldn't waste any more time looking for them. He turned around and walked back along the perimeter. Twice his foot was within inches of the necklace but the boulders and bramble shielded it from his eyes.

His only hope was that she hadn't worn it. The house would have to be ransacked. He'd also have to check the statues in the garden, the caves at Zinzulusa, and hope the necklace and the information turned up. Maybe she'd put the necklace with the incriminating evidence she had been collecting, and maybe he'd find some cash. He still didn't know why *il padrone* wanted the necklace, and he really didn't care. It wasn't his business to care.

But the assignment had been clear—money, information and necklace—the price she had to pay for interfering. But either way, the main goal had been to kill her, and he had accomplished that goal. Her death would be a warning to anyone who might consider tangling with the SCU.

He placed a large boulder inside the tarp, then pulled it tight around her body. The diamond-braid campo rope was meticulously tied before the bundle was rolled to the edge of the cliff. He paused and glanced around the area before shoving her body over. He didn't wait for it to hit the water some thirty meters below.

The plateau was swept clear of footprints and blood without too much effort since another storm was forecast for the evening. By tomorrow there would be nothing suspicious left.

The driver and the bogus photographer were handed envelopes containing forged passports, one-way plane tickets, and money. Night descended as Riccardo watched the two men take separate routes. With the arrangements he had made, it was unlikely they would be found.

Once they were out of sight, Riccardo ran to his car and headed to Stella's house while muttering the rosary under his breath.

CAT

LECCE, ITALY

Rain drums on the roof of the car. Gray sheets of water cascade down the windshield. Instead of driving on to Castello del Mare, I sit in the car in the parking lot in Lecce more confused than ever.

Stella has always been my best friend. Our history began the moment we were born, squalling into life at the same hospital on the same day, born to mothers who were best friends. We germinated into childhood, living next door to each other. We were inseparable during our growing up years. Our families attended the same church, country club, and community activities. Stella and I were enrolled in the same class at Catholic girls' school. We studied catechism and took our first communion together.

Mom used to lament that there had been a mixup at the hospital. Somehow her best friend the shy, dark Angelica left the hospital with the gloriously blonde, already vibrant, Stella. And my mom, the lovely, vivacious Helena, found herself with me, a shy, frizzy redhead. From birth I did not fulfill my mom's expectations. Mom never realized how her words and her disappointment stung. At thirty-seven they still torture me.

"Where did I go wrong," she would wail when I refused to participate in dance or piano lessons, cheerleading, or the school play. Any event or activity where Stella excelled I refused to consider. I loved

Stella and thought that competing with her would be a betrayal of our friendship. But deep down, I believed I could never measure up to her beauty and talent, so why try?

All my growing-up years, I loved and yet was envious of Stella with equal intensity. We had no siblings, only each other. Our blood had commingled over a stolen razor blade. Our fingers pressed together tightly as we swore to be forever friends.

Yet, Stella often let me down. She copied my class notes and homework, not because she couldn't do the work, but because she didn't see the point in both of us doing something that I did better.

She would exclaim in her breathless way, "Cat you have all the brains. You take care of our school work, and I'll take care of our social life." And off she'd go to plan activities that often didn't include me.

Our friendship was lopsided at best. Her niceness ended if she caught any guy or gal glancing my way. She wanted and needed all the attention. I never understood why. She was not only beautiful but she was talented and could easily master anything she put her mind to. Early on, I learned not to question her motives or to stand in the way of what she wanted.

When I was with Stella in a group, I was invisible. Still, I loved her. When she sensed I'd had enough, she would throw her arms around me and weep. She would tell me how sorry she was and how she would do anything if I wouldn't be mad at her. I was too young and inexperienced to understand manipulation.

For a while, she spoke the truth. We would walk to school arm in arm and stop at the corner store on the way home for cokes and French fries. She would ignore anyone else who was clambering for her attention and devote herself to me.

Those were the best days of my life. I gladly let her copy my homework. She would plait my out-of-control curls and slather my face with makeup. She would tell me I was beautiful, pointing out my big green eyes, smooth complexion, and pouty lips. She would remind me over and over that we were forever friends. Then she would drift away, leaving me bewildered and longing for her attention.

Back then, I didn't understand friendship was supposed to be balanced, or that true friends always had your back and your best interest, or that best friends give equal time to listening, comforting, and offering support. It was only recently when I met Cassie that I realized what I had missed all these years with Stella as my one and only friend.

Stella's inconsistencies were painful except for every year for three months when I would have her all to myself. On the last day of school from the time we were five, Stella would turn her radiant smile on me. She would grab my hand. We would run the six blocks home —breathless, giggling with joy. School was out, our bags were packed, our plane tickets secured, and our summer place in Castello del Mare, Italy was waiting for us. Those first seven summers were the best time in my life. Stella and I were inseparable until the adult world intervened and those idyllic days faded away.

It happened the year we turned twelve. Daddy lost his job. Looking back, I realize how demoralizing it was for my family and how uncomfortable for Stella's parents. But in the tempestuous throes of my teen years, I only knew I had to see Lorenzo. My parents after months of discussion finally gave in, and the summer vacations continued for me but never again for my parents.

After Stella became engaged to Antonio, the summer kids were never the same. Lorenzo disappeared, and it wasn't until Stella and Antonio's wedding that I saw him again. My heart still fluttered at the sight of him but my grown up self on the verge of a divorce no longer believed there would ever be a chance for us to connect.

Now years later, I've returned to this place Stella and I loved so well. But the anticipation of being with Stella disappeared when I received her desperate message. Our long-awaited time together is no longer a fun-filled holiday. But what is it? A wild goose chase or something more sinister?

I regret not being honest with Stella. I didn't want to tell her the main reason I resisted staying with her was because I was afraid I'd run into Lorenzo. He's in my past now and that's where I want him to stay. I don't want those volatile emotions ruling my life ever again. But now since Stella has disappeared, I won't be able to avoid him.

Stella's garbled message is never far from my thoughts. I failed her. She called when I had silenced my phone during an event I was catering. My guilt is enormous. It walks with me daily breathing into my ear...hissing the words *I needed you...you let me down.*

I was raised with guilt and only through therapy had I started to recognize that most of it is misplaced and inaccurate. But still it lingers. Its fingers trail down my back as thoughts of Stella consume me.

And now, I'll have to see Lorenzo. And perhaps even worse, I have to see Antonio. I haven't seen him in years—not since their wedding. The few recent conversations have only deepened my lack of connection with him. He was never right for Stella and all these years later, his voice was indifferent, almost spiteful when he spoke of her.

He seemed baffled by my questions, and the information he provided was sketchy. He mumbled something about Stella missing for maybe three weeks, but he wasn't sure. He said he didn't know she was missing until the caretakers at the villa, Gino and Maria, called him when Stella didn't return home after a photo shoot.

When I asked how long she was missing before he knew, he said it had only been a few days. Initially, the caretakers weren't concerned because Stella sometimes went off without telling anyone. They waited a few days before checking on her. When they checked the house, all of Stella's belongings were there—money, credit cards, and passport along with her purse. No clothes or luggage were missing. That's when Gino called Antonio and insisted the police be alerted.

When I asked why he hadn't called me, he said, "I wanted to make sure she wasn't pulling one of her usual disappearing acts or a publicity stunt as she sometimes does. Stella has always been unpredictable. I didn't want you to worry. You were scheduled to arrive in a few weeks, so I asked Lorenzo to check it out first. I was sure Stella would turn up in her usual dramatic fashion and there would be no need to call you."

"But she hasn't turned up, has she? And I have this message on my phone. I believe she's in trouble. The police need to have this message, and I need to know what's being done to find her."

"Don't panic. Lorenzo is investigating. You remember Lorenzo, don't you? Surely you remember him from our summer vacations when we were kids. He was the best man at our wedding. Now he's deputy chief of police at the Guardia di Finanza in Puglia."

Antonio talked at length about Lorenzo and how he had encouraged Antonio to file a missing person report. Lorenzo had assured him that everything was being done to find Stella.

But my mind drifted away from the conversation as soon as Antonio mentioned Lorenzo's name. Of course, Lorenzo would be a high-ranking officer. He'd been a hustler even back when we were kids on the beach. The boy we all adored—slim with a golden darkness and a self-confident smugness. His enigmatic smile and that slightly raised eyebrow when he focused his attention on you were what I had lived for. But he rarely looked my way other than to harass me. I used to dream of him wanting me over Stella. But it was Stella who captured his heart right from the beginning.

When Stella chose Antonio over Lorenzo, I told her she'd lost her pea-brain mind. The magical chemistry between the two of them was so obvious. In one of our whispered midnight conversations, Stella confided that while Lorenzo was thrilling, Antonio's family was richer and connected in some sort of vague way to the last king of Italy, Vittorio Emanuele II. Once she discovered the family connection, Lorenzo didn't stand a chance. For Stella, it had always been about the image and how it would play out on the movie screen of her life.

I would have chosen Lorenzo. During those Italian summers, my heart soared every time I saw him. But he treated me like a kid sister, constantly teasing, pulling my already disheveled curls, tripping me in the sand, or dunking me in the sea. Still, I loved him and took every opportunity to tag along.

A slight cough from Antonio reconnected me to the conversation. The only thing he knew was that no one seemed to know about Stella's photo shoot or even its location. Stefano, her usual photographer, was distraught. He said he hadn't arranged a shoot for her, nor had he talked to Stella in several weeks. His assistant had been out of town on another assignment. Stella's agent offered no clues either. When questioned, he had an alibi as did Antonio who had been in Milan at a conference.

Antonio assured me Stella would return. Then he said, "Lorenzo needs to talk to you about the phone message from Stella. He wants your phone, and he wants to know about any recent conversations you and she had. Maybe something innocuous she said will help the investigation. But Stella is sure to be back by the time you arrive. Please don't change your plans. You know Stella. It's hard to know what she'll do next."

"Of course, I'm changing my plans. Stella's message was urgent. Lorenzo must want the message she left right away. I'm wrapping things up here. I've left a message on her cell about my change in plans. I'll email you my schedule."

I hesitate for just a moment but I have to ask, "Do you have any idea why she disappeared?"

Antonio didn't respond.

"You're not telling me something," I prompted.

Finally, he broke the silence, "Something about her disappearance isn't right. It's just a feeling. Occasionally, Stella does disappear but rarely does she leave without letting Maria and Gino know.

Maria told me that Stella was excited about your visit and didn't talk about anything else. So why would she disappear so close to your arrival?"

"Well, three weeks isn't that close. Maybe she wanted some alone time before I arrived."

"Cat, she didn't take anything with her. Her identity, clothes, luggage—all are still at the villa."

"Do you think she was kidnapped?"

When he didn't answer, I asked, "What kind of people does she keep company with? The circles she moves in have always been suspect, haven't they?"

After a long pause, Antonio said, "There's no trail, no starting point, no evidence other than the traces of fentanyl discovered in the sink in the villa."

"What?" I cried out in disbelief. "I know Stella did recreational drugs but taking fentanyl is dangerous. What else aren't you telling me?"

Bit by bit, Antonio eked out the story of Stella's addiction. A heavy darkness settled in my stomach as I tried to ask him intelligent questions. A vision of Stella's body floating in water blurred my sight. Stumbling through the rest of the conversation, I watched tears puddle on the notepad I kept on the kitchen counter.

During the entire conversation Antonio never once mentioned that he and Stella weren't living together. Yet, a definite tone of hostility resonated in his voice—a harsh, brittle sound with flat notes. An inflection that said he didn't really care whether or not she showed up. The possibility crossed my mind that maybe it wouldn't be a hardship for him if she didn't return.

It all seemed so contrary to the last conversation Stella and I had. She had been jubilant and had raved about the upcoming photo shoot for *Vogue Italia*. It was an important spread and would feature scenes from her latest film, *Stargazers*. It was great publicity. Her elation rushed across the ocean into my ear. Her laughter was strong and healthy. The photo shoot was her last event before I arrived.

But now with Stella's desperate message ringing in my ears, our well-planned reunion has gone off the rails.

Of course, I dropped everything and came. And now what? I'm still sitting in this parking lot in Lecce wondering why in the hell I'm here. My only company is Carlo's warning to be careful and Antonio's blasé attitude. I can only ask myself if the decision I made to change my life for Stella was unselfish or foolhardy.

CAT

CASTELLO DEL MARE, ITALY

I force myself back to the unfamiliar parking lot in Lecce, Italy. The trajectory of the storm has moved to the West. My decision to come here may be foolhardy, but I'm here. I start the car and drive out of town. A black Mercedes pulls out behind me but disappears once I turn onto the highway.

The road produces more white-knuckle driving. It takes my last bit of energy to stay awake but at least it prevents thoughts of Stella from consuming me. After all these years, she is still a force in my life —still deciding my fate.

The storm rolls off as I pull into Castello del Mare. I park in the main piazza and watch the waves pound against the stone wall. Wispy swirls of mist float across the square. They cast unfamiliar shadows on a place I thought I knew—but twenty years away tells a different story. The angry sea swallows the low-hanging black clouds. The windshield wipers slap back and forth. I count until I'm calm enough to turn them off.

The drab gray and brown landscape stretches in front of me. A moist breeze slips through the lowered window, draping the air with heavy dampness. Images of Stella and me splashing through the azure waters invade my thoughts. Those light, breezy days when we were of one mind. Days that braided our lives so tightly that despite our parents falling out we kept the friendship alive even when we were grown and separated by oceans, lifestyles, and careers. The deepest bond was created during those early summers, one that has kept us linked throughout the tangle of our lives. The imprint of the smeared bloody fingers of forever friendship still aches in my heart, validating the reason for my return.

A weak streak of sunlight bounces off the windshield. Exhaustion from three flights and the storm-tense drive crawls across my body. Temptation is luring me to curl up in the back seat and sleep. There's time as I don't meet Gino for another hour, but the watery sun beckons. It invites me to stretch my legs and clear my mind. Before leaving the shelter of the car, I pry open the box of Adam Turoni's chocolates. It had been the worst kind of temptation not to polish off the entire box during the flight. I intentionally squirreled them out of reach in the overhead bin so I wouldn't succumb.

Whenever I'm in Savannah, I stop by the shop on Broughton or Bull Streets and allow myself two or three of these hand-made jewels. But since it will be a year before I return, I splurged and selected fourteen exquisite artisan truffles, two each of Raspberry Chambord, Habanero Caramel, Dark Chocolate Peanut Butter Cups, Roasted Fig and Cognac, Grand Marnier Cherry Cordials, Coffee Caramelo de Luna, and Hazelnut Honey Pralines.

The intense richness of dark chocolate permeates the car. My hand hovers, counting the chocolates as I puzzle over which one to choose. Fearing I might choke on my own saliva, I close my eyes and lift the first piece my fingers touch.

"Hmmmm," mixes with the gooey goodness of crunchy hazelnuts, buttery praline, and a hint of wildflowers. With the first bite the liquid honey bursts out of its chocolate confinement. I sink into chocolate heaven until there's nothing left but licking my fingers clean.

The warmth of the sun strokes my eyelids. I slip into a chocolate-induced stupor. Food is always the first and last thought on my mind. As exhaustion plummets my body, I stop fighting. I hover between unconsciousness and awareness until a blast of wind rattling against the window startles me. A few more cars have pulled into the parking area. It's close to lunch and people move in the direction of a restaurant tucked into the side of a cliff. A black Mercedes stands out among the numerous *Piaggio Ape*.

I need to stretch. My knee is still tender from the encounter with the trailer hitch, and my ego is still bruised from the betrayal by both John Ashley Davenport, IV and his future mother-in-law Mrs. Harrington.

With my chocolate cravings temporarily sated and a surge of sugar energy, I tuck an umbrella under my arm and leave the car. I splash my way through puddles and scattered debris.

The multi-colored houses lining the hill beckon me. One of these could be Casa dei Fiori. My feet follow the cobbled street away from the piazza. Even in January the miniature gardens in the front of each house are full of blooms in scarlet, neon orange, and blazing yellow.

My Italian daydream accompanies me, both the early trips with Stella and our families and my first trip alone as a young adult some fifteen years ago. My connection to Italy has been strong and continuous based on my exposure as a child. Finally, I'm here. But Stella is not. What a crappy way to begin our reunion.

The narrow street winds upward. My eyes soak in the stone houses, the red tile roofs, and the flowering gardens. My heart yearns to belong. This village could be my forever home. Living in Italy has always been my plan, but now I'm torn.

Since I moved to the Lowcountry, a subtle change has taken place. It would be hard to leave, even after my miserable encounter with Mrs. Harrington. The Lowcountry and Castello del Mare play Russian roulette with my heartstrings. This trip was to have been a trial to determine which place has the strongest pull. As I meander through the familiar yet changed village, I feel like a fickle lover wondering which mate to choose—Italy or South Carolina? The question seems obscene without Stella.

Halfway up the steep incline, the cobbled path splits—left or right—which do I choose? The right path curves toward the sea. The pragmatic side of me leans in that direction, toward the pale shades of gray that tickle the foam-crested waves. It's the brightest spot on the horizon in the middle of an afternoon filled with stormy gloom. The road to the right—*a destra*—will lead me back to the piazza where my car is parked and where Gino will meet me and take me to Stella's villa.

The left road snakes up to the old fortress—the place where Stella and I played during those long-ago glorious summers of our childhood. The left—*a sinistra*—is heavy with residual history from the Middle Ages when left handers were believed to practice witchcraft. Buried deep in the same history is the story of the Devil, himself a southpaw.

Travel fatigue makes the slightest decision an effort—right or left? The storm gathers steam. It moves rapidly across the tumultuous waves. Hesitating too long, the rain and wind return with exaggerated fury. The umbrella, once open, jerks me off balance. I stumble toward the left, the decision made for me.

Fog, thick as tapioca pudding, swirls at my feet as I trudge left in evil's embrace. Why not? It seems appropriate based on the heavy load of adversity I've encountered in the past few years. Even in this beautiful place of my childhood, evil has followed me across the ocean.

Buckets of rain spill over me. The wind howls, snatching the umbrella out of my hands. It tumbles in Olympic-style free fall down the narrow street as the village below vanishes in a gelatinous mist. Looking for shelter, I dash from overhang to overhang as swirling water beats against my ankles. The wind cries into empty spaces between the buildings.

A house, seemingly vacant, appears. I dash toward the alcove. The storm rumbles its way across the valley as I lean against the smooth, wet stones and let exhaustion wash over my body. My jacket hood slips off my head. I tug it back in place as rain pellets my face. My heart pounds to the roll of thunder.

Crippled by jet lag, sluggish from sleep deprivation, and ravenous from lack of food, I shudder as the day darkens. Nature lunges into my space spinning my dream of living and working in Italy into a devilish nightmare.

Everything had lined up—the money, my business, someone to rent my house, a chef's job waiting for me in Castello del Mare, and a reunion with my best friend Stella. After all the planning, that one whispered message has changed everything. I pull out my phone and listen again to her fear-filled voice: *Cat, please, please help me!*

For thirty-seven years I've adjusted my life to suit Stella's. I'm her rescuer. It's a role I've played for too long. I had grand plans to point this out during our time together. Now I pray I'm allowed to rescue her one more time.

Wind whooshes through the alcove. I squint until my tears and the raindrops merge. My only wish is to be back in the car. How to accomplish that without swimming to the piazza is a mystery.

I slump into a squatting position. My mind wrestles with the stupidity of the trip. My decision to change my life and live a year in Italy was spurred on by Stella's enthusiasm. The thing is Stella took over my plan. Her celebrity status opened doors so easily and to her it simply didn't matter that La Canzone wasn't my first choice. Another example of our lopsided friendship.

A loose shutter scrapes against the stone wall. Adrenalin lurches through my tired body. Broken flower pots topple across the terrace. I shift deeper into the recesses of the alcove and glance around at my surroundings.

The front door is weathered. A faded symbol catches my attention. Slowly rising from my position on the far side of the alcove, I move in for a closer look. A faint outline of a washed-out sun with a single large blue eye stares back at me. Coiled in the center of the eye is a snake. Its tongue flickers in my direction.

I shiver, pulling back so quickly I lose my balance, stumble on the wet tiles, and fall against the door. It gives under my weight. I yelp and hop backwards as it cracks open a sliver. Rain and wind slam into my back. Desperate to find a dry spot out of this maniacal storm makes it tempting to take a peek inside. My hand gives a little push. A nerve-grating creak cuts through the storm's roar as a dark, dank interior is revealed.

Inside, the darkness shifts. A fetid odor of decay assaults my nostrils. The murky interior vibrates with dark shadows. The door swings wider. A sharp stab of lightning paralyzes me in place as it illuminates the room. A figure shrouded in black leaps from the inky depths and grabs the sleeve of my jacket. I wrench free and tumble backwards. My sore knee collapses. I crash-land onto the pavement. A hand grabs my ankle and drags me back onto the terrace. Kicking with all my strength, I hit a solid body part. There's a yelp and the hand loosens. Jerking free, I roll into the flooded street. Without thinking, I scramble up and run like hell. My ballet flats pound across the wet cobblestones as water splashes up the legs of my already saturated jeans.

I run until the thud of my heartbeat is louder than the thunder. When the pain in my side becomes unbearable, I stop and quickly scrutinize the area before sliding in-between two houses. My breath comes in big panting gasps. Slumping against the wall, I force myself to count until my heartbeat slows into a safer zone.

For a few seconds, I close my eyes. When I open them, the mist and clouds part. A figure materializes through the rain and fog. It floats toward me.

"Oh, no," I whimper as my heartbeat gears back into gallop speed.

My choices are the fearsome vacant house behind me with an attack person waiting or this apparition coming out of the mist. Once again I race through narrow passages until a tiny crevice opens between houses. I shove myself through, praying it's not a dead end. The slap of my feet echoes off the stone buildings as I put distance between myself and any would-be assailants.

Behind me, I hear a faint voice calling, *"Signora! Signora Gabbiano, dove sei?"*

My legs, quivering with a combination of fatigue and panic, give out. There's only one person in this village who knows I'm here—the caretaker, Gino. The person I was scheduled to meet in the piazza before I veered onto the left path.

The voice drifts on the wind and changes direction. My breath heaves in the foggy air. What should I do?

CAT

My choices are limited. The pervert from the house could have followed me. Or, maybe it's Gino. Or maybe not. I rotate my neck hoping to ease some of the tension in my shoulders and the paralysis in my muddled mind.

Heck, I'm going to bet on Gino. He's the caretaker and not a nut case. Gino and my attacker are not the same person. My deductive reasoning, while greatly flawed, is comforting. I step through the narrow opening. Rain and sweat mingle with panic as I call out Gino's name.

My words are shrill. They bounce down the rain-slick cobbled street, "*Gino! Gino! Aspetta! Sono qui*—wait, I'm here."

I race toward the voice. My thoughts tumbling over each other. Should I tell him I was attacked? Will he think I'm crazy? Oh, how foolish I am to have come all this way. It never occurred to me that Stella wouldn't be here.

Puddles impede my progress but I plow through leaving a trail of spraying water behind. My thoughts slide over the abandoned house. I tell myself that once I'm settled, I'll go back. If I find anything unusual, I'll go to the police. A small voice in my head says, or you could contact Lorenzo. You know you want to see him.

Dashing through the rain, I continue to call out Gino's name. The ghostly figure ahead stops and pivots in slow motion. He slushes toward me. Streams of water gush down his black rain slicker. His head, covered by a hood, prevents me from identifying him. Not that

I have a clue what he looks like. A minor detail I forgot to ask Carlo about.

He's within a few feet when he pushes the hood back from his face. He's short, stocky and dark-skinned. He nods and says, "*Chiamo Gino. Andiamo!*"

A little screech of delight escapes from my mouth. Wanting to make contact with another human, I extend my hand. He hesitates for a second longer than necessary before he shakes and drops it.

He moves away while a rapid staccato of heavy dialect flows over his shoulder. While I have a good grasp of Italian from my childhood and later from studying it at university, the Salentino words blowing out of his mouth are heavy with hints of Greek, Latin, Spanish, Old French and Napolitano nuances. The raging storm strings the words into a collage of colorful musical notes. I stumble after him, trusting it's the right decision.

He rushes across the slick, wet cobblestones. Frightened he will leave me behind, I pick up my pace. He disappears around a corner. We almost collide when I turn in the same direction and find he's stopped in front of a small wooden door recessed into a stone wall. Heavy coiled vines, drooping with gray-green wetness, sag over the top of the wall.

Gino whips a keychain out of his pocket and inserts a long, narrow black key into the lock. The door swings open. He zips through at a trot. I follow him inside and find that I'm standing on a stone slab with steps leading upward. The massive door is not the entrance to the house as I thought it would be. But Gino has already disappeared up an old stone staircase. I rush after him.

Rain cascades down the roughly hewn steps—fast-moving water spilling from the terrace above. It swirls around and over my already soaked ballerina flats—a poor choice for this weather. My feet protest as the icy water plunges inside.

On each side of the staircase are more dull, lifeless vines. The thought of touching them is repugnant but the slippery steps require holding on to something. I shove my hands into the wilted, rotting vegetation and hope the slime is only dead vines.

My mind locks into counting as I climb. Nineteen steps later a small landing appears. It continues to the left, leading to another set of stairs. Gino is not in sight. Twenty-three additional steps are counted one-by-one.

At the next landing is a small terrace with stone benches and statues that dominate a bedraggled flower garden. No sign of Gino. This leads to yet another set of steps, twenty-six. I rapidly calculate a total of sixty-eight steps to conquer day in and day out. As I reach the top, a grand, expansive terrace with spectacular views of the sea opens before me. I don't linger as the front door to Stella's *Casa dei Fiori* beckons me out of the storm-filled day.

Little raspy breaths catch in my throat as I cross to the vine-covered pergola. I run my fingers through my out-of-control hair before I remember my hands are covered in muck. There is just no trying to bring order to this miserable day. Before entering the house, I shake off as much water as possible, wipe my hands on my jeans, and step through the door.

Gino doesn't notice that I haven't kept up with him. His muffled chatter reaches my ears as he moves from room to room. His steady stream of words offers instructions on the workings of doors, shutters, and the fireplace. He nods and signals with his hands while shrugging his shoulders. He scurries into the kitchen and lights the gas burners. He opens the cabinets under the sink and points to knobs indicating I must turn them on, off, or perhaps both. It's not clear.

As I watch him, I add to the small list of things I know about him. His hair is turning white and overdue for a trim. The stubble on his face is dark and a day or two old. A bright blue sweater peeks through his now unzipped rain jacket. When he looks up, I catch just a glimpse of the same intense blue in his unsmiling eyes. His weather-lined face and stoic expression do not invite questions. He trots down the hall. I follow.

He pauses at the bathroom door and points to the water heater.

He turns on a switch that's too high for me to reach without a chair or step stool. At the far end of the bathroom there's a washing machine. He moves toward it and twirls the dials. Only a few of his words penetrate my rain-soaked brain. Before I can craft my questions, he turns toward me and points at the keys in his hand and says, "*Le chiavi?*"

I nod, pulling out of my pocket the set of keys Carlo gave me. There are several different keys on the ring. I ask, "*Quale chiave è per la porta d'ingresso? Which one is for the front door?*"

There's no response. When I look up, I'm speaking to his receding back. He sprints down the hall, out the front door, and vanishes down the steps.

I stand rooted. I hold my breath. Surely he isn't leaving? An engine starts. A car pulls away. Seconds, then minutes go by. He's not coming back. A vision of my car packed to capacity back in the piazza spreads numbness through my body. A tear leaks. I sniff it back.

A series of questions parade in front of me: Is there heat in the house or is the fireplace the only source? Where is the firewood or do I have to buy some? Where would I buy it? Can I legally park in front of the villa? Have I lost my flipping mind? The last question is the most important, but there are no answers.

Don't panic, I think. What do I need first? Is it the car, to be warm and dry, sleep? Yes, but what I really need is food.

"One step at a time," I say out loud as the wind blows rain through the open door.

CAT

My clothes, wet and dank, cling to my body. I shut the front door. The rain and wind blast against the house. The shutters rattle. The roar of the storm hasn't diminished. Sinking into a warm bed and pulling the cover over my head is all I'm capable of handling at the moment. Fatigue and despair battle for my attention, but I force them out.

Backing against the door, thoughts of Stella assault me. She should be here, her hand tucked in my arm as she whirls us both about the room laughing and breathlessly squealing, "We're finally together."

Instead of balling into a knot on the floor, I pretend this is our secret place. It's a childhood game Stella and I used to play. Years later it's still a practice that helps me feel safe. It centers me, calms me, and units my fragmented thoughts, at least it has in the past. With fresh eyes, I begin to explore our place–a place that Stella has prepared for us.

A massive fireplace centers the room. If only there were a roaring fire to take the dampness out of the house and my heart. My wish is almost granted when my eyes touch the painting above the mantle. There we are—Stella and me—standing in the surf. Stella's mother took the photograph the summer we were ten. The sea swirls around our feet and laps up our sun-burnished legs. A spray of water leaps in the air. It splashes our faces and leaves glittering trails of diamonds in the air. Our small hands are clasped. I gaze at

Stella while she looks directly at the camera and poses like a graceful swan.

Stella must have had it painted as a surprise for me. I lean in and close my eyes. For a moment, the surf ripples at my feet and the warm salty spray licks my face. There's something vaguely familiar about the painting—something I should know but don't. Tears slide down my cheek. I turn away from the portrait to explore the rest of the room.

Stella's presence is everywhere—in the terra-cotta floors burnished to a rosy glow and in the antique furniture cushioned in royal blue and piled with pillows in sea hues of jade and teal. The coffee table is adorned with a picture-perfect table book on starfish. The familiar elegant style of Stella graces the room.

But what surprises me are the splashes of a different Stella on display. Her usual decor is comprised of pale blues and taupes, and she has never been a collector of anything except jewelry and clothes. In this place, pottery of every size and shape overflows on the mantle and the hearth. Additional shelving almost groans with the overabundance. Local art adorns the walls. The pottery and artwork burst with brilliant reds, yellows, violets, and strong blues—so unlike Stella. The collision of colors creates warmth and energy. It broadcasts a new image of Stella, one that is vibrant and imaginative. The convergence of these bold colors belongs to a stronger, happier and healthier person. My fingertips brush against the lively cups, jars, and vases.

While I love the colors and the possibilities, the room also looks as if Stella had stopped mid-way through her decorating. Stacked in a disorganized jumble against the wall are more paintings and pottery. My overly organized mind cringes at the disarray. This surplus of decorative items will be the first things to tackle. Stella, when she returns, will laugh at me and wave her hands indifferently, saying do whatever.

The next room connects through a wide archway. It's centered with an immense chestnut dining table and hand-tooled chairs for eight. Wide windows allow a view of a side garden. A china cabinet is crammed with more local pottery and an assortment of plates and cups. More artwork hangs on the walls—another hodgepodge to organize. A long, low bookcase anchors the other wall. Again, I'm surprised. Stella has never been a reader. Heavy tomes with titles like *Starfish: Biology and Ecology of the Asteroidea* perch next to *Coral Reef Curiosities: Intrigue, Deception and Wonder on the Reef and Beyond* which is lined up next to children's books: *Stella the Starfish* and *Star of the Sea: A Day in the Life of a Starfish*. They invite me to pull them off the shelves, find a cozy chair, and sink into the wonder of them. But not today.

The dining room flows into the kitchen. I peek in. It's small but adequate, at least for Stella—not so much for me. Stella dislikes cooking and rarely prepares anything other than a smoothie. She loves it when we're together and I prepare our meals. She teases me about becoming her personal chef. She starves herself most of the time but eats voraciously when I cook. We joke about her adding pounds, as if she ever would. She's as thin as a willow branch.

There are no windows in the kitchen, but a French door opens onto the back garden where there's a generous bed of herbs and winter vegetables. This is my comfort zone, meals around the table and conversations late into the night. A smile makes its way to my mouth, the first since my arrival.

My smile fades when I open the cabinets and drawers and a wild assortment of cooking tools jump out at me. Utensils are mangled and tangled, plates intermixed with bowls, and saucers without cups. I take deep breaths while fighting the urge to rearrange the entire kitchen right now. Okay, back off I tell myself. You have plenty of time to tame the disarray. Close the drawers and cabinets and walk away!

Beads of sweat line my forehead. My life had been spinning out of control for years. It was only recently that I sought help. Through therapy I've found tools to conquer my anxiety. While counting and organizing may not be the best coping mechanisms, they work for me.

My therapist has been supportive, giving me permission to claim these tools with the warning that even a harmless coping tactic can become compulsive. I'm grateful to find something other than medication to help. Organizing and counting have become my daily companions in my effort to stay sane.

Wiping the sweat off my brow with my shirt sleeve, I push the drawer. Just before it closes, a gleaming chef's knife catches my eye. Stella has never had a good chef's knife, but she knows I travel with mine. I smile with delight as I'm sure she bought it for me. Her excitement at purchasing the knife spills into the kitchen. I picture her close by, waiting for me to open the drawer. We would both squeal with delight when I discovered it. But without Stella by my side, I curl my fingers around the handle and sob. A crumpled piece of paper is wrapped around the handle, secured by a rubber band. I slide the paper off the handle and open it.

La cipolla a cupola is written in Stella's cursive on the small piece of paper. *The domed onion*, I read out loud. I frown. Did we have a private joke about onions? Does it have something to do with cooking and a particular meal I made for Stella? The guessing games we played as children spilled over into our adult lives. We've never stopped playing them. I smile again and drop the note on the counter to revisit later.

Continuing my exploration, I cross the dining area to reach the hallway. The first door on the left is the long, narrow bathroom. It's lined with shelves of soft towels, shampoos, and soaps. A small Murano glass chandelier with tiny starfish prisms paints rainbows on the ceiling.

Further down on the left side is the guest bedroom. Stella has made it perfect for me. A cream spread and navy throw exude warmth and comfort. There's a small desk, a wardrobe, and a love seat surrounded by floor-to-ceiling French doors opening onto a side terrace.

Last is the master bedroom. The floor-to-ceiling French doors open onto the front terrace. The room is spacious with an intricate rolled-top desk with multiple drawers and cubby holes. There's a large wardrobe, an antique chest, and a small sitting area with a round wooden table and cushioned chairs. The massive headboard is intricately carved with bronze grape leaves. A soft peach duvet and terra cotta colored shams bring sunshine into the room even on a gloomy day.

Returning to the living room, I open the front door and stand outside under the vine-covered pergola. A large table and eight chairs have been pushed against the wall. A cobalt patio umbrella leans nearby. When Stella returns, I imagine we'll share many late-night dinners around this table.

Today the sea crashes far below. The mist obscures all but the sound of rain. My eyes shift back and forth, adjusting to shadowy images of towering stone cliffs. The marina appears and disappears through the hazy fog. The wet air is warm. It coats my face and clothes with damp softness. Gigantic waves swell and crash against the rocks sending spray across the terrace. I sigh and shudder simultaneously. Fear and wonder mingle.

I am finally here. But where is Stella?

Back inside I contemplate what to do next. My stomach gurgles, reminding me that I'm famished. A cup of coffee after deplaning in Rome hours ago and a couple of pieces of chocolate are not going to get me through this day.

Many of the paintings crowding the walls feature tables ladened with platters of food and bottles of wine. Saliva gathers. My first solo trip to Italy as an adult infuses my memory with food.

The rich aroma of a Florentine steak sizzling on a grill floated in the night air. The chef had invited me outside to watch him prepare the T-bone steak. He flipped the red slab of meat with charred grill marks. He dipped rosemary sprigs in olive oil and swabbed each side. When the steak was cooked to perfection, he slid a slice of raw garlic the length of the beef and sprinkled it with chipped sea salt. A plop of Gorgonzola was slathered across the surface, melting into all the things I love about Italy. Before I could applaud his work of art, he passed a nub of truffle under my nose and shaved it over the dissolving cheese.

The memory of that first incredible meal I ordered in Florence never fails to make my mouth water. Food is a powerful force in my life and the reason I return to Italy. This trip was meant to bring me closer to the food secrets I learned from my nonna. I sigh and shake off the visionary feast. It's time to eat.

Earlier when I parked in the piazza, I had noticed a restaurant tucked into the cliff overlooking the marina. If I leave immediately, I can get there before closing time. Eating is mandatory if I'm to settle into my new home today. But then, eating is always mandatory for me.

CAT

Exhaustion and hunger compete for my attention. I grab an umbrella from the stand in the corner of the living room and lock the door behind me. Gino's abrupt leave-taking leaves me suspended between two continents. The purpose of coming all this way dissolves. There's no clear direction on what to do next.

My thoughts flash back to the image of the vacant house and the figure in black. Fear joins me on the terrace. I shudder, too weary to make sense of anything. The combination of travel fatigue, a six hour time change, the brutal weather, and Stella's disappearance invoke kaleidoscopic images and sounds. My mind scrambles to fit the bits together while my imagination, on the verge of meltdown, interferes with logic.

There are no solutions. Leaving the protection of the pergola, the storm penetrates my still-damp jacket. One soggy foot slides forward and the other follows. The sixty-eight steps are far more threatening going down as a stream of water rolls with every step I take. It pours over my sodden shoes and splashes up my drenched jeans.

The heavy wooden gate thuds shut. The lock clicks in place. The wind, a lover of umbrellas, flips mine inside out. It drags me down the rain slick road. My first shopping expedition will include more efficient rain gear.

In the dim, gray light at the bottom of the hill nothing stirs in the lull of the storm. A small sign indicates *Ristorante L'Aragosta.* A faded red arrow points to a nondescript building that blends into the side of the cliff. The entrance leads down three concrete steps into a pool of swirling water. I tramp down the stairs and push through the door. My mangled umbrella drops to the floor. I hang my dripping rain jacket on the coat rack.

Whiffs of freshly baked focaccia linger in the air. The rumbling of my stomach matches the cacophony of the storm. The quiet elegance of the foyer is a welcoming contrast from the downpour. I squish across the carpet and enter the dining room.

Orderly mayhem prevails. Chairs are stacked on blocks next to the floor-to-ceiling windows that ramble across the length of the restaurant. The huge expanse of glass frames a majestic view of the sea. On a sunny day it would be breathtaking. Today with Castello del Mare in the eye of the storm, it's more like chaotic splendor. Giant waves foam and hurl against the rocks. They break against the massive windows. Tiny pinholes around the windows dribble sea water into the dining room.

The waiters move efficiently. They drag heavy red draperies and gauzy sheers away from the persistent leakage. The billowy material is stretched across chairs. It's a race that the sea appears to be winning.

I gasp and all eyes turn toward me. A flustered red-cheeked man, who seems to be in charge of the rescue mission, nods. He stops layering the draperies across the chair and walks toward me.

Benvenuta, signora. Pranzo?

Sì, grazie, è possibile?

Naturalmente, vieni con me.

My shoes or my stomach make strange gurgling sounds as I follow him to a table set back into an alcove. He pulls out the table, and I slip behind so that I'm facing the huge expanse of windows. The rhythmic power of the sea and storm is hypnotic. The waves, each clamoring to be first, race to the rocks. They collide, withdraw, and return, slamming all their energy into breaking the glass. The waiter returns with water.

"*Vino rosso o bianco?*" He inquires.

"*Rosso, per favore.*"

He nods and pours from a carafe of red wine while telling me it's a strong local wine, good for the tempestuous day. The first sip brings a smile to my weary body as the warm rush of intense summer days in Castello del Mare return. Regardless of what happens, I'm here. There's no turning back. I glance around the room and wonder if Stella ever eats here. She will split her sides laughing when I tell her the story of my arrival.

She will say like she always does, "Cat, you need to write a book."

And I will say, "Only if you play the part of the heroine when it's made into a movie."

Tension lifts from my neck and shoulders for the first time since I left South Carolina. The cushiony carpet, if it wasn't damp, would be an invitation to lie down and sleep to the sounds of the raging sea. My eyes glaze over until the waiter clears his throat.

"*Che cosa mi consiglia*—what do you recommend?" I ask.

He smiles and nods, "The special today is *pasta con vongole*."

"Yes, please."

After he retreats, I notice other rain-soaked patrons have slipped in. The tinkle of silverware and the glub, glub of wine pouring into goblets bring me back to the present. My admiration for the owner grows as I cannot possibly imagine opening for business on such a day.

The waiter returns with a small charcuterie board loaded with slivers of peppered salami, a local caciocavallo cheese, and bruschetta topped with local greens. Before I take my first bite, a basket of crusty bread studded with black olives arrives. My early childhood summers in this region of Italy taught me that the olives are not pitted.

The first bite of the bruschetta with sautéed greens bursts with fresh tastes of earth and rain. A touch of roasted garlic and balsamic vinegar tame the bitterness as my teeth sink into the crunchy bread. My plate is clean within minutes. I take a long, deep drink of the robust red wine. A soft lightness moves into my body.

My wiped-clean plate is whisked away. There's a leisurely space of time between courses—time to observe the other patrons. No other thoughts intrude until a platter of crispy calamari sprinkled generously with sea salt and minced parsley arrives. I squeeze a wedge of lemon over the stack and ravenously devour every morsel. My hunger pangs subside. A big sigh of weary contentment escapes.

The third course, *pasta con vongole,* is a favorite. This is a dish I often order as well as make. Plump juicy clams rest on a plate of steaming al dente vermicelli #7. The sauce tastes of garlic, basil, red pepper flakes, butter, a touch of white wine, and a smattering of chopped oregano. My wine glass is refilled.

Outside, the storm rages. Inside, I'm safe, warm, and almost dry. My stomach moans with happiness. The morning's problems soften.

"Dolce, signora?"

"No, grazie, sono sazia. I'm full."

I leave with the second wrecked umbrella of the day. When I pass a large trash container near the restaurant, I toss it in. Quickly, without endangering my life, I splash my way to the car. With great caution, I maneuver it in front of the villa, park it as close to the stone wall as possible, and hope I won't be sideswiped or towed during the night.

The thought of napping in the car is promising. The thought of hauling my luggage up sixty-eight steps in the still raging storm is just stupid. But getting out of wet clothes and sleeping in a real bed overrides all my other thoughts. After transferring only essentials to my carry-on, I gather up my laptop and the box of chocolates. Everything else can wait until tomorrow.

It takes a fumble or two with the lock before the door lurches open. I plunge through and rush up the steps without counting. I unlock the front door and come to a dead stop on the threshold. A fire is blazing in the hearth.

When my heart stops racing, I try to be grateful to Gino for this gift of heat but I'm angry—angry that he has a key to come and go whenever he pleases. But I'm too tired to think about it now.

I drop my carry-on by the door, place my computer and the chocolates on the coffee table, and slam the deadbolt into place. I peel off every stitch of wet clothing. Everything drops in a damp heap on the living room floor. Grabbing a towel as I pass the bathroom, I give a half-hearted swipe to my wet hair and soggy body. The towel drops from my hand outside the bedroom door. I throw back the bedding and crawl in as darkness descends on my first day in Castello del Mare.

CAT

The early morning sun slashes across my eyelids. Squinting and blinking, my eyes pry apart to a strange room with a wardrobe, vibrant paintings, and shuttered French doors. Where am I? Pushing up on my elbows, my eyes slowly wander around the room until they connect to my brain.

Memories of yesterday return. I reach for my phone and scroll through messages, always checking to see if Stella called or texted. Everyday I text and email, always hoping she still has access to her phone. Each day she doesn't respond is a day fear creeps a little closer. Before I'm fully awake, I send another.

"*Ciao mia carissima amica. Sono qui a Castello. Ti aspetto.* Hello my dearest friend. I am here in Castello. I'm waiting for you."

A hand reaches out for the vibrating phone—Stella's phone—and reads yet another text from the persistent Caterina. The phone is turned off and the SIM card removed. A hammer smashes the phone into unrecognizable pieces. Later, after a long drive, a black Mercedes pulls off the road. A car door opens and footsteps echo on boulders. Then, silence at the water's edge. Pieces of glass, plastic, and metal dance in the air only seconds before drowning in the wide expanse of the sea.

I squish the pillow behind my head. Heavy folds of sorrow shroud my body and reside alongside the fatigue still lingering from yesterday. Pulling the covers over my head, I sob out years of suppressed pain. The tears stop when my nose clogs up so much I can't breathe. I lie huddled under the duvet. How do I convince myself to get up and embrace this new life I've chosen? Where is Stella?

Eventually, I stretch to full length and push back the covers and place my feet on the cool terra cotta floor. It's chilly enough to have me speed walking to the bathroom and jumping into a hot shower. Later I wander into the kitchen to discover coffee has been made and *cornetti* peek from a napkin-covered plate. A note on top says, *Benvenuta, Maria e Gino.*

Mixed emotions and thoughts race through my head. Once again they've entered the house without asking, without knocking. The relationship Stella has with these two people doesn't suit me.

Casting my irritation aside, I grab a cup of coffee and a *cornetto* and mindlessly stuff the pastry down my throat. The flaky confection dusted with powdered sugar oozes with thick, creamy Nutella. I quickly finish one and start on the second. I slow down long enough to sit at the table and survey the kitchen. Today is for settling in. Once I've unpacked, the kitchen will bow to my organization skills. As a chef, I cannot abide anything out of place in my workspace.

But before I can start my day, there's yesterday's attack hanging over my head. In the morning light, my fears seem ludicrous. But if I'm to stay, this incident has to be faced. I'm sure it was either a misunderstanding or a figment of my exhausted imagination, but my first goal is to check it out.

The sixty-eight steps are free of flowing water, and the mucky vines have perked up. I close the gate and walk down the hill to the center of town. The main piazza is easy to find but the narrow streets

all look the same. I select one that leads uphill. When the road splits, I turn left and tuck down a narrow passageway.

The terrace is in the same state of disarray as it was yesterday, but there's a padlock on the door. I stare in confusion. It wasn't there yesterday. I'm sure. The corroded lock suggests it's been in place for a while. The buildings on either side of the house don't offer any clues. The strange symbol of the faded sun with one large blue eye protruding with a coiled snake is the same one I saw yesterday.

No one answers my knock. There are no lurking shadows or signs of anything remotely sinister. But then, today is brilliant with sunlit skies. There's a fresh rain-washed breeze from the sea. It's impossible for me to recreate yesterday's scene of fear and violence.

Forget it, I tell myself. A loose shutter taps a sorrowful tune as I walk away. The frightful images are pushed far back into the recesses of my mind as I return to the piazza.

Twenty years have passed since I walked this same promenade surrounding the sea. The small village now sprawls across what used to be farmland. The numerous souvenir shops announce tourism has found this obscure spot in the heel of the Italian boot. The day is warm and business is brisk at the *gelateria*. I choose a cone of pistachio and find a cozy spot along the seawall. My tongue slides around the pale green nutty sweetness.

From my strategic spot, I lick the melting gelato and watch the vendors set up their wares. The papier mache vendor is closest. His movements are steady as he stacks the table with feisty fishermen, beaming bakers, aproned butchers, and snappy soldiers along with dogs, cats, donkeys, cows, horses, sheep, and fish. Salento suns blaze in copper and red. Madonnas are vibrant in robes of blue and gold. The sun caresses my back as I lean forward to get a closer look. Children play an improvised game of soccer, women barter with the food merchants, and a carousel plays Napoletana tunes. I nod in time to the music. A gentle peaceful drowsiness descends. I close my eyes and lean against the stone wall and let yesterday's fears and anxieties drift away.

Maria gave me a day to settle in before arriving on my doorstep. This morning she stands in the doorway with a vase full of wildflowers and a jar of homemade tomato sauce. She growls at me in a dialect that's unfamiliar. It's hard listening to a language you can't quite decipher. But I peel back the words one by one until they begin to penetrate. She says that she rang the bell and no one came. So she let herself in.

She smiles shyly. Her eyes sweep over me from head to toe. She nods and says, "You are Stella's friend."

A strange longing to weep and tell her about the violent attack on my first day surfaces. I force a lid on that thought and continue to listen intently to catch all the nuances of the dialect.

"I was going to leave these on the outside table. I apologize for bothering you. *Domani,* I will bring you fresh eggs and herbs." She looks me directly in the eye and backs toward the steps while she continues, "Gino raises chickens."

"Grazie mille," I respond with my arms full of flowers and tomato sauce. *"Sei molto gentile,* you are too kind," but she is already halfway down the steps by the time I get the words out.

CAT & MARIA

After the first exhausting and fear-filled day, my initial sense of danger diminishes. I call the clinic and leave a message for Antonio. I don't want to see him but if it will help find Stella, then I will. Next, I call Carlo. He answers with that same low hum in his voice.

"Ciao, Cat. How is everything at Fiori? Is everything okay?"

"It's perfect," I say and explain that I don't want to look at any other properties.

"I'm glad you like it. It's a beautiful property and with Stella's touch it's even more so. She threw a party a couple of months back and showed off all the changes she made."

"Oh, how was she then?"

"She was in her element. It was a pretty big crowd, noticeably absent was Antonio. Guess he wasn't invited."

"Hmm. You seem to think he should have been?"

"She usually includes him but you never know with Stella. One day you're on her good side and the next day you're not. It's understandable since they're not living together. I was surprised Lorenzo showed up. The rumor circulating around town indicated that he and Stella were spending time together although I also heard it didn't work out."

I don't wade into this conversation. Stella and Lorenzo, as a couple, are not my concern. Although the thought of them together sends me to a dark place. It's still the same. Stella always gets what she wants.

Carlo and I talk a few more minutes. He promises to stop by soon and insists we have lunch when he's next in Castello.

The days flow easily. I spend my time organizing drawers and cabinets, arranging pottery and art, and clearing the garden of weeds. No other sinister threats occur and there's no progress in finding Stella. What if the attack episode has something to do with Stella's disappearance? As much as I puzzle over it, nothing significant surfaces.

I leave another message for Antonio. I consider stopping by the clinic as I don't understand why he doesn't return my calls. Next, I click on Lorenzo's number. While I don't want to see him, he needs Stella's phone. Reluctantly, I place the call. I'm so relieved when he doesn't answer. I leave a voice message. Of the trio, Carlo is the only one that calls—every couple of days to chat. He seems eager to stay connected. I don't discourage him as he might be the only person I can rely on. There's always a hint in his voice that he wants to tell me something more, but I don't probe.

During one of my conversations with Maria, I asked about Carlo. She and Gino have worked for him for a while. According to her, it's a good arrangement. She rattles on at length about Carlo while I stare out the window, always wondering where Stella is.

When word gets around that I'm Stella's friend, neighbors surprise me with small gifts: a bottle of olive oil, a small bay plant, and bread still warm and fragrant from the oven. All week there are tentative rings of the bell. When I peek over the wall, there's a brief wave of a hand, a smile, and a disappearing face. I rush down the sixty-eight steps to find the person long gone, but there's always a delicious surprise waiting for me. My pantry brims with liters of wine, rounds of soft cheese wrapped in grape leaves, dried salami bound with string, almonds and pistachios, along with homemade sauces and jams.

Maria arrived most mornings–her arms overflowing with food she has prepared or picked up from the market. Sometimes it's a tasty lasagna or eggplant parmigiana still warm from the oven. Other times it's a cherry crostata, or a jar of spicy peppers, or a bottle of local wine from her uncle's vineyard.

She took me to the market and introduced me to the vendors while whispering which ones were the best and which to avoid. She pointed out the fishmonger with the freshest fish and showed me all the best places for wine, olive oil, books, linens, and anything else I might need.

We find common ground in the daily flow of life. Each day I ask her about Stella. My questions are simple as I struggle with the unfamiliar dialect. My tentative probes bring a fresh flood of tears when I ask. Each time, she turns away from me and says, "*Non so*—I do not know."

This morning, I open the last unorganized kitchen drawer and count the utensils to determine which to keep and which to toss. As I pitch a mangled fork into the trash, Maria's voice calls out, "*Ciao Caterina, permesso?*"

"*Sì,*" I respond as Maria enters the kitchen with *cornetti*.

She frowns because I haven't made coffee. It has become a morning ritual to share coffee and pastries over chatter. Once the coffee is made and the pastries plated, we move in front of the fireplace.

Once settled, I say, "I'm thinking about inviting some neighbors over for dinner? Everyone has been so generous to supply my pantry with wonderful gifts of food and wine. I want to thank them. It's just that Stella isn't here. It seems wrong to have a party without her. What do you think?"

Maria nods her head between yes and no. At first, she says *no*. I nod in agreement but she repeats no and follows with, "No, no, it will be good to have a dinner party here. Stella would expect you to meet everyone. If she were here, she would have a party to introduce you. Yes, we will do this."

After I remember that *no* often means *yes*, I ask, "Will you help me with the guest list?"

Maria's smile lights the room. I gather paper and pen and move my chair closer to hers. I scribble notes as she identifies the guests: the butcher and his wife, the retired opera singer, the fishmonger, the widower, the teacher, the lady who makes the pottery, and of course, a couple of local artists. When she stops, there are close to two dozen names on the list.

Over the next several days, the party bonds us. Our friendship grows as we ponder lists of food, wine, flowers, candles, dishes and utensils, linens, tables, chairs, and seating arrangements. We discuss the weather at length. It's the time of year when eating outside is iffy but we decide on outside with contingency plans to move inside if necessary.

The listing and counting give me purpose. I'm calm and relaxed, lulled into believing Stella will turn up. During these days, Maria slowly opens up about Stella. She confides that Stella often disappears for weeks, but she always returns.

As our plans gel, I realize Maria has assigned most of the food preparation to herself. When I mention this, she smiles shyly and says she loves to cook.

"I do too. Could I make the desserts?"

Maria tosses her head severely enough for me to understand she doesn't like the idea.

"I would love to make some American desserts from the south where I live. They would be different and a way I could thank everyone. What do you think?"

"Humph," is all she says.

"Look, I love Italian food. My nonna taught me everything I know about it. But it would be fun to share our cultures. The desserts would be a surprise. Of course, your Italian desserts are far better than mine and my attempts would be inferior to yours, but I'd like to try."

Maria faces me across the table, "Tell me what you would make."

"A triple-decker blackberry jam cake with caramel icing, a buttery pound cake with lemon curd, and a decadent chocolate praline cake."

Maria wrinkles her nose. At first, I think she's displeased. But I'm becoming familiar with her slow way of smiling. It starts when she tilts her lips upward just a fraction. Soon her face is awash in a full out giant smile.

She exclaims, "*Va bene*. You make dessert."

I clap and squeal with delight. The date for the party is set two weeks later on a Sunday evening. Gino delivers the invitations.

CAT

Whenever weather permits, I walk the promenade. It encircles the sea like the tentacles of a giant octopus. It hasn't changed much since our early years in Castello. At dust the dazzling white sails of seaworthy vessels unfurl and billow in the breeze as they leave the safety of the harbor. At dawn the fishing boats return to port. Stella is always with me.

If the day is warm and sunny, I return in the afternoon. I usually bring one of Stella's starfish books and tuck myself into one of the small niches along the sea wall. The stone benches, concealed from view, fold me into a secret hiding place away from watching eyes. Often, I don't open the book. I simply gaze out to sea. Time blends with eternity. Stella sits beside me. I reach for her hand. The day settles heavily around me.

Today when I come to the end of the promenade, I continue on the path until it brings me to the antique lighthouse crumbling into ruins. Stella and I loved this place. We used to pretend that knights in armor were on their way to rescue us from evil men and dragons. The obscure path fades before reaching the water. Large boulders plunge into the sea. They form fortresses, hideaways, and caves that resurrect special memories of our childhood.

The boulders are solid, impenetrable, heated by the sun. In a low crouch I scurry across them, not nearly as agile as I used to be. A small protrusion hides a cozy cove with a swallow pool. Removing my shoes, I sink my feet into the soft sandy base. Pebbles cascade, casting concentric circles that ripple across the surface. The sun penetrates the bedrock and warms my back when I lean into its rough surface. A quiet peacefulness spreads through my body. I close my eyes and sink into nirvana until something scampers across my feet.

Jerking them out of the water, I shriek and fall backwards. I crouch and peer into the pool. A small red starfish clumsily scuttles to the closest boulder and attaches itself. I slide down on my stomach and hold my breath for fear of startling the tiny creature. From reading one of Stella's starfish books, I've learned that the eyes, which only discern light, dark, and large structures, are on the tips of their arms. Bending over the edge of the pool, I regard the delicate arms as they tighten on the rock by using its numerous suctioned feet. Its tiny eyes can't be seen because the curvature in its arms as it grasps the boulder hides them. The starfish lies still. Does it see me as a large obstacle? When it doesn't move, I reposition myself back onto the warm boulder, but I keep my feet out of the pool. I open Stella's starfish book and read.

A starfish is a marine invertebrate...and a predator...they are probably the most important predator in the shallow ecosystem...They eat basically anything they come across. Their feeding activities control the whole ecosystem of the ocean.

It's late afternoon when I awake and drowsily stretch into the last rays of the sun's fading light. The little red starfish had vanished. Tucking the book under my arm, I stroll back to the piazza. Haunting sounds of an *organetto* fill the air. It's joined by the slow beat of a drum. As I enter from the far end of the promenade, I'm sucked into throngs of people moving to a steady, rhythmic march. A statue sways at the front of the column.

I work my way through the crowd until I'm close enough to see the rippled muscles of the backs of eight young men. A saint rides high on their shoulders as they step in time.

"Quale santo?" I ask the person next to me. "What saint?"

"Oh, Sant'Antonio!"

Saint Antonio is a much beloved saint throughout Puglia. He's the patron saint of fires and fireworks and a healer of plagues. In my book of saints, Antonio is one of my favorites. Who wouldn't love a saint of fireworks as well as a healer of plagues? I fall in with the procession.

The crowd undulates toward the cathedral. The low hum of chanting and the woodsy odor of incense float in the air. Small beads of sweat gather at my hairline as the throngs push to get closer to the statue. The masses of humanity are suffocating. I extricate myself and search for a place where I can watch without participating.

A small stone bench at the perimeter of the piazza is empty. I grasp the edge and pull myself into a standing position. The strong backs and arms of the young men strain. The statue tilts from side to side until it's perilously close to wobbling off the platform. I like to think it's the magical chanting that keeps the statue and the men from toppling over.

Columns of bodies weave into the church. The piazza is left empty and quiet preveils. I slide into a comfortable sitting position. The stone is still warm from the last burst of the sun's heat. The tinny music fades. Once again delicious drowsiness returns. I close my eyes for just a moment to lock into place the memory of S. Antonio before heading to the villa.

Every nerve in my body jerks when a hand tightens on my shoulder. I struggle to pull away, but the first hand is joined by a second. My neck locks into place as the pressure increases. I claw at the hands, but they are clasped firmly and painfully around my throat. A small noise like a muffled scream puffs from my mouth. A rough unshaven face presses against the left side of my face. I wheeze and flail, but the world is already fading. A knee pushes into my spine. A deep, guttural voice comes at me from a distance.

Non muoverti, non parlare. Ascolta attentamente. Devi partire. Andare a casa. Morirai se rimani.

"Do not move, do not speak. Listen carefully. Leave. Go home. You will die if you stay."

The piazza dissolves and distorts and then comes back into view.

I struggle to stand on jello legs. They wobble as I frantically search in every direction. My neck throbs. My legs crumble. I sink back onto the bench and position my head between my knees to keep from fainting.

Movement shifts next to me. I scream before I open my eyes. A woman attired in black has a bewildered expression on her face as she says, "*Mi dispiace. Ti ho spaventato*? I am sorry. Did I startle you?"

I shrill, "Did you see anyone? Did you see a man standing behind me?"

Non capisco l'inglese is all she says as she rushes off to tell her family and friends she was harassed by a crazy American woman.

My heart pumps painfully as I push through the dense crowd gathered outside the cathedral. Each face looks sinister. They leer at me. I stumble. A hand reaches to help me. I bolt without a word of thanks or apology. My head spins as I race away from the piazza. Unraveled and breathless, I arrive at the villa. I tear through the gate, up the stairs, and frantically fumble to unlock the front door. Only after I'm inside and the deadbolt is secure do I allow my knees to give way. I slide down the wooden door and dissolve into a puddle.

What is going on? Am I losing my mind? Stella, where are you?

CAT

Fortified with a glass of wine, I adjust the cushions and take my usual place on the terrace. I imagine Stella doing exactly the same thing. My eyes lock on the lone tree on the small barren peninsula jutting into the sea, the same tree her eyes would contemplate. A hush descends at twilight. Children and pets have been called in for the night. Aromas of roasted meats and wood-burning fires circle in the air. The lone tree represents my personal angst—a sentinel with its awkward arms stretched in supplication, praying for what?

The incident in the piazza spirals my thoughts in every direction without formulating a conclusion or coming up with a plan. Should I tell someone? But who? Lorenzo?

A regiment of ants marches across the baluster while I create an imaginary conversation with him.

Someone tried to choke me.

Cat, who tried to choke you and why?

I don't know.

What happened?

One moment I was sitting in the piazza watching the St. Antonio celebration, and the next minute someone was choking me. They threatened me and told me to go home.

Did you see the person?

No, but it was a man.

How could you tell?

I could feel the stubble of his beard when he pressed his head against mine.

What else?

His hands were big, rough.

Did you see his hands?

No.

But you know they were big and rough?

Yes.

What did you do?

Nothing. I couldn't breathe. Oh wait, I may have scratched his hands.

Did you draw blood?

I don't know.

What else can you tell me about this man?

Nothing.

In review, you want us to look for a male with big rough hands, maybe scratched with stubble on his face? That would be the entire male population of Castello. Of course, we would eliminate anyone under twelve.

I don't call Lorenzo. We've had one brief conversation since I've been here. He returned my call, but he sent one of his officers to pick up my phone. My disappointment was huge. Actually, I was devastated. Stupidly, I had hoped he wanted to see me. But instead, he sent a young officer who swapped my phone for a burner phone and said mine would be returned in a few days.

The only thing I know to do is record both incidents in my journal. I jot down every detail about the attack at the dilapidated house with the symbol of the sun and the snake emerging out of its blue eye. I do the same for the encounter in the piazza. Stella hovers in the background of my mind. Fear is in her eyes.

CAT & MARIA

This morning when Maria arrives for coffee, we decide to sit outside despite the chill in the air. We bundle up and drag our chairs into the sun. We sit on cushioned lounges next to each other. The pale sun paints an angelic glow on Maria's face. The breeze pauses, leaving the sea to slumber like a giant asphalt parking lot.

My ears are slowly becoming attuned to Maria's dialect. Recently, she's been adding English words to her sentences. But I'm surprised when she asks me in English, "What's wrong? You look exhausted."

My mouth opens. There's only a brief pause before my story tumbles out. I tell her everything that happened yesterday and the day I arrived in Castello. The words keep pouring out along with all my fears. She doesn't speak, not even to ask a question. She listens and nods from time to time.

When I finish, she takes a deep breath and says, "You are Stella's best friend, *vero*?"

Before answering her question, I say, "You speak a lot more English than you let on."

For a moment, a mischievous grin flits across her dark, lined face. "*Sì, un poco*. Stella helped me. She used to talk about you all the time. She said I could trust you, but I was afraid. After Stella disappeared, I didn't trust anyone but Gino. I have many fears and worries about

Stella. Now you are telling me that bad things are happening to you. These must be the same people who threatened Stella."

Panic rises in my throat, exactly the way it did in the piazza. Knots twist in my stomach. Whatever Maria is going to tell me, it's something I don't want to hear.

She lays her hand on my arm and says, "From time to time Stella disappeared."

I nod and stay quiet as she concentrates on her phrasing. I can almost hear the voice in her head as she struggles to translate from her guttural dialect into English.

She starts, stops and then begins, "Stella has—had problems with addiction. You know this but perhaps not the full picture. Often, particularly when she was here, she was able to control her desire for the drugs. She also controlled it whenever she was with you. You are a strong force in her life. She never wants to disappoint you."

Maria pauses and takes another deep breath, "She has been in and out substance abuse clinics, and lately she's been seeing a drug therapist in Lecce. She has worked hard to overcome this difficulty and has made progress. This is the reason for her frequent disappearances. As far as I know, she only confided in Gino and me.

"Stella has not been on drugs for a couple of months. She was determined to be clean when you arrived. The strange thing is that neither her agent or her photographer knew about her last assignment or the location. Stella said it was publicity for her new film which releases in a few months.

"When she disappeared, we thought maybe she had returned to the clinic. But she was doing so well with her recovery that it didn't seem right. I asked Antonio if she was in rehab as he always seems to know. I imagine his medical friends keep him informed. He only worries about Stella because he's afraid he will lose his license if the authorities find out he was complicit in providing the drugs. Gino and I think Lorenzo knows about Antonio and the drugs, and we believe Lorenzo is protecting Antonio. We don't know why."

It's difficult not to interrupt with my questions, but I don't. I take a sip of my already cold coffee and shudder as a sudden burst of wind blasts across the terrace.

"A few days before the photo shoot, Stella asked me to come to the villa. She showed me a secret drawer in her desk. She was nervous and very agitated like she wanted to tell me more. She revealed what was in the secret drawer and told me if anything happened to her, I was to give this to you."

Maria reaches into her bag and pulls out a ceramic box. She pushes it across the table. The lines between her eyes are deep. I look at the box and back at her face.

She simply says, "Stella."

A chill races down my spine. It reminds me of Pandora's box waiting to release the evil contained inside. Instead of opening it, I touch it. With my finger, I trace the inlaid mosaic pattern. The cobalt background radiates intensely like a brilliant summer sky. Two white doves perch on a birdbath trimmed in gold leaf. One bird drinks from the vessel, the other stands guard. The cobalt fades into a tempestuous gray-green color like a storm-tossed sea before softening into the palest green bordered in the same gold leaf. My eyes lock with Maria's.

My fingers tremble as I lift the lid. On top is a small red packet containing a key. I set it aside and pick up a tightly rolled piece of parchment tied with twine. I unroll it but tears gather making it difficult to read the words.

"It's something about the necklace," I say as I recognize the words *la collana con la stella marine.* "Would you read it to me?"

I hand Maria the message.

Stanotte verrai alla grotta progettata. Riceverai il tuo primo incarico. Devi portare anche la collana di stelle marine. Sarà il tuo primo pagamento per cancellare il tuo debito. Garantirà protezione a te ed Antonio. Se non vieni, veniamo noi per te.

She translates, "Tonight you will come to the designated cave. You will receive your first assignment. You must bring the starfish necklace. It will be collateral against your debt. It will guarantee protection for you and Antonio. If you do not come, we will come for you."

My mouth drops open in astonishment, "Stella would never give anyone her necklace. Who would want it? She has plenty of money. This doesn't make sense."

Pain flits in Maria's eyes, "I'm not sure. She told us she owed money for drugs because she decided to buy this villa instead of paying off her debt. She said she was working on an arrangement to pay off her debt. This message must have frightened her."

I turn back to the ceramic container. A faded royal blue velvet box brings back a flood of memories. It's been twenty years since Stella rushed into our shared room clutching this box in her hands.

Her seventeen year old eyes brimmed with tears of joy, her breathy voice exclaiming, "Oh Cat. He asked me to wait for him. He wants to marry me."

"Look!" she'd exclaimed through the tears trembling down her cheeks.

She had opened this same box although twenty years ago it had been a deep royal blue. Nestled in the folds of white satin was a spectacular bracelet.

With jubilation she continued, "Antonio had it custom designed for me by the most famous Italian jewelry designer, Aldo Cipullo. It's for me, Cat! Look at it! Can you believe it?"

At seventeen we had no sense of what that meant. To us it was the essence of romance, a shimmering declaration of love straight from our childhood fairy tales. We knew without being told that it was expensive and that the delicate natural red ruby shaped like a starfish was one of a kind. We stared at the exquisite piece of jewelry —spellbound and wordless.

Twenty years later, I open the same box. A small card with Stella's name engraved on it lies on top. I turn the card over. Stella's bold handwriting invades my soul—*amiche per sempre*—forever friends. The diamond clusters sparkle in the sunlight until a cloud passes. A chill starts at the base of my spine and rolls up to the back of my neck. My own tears tumble onto the red starfish. The bracelet and the note mean only one thing. Stella will not return.

My hands shake as I set it aside, lay my head on the table, and sob.

Maria folds me into her arms and lets me cry. The wind turns cold. It penetrates my jacket and wraps its icy hands around my heart. I scrunch up my eyes and see Stella standing on the terrace. I hear her voice entertaining me with stories about her latest film or the splendid place she and I will have lunch today. I open my eyes. She's not here.

Maria shifts her weight. She brushes my hair out of my eyes and says, "Let's go inside. We need a fire and fresh coffee. Then we'll finish looking through the box."

She stands, pulls me up, and leads me into the house. She plumps the pillows on the sofa and gently guides me to sit. She places a blanket around my shoulders and tucks it in. Soon a fire is blazing and a steaming cup of coffee is in my hand.

The ceramic box sits on the coffee table in anticipation. Under the velvet box there's a scrap of paper. As my fingers pick it up, they scrape against cold metal. A Mary Magdalene medallion is stuck in one corner. I pry it out and clasp it in the palm of my hand. My fingers trace over its rough, tarnished surface. Memories of our first holy communion and Stella's refusal to wear the medallion invade my thoughts. Our giggles had turned into tears when the sister had cracked a ruler across Stella's knuckles.

Next I reach for the paper and press it flat. It lies silent on the table. It waits to tell a story. But, the message has no meaning. It simply says, *Trova gli indizi*—Find the clues. *Ce ne sono tre*—There are three.

"Maria?"

Maria's usual dark complexion becomes pale and splotchy. She inhales and slowly expels her breath. Sadness creases her face until she looks like Picasso's *Melancholy Woman*. She shakes her head in bewilderment and says, "I don't know. But Stella thinks you will understand what she means."

CAT & MARIA

Find the clues—the words bounce back at me from the scrap of paper. Something tickles at the back of my mind, a long-ago memory of a game we played where we left trails of paper with clues written on them. But now, after all these years? What made Stella think of this? Where would I look?

I gasp, jump up, and run to the kitchen. Where did I put that scrap of paper? What did it say? I jerk out drawers and fling cabinet doors open. I check the wastebasket and the top of the table where I sometimes put odds and ends. I sprint to the bookcase and wildly throw starfish books on the floor until I find the one I was reading last. There, wedged between the pages of *Starfish* by Akemi Dawn Bowman, is the sliver of paper I found wrapped around the chef's knife in the kitchen drawer.

I rush back to the living room where Maria sits on the edge of her seat.

"What?" She asks.

"Look, this has to be one of the three clues." I hand her the tattered scrap of paper.

La cipolla a cupola

She frowns and asks, "A domed onion? What does it mean? Where did you find it?"

"It was in the utility drawer wrapped around a chef's knife, a new knife. I'm sure Stella bought it for me. I don't know what it means. A domed onion? What sense does that make? I thought maybe you would know?"

Maria and I sit side by side. We stare at the piece of paper.

Finally, she places her hand over mine and says, "You must look for the other clues. Maybe when you find all of them it will make sense."

"It's only a scrap of paper. Maybe it's not a clue? Where would I look for the other clues?"

"Stella is clever. She put the first clue exactly where you would look—in the kitchen around a chef's knife. The other two clues will be in places where Stella believes you will look."

I nod. Maria is right.

"Do you think I should tell anyone? Lorenzo? Antonio?"

A whispered *no* escapes from Maria's lips. "No, no, no. Look at the words. Stella wants only you to know."

I pick up the paper as Maria continues, "The onion dome means something to only you and Stella."

"I'm not sure what. We had so many secret hiding places during our summers here. Maybe it's one of the caves. Did she ever mention any of this to you?"

Maria shakes her head no, but then she says, "Recently, Stella was suspicious of everyone. After her disappearance, I feel the same. Don't talk to anyone until you find all the clues and have some idea of what to do next."

"Okay, but what, other than Stella's disappearance, makes you suspicious?"

"A few days after Stella disappeared, Antonio came to the villa. He packed up some of Stella's belongings. Later, I saw Carlo stop by. He was only inside for a few minutes, but it didn't make sense for him to be there. Then, Lorenzo showed up. At least his visit was official. He taped off the house and then stopped by to talk to us. He asked us questions about Stella. I told him about Antonio and Carlo being in the house, but I don't know if I can trust him."

I puzzle over Maria's comments before saying, "It's strange isn't it? It seems suspicious that Antonio would go in the house before Lorenzo searched it. It's also odd that he would take anything of hers. I mean, they are separated, aren't they? And Carlo—it makes no sense at all. Why would he be at the house?"

Maria shrugs. I continue, "I can understand Lorenzo searching, but I don't understand anything else. Did you know that Carlo had Stella's house listed as a rental?"

"Oh, no," Maria says and squirms in her seat. "You know we are close to Carlo. He's always been good to us. He keeps Gino out of trouble. But it's Stella's house. No one except Stella or her executor has the right to rent it or sell it. Oh Caterina, this is a big mess. And Gino and I have added to the mess."

I silently wonder where and when this craziness will stop? Everyone is involved. Yet we are no closer to finding Stella.

I catch up with Maria's words as she says, "A few days after Stella's photo shoot, I became worried. I stopped by to see if she needed anything. She didn't answer, so I went home. That evening I told Gino that Stella had not returned. The next morning we went together. We used our key to open the door and were shocked. The place had been ransacked— drawers were open and her clothes and jewelry were scattered on the floor. I knew something was wrong, so I quickly removed a few personal things Stella told me she would like for you to have. And I removed the ceramic box from the desk. We found her purse but nothing had been taken. That's when we notified Antonio. A few days later he showed up, then Carlo, and finally Lorenzo."

"So you don't really trust any of them, do you?"

"No, I do not. Someone was spying on Stella. I never told Stella because I wasn't sure, but on several occasions I saw the same person watching the house. There is no reason to patrol this area. At first I thought Lorenzo was having her watched or maybe he was trying to protect her. But it could have been any of them."

"Why was your first reaction to think it was Lorenzo?"

"He was still in love with Stella even after they stopped seeing each other. He wouldn't want anything to happen to her."

"But something did happen to her. If he was having her watched, wouldn't he know something?

"I don't know. Maybe it wasn't Lorenzo who was watching. I didn't ask him about it because he could easily lie. I did ask him why Carlo was at the house. He said maybe Carlo needed to take photos in case Antonio wanted to sell the house. It seems both Carlo and Antonio have keys. Why would Stella give keys to either one of them? Of course, I'm sure Lorenzo still has his key."

Gracious, I think, what a mess. Lorenzo or one of the others may have had Stella followed; Carlo has keys to her house; Antonio is already removing Stella's belongings as if he knows she's dead. What else?

I'm still lost in thought when Maria continues, "I suspect I'm in trouble for removing things from Stella's house too, but only you and Gino know. Because we're the caretakers, our coming and going is routine. If they check for fingerprints, it would be normal to find ours.

"I waited for a few days, and then I contacted Lorenzo and asked him if I could enter the villa to do my regular cleaning. He said to wait until he removed the yellow tape from the door. When he did, I went back. The house had been straightened. That frightened me even more. Which one of them would have done that?"

Shaking my head, I pick up the ceramic box. It shimmers in the afternoon sunlight filtering through the window. My fingers trace the outer edges. Perhaps if I rub hard enough, a genie will appear and help us sort this out.

"So far here's what we know: sometimes Stella disappears, she may or may not have had a relapse with drugs, and she's made enemies. Which of those enemies would hurt her? Who would benefit the most if she wasn't around?"

Maria considers my questions before answering, "After Stella moved into the villa, she talked to Gino and me about her relationship with Antonio.

I frown and ask, "Was she scared of Antonio? Would he hurt her? Do you think it was the drugs? Do you know who was supplying her?"

"Stella had everything, but she was *infelice*—unhappy. When she was working, she needed the drugs. When she was not working, she sometimes did not get out of bed for days. She and Antonio fought over the drugs. That's when she left him. Around the same time, she decided to break the addiction. It's also the same time Lorenzo came sniffing around."

The hard way Maria says Lorenzo's name warns me that I do not want to hear whatever comes next. Stella is still breaking my heart and scattering the fragments into the wind. I have never felt whole in her presence or in her absence. She always took what I wanted. I never fought her for anything—not even Lorenzo. There was no point. Besides I don't want a man I have to fight someone for. Seems like it would be a very lopsided relationship. I've already had my share of those.

A small sneer tugs at Maria's lip. I watch while she struggles to get it under control. She doesn't notice my pain and continues, "Stella told me she had married Antonio for his money and his family connections. Eventually, she told me that she had always loved Lorenzo.

"Lorenzo expected us to keep quiet about his seeing her. We did for Stella—not for him. But Stella slipped with the drugs, and Lorenzo's position in the Guardia made it impossible for him to stay with her. When Lorenzo told Stella he was leaving, she stopped caring about anything, including herself for a while. Gino and I were glad to see him go, but it was hard watching Stella suffer.

After she knew you were coming to stay with her, she was different—happier, healthier, and certainly anticipating your arrival. That's why her disappearance does not make sense."

"So any or all of them can be involved. What a mess!" I exclaim.

"Just before Stella disappeared, she told Gino and me she was frightened. She had received several threats. She told Lorenzo, but he said it was probably a prank from a fan. Stella didn't think so."

I interrupt, "Do you know what the threats were? Phone calls, texts?"

"No, those would not have frightened her. These were evil threats—a dead bird with an arrow in its heart, a black rose—terrible omens of things to come. They each contained a note with one word only—*Omertà*. This word is used as the code of silence. It was a warning to her about what would happen if she talked. Several times after these horrendous messages, she asked me to stay with her. The last time I did, she told me she was in a difficult situation, but it would soon be over. Gino and I do not believe Stella disappeared on her own. Of course, Gino knows more, but he's not talking."

I shake my head in bewilderment. Maria keeps talking.

"Gino was often away at night. He was helping Stella, but he wouldn't tell me what they were doing. He said it was too dangerous for me to know. My fear is Stella may have used whatever information they found to threaten someone."

"Where do we start? Who can we trust?"

Maria remains silent. My thoughts wander off to dark places. I'm angry with myself for not probing deeper when Stella and I met in New York. I knew something was wrong, but I let hurt feelings and resentment prevent me from questioning her. I'm her best friend, yet I didn't care enough to really listen and offer help. Guilt gathers which only makes me more resentful toward Stella and angry at myself.

Maria's words break into my devastating thoughts.

"Perhaps we start with Carlo. He has been very good to us. He knows a lot about the local mafia. After all, he is an attorney, and he owns a lot of property. He might not talk to us because we work for him, but you could ask him discreetly. I am suspicious of him too except I never saw him alone with Stella, and I never noticed her paying him any attention.

"Antonio is afraid of losing his practice, so he's no help. And

Lorenzo, I'm not sure. Stella was so angry when he left her. She told me he didn't give her a chance. She only took a couple of pills one time before an audition, and he was all over her. You know how vindictive Stella can be. Yes, I know you love her enough to overlook that part of her personality. We love her too, but her behavior was out of control when she didn't get what she wanted. She changed from a beautiful woman into a screaming *strega*."

Images of Stella screaming at me flashed before my eyes. It wasn't the first time that she'd done it, but it was the first time it mattered to me. It had been after she had slept with Lorenzo. She'd rushed into the bedroom we shared, radiant and breathless, expecting me to be happy for her. I told her I hated her. She screamed and pushed me. *La strega,* the witch, came out in full force. We fought like two wild animals until I realized that no boy or man was worth wrecking our friendship. We cried, laughed, and hugged each other fiercely. And at sixteen, we recut our fingers and mingled our blood and pledged all over again to be forever best friends. That was when I let go of loving Lorenzo.

Maria nudges my hand, "Are you okay, Caterina? You are far away."

"Sorry. What about the mafia? They pretty much control the drug scene. Who has mafia contacts? Antonio? Lorenzo? Carlo? Someone else?"

"Gino knows. We can ask him. Can we show Gino what's in the box? He can help us. He has connections."

"Connections? What does that mean?" I shriek like a game show contestant.

"He knows people. He can ask questions, snoop around, and look for evidence."

"Maria, if Stella has been kidnapped or worse that could put her life in danger. It would be insane for you, me, or Gino to start asking questions or to hunt for evidence. We have to take this to the police."

"Do you think that is what Stella would want you to do?"

A warm blush spreads across my face before I say, "You're right. We do need more information. What else did Stella tell you?"

"I don't want to tell you more. You might disappear too. If Stella turns up and you are gone, her anger would be worse than anything I can imagine."

I shake my head, "Maria, you have to tell me. If Stella disappeared because she needed to or wanted to, then she will never know you told me any of her secrets. I would never betray you, and I would never betray Stella. So tell me everything you know."

Maria sighs with relief and looks at me intently, her eyes filled with fear.

"Stella told us the Sacra Corona Unita had contacted her demanding payment. She also told Lorenzo. He told her not to worry as soon he would incapacitate them. The SCU is an oozing sore in the flesh of Puglia, but the backlash would impact the entire town. The mafia touches all of our lives."

Maria stops talking and sinks back against the cushions. She rubs her fingers across her forehead. I wait until she speaks.

"Would you be willing to let Gino ask a few questions first? He knows people in the local SCU."

"Ask someone in the mafia, really? Maria, we could get ourselves killed," I stammer as my heart gallops. "This isn't what I expected. It's too dangerous."

I shrink back in the chair and tell myself to book a flight home. This is insane. My brain scrambles through layers of questions while my voice of reason tells me that leaving this place would be the best thing to do.

Before I can stop myself, words fly out of my mouth, "Okay, tell Gino to ask around. Then what?"

"Well, you know the party we are planning?"

"Sure, but what does that have to do with Stella's disappearance? In fact, we need to cancel it. I can't celebrate anything knowing Stella needs our help."

"But we must go on if we are to help her. Everyone loves *una festa*, a party. We already have one in the works. People have already been invited. What will you tell them if you cancel it? What we can do is add a few more names to the guest list like Lorenzo, Antonio, Carlo, and maybe one or two people we know who have connections to the mafia. Gino can give us some of those names."

"I don't want mafia types at our party."

"Caterina, we must do everything to find Stella. This small party for the neighbors can easily include some others. Stella was well liked. She was not here all the time, but she was generous. She insisted I tell her who was sick, or pregnant, or if there was a death in the family. If she was not in town, she told me to take food or flowers or find a way to subsidize someone who needed help. These people keep their ears open. If we listen and probe gently, we might learn something. No one will know our intention."

"Holy crap," I gasp.

A faint smile turns up the corners of Maria's mouth as a tear slides down her face. I reach across to her. We join hands.

"Okay, let's extend the guest list."

CAT

This morning after my run, I change into a pair of jeans, an old shirt, and grab my rain jacket. My job is to come up with flowers for the centerpieces for the dinner party.

During my drives up and down the coast, I discovered a place where masses of red blossoms waved at me from the high crevices of volcanic cliffs. My mind is already busy arranging the spectacular red flowers in some of Stella's rustic pottery pieces with a little ivy and rosemary from the garden. At yesterday's market in Lecce, I found white tablecloths and material to make green runners. The red flowers will pull everything together.

As I count my way down the sixty-eight steps, a muggy breeze stirs and a faint trace of sunlight wobbles its way across the horizon. A chill hangs in the air. Intermittent days of downpours and winds have made walking around town impossible.

The weak sun disappears and a fine mist smears the windshield. I turn on the wipers and count ten whacks before pulling onto the road. It's early so the barren stretch of highway is free of traffic. I have plenty of time to pick and arrange flowers before Maria arrives for lunch. Our plan is to review the menu one last time.

Maria's daily visits are now an integral part of my life. If I don't accompany her to the market, she stops by for coffee. She shares local gossip and asks me about my life in America. Her vivacious and sunny disposition are a sharp contrast to Gino's dark, silent personality. But every once in a while, he presents me with a shy smile and an occasional nod. That simple acknowledgement from him is like hitting the jackpot.

Every morning Maria asks me if I've found another clue or if I've made sense out of the one Stella left wrapped around the knife. Every morning I say no. We both know finding the two other clues is crucial to unlocking the code. Stella, I hope, is guiding me to the next clue, but she's been very silent.

My thoughts are so distracting I almost drive by the burst of red flowers bobbing from the cliffs. There's no parking, but I've watched locals make their own parking rules when they forage for bitter greens, mushrooms, and asparagus that grow wild in the area. I pull off the narrow, winding road and lop-sidedly park on the shoulder.

My rain jacket and my good sense I leave behind in the car. The rocky terrain is slick as I place my foot on the first ledge. About halfway up, soft rain shrouds me in a fine mist. My shirt clings in sloppy wetness, but I continue to climb. Each foothold is counted. Pulling myself from crevice to crevice, I secure each foot and hand-hold before moving on. It's slow and tedious as rock climbing isn't on my usual list of activities.

The flowers are not nearly as close as they appear from the road. As the pitch steepens, the rocks, sharpened from thousands of years of wind, rain and the sea's endless beatings, cut into my hands and scrape against my shins.

Steadily I plod on with the words from *Climb Every Mountain* pulsating in my head. The crest of the rock formation and the flaming blooms are only a few feet above my head. My normal jogging routine has suffered since I arrived, and I'm winded from the climb. Pausing to catch my breath, I evaluate my next move.

The step up to the next crevice is awkward. I brace my left knee into the rock and lunge at the protrusion above my head. As I pull myself up, the rock wobbles, causing me to slide backwards. I land with a thud on a lower ledge with torn jeans and bloody knees.

Dr. Ginny's voice shouts in my ear, "Cat, what are you doing?

You have enough issues and fears without doing your darndest to create more."

Intellectually, I understand that, but emotionally I have a lot of work to do. I scoot across the ledge and look for a less treacherous approach. The cliff levels out as I move to the left.

The path deviates away from the flowers but it looks like a more direct route once I reach the top. With one big thrust up I land in a crumple on a small clearing. I push into an upright position and scream. Pain ricochets through my hand and up my arm. I jerk away from the spot. I teeter on the edge of the cliff. With a lot of arm waving, I regain my balance and notice blood oozing from a cut on the soft padding on the outside edge of my hand. In the misty drizzle, deep red drops hit my white shirt and fade into splotchy pink puddles.

Leaning against a boulder, I remove my shoe and sock. It's not the best plan to stop the bleeding, but it's all I have. I wind the sock around the cut while I count. It throbs as blood seeps through the cotton and trickles down my arm. Treatment, possibly stitches, and I fear a tetanus shot are in my future. I tighten the sock and slide into a squatting position which creates an involuntary moan as even the simplest movement slams pain up my arm.

The small clearing where I landed opens into a large plateau that overlooks the sea. It's sparsely covered with vines, dried grass, and brambles twisted by wind and rain. In the crevice closest to where I cut my hand, tiny shards of glass stick straight up.

Maybe, it's a broken bottle. I pick up a piece and see my reflection. Maybe a mirror? But why would a mirror be in this obscure place? I pull several shards out of the ground and place them side by side.

A light bounces across my face. I glance up and gaze across the plateau to the villas lining the hill above the marina. There's a large villa at the top away from the others. A circular balcony wraps around before disappearing into the side of the hill. The light came from that direction. I wait but the light doesn't reappear. Maybe I imagined it. A cold chill runs up my spine as the mist plasters my shirt to my back.

My eyes sweep back to the plateau. There's an overgrown path on the other side which appears to lead to the marina. I'll feel pretty stupid if it does since Stella's house is within easy walking distance of the marina.

I inspect the area one last time. My sock-wrapped wound continues to ooze. With a sigh and a promise to come back, I turn to leave. A small shiny object, emerging from the dirt, catches my eye. I poke it with my shoe, but it's solid and doesn't move.

I kneel into the muddy earth and use my fingers to dig. My movements are slow and clumsy, my breathing—erratic and shallow. Although I'm using my right hand, the left one throbs with every move. When my fingers begin to ache, I pick up a large piece of glass and probe in a wider circle. I carefully brush the dirt away from the object until mud-crusted diamonds and a red starfish pendant surface.

Every nerve in my body wails, but I continue to push the dirt away. My wet clothes meld into my flesh. Shivers involuntarily jerk through my body. Little by little clusters of diamonds emerge. The soft, wet earth gives way. Stella's diamond necklace with the delicately carved red starfish stares back at me. *La stella marina rossa.*

Stella, I whisper into the wind.

A sudden burst of rain pelts my back. The throb in my hand starts an agonizing journey up my arm. The road below seems far away and the incline of the cliff seems steeper than when I climbed up. The wind whips around the boulders, each one a possible hiding place for silent eyes that seem to watch my every move. My heart rate accelerates as a movement above causes pebbles to cascade down the cliffs. I crouch into the rocks. Was it the wind or is someone up there watching?

The rain intensifies. I quickly unearth the necklace. It's twisted and the clasp is broken, but it seems intact. It's too big for my pocket, so I awkwardly tie it in the tail of my shirt.

Il padrone frowned. He turned off the light on the telescope but continued to peer through the lenses. What in the heck was that woman doing? It looked like she was picking up something—maybe something Riccardo left behind? Her body blocked whatever she was digging up. A white sock was tied around her hand but that was all he could see. Her movements were jerky. He watched as she stood up and appeared to wrap or tie something into the hem of her shirt. Then she was gone. He texted Riccardo. *Take another look at the plateau and keep a close watch on Stella's friend.*

Now what to do? Who should I take it to? Should I leave it here? After all, it's evidence.

The gathering storm settles the question for me. Antonio gave the necklace to Stella. Maria won't agree, but it's rightfully his. Since I need to see a doctor, the decision is made.

Steadily, I descend, the flowers forgotten. The wind gathers strength, herding my feet into tangles. I'm airborne—falling on my butt, sliding sideways and arriving in a heap at the bottom of the cliff. There's no time to inventory the damage as the rain beats unrelenting staccato notes on my head.

My hand slams against the car door as I rush to open it. I swear out loud and tears gush. I simply cannot show up at the clinic sobbing and feeling sorry for myself. I grit my teeth, put the car in gear with my right hand and try to steer with two fingers.

It's close to one o'clock, the time most businesses in Castello close. I gun the accelerator. The car lurches across the narrow road. It takes death-defying seconds to correct it from pitching down the embankment. Thoughts of Stella and death filter through the pain as I reel the car back onto the rain-slick road.

I count—leaves falling, the thump of the windshield wipers, even roads that intersect. The clinic comes into view. I park in front of the clinic and stumble into the empty waiting room just as the receptionist turns the lights off in her office. Her mouth opens to speak, but no words come out. For a brief moment, I imagine what she sees—a wild-eyed woman with out-of-control hair garbed in muddy, blood-soaked clothes.

We stare at each until I say, *Per favore, vorrei vedere il dottore,* praying that the words *please I want to see the doctor* are enough to gain access to Antonio.

She turns her back to me while gathering her coat and purse. She shuts the door to her office. "I'm sorry, we're closed for lunch. Is it an emergency?"

Her unexpected English causes me to stammer.

"Please, I need to see Antonio. This is his clinic, isn't it?"

"Yes, it is. But I'm sure Dottor Moretti has left for the day. It's Friday. He won't return until Monday."

Her lips form a firm straight line as she guides me to the door.

"It's an emergency! Please check to see if he's still here. Tell him Caterina Gabbiano—Cat—is asking for him. Please?"

She opens the door and starts to usher me out. I lift my bloody sock-enclosed hand into her face.

With a quick intake of breath she says, "Take a seat. I will check. But if he's not available, you will have to go to the emergency unit at the hospital."

CAT & ANTONIO

With one hand, I struggle to pull my hair into order while rain-diluted blood drizzles down my arm. My shirt is soaked, and the knot securing the necklace is slathered with mud. A small puddle collects at my feet. Dragging my shoe through the water doesn't do anything but make it appear bigger. Fatigue crawls over my skin like shards of glass. I glance at the pristine surroundings not sure I won't be penalized if I sit on the immaculate furniture.

Stella's presence is everywhere: in the pale shade of sage on the walls, the off-white leather chairs, and the magnificent artwork perfectly balanced around the room. Gilded mirrors create light where there are no windows. Upscale magazines rest on the intricately carved round table in the center of the room. After brushing off my butt, I sit on the edge of a wooden chair that is artfully placed at an antique writing desk. The world becomes smaller as I withdraw into a safe place in my mind.

When a warm hand touches my shoulder, I jump. It's been years since I've seen Antonio. His amber eyes are dull. Tiny lines zigzag around his mouth. A dark stubble on his chin acerbates his gaunt appearance. Exhaustion, probably caused by long hours at the clinic, etches shadows across his face. His hair needs combing. His white coat is dingy. The tense grip of his facial muscles, his furrowed brown, and his vapid eyes send out messages tinged with pain and guilt.

"Cat," he says as he lifts me into an embrace and plants a kiss on each cheek, "What happened? You're a mess. Are you okay? Don't answer. Come with me."

He leads me through the waiting room and into his office while calling for someone named Sylvia. A smiling face peeks in the door. The face is surrounded by wispy curls escaping from a coiled braid.

Looking her over, I think this must be the person he's having an affair with. Crap, Stella will be furious if I'm nice to her. The woman tries to include me in conversation. When I don't respond, she turns to Antonio and asks, "What do you need, doctor?"

Antonio unwraps my sock-clad hand and inspects the wound. "A numbing shot, antibiotics, sutures, bandages, antiseptic pads, and something for pain."

My head stays down. I stare at the floor until the door closes. He gently places my hand on a sterile towel and reaches across me to open the desk drawer. Out comes a shot glass and a bottle of grappa. He pours, hands me the glass, and says, "Drink, then tell me what happened."

I sip the grappa and shudder as the harsh liquid hits my empty stomach, "I was climbing up the side of a rocky slope to pick some flowers. Instead, I cut my hand,"

"Hmm," is all he says as he guides the grappa back to my mouth. I slug the rest of it down in one swallow, sputtering and gagging as the raw alcohol churns and burns its way down.

Sylvia knocks and enters. The pattern on the floor becomes my focus as I refuse to acknowledge her. Yet, I'm curious. I shift my eyes enough to take a look as she hands Antonio a metal tray with supplies. She has one of those sweet faces, all innocent and glowing. She positions herself next to him and acts all professional while keeping her eyes fixed on my injured hand.

Antonio cleans the wound. He glances at me from time to time but never looks at Sylvia. When he finally speaks, his voice is serious.

"The karstic cliffs are dangerous. You have to be careful. Stay away from rock climbing for a while," he looks up, grinning in the way I remember. It softens his face and erases some of the anger and fatigue.

"How are you, Antonio?"

Instead of answering he says, "Sylvia, go ahead and leave. I'll finish up."

A red flush spreads across her face, "You usually let me finish the stitching. Aren't you supposed to be on your way to Gallipoli? I can take over."

His jaw clenches, "No, you go ahead. Cat and I need to catch up. Lock up when you leave."

She shrugs and shuts the door a little harder than needed.

Antonio waits until the door closes and says, "I guess you want to know why I didn't return your calls?

"Yes, I do. I thought you didn't want to see me—had maybe changed your mind and didn't want me here."

"It isn't that—it's just I don't know what to say. It's awkward. Stella and I are separated. Now she's missing. I knew you'd have a million questions."

He looks at me from under a clump of hair that partially hides his eyes.

"I don't have any answers. It's absolutely crazy, Cat. I'm stuck in this void."

"What about Stella? Don't you think she's stuck somewhere far worse than a void."

Antonio lowers his head. Little beads of sweat line his forehead. His hands tremble enough to make me worry about his stitching me up.

There's no point in castrating him. He's probably already been down that road.

"Maybe we should start with what happened to you and Stella?"

"Uh, okay." He breaks off then continues, "You know about the drugs. It wrecked our marriage. I was willing to try again, but she turned to Lorenzo instead. Then she vanished. Initially, I thought it was her usual disappearing act, but now I don't think so."

I wait for him to continue. When he does, he mumbles, "Sorry I didn't return your calls. Are you settled? Do you need anything?"

My thoughts stew a bit before I answer, "It was uncomfortable when you didn't return my calls. You knew I was coming and still you left me in a lurch. If you don't want me staying at Stella's, tell me."

He doesn't respond.

"Antonio, is it okay for me to stay at Stella's house?

He inspects his nails and pushes the clump of hair out of his eyes.

"I guess that means you don't want me there. Would you at least tell me why Stella's villa is listed as rental property on Carlo's website?"

His elbow bangs against the table. Supplies bounce before settling back down. His fingers randomly fumble through the assortment of items on the tray.

"That day I met Carlo to pick up the keys, I asked him about the villa. He said he'd forgotten to take it off the rental listing. He offered to find me another place to stay. Antonio, I want to stay at Fiori. Before Stella disappeared, she invited me to stay with her—insisted. It feels right for me to follow through. I want to be there when she returns."

"Yes, yes, of course. If that's where you want to stay, then it's fine. I know Stella would be upset if you didn't."

Again silence. I continue to randomly chatter. Maybe I'll hit on a topic that will somehow persuade him to join the conversation.

"Okay, the only thing I need is information. Tell me everything you know about Stella's disappearance."

No response. My nonstop chatter escalates as the sting of the numbing needle and Antonio's nonverbal approach leave me floundering. Thankfully, his hands are steady as he draws the thread through my flesh creating tidy, evenly spaced little stitches.

When he finishes, he hands me a couple of tablets and says, "Slide your shirt off."

I glance up and see a needle pointed at me.

"It's an antibiotic," he says. "The next one is for pain. You're going to need it. As soon as you get to the house, take these pills. They'll help you manage the pain for a couple of days.

There's a knock at the door. Sylvia enters and gathers up the instruments and nods at me, which I ignore. It's against my southern sensibilities but necessary for Stella's sake. Irritation crosses Antonio's face.

"You haven't left?"

"I thought you might require assistance or need additional supplies. But since you don't, I'm off to lunch now."

She lingered and waited for him to say he'd meet her for lunch at their usual place. When he doesn't, she stammers, "Unless there's something I can do?"

"No, go to lunch. If you need me this afternoon, you know where I'll be."

Her smile gathers him in a warm embrace, but he doesn't return the smile. He fidgets until she leaves.

"Is your car outside?"

"Yes."

"Leave the key with me. I'll have someone drive it over later. You can't drive a manual until the wound heals. I don't want you breaking open the stitches."

"I managed to drive here. I'm sure I can drive back to the villa. But before I go, I need to show you what I found today."

Unsteadily, I stand. He reaches out to keep me from falling. His touch is warm and firm, anchoring me. With my right hand I fumble with the knot in my shirt tail. The muddy necklace spills into my hand.

Antonio's sharp intake of breath startles me. When I look up, his face is a deadly shade of white. His forehead creases into a scowl. His mouth drops open. Since he is only a few inches taller than I am, our faces are close. His eyes harden as they lock on the starfish. His grip tightens on my arm. A small whisper escapes through his clenched teeth, "*Stella*."

His voice turns steely as he reaches out and lightly touches the necklace with his fingertips, "Where?"

"On one of the cliffs overlooking the marina. Where I cut my hand. There were tiny shards of broken glass everywhere. I saw something poking through the dirt and dug it out. It was Stella's necklace. She would never discard it in the place where I found it. Something has to be terribly wrong for it to be there. All the way to the clinic I kept asking myself, 'What made her take it off? How long has it been there? Why wasn't it found by the police?' Antonio, what's going on?"

I glance up. His mouth flatlines. His face sags. He starts to speak but stops. The silence hovers like thick fog until he says, "I need to call Lorenzo. As much as I want to keep the necklace, it's evidence. He'll want to talk to you, and he'll want to see the location."

He shakes his head and continues, "It just seems strange that you found it. Lorenzo told me he searched everywhere. But now I wonder if he did."

"Why would you think that?"

"Why wouldn't I?"

I'm confused by the remark, but Antonio doesn't answer. He abruptly releases my arm and walks out of the room.

The diamonds, although laden with dirt, gleam in the muted light. Two little girls swim into my thoughts, one golden haired and one with a crown of strawberry curls. They giggle and stumble but never release each other's hands. As their toes touch the sea, they turn simultaneously to see if they are still being pursued by the young boys. They stand suspended in the surf as waves crash against their sun-bronzed bodies. One boy catches up to them. He brushes his hair away from his amber eyes and stares at the girl with the golden hair.

CAT & ANTONIO

"Lorenzo didn't answer, so I left a message. He'll want to talk to you right away, but I asked him to wait until tomorrow morning. If you're ready, I'll drive you home. You need to rest for a few days."

"What?"

I drag myself back to the present, barely aware that I had drifted off or that Antonio had left the room.

"Lorenzo," he says softly with a puzzled look. "He'll stop by the villa tomorrow. Cat, you're exhausted and none of this makes sense. Don't argue with me about driving, You can't shift gears and steer with a stitched hand."

He takes off his lab coat, runs his hands through his hair and helps me down from the exam table. He places his hand on my back and steers me to his car. As we approach the house, Maria is waiting by the gate with several shopping bags.

"Grazie, Antonio. You were right, driving would have been difficult. Drop me off here. In all the confusion I forgot Maria was coming. We've having a dinner party next Sunday night. I'd love to add your name to the invitation list."

He pulls off the road and shifts into neutral, "I haven't gone out since Stella left."

"Maybe it's time, Antonio," I respond as his face struggles with the decision.

"Is Lorenzo invited to the party? It might be helpful for the three of us to connect again. It has been a long time, hasn't it? Stella never included me when you two met. It was the wedding when I last saw you."

"It's been at least ten or twelve years. Yes, I'm inviting Lorenzo and also Carlo. Please come."

"I don't know, Cat. Can I bring a guest? I'd feel more comfortable having someone with me."

Oh drat, I think. Why does he want to complicate things? There's no way I'm going to let Sylvia into Stella's house.

Out loud I say, "I hope you understand, but the guest list is limited. There's only room for twenty-four. I can't possibly add anyone else. I hope that won't make you stay away. You'll know everyone. You must know Stella's neighbors? Right?"

He looks down at his shoes and doesn't say anything.

"Antonio?"

"Maybe, I'll let you know," is all he says.

"I'll count on you coming. If you can't, then call me."

I inch toward the door, but he stops me with his hand on my arm.

"Cat, I told Lorenzo he could pick up the necklace from you tomorrow. It makes sense as I'm leaving for Gallipoli and will be there all weekend."

He places the necklace in my hand. His fingers drift over the dirt-covered stones. He searches my face, "Oh, Cat, I couldn't give Stella what she wanted. She never understood my passion for my studies and my patients. She wanted all of me, all of the time. She drained me with all her drama and her constant need for attention and for publicity. Everywhere we went the cameras followed us. She was always angry with me and accused me of so many things—whether or not I was guilty. Once she started taking drugs, I couldn't help her. I tried, but I wasn't capable."

There are no words to ease his anguish. Our hands close around the starfish necklace. A slow, warm vibration hovers over the necklace until Maria taps on the window. Our hands separate as I stuff the necklace back into my shirt tail and tie an awkward knot. I slide out of the car into Maria's path. She surveys my bandaged hand and scraped knees.

"*Dio mio*," she whispers as she rushes to help me. "*Dio mio*, what happened?'

"*Allora*, I took a tumble."

"Hush." she says. "Hand me the keys. You can't possibly talk about the party today. In fact, we need to cancel it."

"Oh no, Maria. My hand will be fine in a few days. I'm really okay. Dr. Moretti fixed me up. With a little rest, I'll be back on track in a day or maybe two."

Maria doesn't acknowledge Antonio which puzzles me. She keeps her eyes on me and makes endearing clucking sounds and says, "We'll see."

The sixty-eight steps confront me, but the counting keeps me focused. Sweat collects on my forehead and leaks down my face. I plant each foot firmly and move woozily up. By the time I reach the top terrace, my knees are quivering. I lean into the wall while Maria opens the door. She guides me to the sofa and brings me a glass of water. I swallow one of the pills and hope for quick relief.

"Stay here. I must put the food away before it spoils. When I finish, I will wrap your hand in a plastic bag and put you in the shower. Leave your clothes on the floor. Then go to bed. I will take care of everything."

Holding my plastic-wrapped hand out of the water, I lean against the shower wall and let the dirt and grime of today's adventure wash away. Little by little my muscles untangle and the pain medication kicks in.

CAT & MARIA

During the night, a pinpoint of light from a laser flashlight waves across the tiles in the bathroom. It sweeps across the pile of damp clothes lying on the floor. A hand searches through the pockets of the jeans but drops them on the floor when a low moan floats from the bedroom where Cat sleeps. The flashlight switches off. The bed creaks and groans as her body weight shifts on the mattress.

The man in black crouches on the floor and doesn't breath until the silence of night once more hangs in the air. He reaches for the jeans again without turning on the flashlight and continues to search.

The creaks from the bed grow louder. On all fours he scrambles out of the bathroom and into the dining room and slides behind the china cabinet.

I stumble into the bathroom and trip over the pile of clothes I left on the floor. My head is heavy, my thoughts groggy, my muscles limp. Something woke me, but what? I grope my way into the hall and listen. The house whispers. Shadows move across the walls. I can't remember why I'm in the hallway. Using my hand as a guide along the wall, I shuffle back into the bedroom and fall across the bed. Heavy darkness descends.

He waits until a gentle snore echoes from the bedroom before slipping back to the bathroom. He continues to search but finds nothing. *What did she do with the necklace?* He sets back on his heels, picks up the jeans and shakes them. He pulls the still-damp shirt forward and checks the breast pocket. Nothing. He drops the shirt on top of the jeans and pushes up from the floor. His hand hits a lumpy wad. He squats back down, grabs the shirt and pulls the knot apart. He longs to look at the necklace. Instead, he slips it in his pocket and quietly makes his way to the back door. He pauses long enough to lock the deadbolt before vaulting over the wall and disappearing into the moonless night.

I don't remember getting out of the shower or going to bed. I only know when I awake the sun is shining through the shutters, and Maria is banging around in the kitchen. I wiggle my fingers and toes and concentrate on a spot on the wall to stop the low moan in my throat. Little by little I stretch. My body howls as I determine which parts are still working. Initially, all movements equal throbbing, but I continue flexing arms and legs until I'm limber enough to sit up.

When my feet touch the cool terra-cotta floor, I remember the dinner party and that I forgot to pick the red flowers. My stomach snarls in angry protest as I realize I haven't eaten since breakfast yesterday. I brush my teeth, run a comb through my hair, and shuffle into the kitchen. A cappuccino pod is waiting. I pop it in the coffee machine before I say good morning to Maria.

She looks over her shoulder as she stirs some divine concoction on the stove. "Buongiorno, Caterina. Did you sleep well? Go back to bed. I'll bring you coffee and something to eat."

Before I answer, it occurs to me that I didn't see my dirty clothes in the bathroom. "Shit, the necklace," I mutter as I hobble down the hall.

The bathroom is spotless, all tidied up by the ever-cleaning Maria. I rush back to the kitchen.

Maria growls at me, "What are you doing? You need to be in bed. Go."

"Maria, I'm fine. What happened to my clothes, the dirty ones I had on yesterday."

"I washed them. What else would I do with them?"

"The necklace! Stella's necklace was tied up in my shirt. Where is it? What did you do with it?"

"What necklace? There was no necklace. I checked your pockets. I always check your pockets because you leave stuff in them—money, chocolates, keys, notes. There was no necklace," she sniffs, clearly annoyed.

"Maria, I found Stella's necklace yesterday. I tied it up in my shirt. I meant to tell you, but Antonio gave me that pain shot and then I took one of the pills. I forgot to tell you. Oh crap, we have to find it. It's a major piece of evidence in Stella's disappearance. Lorenzo is coming by this morning to pick it up. It has to be here."

Maria's mouth opens and closes. Her eyes squint and her nostrils flare. "Stella's necklace, the red starfish one? Where did you find her necklace? There was no necklace with your clothes. Do you think I took it?"

Now my mouth falls open. "I would never think that, Maria. Why would you even ask such a question? But it's crucial we find it. Lorenzo is on his way. Help me look, please."

We scour the bathroom, the bedrooms, and the kitchen while I fill Maria in on what happened yesterday. Maria runs back to her house to make sure the necklace didn't get mixed up with the other laundry.

What do I tell Lorenzo—what do I tell Antonio? That somehow I lost the necklace? Who is going to believe that?

My thoughts plow through every corner of the house.

Did I put it somewhere for safekeeping last night when I was too groggy to even remember putting myself in bed?

The gate clanks shut. Maria's footsteps race up the stairs. She rushes into the kitchen breathless, "The *Commissario* is right behind me. What do you want me to tell him?"

"Seat him at the table on the terrace. Give him coffee and pastries. Tell him I'll be right out. I need a few minutes to think before I see him."

"*Si,*" she says as she moves toward the terrace and stops him before he enters the house.

CAT & LORENZO

Dashing into the bedroom, I grab a soft, blue knee-length tunic that slips easily over my head. A quick comb through my wild standing-on-end hair has me sighing with regret at my always unruly appearance. It's been years since I've seen Lorenzo, but my heart races as recklessly as it did all those summers ago. I had imagined our first meeting after all these years—a look, a touch, a new beginning. Instead, I'm in panic mode and there's no hope of taming my unruly curls. It won't matter anyway since he'll be furious when I tell him the necklace has vanished. I place the hairbrush on the credenza and tiptoe down the hall.

Maria has settled him on the terrace with an espresso and *cornetto*. I pad softly across the living room and stop short of the doorway. From my vantage point Lorenzo, now a full-fledged *Commissario at the Guardia di Finanza*, scrutinizes the sea. Stella's wedding was the last time I saw him. My heart had fluttered back then. Now, it's thundering.

His appearance surprises me. I expected him to arrive in uniform or at least a suit, but I didn't expect his casual appearance. Living in Castello has changed him, maybe for the better. There's no formality in the blue jeans and the dark pullover. The only touches of his former life in Rome show up in the Italian loafers that are polished to a shine so brilliant they are reflected in his navigator Dolce & Gabbana sunglasses. His job pays well, or perhaps the family money continues to support these pricey extras. As I feast my eyes on him, it occurs to me that I don't care what he wears, because my heart still gallops like a wild horse breaking free of restraints. Ah, if only, I think. Then I take a few deep breaths and join him on the terrace.

"*Buongiorno, Commissario*. Are you enjoying the view?"

He turns and stands. The electrical charge consumes me as he wraps his large, cool hand around mine. The thick dark hair, aquiline nose, and intense blue eyes search my face. His stunning good looks are intact, and my sixteen year old self blushes from head to toe. The only way I can pull myself back from the edge is to remember that he always loved Stella—never me.

Still holding my hand, he pulls me into his arms and says, "*Salve, buongiorno, Cat. Si*, yes. The view is exceptional, just as you are. It has been so many years since we last met. Stella and Antonio's wedding, right? I'm surprised you're staying in Stella's villa, but I'm glad you are. I cannot remember the last time I was here. Maybe some party Stella threw. But her parties were so packed I never noticed the superb view of the marina. It's a busy place today with the fishing boats and the restaurant owners haggling over what will be on today's menu."

He takes a deep breath and continues at the same fast-forward pace, "But that's not important. You must tell me what happened yesterday. Antonio and I connected late last night. He said I needed to speak with you immediately. I apologize for not contacting you sooner about Stella's message on your phone. Let's start there. The lab results are back and I could use your assistance in putting a timeline and other pieces together, *va bene*? Not today since clearly the necklace is more important. But in a few days?"

His rambling speech leaves me confused. Lorenzo was never a conversationalist. I move out of his embrace and study his face. Maria believes that any one of the men in Stella's life could be involved in her disappearance. Plus, she told me that Lorenzo had stayed here with Stella. That means he's already lying to me when he says he can't remember when he was last here.

I nod in answer to his question and say, "Please, sit."

Before he does, he pulls a cushioned chair out for me. He eases into the opposite chair and pulls it close enough so that our knees brush.

"Antonio told me about the tumble you took yesterday. He said he stitched up your hand, and he wanted me to check on you today. He said you found Stella's necklace. Tell me what happened."

My mind reels from the rapidity of his moving from one topic to the next. How is it going to sound when I tell him I can't find the necklace? But he's not through and keeps right on with the nervous chatter, so I don't have to admit anything yet.

"Cat, you can imagine how Antonio felt when he saw the necklace. My officers searched everywhere and couldn't find her or the necklace. You arrive in town and immediately find the necklace. I might have to hire you," he says with an ironic smile.

Another flush creeps up my chest and throat, a red-head trait I despise.

Lorenzo does not seem to notice and continues, "So tell me everything. How and where did you find the necklace?"

"I'm not sure what you want to know, so I'll start at the beginning."

He leans back in the chair and finally stops talking.

"Yesterday I was foraging for flowers out by the cliffs. But instead of flowers, I found the necklace. Antonio was the only person I could think of to take it to. It wasn't my intention to upset him. It all happened so fast: first cutting my hand, then discovering the broken shards of glass, and then Stella's necklace—all within minutes of each other."

"Hmm, Antonio didn't say anything about broken glass or how you cut your hand. Let me see."

I hold up my bandaged hand.

"A few stitches is all. I'm fine."

"I'm glad because it's important we return to where you found the necklace. Do you feel well enough to show me today? I have to take a look before anyone else finds out about it. Of course, it has been several weeks since Stella disappeared. We don't know if she was there or if someone planted her necklace in that spot. The storms will have washed away any evidence. But it won't hurt to look."

What a pickle, I think before saying, "I'm still exhausted but I'll show you today. Maybe finding the necklace will lead us to Stella, and I can still pick flowers."

He frowns and says, "I don't understand what this has to do with flowers."

"I don't mean to be glib but that was my sole purpose for being in that location. Haven't you noticed those gorgeous red flowers that grow on the cliffs. Would you like to go now or later? I'll need to change."

"Yes, I'd like to go now. But show me the necklace first. Finding it means I can put the investigation back on the priority list. Stella wouldn't take off her necklace particularly in an isolated location. Your discovery substantiates that she's truly missing."

"Do you think she's been kidnapped?"

"Could be but so far we haven't received a ransom note. Maybe the intention was to steal the necklace but somehow Stella managed to hide it. It's hard to say. But if she was kidnapped, they'll want something."

"Stella's been missing for over three weeks. Doesn't it seem strange that no one has heard anything from her or from someone who might want something?"

"Yes, if the kidnappers wanted a ransom, we would have heard by now. There is a positive side to all this. Since Stella is still considered missing, I can reopen and control the investigation. If it becomes a homicide, I'll have to turn the case over to the *Polizia di Stato*. I don't want to do that, but they'll question the three weeks as it's a long time not to hear anything."

My breathing quickens. Lorenzo's words hang heavy in the air. I shift in my chair and look away from him.

When I don't respond, he stands and offers his hand, "The necklace is crucial evidence. Let me see it."

Wishing with all my might that the necklace would drop out of the sky but knowing it won't, I say, "Well, that's a problem."

One eyebrow raises. His eyes narrow as he searches my face, "What do you mean?"

"I mean, when I got up this morning, the necklace was gone. No trace of it. I left my dirty clothes in the bathroom last night. Stella's necklace was tied up in my shirt. Maria said she picked up my clothes from the bathroom floor last night and washed them. She said there was no necklace with the clothing."

"What? You're joking, yes?"

"No, I'm not. Antonio gave the necklace back to me just before I got out of his car. It was too big for my jeans pocket so I tied it in my shirt. I was groggy from the pain shot he gave me. I simply forgot to tell Maria I had it. This morning I realized the necklace was gone. Maria and I searched the entire house and grounds—even where Antonio parked his car. We found nothing. The only other possibility is the necklace fell out of my shirt in Antonio's car or on the ground and someone picked it up. Antonio is in Gallipoli. I haven't had time to call him. If it's not in his car, I'm afraid it has disappeared again. You're welcome to search the house yourself."

"Where is Maria?"

"In the kitchen."

We follow the aromas drifting across the terrace. Maria's hands are thick with flour as she rolls out pasta. A wild mushroom sauce simmers on the back burner.

"Yum," I say. "Can I taste?"

She looks up and says, "*Si*. You must be starving."

I take a spoon out of the perfectly organized utensil drawer and dip it into the fragrant sauce. "Oh Maria, it's heavenly. I know it's for tonight's dinner, but maybe we could have a little for lunch. Lorenzo, would you like to stay?"

Before Lorenzo can respond, Maria snaps, "The *Commissario* does not appreciate peasant food. His tastes are more refined. Plus, there is only enough for tonight. There is a plate of cheese and salumi on the counter if you want something now."

Maria's response shocks me. Her shoulders tense, and a frown creases her brow. I'm on unfamiliar ground, so I shrug and say, *va bene.*

Her shoulders stay hunched up around her ears as she continues to roll out and cut the pasta. She turns her back to us and hangs the strips of dough on a wooden drying rack.

Lorenzo leans against the door frame and asks, "Maria, did you find Stella's red starfish necklace mixed up in Cat's clothes? Cat said you washed her clothes. Did you check the washer and the area where you hung the clothes to dry?"

She avoids looking at me as she responds in a hard clipped cadence, "I found nothing. I told Caterina I always check her pockets. She collects things. Last night there was nothing in her pockets. There was no knot in the shirt, and there was no necklace. Go ahead, check this house, my house, or wherever you want. I never saw Stella's necklace."

"Are you sure?"

"There was no necklace. Cat was exhausted when she got here. She did not eat, just fell into bed and slept. I picked up her clothes and checked them. There was nothing. I am sure."

"How long was it before you picked up the clothes and washed them? Was Gino around last night? Perhaps he will remember seeing the necklace. Where is he now?"

"Once I got Caterina to bed, I went home to cook for Gino. When I left, the clothes were lying on the bathroom floor, undisturbed. Caterina was asleep. I checked on her before I left. Gino was late coming home. Dinner was delayed, but he did not go back out after we had eaten. Later, maybe around ten, I came back here and got the clothes which were still on the bathroom floor. Gino does not know anything about the necklace. Neither do I."

I catch Maria's downcast eyes and furtive glances. Some kind of warning, but what?

My stomach lurches as I turn to Lorenzo, "Do you want to search? I could have misplaced it. I was exhausted. Not only did Antonio give me a shot for pain, but he also gave me painkillers which I took. My mind was groggy. I don't remember anything."

"Nothing at all? Did you get up during the night?"

"Wait, yes, I did wake up. I thought I heard something. I remember stumbling over the clothes, so they were still in the bathroom. But I have no idea what time it was. I was in a medicated fog. I don't even remember how I got back to bed."

Lorenzo stares at me. Frowning, he pushes away from the wall.

"I don't understand. How could the necklace disappear? Who would take it?"

"How would I know? But you're welcome to look for yourself."

"Yes, thank you, I will. Come with me. Maria, you come along too but call Gino first. Tell him to get back here now. I need to question him."

Maria turns her back to Lorenzo and continues to stir the mushroom sauce, "I already told you Gino is not here. I do not know when he will be back."

Lorenzo's face flushes. He walks past me and lightly touches Maria's shoulder and says, "Call him. Now. He needs to change his plans."

He turns and pushes past me and strides down the hall. I trail behind until I realize Maria is not with me. I turn around. Her back is to the door. Her right shoulder scrunched to her ear. I lean against the wall out of sight. Her whispers barely reach my ears, "The *Commissario* is here. Do not come back. I will call you later."

When the drum beat of my heart settles, I back away and then intentionally hit the table by the hallway door, "Maria, can you stop what you're doing? Lorenzo really wants both of us to accompany him while he's searching."

Maria's head, then her body, appears in the doorway. "Why does he want to search the house? You need to refuse. Tell him to go away and come back with *un mandato di ricerca*. Do not allow him to do this."

Her angry response startles me. I've never seen her cross or ruffled. What in the crap is upsetting her? Is it Lorenzo? Is it the search? Maybe Gino? What's happening?

Everyone but me seems to understand. It reminds me that I don't know these people. Their ongoing relationships are something I've not been part of. The undercurrent is strong. I'm alone in this, and I don't have a clue whom to trust.

Maria turns her attention to the stove. The tension in the kitchen gathers. I break the silence by asking, "Can you call Gino and ask him to come back right away?"

"I just spoke with him. He has been called away to his brother's house in Martano. He does not know when he will return. His brother is ill. It could be late or maybe not until tomorrow." Maria says, as her features flatten into stone. Her nostrils flare. Tiny beads of sweat collect over her upper lip as she removes her apron.

"Maria, we have to find Stella's necklace. Please help me with the search."

Lorenzo's footsteps echo down the hall and stop when he enters the dining room. His gaze moves from my face to Maria's. His smile is only in the curve of his lips, "If you prefer, I can call Antonio. He would not have a problem with me searching the house and grounds. Or if you like, I can call the office and arrange for someone to deliver a search warrant. But you know I can search without one."

The two of them glare at each other until I break in, "But I've already said you can search. I have nothing to hide. Antonio gave me the necklace. If it's lost, then it's my fault. What else can I tell you? Call Antonio."

"I called him while I was waiting for you and Maria. The necklace is not in his car. Now, would you please lead the way? Maria and I will follow. My visit has been tiring for you, and I still need to see the spot where you found the necklace."

At the bedroom door, I stand back to let him pass. Maria's face is sullen. She lowers her eyes but follows his every move.

Lorenzo shakes the covers and pulls back the bedding. He moves the pillows and looks under the bed. He searches the wardrobe, the two nightstands, and the dresser. I force myself not to register any emotion when he sorts through my underwear. His cheeks flush as his fingers slide over and under silky undergarments.

We continue to Stella's room. He tackles the rolled-top desk first. Maria and I avoid looking at each other as he raises the top and one by one pulls out each drawer. Each one brings him closer to the drawer with the false panel and the secret hideaway. Most of the drawers are full of newspaper clippings of Stella. A few contain papers and office supplies. Lorenzo's hand quickly scans the top, bottom, and sides of each drawer. I could kick myself for putting the ceramic box back in the cubby hole. Holy moly, I think as I gaze at the stack of papers Maria took out of the drawer in order to reach the fake panel. They are still on the desk in front of the drawer.

Lorenzo notices the stack of papers the same time I do. As he picks them up, I literally fly across the room. I arrive at his side as he turns. We collide and paper sails from the pile. We move apart and grab as they float to the floor. A scrap of paper lands by my foot. I quickly step on top of it.

When I look up, Lorenzo is watching me. "What's that?"

"What?"

"The paper you're standing on?"

"Oh," I say as I move my foot away. Without my reading glasses I can't make out the words although I know it's Stella's handwriting.

We both reach for the slip of paper lying on the floor and find ourselves staring into each other's eyes. Our fingers simultaneously touch the paper. Desperate to read its message before Lorenzo does, I grab it first.

The words *Veni, Vidi, Vici* cross in front of my squinted eyes. With a half laugh and a half snort, I slap the paper in Lorenzo's hand.

"Looks like Stella is still studying her Latin."

Lorenzo frowns as he reads the words and drops the scrap of paper on top of the pile. "Why would she be studying Latin? Stella was never interested in school. This seems strange to me."

"It's not strange. Stella and I took Latin for all four years of high school. Believe it or not, she excelled in languages, and she loved to memorize catchy phrases. This one by Julius Caesar was her favorite. If we look long enough, we'll find other phrases in Latin."

My story is so spontaneous that I almost believe it myself. My brain is scurrying with the words: I came, I saw, I conquered. Is this another clue? What does it mean? There's no time to ponder the possibilities as I need to get Lorenzo out of the bedroom.

In desperation I clutch his arm and lean into him.

"Lorenzo, I'm exhausted. Why don't you finish searching the rest of the house while I change clothes. I have just enough energy to take you to the location where I found the necklace. But if we don't go soon, it will have to wait until tomorrow.

He straightens his body and gently removes my hand from his arm. He holds it with both of his.

"You're right, Cat. The necklace is not here. I'll do a quick check of the rest of the house to make sure. There's no need for all three of us to search. Why don't you rest? I'll knock on the door when I'm ready."

He pulls me closer. The sleeve of his soft cotton pullover brushes against my arm, and his breath lands in warm puffs on my cheek. My body automatically stiffens. He drops my hand.

"*Scusami.*"

"It's ok. My mind is still fuzzy from the meds. This is all too much to take in. It seems crazy now, but Maria and I are planning a dinner party," I say in one breath.

In the next I ask, "If you don't already have plans, I hope you'll come. It's next Sunday night at eight.

Maria's face darkens. Lorenzo's lights up as I continue, "Antonio's coming, and I've asked Carlo too, as well as a few other people."

"Of course, I would love to come. Let me help. I'm a pretty decent cook," he says with an eyebrow cocked.

Maria mutters under her breath. I fear she is going to blurt something out. So I rush on, "Thank you, but there's no need. Maria and Gino are magicians. Whatever I need, they take care of it. Maria's cooking skills are exceptional. Just show up for the party."

"Yes, I would love to come. Grazie."

"Please, continue your search. I'll change my clothes. Let me know when you're finished. I'll be ready."

Lorenzo strides down the hall. Maria and I lock eyes before she closes the bedroom door and follows Lorenzo. I lift the scrap of paper from the pile and dump the rest of the papers back into the fake drawer. Lorenzo's footsteps echo across the terra-cotta floor and into the next room. I open the wardrobe and stick the scrap of paper into the pocket of a black vest.

Lorenzo's footsteps fade as he moves into the living, dining, and kitchen areas. My body trembles. I lean against the wall and close my eyes. His voice outside the door surprises me.

"I'm ready whenever you are."

"Almost," I call back, praying my voice doesn't crack.

I cross the hall to my room and slide into a pair of jeans and a black sweater. My feet find shoes suitable for rock climbing. I join Lorenzo on the terrace.

CAT & LORENZO

There's no conversation other than when I say turn left or right. It makes the short drive very long. But I have no desire to talk. I sneak a few side-long glances at Lorenzo's face, enough to know he isn't happy with me.

The sun is sparkling as we drive past small signs of spring. Wild asparagus shoots sprout up along the road in the midst of tiny white blossoms of alpine strawberries.

The silence is broken when I say, "Park there."

We walk across the road and stop at the bottom of the cliffs. Lorenzo tilts his head back and surveys the steep incline before saying, "Wait here."

He analyzes the situation with a furrowed brow. He's probably looking for another way for me to scale the cliffs with an injured hand. He trots down the road a few paces and calls to me, "I think I've found an easier way up. Give me a few minutes, and I'll let you know."

He disappears around an outcropping of rock. I don't bother to tell him there's an easier way to scale the cliffs—that all we have to do is use the path from the marina. I slowly trudge in the same direction with my body screaming to lie down. By the time he returns, I'm standing at the base.

He points toward the large boulders that have been beaten into stepping stones by wind and rain and says, "This way looks less complicated,"

It looks like a precarious stairway, but certainly less of a challenge than yesterday's trek. It also leads directly to where the red flowers grow.

I brush past his outstretched hand and begin to ascend, not stopping until I'm standing among the large nodding blossoms. He quickly catches up and stops next to me as he scouts for a route back down to the plateau area. Both of us have competitive personalities. I push past him, but he stays close on my heels.

As I pick up speed, my foot hits a loose patch of rocks. They scatter under my feet as my arms and legs flail into empty space. Lorenzo grabs the back of my sweater and swings his arm around my waist. My feet dangle briefly over the side of the cliff before he pulls me close against his chest. Our breaths come out in short puffs as we balance dangerously close to the edge. My head is tucked under his chin as we allow our collective heartbeats to settle into a more normal rhythm. I relax into his body until his words, muffled against my hair, send me right back into a defensive position.

"You are crazy, Cat. Quit being so damn independent. There's no point in killing yourself."

He's right, but men bring out the worst in me. And Lorenzo is at the top of the list. He creates all sorts of problems. I want him. He doesn't want me. He loves Stella but she made his life too complicated. Stella thinks she loves Lorenzo, but Stella has never loved anyone but Stella. What a crock.

He releases me and tells me not to move while he maneuvers the few steps down to the plateau. Once there, he extends his hand. I let him guide me through the last few steps.

When I arrive beside him, he says, "How difficult was it to let me help you?"

He smiles that half smile that radiates in his dark blue eyes. He's so damn hard not to like.

He turns aways from me and strides into the clearing and calls back, "Cat, did you see the path leading down to the marina? Is this a joke?"

He runs his hand through his hair and continues, "You did this on purpose, didn't you? You must have seen the path? So tell me why we had to scale the cliff? Was that to prove how tough you are?"

I squint in the afternoon sun before saying, "Of course, I saw the path. I'm not blind. But if we came up from the marina, the exact spot where I found the necklace would be skewed. If you want accurate information, it means approaching the plateau from the same direction as I did yesterday. Surely you want accuracy, right?"

He smiles slowly. "You're still the same brat you always were. Now show me where you found the necklace."

I point to the spot. The earth I dug up yesterday is clumped in a small pile next to the hole. Lorenzo nods and squats to examine the shards of glass. "You're right. It looks like a mirror."

He shakes his head and mutters, "I assigned a couple of new officers to this area while I concentrated on the last place Stella was seen. I was sure that's where I'd find clues to her disappearance. I really screwed up by not coming here."

"How could you know? This seems like a crazy place for a photo shoot."

I slowly turn in a circle as I try to see the area with new eyes and clear thoughts. The waves below crash hard against the jagged rocks. The wind whooshes in and out of the boulders.

"That's the background sound we picked up from Stella's call to you."

"What?" I say coming to a standstill.

Our eyes lock.

"I'm sorry, Cat. But this is probably where Stella was killed. I'll have forensics up here tomorrow although it's been too long. I doubt that we will find anything. But we'll check it out thoroughly. Two shots were picked up on the message Stella left you along with a garbled conversation, and what sounds like a struggle. Then another shot occurred before the phone was shut off."

I turn away from him and continue to move in a circular motion. Crying now doesn't seem helpful. I'll come back another time to be alone in this place with her. *Stella, Stella,* I whisper in a low steady hum. I track the houses scattered in the hills—all so peaceful. It's another ordinary day with the weak sun throwing flashes of light in my eyes. Another flash of light crosses my face. I pause, looking for the source as I remember with sudden clarity a similar light flashing across my face yesterday.

"Did you see that?"

"What?"

"A light or a flash—something like a reflection. I suppose it could be the sun bouncing off glass but it happened yesterday when it was raining. That seems suspicious to me, doesn't it to you?"

Lorenzo shrugs and continues to prod the dirt with a stick he picked up somewhere. He glances up at me, but I continue to squint at the hillside and don't notice when he picks up a smashed bullet and pockets it.

"Why do you think a light flashed from that large villa on top of that hill?"

There's no answer. I turn back and see he's rubbing his hand over a large boulder.

"Did you find something or are you just into petting rocks?"

He grins like a Cheshire Cat and walks toward me. He stops almost but not quite in my space. His eyes are soft but troubled as he looks at me.

"Hey, you're exhausted. I'm taking you home now. I'll come back tomorrow and finish up. Nobody is going to scale these cliffs between now and then."

This time I let him assist me from rock to rock. When we approach the red flowers I ask, "Do you mind if we stop here? These flowers are the reason I found Stella's necklace. I came here to pick them—for the dinner party. Can you wait?"

The scowl is back on his face, "You sit right there on that boulder. Don't move."

I do as he says. He removes a Silca army knife from his pocket and precisely clips a bunch of flowers and hands them to me. He keeps on clipping until I have an armful. Before he hands me the last batch, he bows deeply.

"*Signora*, you are more beautiful than the flowers."

I dissolve into a flood of tears. He swoops me up in his arms. "It's okay, Cat. Somehow it will be okay. I promise."

He holds me for an endless period of time. His strength seeps into my body until my sobs subside and he whispers against my hair, "I'm taking you home."

He puts his arm around me and gently guides me back to the car. The drive back is quick. We walk up the steps. He takes the key from my hand and unlocks the door.

To gain control, I ask, "Why don't you stay for dinner? I'm sure Maria made enough for two. All I have to do is cook the pasta and make a salad."

"Cat, you are crazy."

His voice is soft, gentle—a caress that I want to wrap myself in and never leave.

"I wish I could stay, but I still have a ton of paperwork to complete. You've had enough for today. Promise me you'll eat and then go to bed. I'll check on you tomorrow. We'll make plans for dinner for another night. Rest. I'll call you."

"Thanks for not letting me fall off the cliff and for the flowers. I'm glad you're coming to the dinner party. I'll see you then."

He holds my gaze for a few seconds, then he's gone. The gate clicks shut. The tears start as soon as I close the door until I remember the clue. I fill a jug with water, dump the flowers in, and rush to the bedroom. The closet door is open just as I left it. I reach in and pull the scrap of paper from the vest pocket.

LORENZO

Lorenzo hated driving across Puglia. He found the endless olive groves and barren scrubby land tedious. The small towns and villages white-washed the poverty in the coastal area. But take a drive into the interior of Puglia and it was a different story. Life stood still in its dusty forgotten past. Tumbled-down walls and half-finished houses slumped in fields of overgrown weeds and trash-filled roads.

He wished he had time to take the longer scenic route, the one that wrapped around the Adriatic and took him to his house in Leuca. His beautiful hideaway languished from lack of use because he rarely took any time off and usually stayed at his apartment in Castello.

He had chosen Leuca because it was less expensive than the better known tourist towns like Aberobello, Ostuni, San Cataldo where Carlo's second home was located, and Gallipoli where Antonio had his villa. The other irritating fact about Gallipoli was the continuous confusion with the city in Turkey. He didn't understand the logic since Gallipoli, Turkey would take eighteen hours of non-stop driving plus a ferry ride across the Adriatic. It was a standing joke with southern Italians much to the chagrin of tourists. As far as Lorenzo was concerned Gallipoli, although filled with a certain charm, didn't come close to Leuca.

Lorenzo loved the quiet, quaint fishing village. It was located on the southernmost tip of Italy where the Ionian and Adriatic Seas merged. He had noticed on his last visit that tourists were beginning to vacation in what had once been an obscure place. He had invested a lot of money in renovations and was concerned that one day he would be surrounded by high-rise apartments. His villa was small but his property rolled into the sea with unobstructed views. The sun sunk in spectacular fashion outside his front door.

There was a flower and vegetable garden, and last year he installed a swimming pool. But the first renovation had been the kitchen. There were no girls in his family but that made no difference to his nonna. She had introduced him to every aspect of cooking until he could crank out a meal for thirty without breaking a sweat. When he came home at the end of a long grueling day, he headed to the kitchen. He didn't stop until the grime of the day fell away through chopping and dicing, sizzling garlic and onions, and creating tantalizing aromas of exotic spices to fill the air.

Today, with a hint of spring popping out of the earth, he could only wish to be in Leuca. Instead, he had promised to meet Antonio for lunch in Gallipoli. He longed for time away but that would have to wait for another day.

Before leaving the station, he swapped out his official car for his custom painted royal blue 2007 *Alfa Romeo 8C Competizione* convertible. Both he and the *Alfa* need their pipes cleaned out. He grinned with pleasure as he shifted gears and eased onto the highway and settled into a smooth cruising speed.

Anticipating a sunny day, he had the top down. It was the end of January, but it was much warmer than usual. He glanced at his watch and thought, *just enough time to drive to Gallipoli, have lunch with Antonio, and make it back in time for the aftermath of last night's drug bust.*

He turned off the roundabout at Maglie and let his thoughts ramble back to the previous day's encounter with Cat and Maria.

Strange, he thought. The necklace disappeared without an explanation. Why? Could one or both of them be hiding something? He shook his head. More than likely it was Gino. He was the one with connections to the mafia through his uncle. Lorenzo had seen him hanging out with some of the mafia riffraff. Maybe they put him up to it. But it would be hard to peddle a piece of jewelry like the starfish. When Stella disappeared, her photographs were posted everywhere. She was wearing the necklace. So what was the point? Who would profit from having it? And who wanted Stella dead and why?

For a second, he wondered if Antonio had stolen the necklace. It would be easy enough. He had a key to Fiora, but then so did a lot of other people, including himself. He doubted Cat knew that. She would pitch a fit.

Yesterday when he questioned Cat, she seemed genuine. But maybe, like Stella, she was an actress. He remembered Cat being so open and vulnerable when they were kids, but they had all changed—become jaded by life. He had wanted to ask her what she had been doing since those sun-filled summers at the beach, but he hadn't. He felt inadequate around her. He wasn't used to a woman being so damned defiant.

He had barely spoken to her at the wedding. He had been too unhappy to speak with anyone when Stella chose Antonio over him. In the end, Stella valued Antonio's money and family connections over Lorenzo's love. While Lorenzo's family was well connected and well respected, they didn't come close to the power and financial assets of the Moretti family.

Somehow he and Antonio managed to bridge the gap and remain friends, but after the wedding they were never as close as they had once been. He was never sure if Antonio knew how much he loved Stella.

The summers came back with a rush as he rounded a curve and a snapshot of the sea came through the windshield. Seeing Cat again had been a surprise. She had retained those unruly red curls and self-confident swagger in her grown-up body, but she was no longer all arms and legs. He had barely noticed her at the wedding although he had overheard the male population commenting on her stunning looks.

Yesterday she had scaled the cliffs even with her injured hand, never complaining. And she'd insisted on accompanying him to the spot and had been meticulous about the exact location.

What did he know about her? Divorced, same age as Stella. First a fancy corporate accountant and now a full-fledged chef, living in a place called the Lowcountry. He had never heard of it. These details weren't much, and he had learned that little bit through Stella. She had been so excited when she told him Cat was coming to stay with her for a year and would be working at La Canzone. He tried to remember his last conversation with Stella, but he only saw her big blue eyes full of tears. He shook his head in futility and thought about Antonio and lunch. But the memories of what used to be were too strong.

They had become inseparable friends during those summer vacations and all of them had fallen under the magic of Castello del Mare. He wasn't surprised when Antonio and Stella had moved back after their marriage. Lorenzo hadn't anticipated ever returning to Castello. Rome was his home. But the *Guardia di Finanza* had promoted him to this region.

Once he arrived, he reconnected with Antonio who had introduced him to the movers and shakers in the region. Both of them had been eager to make a name for themselves. They had respected each other's work and had settled into a somewhat uneasy companionship based on those long-ago summers. Sometimes they met for drinks after work and sometimes they attended the same social events.

But Stella continued to be the wedge between them. A few years into their marriage her beauty had become raw, an open wound for his eyes only. He had watched in pain and silence as she suffered. There had been a deep and restless tension in her movements and conversations. She smoldered at the edge. Waiting to explode. He had maintained his business relationship with Antonio by avoiding her. He had managed until she left Antonio. He and Stella had immediately reconnected until he realized it was a huge mistake. They couldn't recapture the magic of those endless summers of their youth. They had changed too much.

Now he had to consider Antonio as a suspect and that was giving him heartburn. He was sure Antonio suspected him as well. They both had good reasons to want Stella to go away. Antonio's reasons were well known. The ferocious argument he and Stella had just before she disappeared was not a secret. Everyone in town knew about it and about Antonio's affair. The problem was Antonio's family would not allow him to divorce Stella. The only way he could be free of her was if she was dead. Lorenzo didn't believe Antonio was capable of murder, but around here it was easy to find someone else to pull the trigger for you.

Lorenzo also had a fight with Stella. The difference was only Maria and Gino knew. He had been sure they wouldn't say anything. But after yesterday, he wasn't so sure. Maria had been openly hostile and suspicious. He wondered if she believed he had a hand in Stella's disappearance. She would be right. His mistake was one of omission —not telling Stella he planned to protect her without her knowledge. He thought by cutting off their relationship and pushing her away, she'd be safe. He had been so wrong.

During the initial investigation into Stella's disappearance, some s.o.b in the office had informed Rome that he and Antonio were close friends. But before Lorenzo had been taken off the case, he had been able to view the microscopic traces of blood in Antonio's kitchen. When questioned, Antonio said he had cut himself while chopping vegetables. The lab confirmed that only Antonio's fingerprints were on the knife. Lorenzo had not found any hard evidence of Stella's involvement. The problem is Stella had told him she stabbed Antonio in a moment of fury when she discovered him with Sylvia. Stella's fingerprints should have been on the knife, but they weren't. That meant Antonio cleaned the knife and then lied about it which was an obstruction of justice. That had put a huge strain on their relationship.

Lorenzo's anger had boiled over when the Rome office pulled him off the investigation and put one of his colleagues in charge. He understood the necessity but being on the sidelines had made it difficult for him to protect Stella. She needed protection. He along with everyone else had failed her.

Rumors had swirled about the ruthless behavior she exhibited to get drugs. She pushed people too far and had made a lot of enemies. She was no fool and used men as freely and randomly as they did her. When she wanted something, she went after it with her eyes wide open. In retrospect, he wished he had stayed with her and supported her. His idea of helping her had been to cut all ties. That had backfired.

Lorenzo pushed Stella out of his mind and focused on his lunch with Antonio. He knew Antonio was not telling him everything, but then none of Stella's colleagues were. Everyone has alibis and adamantly denied knowing anything about the photo shoot. Each one swore they had no part in the arrangements. No amount of research revealed anything of value. It was another cold case. Like so many others, it had been buried under the next batch of cases.

The discovery of the necklace would bring the case back to the top of the heap. Although the evidence had disappeared, they had witnesses. Cat and Antonio would testify. Both had been in possession of the necklace. He also intended to thoroughly search the area where the necklace and now a bullet casing had been found. He was sure there would be more evidence, particularly if there had been a struggle. Although it made the case more difficult, there could still be a conviction without the necklace. Perhaps this time he could convince his boss in Rome to put him back on the case. If not, he'd work it from the sidelines.

The puzzle was to find the necklace and the person who stole it from Cat. He smiled as she made her way back into his thoughts. He wanted to know her better. Although based on the little bit of interaction they'd had, he suspected she was not interested. He felt a slow flush move up his neck as he remembered her silk underwear. He dismissed the thought immediately.

His only focus was the necklace and finding Stella. He hoped Antonio would be more open and fill in some of the missing pieces.

ANTONIO

G*ALLIPOLI, ITALY*

Dottor Antonio Moretti stared at the untouched glass of Primitivo di Manduria. The dark purple hues shimmered in the sunlight. His fingers caressed the hand-blown Murano wine glass but he didn't pick it up. The angry gnawing in his stomach made it unappealing.

Besides, it was too early to start drinking. He was drinking too much: a splash of grappa in his morning coffee, several glasses of wine with lunch and dinner, and a glass or two of brandy in the evening for relaxation.

He pushed back from the table and drifted down the steps to the water's edge. This house in Gallipoli was his only sanctuary. It was a fifty-minute drive from the clinic, far enough away to allow him to briefly forget about work but close enough to get back quickly if an emergency occurred.

Today, instead of relaxing, Stella crowded his thoughts. Her startling blue eyes accused him of deserting her—of not loving her enough. He had failed her.

He wondered how the conversation went between Lorenzo and Cat. How stupid he had been not to keep the necklace. After all, it belonged to him. His fingers touched the cell phone, but he decided against calling. He had to stay calm and put together a plan.

Stella had been his brilliant starfish—beautiful, but in the end, broken. Was he to blame? She said he was. Her image taunted him.

He'd been consumed by his education, research, and practice all which had made him careless about loving her. He'd turned a blind eye to her drug usage, and he'd even provided easy access for her to steal drugs. If only he'd been stronger, less distracted maybe none of this would have happened. Maybe she'd still be here.

He looked out across the water and saw her as he had that first time on the beach. She was just a child. The sunlight bouncing off her golden hair had sent sparks into his heart. She wasn't aware of him as she fought to save the red starfish that had washed ashore during the night's storm. She delicately picked each one up, brushed the sand away, and carried them one by one back into the sea. The sight of her had filled his chest and cut off his breath. His young heart pounded to the sound of the surf. His eyes followed her every movement.

Later, he asked his mother if she knew the family staying in the house next to theirs. "Of course," she said with a smile, "The Lombardi family has been vacationing here for years. They are from America, Italian Americans. They stay every summer, but I guess this is the first summer you've noticed."

She laughed when he blushed and tousled his hair before continuing, "The mother and the little girl are here all summer. There's another family who comes with them. They have a child the same age, an adorable redhead. The fathers come and go. I think they work for the same international company. They are lovely people. Why do you ask?"

"No reason," he said, fleeing the kitchen before his mother probed deeper.

Summers became the most important part of his life. Each year he waited for the last day of school. The train ride from Milan to

Rome was endless. He hated the time they wasted stopping in Rome to visit relatives before continuing on to Castello del Mare.

Each year she grew more beautiful. The girl, whose name was Stella, was rarely alone. The little red-headed girl was always with her. Every night before he closed his eyes to dream about her, he reviewed each detail of his plan to meet her. It would be accidental and on the beach. It took a while for him to work up the courage. In the end, he asked his best friend Lorenzo to go with him. What a mistake that turned out to be.

The morning dawned like a golden orb. The sun was shrouded in a coppery red cloak against a vast blue sky. The cool breeze fresh off the water kept the sand from burning his feet. He wanted to look strong, manly, and sure of himself. Hopping from one foot to the other on hot sand would create a bad first impression.

Walking beside him, Lorenzo was restless. He wanted to play ball or swim and kept asking what they were waiting for. Antonio shrugged and walked toward the beach. As he reached the area where the girls were playing in the surf, he slowed his pace so he wouldn't appear flustered. The girls were tossing a large red, white, and blue beach ball in some whimsical game. Their shrill cries of happiness rode the waves.

Unexpectedly, the ball landed with a soft thump at his feet. He reached for it, but the wet ball slid out of his grasp and was carried away by the surf. His face flushed with splotches of red as the girls watched and giggled at his clumsy attempts. He raced into the water after the ball but failed to capture it for a second time. The sun's friendly rays turned hot and heavy on his shoulders as he waded deeper into the sea. The second time he used both hands and seized the ball. He tucked it into his chest and turned back to shore. That's when he saw Lorenzo standing in a trance like Michelangelo's David. Antonio let his gaze follow the immovable stare. Lorenzo's eyes were locked into Stella's. Antonio reacted, throwing the ball with such force it knocked Lorenzo off his feet.

But the girls had lost interest. They turned their backs, grabbed hands, and raced into the waves. He could hear their laughter, ethereal musical notes wrapping around his heart.

The beach ball slammed into his head and knocked him down. Lorenzo laughed, ducked him under, and wrestled the ball away. With disappointment, Antonio focused his thoughts on not drowning. But when he bobbed up, he could see the girls running toward the large umbrella where all the adults were gathered. In a flash he knew what to do. He scuffled with Lorenzo until he captured the ball. Securing it under his arm, Antonio walked out of the water and trotted toward the people under the umbrella.

Antonio sighed, returned to the terrace and reached for the waiting glass of wine. He noticed a button missing from his cuff. He rolled up the sleeve but forgot to do the same to the other sleeve. Lorenzo had impeccable taste and would show up for lunch with the correct outfit for the occasion. But Antonio no longer cared about how he looked. He couldn't remember when he last slept, ate a decent meal, laughed, or even cried.

"Stella," he whispered, but the wind captured her name and flung it into the sea.

His buzzing cell phone brought him back to the water's edge.

"*Pronto.*"

"*Ciao Antonio*, I will be in Gallipoli in fifteen. See you at *L'Acchiatura?*"

The phone went dead in *Antonio's* hand.

ANTONIO

Antonio dropped the phone on the table and glanced at his watch. He noticed one sleeve of his shirt was rolled up and the other wasn't. He wasn't sure why and wondered if he should change his clothes but decided not to. It was time to leave, but he remained in the chair. He stared at the sea and let the memories uncoil.

Years later he still marveled at his courage that day on the beach. He trotted across the wide expanse of sand and deposited the wayward beach ball on the blanket and introduced himself to Stella's parents. It worked. He was invited to the house for picnics and asked to bring his parents. His parents were doctors, both had studied medicine at Oxford where they met.

During those summers, the households flowed back and forth. His only fear was Lorenzo, whose eyes never left Stella. Lorenzo had a thick mane of black hair, intense blue eyes, and dark olive skin. His family was prominent in politics and in the *Guardia di Finanza*, and they had a grand palazzo in Rome. Like Antonio, Lorenzo was an acceptable admirer. But Antonio's ace was his family connections. He played that card so often he now thought Stella married the royal connection instead of him.

He and Lorenzo met in Castello del Mare when they were little boys. They had been best friends during those summer vacations. But the relationship began to deteriorate as each ratcheted up their pursuit of Stella.

Stella's red-headed friend Caterina was part of the group. She was bubbly and fun. They shortened her name to Cat to torment her, and it stuck. Antonio tried to convince Cat that Lorenzo liked her, but she tossed her red curls and snarled at him. She wanted nothing to do with Lorenzo or him. She was faithful only to Stella. He saw how Stella used Cat to distract her parents or Lorenzo when she wanted to slip away with him. In his heart he was fearful on the days Stella sent Cat to distract him. He was sure this meant Stella was with Lorenzo.

The summer he turned eighteen he announced he was leaving for the University in Padua for six years of pre-med studies. Although Stella was too young, he asked her to wait for him. He called her *Stella del mare*—his star of the sea—his little starfish—*piccola stella marina*. He thought of her that way since he had witnessed her saving the red starfishes. Her smile and lingering hug radiated her approval of the name.

Four summers later, he came for his last summer in Castello. He was moving to London for his residency. He had a week to be with her. He was devastated to tell her he would not see her again unless she came to London. The next five years would be difficult. He thought she would weep and cling to him when he told her. Instead, she'd shocked him by saying it was okay because she had decided to model full time. He was surprised and unprepared. Before he left, he asked her not to pursue that career. She was fragile, and he thought it would not be a good life for her. But most of all, he knew his parents wouldn't approve.

She was adamant about the modeling adventure and did not seem concerned about their separation. She explained to him that she would be allowed to finish her last year of high school while on the road. It was part of the contract her parents had negotiated for her, along with college, if she chose to continue with modeling. She said it would be a distraction while he was studying. She convinced him it wasn't anything to worry about, just something to pass the time.

His parents spent endless hours suggesting he choose an Italian girl, someone more suitable to the life of an Italian doctor's wife. He didn't need an independent American woman like Stella. They pointed out she was embarking on a lucrative career and would not have time to give him the support he needed. But for him there would never be anyone but Stella.

He searched for a unique gift to announce their pre-engagement. He found it in the starfish bracelet created by the famous Italian designer, Aldo Cipullo. The starfish was meticulously carved from a natural red ruby. He chose perfect diamonds to form the circle holding the starfish. Then pear- shaped clusters of diamonds were added to one side with coiled white-gold bands on the other. Never doubting that he and Stella would be married, he commissioned Cipullo to design a complimentary necklace as his wedding gift to her.

When he clasped the bracelet on her arm, she said she would wait for him. The next five years were a blur. He studied and worked endless hours. Stella grew from a sweet, demure teenager into a stunning woman.

Little by little subtle changes worked their way into the relationship. The fast-paced fashion world had swept Stella into a jungle of anorexia, alcohol, drugs, sex, and money. Initially, he was too tired and self-absorbed to notice, but gradually her edginess had broken through his consciousness. Whenever they were together, she was listless, pale, and unusually thin. He noticed her hands often shook. At first he thought she was working too hard and suggested she take some time off. She snapped at him and then begged him to forgive her. She said she was exhausted and not sleeping well. That was the first time she asked him to give her something—just a few pills to get her back on track. It was easy to do. He, like all of his buddies studying medicine, kept supplies of pills for sleeping, staying awake, and for boosting energy.

He gave Stella a stockpile of sleeping pills and asked her to use them with caution. It was after he returned to Oxford he discovered other pills were missing from his bag, not enough to be harmful, but enough to cause concern. That was the start of losing her, even before they were married. Whenever he questioned her, she lied. Fear crept into his heart. He insisted on moving the wedding date up. If he had not been so besotted and fearful of losing her, he would have waited.

Planning the wedding made her happy, and she seemed to get better. Cat came back into her life and together they arranged the grandest gala of the year. It was spectacular. But when it was over, she flew off to her next gig, and he went back to his world of medicine.

The next time they were together, she asked for more pills. She said sleeping was still a problem. When he told her he didn't have any pills to give her, she accused him of lying and said he no longer loved her. He relented. The downward spiral began.

When she didn't show up for her assignments, the studio would call him. He would rush home and find her stoned. She promised she'd get help. When she didn't, he forced her into a rehab center. For a while she stayed off the drugs, but the job was too much for her fragile ego and soon she relapsed.

When he finished his residency, he bought a practice and a house in Castello del Mare. It was where they had always planned to live—in the beautiful village where they met. Their marriage unraveled slowly. She was in and out of rehab, always promising this would be the last time. Then one day she rented a house from their friend Carlo without telling him. Carlo had casually mentioned it over lunch one day. Antonio responded as if he knew, but he was furious to be blindsided by someone he considered a friend.

When Antonio asked her why, she said because he was never home, so she might as well have her own place. On rare occasions she would turn up, asking him to forgive her and let her move back in.

Eventually, she confessed her addiction. She promised him that after her next gig, she would take a break and stay in rehab until she was cured. He believed her until the next night when the lock to his clinic was broken and the place was ransacked. He found the glass-shattered drug cabinet empty, every opiate gone. He cleaned up the mess and didn't report it. He knew it was Stella.

Shortly before she disappeared, she barged into the house and the bedroom. Sylvia was with him. Stella turned into a raging maniac. He pushed her out of the bedroom into the kitchen. They accused each other of unspeakable things. But when he blamed her for breaking into the clinic, she pulled a knife out of a drawer and lunged at him, slashing his hand. He told her if she didn't leave he would call Lorenzo and have her arrested. She laughed in his face. They both knew he wouldn't call Lorenzo. If he did, she would make sure the medical board knew about the drugs he had given her. He would lose his medical license and his practice. He would die if he couldn't practice medicine. That was the last time he saw her.

Now both Stella and the necklace were missing. So far, there was zero evidence to link anyone to her disappearance. She had simply vanished.

ANTONIO & LORENZO

Lorenzo parked in the lot next to the sixteenth century bridge and walked to the old historic town of Gallipoli. *L'Acchiatura* on via Marzani was a favorite restaurant of his and Antonio's. Over the years it had morphed from a simple trattoria with vinyl tablecloths and Mama's home cooked meals into a Michelin recommended restaurant. The ancient tiled floors were burnished to a high luster, the walls whitewashed, and the old bricks lining the ceiling had been restored to their former glory. Even the artwork was noteworthy.

Lorenzo strode through the door and glanced past the bar. His eyes swept the room until he spotted Antonio nervously drumming his fingers on the table. It had been a while since they'd seen each other. Lorenzo positioned himself inside the door and observed Antonio's state of mind. The disheveled hair and a jacket that looked like it had been pulled off the floor painted a grim picture. None of it bode well for their meeting.

He nodded at the bartender and pointed to the table. Then he glided through the crammed-to-capacity restaurant. Many of the diners acknowledged him with a nod, handshake, or thump on the back. By the time he reached the table, a bottle of his favorite white wine was waiting.

Antonio stood, reaching out his hand, "It has been too long *Renzo*."

"*Sì*, it has Tony. It's hard for me to get away. Today's no different.

The paperwork for another drug bust is waiting at the office, so I can't linger over lunch. Let's order and then talk. What did Mario suggest?"

"The special is *spaghettini al limone con gamberi rossi.* The shrimp were caught this morning. I ordered it for both of us."

The conversation was stilted. They were both glad when the waiter arrived with a steaming platter of antipasti: sea urchins, succulent octopus, mussels, and potatoes. The waiter drizzled golden-green olive oil over the seafood along with a squeeze of lemon. The bottle of Tenute Serranova that appeared on the table with Lorenzo's arrival was opened and their glasses filled. Lorenzo rarely drank white wine. But when he did, it was always 100% Fiano grapes. He swirled the glass, sniffed the complexity and structure of the wine, then nodded and raised his glass to Antonio.

They plow through the seafood antipasti while Lorenzo questioned Antonio about Cat's surprise appearance at the clinic.

"You actually saw the necklace?"

"Of course, I saw it. Cat drove to the clinic right after she found it. The wound in her hand was nasty, enough for stitches. Once I stitched her up, she gave me the necklace."

"Why did you give it back to her?"

"You know why. I always drive to Gallipoli every Friday as soon as I see the last patient. I tried to call you while she was still at the clinic. I figured you would want to talk to her, and you would want the necklace. Since I was leaving town and you didn't answer your phone, it made sense to ask Cat to keep it until you picked it up from her. It's too bad you didn't answer your phone or check your messages until after midnight. But what happened yesterday?"

"That's the problem, Antonio. There is no necklace."

"What do you mean?"

"After you dropped Cat off at the villa, she claims she took a shower and went to bed. She swears she left the necklace tied up in her shirt. In the morning when she checked, it was gone."

"*Andata*? *Pazzesco*! Gone! That's crazy! If she wanted to keep it or give it to someone else, she wouldn't have shown up at the clinic and handed it over to me. How could it disappear? What's going on?"

"I'm not sure. The entire story is skewed. First, Cat gave you the necklace. Then you gave it back to her. No one seems to know what happened after that exchange in your car. We searched the ground where you parked, and I tore the house apart. Cat said you administered a shot for pain plus pain meds. She was fuzzy about what happened after you dropped her off. She vaguely remembers getting up in the night but couldn't remember why. When she woke up the next morning, the necklace was gone.

"Maria admitted to putting Cat to bed but said she didn't pick up the dirty clothes on the bathroom floor until hours later. She swore she checked before she washed them and found nothing. She also said Cat did not show her a necklace or say anything about a necklace. She said she certainly would have noticed if Cat had been wearing Stella's necklace."

Antonio's fork stopped in midair as Lorenzo continued, "Maybe the missing link is Gino. He seems to have disappeared along with the necklace. But according to both Cat and Maria, Gino had a family emergency. No one has seen him since, which seems suspicious. I have a couple of officers looking for him."

The conversation halted as sizzling plates of *spaghettini al limone* materialized with piles of red shrimp stacked on the mound of pasta. Silence ensued except for the occasional slurp.

After his first bite, Lorenzo smiled and wiped traces of buttery sauce from his mouth, "It's been too long since I have eaten here. This *spaghettini* is the best I've had in years. I wish I could get over here more often."

Antonio didn't look up but mumbled,"Yes, you used to come often, but you haven't bothered for a long time."

Lorenzo pressed his lips together in annoyance but responded. "I rarely have time off. When I do, I head for Leuca. But since the case is once again a priority, there might be a need for me to come this way."

"Are you sure this is enough to reopen the case? I mean, the evidence is missing. More importantly, will you be allowed to lead the investigation this time?"

"I'll find out this afternoon. It would help if I had something solid to present, but it's a start. While I don't have the necklace, both you and Cat can substantiate the evidence. I'll send a request to have the case reopened. Unless you object, I plan to lead the investigation."

Antonio hesitated before he said, "I owe it to Stella to open a new case. But I would prefer you not lead the investigation."

Lorenzo puts his fork down, "Something you need to say to me? Or do you want to wait until you come to the station to make another statement?"

Antonio didn't respond. Lorenzo swallowed the last of his wine, "Tony, what's going on with you? You're holding back. Maybe you forgot to tell me something the last time you made a statement? Maybe you ought to tell me about the night you and Stella fought?"

Antonio dropped his eyes to his plate, "There's nothing Lorenzo, nothing you don't know. I'm sure Stella told you all about that fight. Do you think I'm so stupid that I didn't know what was going on between you and Stella? I'm not a fool. It's a small town. One too many visits to her villa puts you under suspicion as well, doesn't it?"

A muscle pulsated in Lorenzo's forehead. He pushed back from the table, "I have to get back to the station—another drug bust in the wee hours last night. Reports are waiting for me to review, and I have to determine if we can actually convict someone. By the way, thanks for passing us the info. It has been a lot easier to take some of the dealers off the street since you and Carlo have been working with us."

Antonio nodded, "It used to be fun, but I'm not part of your team anymore. I don't have the heart for it. Finding Stella's necklace seals her fate, *vero*? She's been murdered. If she had been kidnapped, we would have heard by now. Somehow, I think Carlo's and my work with the police is tied up in her murder. I hold you responsible. That's why I don't want you leading the investigation."

The pause hung heavy in the air before Lorenzo said, "It's your decision not to participate in passing me information but what you and Carlo do is invaluable to the Guardia. I would like you to stay on, but I understand if you no longer wish to collaborate."

Antonio nodded and Lorenzo continued, "I'm sorry, Tony. You've always known how I felt about Stella. I never had anything to do with her until after she left you. But I regret that I did. Stella wasn't stable. She had changed too much and so had I. In the end it didn't work for us."

They stared across the table until Antonio shrugged, "It doesn't matter, does it? Neither of us have her now."

They stood, more enemies than friends. Lorenzo said, "I have to get back. The reports must be filed today in order to hold the drug suspects overnight. Plus, reopening Stella's case will require a ton of paperwork. I'd appreciate it if you don't mention the possibility of murder in your statement. If you do, the case will be turned over to the *Polizia*. You know what that means. We'd lose control of the case. That's not what you want, is it?"

Antonio looked down. He backed away from the table. "No, you're right. At least I know what's going on if you're in charge,"

Lorenzo nodded and turned to leave but stopped and looked at Antonio. "Cat said she'd invited you to her dinner party. Will you be there?"

Antonio shrugged.

"Look, Antonio, we need to move forward on Stella's case. We need to put our differences aside. Can we do that for Stella's sake?"

"Perhaps one day we can. Just not at the moment."

Anger flitted across Lorenzo's face. He glared at Antonio, "I took care of the bill when I came in. The station will call you to come in for a statement."

Lorenzo moved rapidly through the restaurant. He didn't stop to acknowledge the many hands grabbing at this coat sleeve. He knew if he stayed he might say something he would regret.

Antonio nodded at the bartender and another bottle of wine was delivered to the table.

LORENZO & RICCARDO

Once in the car, Lorenzo called the station.

"Luca, I'm on the way back. Make sure all the paperwork from last night's bust is on my desk. And pull Stella Lombardi's file. Mark it priority. Grazie."

He shook his head to quiet his spinning thoughts, maybe from the wine, but more likely from the memory of other paperwork that had recently crossed his desk. A missing drug statement had been submitted by Antonio's nurse, Sylvia. It was apparent to Lorenzo that Antonio had not seen the report as his signature was not on the document. Sylvia indicated on the report that she had not used these particular drugs in several months, and she did not know who had taken them since no forms had been completed. She mentioned that only she and Antonio had keys.

Lorenzo was reasonably sure these were the drugs that Stella had stolen from the clinic—the theft Antonio covered up. What he couldn't understand was why Sylvia wanted to implicate Antonio. Stella had told him they were having an affair. Now he wondered if that was falling apart as well. Maybe that's why Antonio was in such a foul mood today.

God, sometimes he hated his job. Hated he had devoted so much of his life to uncovering the slimy underbelly of humanity. From an early age he had wanted to follow in his father's footsteps—to rid Italy of the mafia and all the tentacles that were strangling this place he loved so much.

He remembered the day he had been promoted to Chief Inspector. After ten years of grueling work and due diligence, his position in Rome was finally secure.

He'd been more than shocked when the Chief Deputy called him in and told he was being posted to Puglia. Although a promotion went with the transfer, Lorenzo thought it was a demotion to be pastured away from Rome. He'd been furious. And even worse, he had to spend time at the Southern Regions HQ in Naples. Nobody in their right mind wanted to work in Naples after being at the home office in Rome.

Lorenzo had been first in his class at the Academy and had gone on to obtain his Masters in Economic and Financial Security Services before joining the ranks of the Guardia di Finanza in Rome.

His division had been given the toughest, dirtiest assignments. He'd been saddled with a team of trainees no one else wanted in their squadron. He was sure it was because the old guard wanted to see if he could live up to his father's reputation. Instead of throwing up his hands in despair, he had worked late every night and through weekends to gain the trust and respect of his team. It had paid off when they nailed one of the larger drug and prostitution rings in the city.

From that point on, he had been called into the Chief's office on occasion for late evening chats. At first, he thought maybe his father had put a word in the Chief's ear. That made him tense and uncommunicative. But after a few of these sessions, he realized he was the eyes and ears for the Chief on subjects of drug trafficking, illegal immigration, money laundering, terrorism, cybercrime, miscellaneous mafia operations, and what was really happening in the ranks.

During the next five years, Lorenzo devoted all his time to making a name for himself while trying to avoid treading on sensitive toes. Keeping a low profile and his ears open presented him with an education on the ins and outs of the political hierarchy of the *Guardia di Finanza.*

When he received an urgent message to come to the Chief's office, he thought it would be another update along with a glass of grappa before heading home. He'd been blindsided by the posting to Puglia.

He resisted. Rome was his first love although he had not revealed that to Donatella. Not that she would care. Their on-again, off-again engagement was more to please their parents than themselves. The one good thing about the posting to Puglia, it ended their engagement permanently. She was part of the big city life and would never leave Rome. And he had known all his life the only person he wanted to marry was Stella.

He didn't want to leave Rome but more importantly he didn't want to leave the Guardia. The thought of transferring to a remote station seemed contradictory. He asked the Chief if he had committed some grave misstep along the way.

"Lorenzo, I would never give you this posting if I didn't believe it would help you. Every officer in Rome is jockeying for the same promotions. Sooner or later you will step on someone's toes. A stint away from Rome is a good thing. You're young. This promotion will give you time to make a scandal-free name for yourself in the province. Plus, it's time you separate from your family connections. Taking a post in another region will ensure that those battling for the same promotions will not be gossiping about your family paving your way to the top."

Before Lorenzo left for what he considered to be the outpost, the Chief Commissario told him that the Sacra Corona Unita (SCU), who were operating in Puglia under the Sicilian Corleonesi clan, were making noises. He said if Lorenzo cleaned up some of the mess, he'd be promoted and back to Rome in a few years.

Lorenzo accepted and was promoted to Deputy Chief Inspector. He had barely survived the time in Naples. Thankfully, the need was great in Puglia, so after a few months of study, research, and endless dinners in loud, crowded restaurants with the Neapolitan Chief, he had been sent on his way.

Little by little he found ways to gain footholds in stopping some of the illegal activities in the hotels, restaurants, supermarkets, construction firms and waste disposal companies in the larger cities of Brindisi, Bari, Lecce, and Taranto. His investigations led to numerous arrests of petty criminals in the lower levels of the SCU. He was promoted along the way until he was made Commissario over the region of Puglia. With this promotion he had the ability to live and operate anywhere he chose.

He chose to live in Castello del Mare for a myriad of reasons: memories of those long ago summer vacations, the Guardia already had a fleet of boats in the marina which meant he could reach any part of the region quickly, it was close to his cottage in Leuca, and most of all because Stella was there.

It was enough to be near her. He hated himself for loving her so much. But as long as she'd stayed with Antonio, he avoided her. He settled into his new life and discovered he loved the area and the laid-back lifestyle that was so different from Rome. He took his time collecting information on the SCU. He cultivated some of the street mules and penetrated the lower levels. It was risky but necessary to connect with someone on the inside of the organization. He worked steadily to develop relationships with several of the promising younger members who were designated to move up in the organization. Riccardo appeared to be one of those. A small favor here and there by looking the other way or by sharing some information that was helpful but not harmful.

He was a few years into his job when Stella left Antonio and moved to Casa dei Fiori. He believed he finally had a chance. Their relationship was all he had hoped for until Stella found out he was recruiting informants from the SCU. He never discussed work with her so he was unsure how she found out. He thought Gino might have told her. She tried to use the information to bargain with him. She wanted inside information on the mafia. He refused and that, along with her addiction battle, ended their relationship just as it was beginning.

He couldn't believe how long he had waited for her only to discover that love was not enough to pull them through the mess they were mired in. Still, he had hoped by letting her go and keeping a close watch on her, she'd be out of harm's way. She told him the SCU had a personal vendetta against her, but she had told him so many stories by then that he didn't believe her. He, like Antonio, failed her.

Lorenzo glanced in the rearview mirror. Someone had been tailing him since he left Gallipoli. The cross-country road was too isolated for random travelers. Just before the turn off to Galatone, he pulled off on the shoulder, got out of the car, and waited. A few minutes later a black Mercedes pulled up behind him. Puffing on a cigarette, Riccardo stepped out of the car.

"*Commissario*, what brings you out this way? I don't usually have to work so hard to keep up with you. Must be something personal since you're driving your baby."

Riccardo laughed nervously, running his hand back and forth through his mop of jet-black tousled hair. His dark, beady eyes shifted away from Lorenzo's face. His black leather jacket swung open. Lorenzo could see the APX Centurion Beretta nestled against his red shirt.

"Riccardo, if you think I'm on personal business, why are you following me? My social life has never interested you before."

"Just a joke, Lorenzo. You are always working, but you rarely head out this way in the middle of the day. I was tagging along to see what you're up to. You heard the rumor that Stella's necklace was found? What do you know about that?"

"Not much. As fast as it was found, it disappeared. What about you—have you heard any conversations about what happened to it?"

"No, the scuttlebutt says Stella ran off with some billionaire Arab, and she's locked up in a palace counting his money."

"I see the usual nonsense still abounds in a small town. What else have you heard, Riccardo?"

Riccardo hesitated, shifting uneasily before adding, "It might be that one of the street mules lifted the necklace, although I think someone higher up ordered it done. I don't think the transfer has been made yet, but I did hear the mule is nervous about having it. He might drop it off to his brother in Martano. Since you are close to the turn off, you might want to drive in that direction."

"Does the brother have a name?"

"Bastia. Franco Bastia. When you get to Martano just ask around. Someone will point out his house. It's a big villa, but he's a small-time operator who's overstepping his boundaries. You don't want to stay too long. It won't be safe for you."

"Anything else, Riccardo? Anything that might help me? This is a pretty cold case."

"Make sure that the American girl staying in Stella's house is not messed up in this. I've heard that Franco's little brother and his wife were hired by that Lecce attorney to take care of her. That seems like something you might find interesting."

"Thanks, Riccardo. I owe you."

"You sure do Lorenzo. I'll let you know when I need something. *Ciao*."

Riccardo flipped the burning cigarette into the dried grass. Lorenzo watched as the sedan pulled back on the road and continued toward Castello. When the car was out of sight, he pulled out his phone and called the station as he ground the flaming cigarette into the dirt.

"Get me whatever you have on Franco Bastia. I need it right away. I'm on my way to see him."

LORENZO & FRANCO

M*ARTANO, ITALY*

Twenty minutes later Lorenzo drove past the battered sign announcing Martano. His earlier call to the station provided him with nothing new on Franco Bastia. He wondered why the report didn't mention the connection to Gino. Maybe Franco was only a fringe player in the local mafia, and his connections weren't that important. His mediocre wealth came from money laundering and some double-dealing with both the government and the mafia, perhaps even the police.

Lorenzo turned off the paved road onto a dirt driveway barely large enough to accommodate his car. A wrought iron gate with elaborately carved serpents came into view along with a disheveled villa. Chickens scratched on the front lawn. A couple of flea-bitten old dogs slept in the dirt. They sluggishly raised their heads as he pulled up to the gate. At one time the villa would have been elegant. Now sagging rooflines, crumbling walls, and choking weeds cast shadows of neglect into the sullen air.

Lorenzo rolled down the window and pressed the intercom button on the tumbled-down brick column. There was no response. He waited a minute and pushed it again. A slight movement at one of the curtained windows grabbed his attention but still no response. The third time he pressed, he spoke into the intercom.

"Come on Franco, open the damn gate. I'm not leaving until you do."

A pause, then a spine-chilling screech as the gate crept open. Lorenzo patted his pocket where his small Beretta Nano rested. Unlike Riccardo, he kept his weapon concealed. He didn't need to prove anything.

He checked out the area surrounding the villa as he drove through the gate. He left the protective cover of the car and strode up the buckled walkway. It was eerily quiet as he approached the veranda.

The front door was long overdue for an update. Faded streaks of red peeked through the overlay of chipped black paint. The brass door handle and knocker were corroded from years of neglect. Leaves scuttled across the wide veranda whispering a crackly message. Sensing movement, he checked behind his back. Nothing was visible, but he knew someone was there, probably with a gun pointed in his direction.

An old woman opened the door a sliver and poked her nose through.

"*Permesso?*" he asked, pushing the door wider before stepping across the threshold.

The faded hallway reeked of mustiness, mold, shutters never opened, and sunlight never seen. She drifted down the hall, a whisper of a shadow. Lorenzo's heels clicked in stereophonic sound as he followed. Her movements ceased as she turned toward a pair of burled walnut pocket doors. Her gnarly fingers separated the doors a fraction. She tilted her head and disappeared into the gloom of the hallway.

Lorenzo paused before placing his hands on both doors. He swiveled his head left and right before he slid them open and stepped inside. A flame flickered in the fireplace. His eyes adjusted to the dim light as he glanced around the room. A door on the far side of the hearth vibrated. Probably from someone just leaving.

An oversized hand-carved desk dominated the room. It was an

expensive eighteenth century walnut, rosewood, and boxwood combination. It was patinated and gilded with four cabriole legs entwined in hand-carved acanthus leaves. Lorenzo noted the center drawer was opened a small fraction, just enough for a hand to slip in.

His eyes rested on the hands folded on the desktop. Thick, meaty fingers extended into chewed nails with bloody quicks—hands accustomed to dirty work.

"Signore Bastia?"

"*Si,* how are you Commissario? I don't believe I've seen you in Martano before. What brings you here?"

"You know why I am here."

Lorenzo paused. Bastia said nothing.

"You don't look surprised by my visit."

"Surprises aren't good for my health, Commissario. You know what I mean? This part of the country is desolate. The whole town saw you coming from miles away. Surprises do not happen on my turf. Everybody tells me everything. It would be detrimental for them not to."

"Since you are so well informed, tell me where the starfish necklace is."

"A starfish necklace? What is it and why do you want it?"

"An American movie star was wearing a starfish necklace the last time she was seen alive. A few days ago, another American lady found the necklace on a cliff not too far from the marina. But right away someone relieved her of it, stole it right from under her nose while she was sleeping. Your brother, Gino, has disappeared. I thought you might know where I can find him."

"Gino, ha, Gino wouldn't know a starfish necklace if you gave it to him and told him what it was. Gino minds his own business, always has. Haven't seen my brother in weeks. I did hear that a hot looking American lady is living in Stella's villa and Gino and Maria are her nursemaids. That's all I know. Why would you drive all the way out here to ask me about a necklace? It can't be good for that swanky car of yours to travel on these roads. You could easily pick up nails or glass. You don't want to come here again."

"Well, Bastia, it's strange that you haven't seen Gino since Maria told everyone your health is failing and Gino is taking care of you. You look healthy to me, but I can't guarantee you'll stay healthy. If you happen to see Gino or the necklace, it would be in your best interest to contact me."

Lorenzo reached into his coat pocket while watching Franco's hand slide off the desk and move out of sight. He tossed his card on the desk, "Don't wait too long to be in touch. If you don't have the necklace yet, it could be on the way to you. We'll be watching Gino round the clock. You too."

"You threatening me?"

"Why would I do that? Just telling you what the deal is. The necklace is evidence. You don't want to be tampering with evidence, Bastia. Your friends would not look kindly on you if you were hauled off to jail, would they?"

Lorenzo turned his back and headed for the door. The soft sound of wood against wood alerted him that the desk drawer was opening. In a single smooth movement Lorenzo whirled around, his Beretta pointed at Franco's head.

"It would be a shame to have your brains all over that fine desk. Open the gate and call your people off. If I don't show up at the station, my colleagues will ensure that what is left of you will not be enough to feed fishes."

Their eyes locked. Franco shrugged and placed his hands on the desk. Lorenzo slid the Beretta back in his pocket, pushed the doors apart, and stepped into the hallway. When he reached the front door, it was open. He stood for a moment on the veranda, alert to his surroundings as the creeping grind signaled the opening of the gate.

CAT & MARIA

CASTELLO DEL MARE, ITALY

"Have you heard from Gino?" I call from the dining room.

Maria's back tenses, "No, Caterina. I'm worried. He hasn't answered any of my messages."

The air is thick and heavy between us. Maria stirs a rich seafood sauce for tonight's dinner party. I arrange the red flowers, tucking in rosemary and ivy. Stella's necklace hasn't turned up which is creating tension for all of us. With the flower arrangements finished, I turn my attention to the mismatched china, soft linen napkins, and antique silverware lined up at the end of the table. For all my counting and organizational obsessions, I love the uniqueness of each piece. The mishmash of items gracing the table brings back the fun day I had in Lecce shopping at the big antique market.

A few days ago I decided to drive to Lecce. While there, I had impulsively texted Carlo and asked if he was available for lunch. When he arrived at the restaurant, I was already seated with stacks of shopping bags surrounding me. He laughed long and loud and asked what I might be celebrating. He was delighted when I told him about the party and invited him to join us.

"Is that what all these packages are about?"

"Of course, the villa has a definite shortage of plates, glasses, and utensils. There is not enough of anything to give a proper party. I hope you don't mind. I'll leave everything at the villa when I leave. I'll tell Antonio too."

He shook his head, "That's not a topic we're going to discuss. But let me pay for your purchases; otherwise, I won't come to your party."

We teased and bargained with each other until Carlo agreed we would be even if he paid for lunch. Then he asked me to promise I'd share another meal with him when he was next in Castello.

"Look," I exclaimed as I reached into one of the bags and pulled out an elegant black box tied with a lime ribbon. "I found *Maglio Cioccolato* on via Templari. It's the best thing that's happened to me since I've arrived."

"What? You're a chocolate connoisseur. Why didn't you tell me? Now I know what to bring you when I come to Castello."

We laughed easily. Tension eased from my neck. Even happiness seemed possible—a glass of wine, a likable companion, a plate of pasta brimming with shrimp, octopus, and clams followed by sea bass on a bed of crispy sliced potatoes surrounded by black olives, capers, and tomatoes. It had been an afternoon to linger. Carlo was fun and gracious. I was disappointed when he excused himself, saying he wished he could stay but a client was waiting for him.

The drive back to Castello was full of sunshine. The world felt light and airy as I parked in front of the villa. Humming *That's Amore*, I stacked the packages against the wall while I rummaged through my purse looking for the key. Once found, I looked up to insert the key into the lock. My eyes fastened on the mangled body of a sparrow dangling above the keyhole—a nail piercing its tiny heart. Pain seared in my head as I jumped away from the tortured creature and screamed.

Windows and doors opened. Neighbors rushed to my side. The

bird was whisked out of sight. Someone found my key, someone gathered the packages, and someone had their arm around me as I climbed the stairs.

Maria and Gino arrived soon after. A fire roared, a cup of tea had been placed in my hand, and Lorenzo was on his way.

I'm startled out of these bleak memories when Maria says, "Caterina, do you believe that Gino or I took the necklace?"

My thoughts of the harrowing moment I saw the dead bird have taken my attention away from the centerpiece. My dark thoughts have overworked it. A big lump lodges in my throat. I swallow hard but it remains stuck.

"Maria, of course not. What would be your motive? Neither of you would ever do anything to hurt Stella."

She simply says, *Grazie* and returns to her work.

"Maria," I say softly, "It's okay. The necklace will turn up. Now, what else can I do? The desserts are ready, the arugula washed, the fennel sliced, and the tomatoes chopped for the salad."

As the sun dips its toe into the Adriatic, Maria brings out a large seafood lasagna. I follow with platters of roasted meats. We add sides of crispy potatoes, spinach with pine nuts and raisins, eggplant parmesan, and roasted peppers with a drizzle of olive oil and grated ricotta salata.

When I finish arranging the platters, I check the antipasti table. It's weighed down with olives, taralli, sun-dried tomato tapenade, and caramelized onions. The grilled bread is piled high in a basket next to the mozzarella and burrata and a plate of thinly sliced prosciutto. The cured meats are plated and the pickled veggies are little jewels arranged in colorful crocks from Stella's collection of local pottery.

Maria joins me, inspecting my placements of platters and bowls.

"How does it look? I put the Prosecco and wine glasses on the table overlooking the sea so we don't bottle-neck the food. The three tables pushed together seat twenty-four."

Maria moves a platter and rearranges several bowls, angling them away from the large pot of rosemary I selected as the centerpiece.

"Where are the candles?" she asks.

"There's a small collection of little plates on the shelf over the sofa." I say, trying to ease her thoughts away from the missing necklace as well as Gino and Stella. "I'm using those for the candles."

"Yes, I like those little plates. Maybe circle the candles around the rosemary and some on each table."

"Isn't it splendid? The weather is ideal, mid-February and so warm. No wind, rain, or fog," I feebly attempt to keep the conversation going.

Maria only nods and heads back to the kitchen. I realign the platters and bowls and recount the plates, napkins, and utensils.

Glasses brim with Prosecco, candlelight brushes soft shadows across the terrace. The marina glows with twinkling lights. Whiffs of rosemary and lavender wrap around aromas of tomato sauce, grilled seafood, lemon and garlic. Voices linger in the evening air as guests gather in clusters.

Maria darts in and out of the groups. She chats and expertly keeps glasses filled. Sometimes she singles someone out and their heads bend close together. If anyone can uncover a clue to Stella's disappearance, it will be Maria.

I breathe in the cool air and put on my hostess smile. A hand caresses the back of my neck. I jump ready to smack. When I turn around, Lorenzo backs away with his hands up.

"Sorry, I didn't mean to startle you. Why do I always make you jump?" his voice, deep and sultry whispers in my ear.

"No, it's me. I've been tense ever since I arrived in Castello. Stella is always on my mind. Her disappearance, then the disappearance of her necklace, and now the dead sparrow. I'm a bit on edge. Any news?"

He doesn't respond right away. Instead, he looks across the terrace down to the marina and says, "There's a lot going on, Cat. Stuff that may or may not involve Stella and the missing necklace. The dead bird is a warning. Would you object if I posted someone outside the villa tonight?"

"Yes, I would. Why do you think I need to be under surveillance?"

"It would be for protection, not to spy on you. I'm concerned for your safety. If neither Gino nor Maria took the necklace, it means someone else came inside the house. Have you considered that?"

"No," I say, as a painful knot develops in my stomach.

Lorenzo leans in close and says, "Sometime after you dropped your clothes on the bathroom floor and the time Maria returned to pick them up, someone was in the house. You could have been hurt. That's cause enough to be concerned. The sparrow with the nail piercing its heart specifically targets you. My job is to keep you safe."

People gravitate toward the tables, casting sideway glances at the two of us with our heads close and our voices low. Both Antonio and Carlo look our way—Antonio in surprise, Carlo with annoyance.

"Do you think Gino took the necklace?"

"I'm not sure. If he did, I believe someone asked him to or maybe he did it to protect you. If he shows up tonight, I plan to ask him. He knows about the party, and he knows Carlo is here. He and Carlo are thick. Carlo has given him a cushiony job. I don't think he'll screw around. He wouldn't want to lose the job. Maria, well she's always been honest. As much as she cares for Gino, I don't think he could persuade her to do anything dishonest. They're good people but sometimes good people can be led astray."

I nod and say, "Looks like folks are getting hungry. Do you want to help Maria and me bring out the rest of the food?"

He places his hand on the small of my back. The heat radiates up my spine into my shoulders and neck. It's so tempting to lean back into his arms.

As we reach the door, Maria rushes out of the kitchen, "Gino just texted. He's on his way. His brother is very sick. He had to wait for someone to relieve him. But he will be here soon."

Words gush from Maria's mouth as a brilliant smile flashes across her face. "He did not take that necklace Commissario. I promise you he did not."

Lorenzo looks Maria in the eye and says, "Strange that his brother is ill. He was just fine when I visited him yesterday."

Before Maria can answer, he turns and walks away.

"Well, I thought he was going to assist us with the food. Looks like it's just you and me, Maria."

But Maria had already fled to the kitchen.

Lorenzo steps through the open door onto the terrace.

"You sure are cozy with our hostess," Carlo says as he joins Lorenzo.

Lorenzo raises an eyebrow but doesn't respond.

Carlo continues to poke, "Is there something going on between you and Cat?"

"Why would that be of any interest to you?"

Carlo smiles, "I thought you would still be grieving for Stella."

"Carlo, are you trying to provoke me? Our working relationship is good, but it's strictly business. My personal affairs aren't your concern."

"Pretty touchy. Guess I hit a sore spot. How does Antonio feel about you and Stella? I thought you and he were best friends. Sleeping with your best friend's wife is an insult. I'm surprised Antonio still speaks to you, and I'm more surprised he hasn't blown your head off."

Lorenzo clutches Carlo's shirt and pulls him in close. "You sorry bastard!"

Antonio eases his way between the two. He puts his arm around Carlo's shoulder and his hand on Lorenzo's chest.

"You guys do not want to create a scene at Cat's party. Leave it alone."

Carlo jerks out of Lorenzo's grasp, straightens his shirt, and storms off.

Lorenzo wipes his hands on his trousers and turns to Antonio. "Thanks. Did anyone else notice? Did Cat?"

"No, I just happened to see the look on your face as I was making my way to join the two of you. The tension was obvious to me, but everyone else was busy with food, wine, and conversation. What's the problem between you and Carlo? You work well together. What has changed?"

Lorenzo looks at the grimace on Antonio's face. "Nothing serious. Just a difference of opinion. I will handle it. But thanks again for stepping in. Cat would have never forgiven me if I knocked him senseless on the terrace."

Maria hands me a platter. As I reach the door, I notice Lorenzo, Carlo, and Antonio in a cluster. It doesn't look friendly. Carlo stomps off leaving Lorenzo and Antonio staring after him. Lorenzo folds his arms across his chest, his glare follows Carlo.

There's a subtle shift in conversation and movement. I glance away from Lorenzo and Antonio and continue to the food table. The crowd is congregating, ready to eat.

Maria and I replenish platters as quickly as they are emptied. On our last trip to the kitchen, we both yelp with surprise. Gino is leaning against the table. Skin sags under his eyes. Weariness seeps out of every pore.

Maria sputters with joy as she embraces him, "Gino, Gino, where have you been? What happened?"

Gino slips his arm around her ample waist and says, "We will talk about it later. Now is not a good time."

"Gino is right," Lorenzo says from the doorway.

Silence, dense and stifling, descends. Maria and Gino freeze.

"I won't haul you to the station now because I don't want to ruin Cat's party. But as soon as everyone leaves, you're coming with me. Until that time, do not leave the premises. Do you understand?" Lorenzo walks away, as Maria and Gino clutch each other. Lorenzo returns to the terrace and piles his plate high with food before finding a seat.

"I am going with you Gino," weeps Maria.

"I will take you," I say. "Neither of you are in any shape to drive."

"No, you don't need to be involved. We are the ones suspected of stealing the necklace. We will be okay."

Carlo strolls into the kitchen, "Cat, everyone is waiting for you."

He stops, noticing Maria's tears and Gino's crumpled face. "What's going on?"

I struggle with words and then say, "Maria and Gino just need a few minutes. Do you need a refill? I haven't eaten yet and could use the company."

I deftly maneuver him toward the terrace as he leans in close, "Okay, what is the problem? Let me help, please."

"It's a long story, Carlo. I don't have time to tell you now. I need to be visible. Sit by me. If there's time, I'll explain but it may not be tonight. Maybe you can help sort things out before it all falls apart. I should have told you when we had lunch, but I didn't want to spoil the day. I thought Gino and Maria would contact you. I guess they haven't?"

"No, they haven't, and you're going to leave me hanging, aren't you?"

I nod, tucking my hand under his arm. We walk out to the terrace. Everyone stands and claps. I'm expected to say something. I look at Carlo. He nods and gives my hand a squeeze before releasing it. I gaze around the table until my eyes are stopped by the anger in Lorenzo's.

I stutter a short welcome and thank everyone for their gestures of friendship. There's much laughter and clapping. Before I sit, I offer a toast to the friends gathered and to Stella.

CAT & LORENZO

"You believe them, don't you?" I ask as Lorenzo joins me in the so-called conference room where I've been in limbo.

It's close to two in the morning. The air is stale, the glass of water I've been sipping is tepid. I rotate it, creating overlapping circles. I count them to avoid thinking and to stay awake. We've been at the station for several hours. My body aches and there's this weariness that comes and goes with every breath I take.. After cleaning and cooking for days, all I want is a shower and the comfort of bed. Instead, I visualize the stacks of dirty dishes waiting at the villa. The glass in my hand creates more wet circles on the table.

"I believe Maria, but word's out that Gino took the necklace. Rumor says he handed it over to his brother, Franco Bastia. I got a tip from one of our informants."

"Are you going to see Bastia?"

"I've already been. Of course, he admitted nothing, and there was no sign of Gino. He could have been there, but I don't think he gave his brother the necklace. His brother is a jerk, but Gino is a decent guy although he lied about his brother being ill."

I stop in the midst of my wet circular creations, "What happened?"

"I went out there without backup, not exactly a smart move with a gangster. Franco is a small cog in a big wheel. I'm reasonably sure he doesn't know about the necklace. Based on my conversation with Gino, I believe he has the necklace. But I can't pry it out of him. Why would he take it? And, if he did, what has he done with it? He refuses to talk other than saying he doesn't know anything about the necklace."

"Can I take Maria and Gino home?"

"I would like to keep Gino for further questioning. I could charge him with making a false statement about his brother, but that's pretty flimsy. There's really nothing to warrant an overnight stay. Would you consider talking to Gino? He might open up to you."

"I can't do that Lorenzo. Gino and I are just beginning to trust each other. If I start asking questions, he'll know you're behind it."

"*Va bene*, you're right. Take them home. This is a mess, Cat. I'm sorry you are a part of it."

"Lorenzo, I've been part of it ever since Stella left that message."

He reaches across the table and takes my hand. "It's a nasty business. I don't want you involved."

"But I'm involved and have been right from the beginning. Initially, I thought it was just Stella in one of her dramatic moods. When she didn't answer any of my messages, I called Antonio. When he finally returned my calls, he confirmed Stella had disappeared."

"You talked to Antonio? I didn't know that. Why didn't you call me?"

I hesitate, wondering how to answer. Do I trust Lorenzo? He and Antonio are friends. He's been in love with Stella since we were kids. Would he hurt her? And what about Antonio? He had every reason to hurt her. His practice might be shut down if anyone discovered he had given her drugs. And what about Gino or Maria and all the others? Who can I trust?

Finally, I answer, "When Antonio returned my call, he suggested I wait before changing my plans to come earlier. Actually, it was his indifference that spurred me to change my flight. I came knowing Stella had disappeared. She must have told you we've been planning this trip for a while. It was only recently that I made the decision to stay with her. My original intention was to work in Rome. But you know Stella. She wanted me in Castello. She made all the arrangements and secured a job for me at La Canzone del Mare without regard to what I wanted. Even removed my name off the waitlist in Rome at the restaurant that was my first choice. Initially, I was furious as I didn't want to return to Castello. But it was a chance for us to reconcile. We both wanted that. Once I accepted the job, it made sense for me to stay with her. But I made it clear that if it didn't work out, I would find my own place.

"I didn't call you because..." My mind shut down. What can I say? There's no logic to my feelings. I shrug.

Lorenzo's angry stare penetrates to the core, but I don't flinch. I have no idea why he's angry. It could be me, Antonio, Gino, or any number of things. I keep silent, hoping he will let us go home.

"I wasn't aware you and Antonio had talked."

"Does it matter? It doesn't shed any light on Stella's disappearance."

"I'm not sure Cat. It just seems unusual that Antonio would ask you to wait."

"I thought so too. I was sure you'd want Stella's message as quickly as possible. I'm sorry I didn't call you directly. That would have been the wiser choice."

Lorenzo continues to hold my hand. With my free hand, the one holding the glass, I persist in creating more wet circles. I watch and wait. His mouth is grim but his eyes are warm as he searches my face.

"Okay, I'll release Gino for now. You're exhausted. Leave your car here. I'll have one of my officers drive all of you back to the villa."

"No, I'll drive. It's not that far. I think Gino and Maria might not want to be escorted home by the police."

Finally, a smile shifts briefly across his haggard face, "I'll be in touch soon. I have more questions for you. But even if I didn't, I'd like to see you. Is that okay?"

"You have more questions for me? Why not ask them now."

"My questions are for you, about your life since I last saw you. Do you think we could talk over dinner one night? I'd like to cook for you."

I'm so surprised I don't have a comeback. I nod and back out the door. As it eases shut behind me, I run down the hallway where Gino and Maria are waiting.

Lorenzo watches, longing to run after her. Instead he walks in the opposite direction and opens a heavy metal door that leads out back. He leans into the wall and pulls a pack of cigarettes from an inside pocket. *Hell,* he thinks. *I haven't had the urge to smoke in weeks and now I'm going to let that red-headed temptress bring me down.* He chuckles and drops the pack in the trash bin.

CAT

The shrill ring of the alarm rouses me from a rain-filled mountain climbing dream. I peel the damp twisted sheet off my body and hit the off button. Night blackness still hovers. It tempts me to crawl back into bed. It was well after two when we returned to the villa last night. I'm exhausted, but something keeps whirling around in my mind—some clue or something I saw but missed. Ever since the day Lorenzo and I went to the site where I found the necklace, I've had an unrelenting urge to return. Today is the day I had planned to do this but that was before I knew I would be up half the night at the police station.

Maria and I had only minutes after we left the station to compare notes from the dinner party. She quickly filled me in. Signor Zappia had remembered seeing Stella being picked up for her photo shoot. He recounted how he'd often seen her leaving in a limo but this time *un'ape* was waiting for her. He found that strange. He recalled the driver did not get out to assist her and had taken off so fast that Stella's dress was still outside the vehicle. He hadn't seen the driver's face because he wore a hat pulled low. The day was warm and he noticed the driver had on a dark long sleeve pullover.

The only other conversation of interest was with the local artist—the one Stella commissioned to paint the portrait of the two of us. He told Maria that Stella had put a lot of pressure on him to finish it ahead of schedule. He wasn't satisfied and had asked her to give him more time. But she was adamant that the painting was to be finished and hung before I arrived. Once he had hung it, Stella asked him to take it down. He was confused and asked her why? She told him she wanted to look at it for a while, and she would rehang it later. He thought it was an unusual request. We puzzled over this for a few minutes but neither Maria nor I could decipher the significance.

I told Maria about the tension I witnessed with Lorenzo, Carlo and Antonio. I had no clue what it indicated, but it seemed significant.

By the time I'm fully awake, streaks of grays and pinks etch the sky. I throw on jeans and a sweater, grab my camera and slip out into the early morning light. The overcast sky portends rain on the menu today. No one, not even one of the mangy neighborhood cats, is stirring at this hour. I shiver in the misty morning and pick up my pace as I jog to the marina.

Once there, I sit on the wall with my back to the sea and look for a path leading to the plateau. From my position, the landscape either rambles off into the sea or straight up the rocky incline. I methodically scan the hill. Tall grasses, rambling vines, and who knows what else sway in the morning breeze. Maybe this early in the morning all the critters are hunkered down and my trespassing won't disturb them. I hope that's the case.

Several rudimentary pathways look promising. I hop off the wall and begin to search. My first attempt is a dead end. The sky lightens. My heart races as anxiety ratchets up. If I don't find the path before it's light, the entire village will see me and wonder what I'm doing. That thought pushes me forward. I stand in front of another patch of thorny shrubs. Why didn't I tell Lorenzo about my plans to return to this place? He'll be furious. But I won't tell him unless something suspicious turns up.

A slight movement in the tall weeds further up the hill catches my attention. A small critter plows through the undergrowth. Its speedy movements push down the grasses revealing something that looks like a path. The thorny vines and tall grasses wrap around my jeans as I tread cautiously through the undergrowth. The path isn't much but little-by-little a sandy trail appears. My feet maneuver with caution between boulders and small crevices to avoid another tumble.

The view from this side of the plateau is expansive. The sea and sky spread to eternity. The wild beauty is in sharp contrast with murder. Yet, this is probably the last view Stella saw before she died. I close my eyes and listen. Stella and I had different DNA, but she was my sister, my forever friend. My spirit tells me she has left the earth. The emptiness gathers and hums. The haunting tune *Stella by Starlight* plays in my head as I see Stella at her wedding dancing, not with Antonio but with Lorenzo.

Ella Fitzgerald's rendition of the melancholy tune floats on the air. "*...That's Stella by starlight, And not a dream, My heart and I agree, She's everything on this earth to me.*"

A cool breeze rises and seagulls circle. The music dies in the wind. I open my eyes and breathe in the thick salty air. The sky brightens as the soft glow hovering over the horizon signals daybreak. I remove the lens cap from the camera and systematically take photos of the area.

The zoom reveals minuscule shards of glass lying shattered along one side of the stony hill. It would be easy to miss it if I didn't know what I was looking for. I pick up a shard and turn it over. The black underside reveals the silvering on the back of a mirror. I squint, imagining this magnificent location with a mirror as a dramatic backdrop. It was so Stella.

But it's also evidence. I should leave it, but I pocket the piece of glass to study it later. It's puzzling that someone wouldn't have noticed a large mirror being transported up here? Perhaps it was brought up during the night. However it got here, no one's talking. It just seems like such an elaborate and nonsensical way to kill someone.

Even if this is a desolate place, there's a clear shot of the marina and there are houses on the far hillside. I glance in the direction of the penthouse. Surely someone saw something. Did Lorenzo think to interview the occupants?

My gaze slides back to the sea. The black, brooding sky dips low into the water. I finish taking photos and clumsily smudge my footprints as I step around the outer edges of the perimeter overlooking the sheer drop.

Something small and twisted is wedged in the rocks just out of reach. I lie on my stomach and inch my way until the land under my head and shoulders drops away. I snap several photos before dizziness overcomes me. Beads of sweat gather and my stomach slushes over. I close my eyes and slide backwards away from the drop off. I do not have time for one of my occasional brushes with vertigo. Rocks scrape across my bare skin as my sweater bunches up. When my head and shoulders find solid ground, I open my eyes, scoot into a sitting position, and wait until the merry-go-round in my head stops spinning. I make an attempt to brush the sand and twigs from my jeans and sweater then balance the camera on my knees and enhance the images.

A gray, contorted object appears in the frame. I adjust and readjust until a crumpled once-white ballet slipper stares back at me. My heart knows it belongs to Stella. Wailing is what I want to do, but first Lorenzo must be called. He'll be so pissed when I tell him I came back to search on my own. But the shoe will be more than enough evidence to reopen the investigation. Surely it's as good as the necklace.

When Lorenzo doesn't answer, I leave a message for him to call me.

The path down requires concentration. More than once I'm on my butt as rocks slide out from under my feet. If that isn't enough, the shrill jangle of my phone throws me off balance. My body spirals toward the earth. I manage to land in a squatting position instead of face down. As I pick myself up out of the sand, the phone erupts again.

"Pronto."

"Ciao, Cat. It's Carlo. How are you? I enjoyed last night, in spite of the intrigue. You promised to fill me in on what was happening with Gino and Maria. Would today work?"

Before I can answer, he continues, "Look, I stayed overnight in Castello because I have to check on some rental properties. If you aren't busy, let's have lunch. Can I pick you up around one?"

My mind fast forwards through the events of last night and what I'm willing to tell him.

When I don't answer, he says, "Cat, say yes. I want to spend more time with you, but my schedule has been crazy. You have to eat. There's a great seafood restaurant in town, the one where you'll soon be working. If you haven't met the owner, you are in for a treat. After lunch, I'm driving to San Cataldo. I'd like you to go with me.

"Sure, it sounds wonderful. I'll expect you around one. Thanks, Carlo, ciao, ciao," my words spill out in a rush to get off the phone.

I managed to scoot down the rest of the path without falling or hurting myself. As I reach the marina, the soft plop of raindrops dot the dirt.

Riccardo lowered the binoculars and snorted. He turned from the window and spoke, "She's trouble just like Stella. I knew it the first time I saw her. She's nosy, and a nosy woman is dangerous."

"Don't upset yourself, Riccardo. You can use the penthouse to keep an eye on her and Lorenzo. See how many times he stops by to visit her. That first day he saw something that interested him. He stayed on that terrace for a long time, and he was staring at the marina. I don't know what he saw—but we need to steer clear of the area for a while, until things settle down."

"Look, I don't want to babysit the girl," snarled Riccardo. "I'm already in too deep. You know that attempt to scare her on her first day in town didn't work. She kicked the shit out of me. The second threat in the piazza didn't slow her down. Even the dead bird didn't send her packing."

"You have no choice, Riccardo. You will keep her in your sights at all times. You hang out at that restaurant where she will be working, right?"

"Sometimes," Riccardo muttered.

"Well, meet her. We need to find out if she knows anything. Either that or snuff her out. Since the necklace was found, the Guardia is going to be on our tail. I want that necklace. Somebody has it. Since you screwed up with Stella, it's your job to find it. Stella's friend is the only one who might know where it is. If she knows, then she probably knows where Stella hid the information she collected on our operation. If you can't get the girl to cooperate, you know what to do."

Riccardo shifted his dark, beady eyes from the window to his boss, "I don't like it. You know Stella lived in that house before—you know, before she went missing. What if we missed something when we searched the place, something that can be traced to the photo shoot?"

"You're the one who screwed up the photo shoot. If anything is found, your name will be on it. The only reason you are alive is because you found enough cash to cover her debt. I still don't understand why she had so much stashed away. She could have paid off her debt."

Riccardo stared out the window. He hadn't told anyone, not even *il padrone*, that the money he found was in an envelope addressed to Gino. A note was attached saying it was for little Gino's new experimental treatment. He'd felt shitty taking it, but his choices were limited to taking the money or being killed. An easy choice that allowed him to stay in Castello instead of on the run.

"We'll never know why she didn't hand over the money, but it doesn't matter now. What does matter is the necklace. We'll hit Antonio up for more money—call it Stella's past debts. But I want that necklace to dangle in his face when I tell him he's to blame for her death. He has no idea I know he supplied Stella with drugs. If he refuses to play with us, I'll threaten to turn him in. It would kill him to lose his practice. That knowledge will keep him in line. He'll pay up until I bleed him dry."

Il padrone downed a cup of espresso before continuing, "Perhaps you would like to tell me why you think Gino has the necklace? According to Franco, he doesn't. The girl is smarter than we think. You need to search the place again. What about Lorenzo? Can you feel him out about the girl? He owes you a few favors. Maybe she's confiding in him the same way Stella did. Lean on him."

Riccardo turned back to the window and lifted the binoculars, "This is too big to pull in any small favors Lorenzo owes me. He wants to make a big name for himself and solving this case and busting a big drug network would ensure his promotion back to Rome."

"He doesn't have enough information to bust us although it would be a blessing if he were called back to Rome. Things would go back to normal. But I'm sure he told the *Guardia* in Rome what he's planning, so a big-time failure will knock him down too. It might be enough to have him demoted and out of our hair."

Riccardo nodded and said, "Normal would be nice—like it was before Stella caused all this mess. Lorenzo is okay, you know."

Silence reigned until there's a cough, "Are you getting in too deep with Lorenzo? Your job is to take him down. If it hadn't been for that stupid bitch, we'd have nailed him. She got in the way when she decided it was her civic duty to spill her guts. If Stella had lived, she would have testified. It would have taken us years to recover. Killing her was the only answer. She may have told Lorenzo what she suspected, but I'm pretty sure she didn't give him the documents. That means they're hidden somewhere."

"I tore the house apart. There was nothing there."

"Then start following the red-head. We need to find it before she does. She's always snooping. With the case reopened, you need to tread carefully. I would hate for Lorenzo to find out you killed Stella."

Riccardo shifted uneasily and said, "Killing her was what you told me to do. I don't need another murder hanging over my head. It's too soon."

"Then maybe you ought to contact Lorenzo. Find out exactly what he knows."

Riccardo grunted, "What do you suggest I discuss with Lorenzo? If Stella's body turns up or if that girl uncovers anything else, it will lead to us."

"Nothing is going to lead to us," *il padrone* growled. He stood and strode across the room. He grabbed the front of Riccardo's shirt and jerked until their foreheads bumped. "Do not screw this up. If Stella's body hasn't turned up after all this time, it's not going to. Make sure the girl quits snooping around in dangerous places. She could get hurt. She could stumble and fall into one of those sea holes. Nobody would find her, would they?"

"You want me to get rid of her?" Riccardo's beady eyes widened.

"I'm saying stay close. You'll know what to do and when."

Riccardo grunted and returned to scanning the hillside until Cat disappeared from view.

CAT & CARLO

The long, hot shower paints the world nice again. The lime green skirt flares over my head settling around my waist. I pull on a white V-neck sweater and twist a green and turquoise silk scarf around my throat—a steal at the market for five euros. Even my squirrelly hair is behaving today. I push silver loops in my earlobes as a shiver of anticipation crawls down my spine. It has been a while since I've felt like making myself presentable. It's not a date, but still.

I peer into the mirror for a last check. Stella's pale face gazes back at me. Sweat gathers in my armpits. My heartbeat rumbles in my ears. My eyes snap shut. I breathe deep, sucking in air until my courage returns. When I open my eyes, I'm alone with only my reflection.

I sink onto the bed. Is Stella warning me to stay away from Carlo? Why? Gino and Maria insist Carlo is trustworthy. But it could be Antonio or Lorenzo, particularly Lorenzo as the blind spot I have about him could lead me in the wrong direction.

A sudden chill enters the room, moving the hairs on the back of my neck. It takes a few minutes for me to regain my composure. I glance at the time. Carlo will arrive in a few minutes. I open the door and count as I drift down the steps. His car pulls up, and I slip out the gate.

"Wow, you look spectacular," he blurts out.

Blushing like a thirteen-year old, I say, "Grazie Carlo, you're looking smart yourself."

He has the good graces to blush as well. My eyes take in charcoal gray slacks, navy blazer, and an immaculate white shirt with enough buttons open for me to quickly shift my gaze to the ground. That gives us both time to regroup into our adult selves.

"How are you today? Did it take long at the station last night?"

"Yes, it did. I'm not exactly good company as I didn't get much sleep. But I'm hungry. Let's wait to discuss last night over lunch. Or, we can keep standing in the middle of the road."

"Sorry," he says as he approaches the passenger side of the car and opens the door.

"What? We're not walking?"

"*Allora*, if you're tired, wouldn't driving be better?"

"No, the walk will do me good."

He asks me about Gino and Maria, but I stop him with a gentle reminder and a change of subject, "Please, we agreed to wait. I'm glad you chose La Canzone. I've stopped by several times, but it's always closed. I haven't met the owner yet. Signor Piestrada, isn't it?"

"Yes, Giorgione is a great guy. You'll love working for him. When I called for reservations, I told him you were my guest. He was delighted. He said he had meant to call you, but he's been busy renovating the restaurant. He usually closes in January and sometimes February so he can freshen the place up before the new season starts. But whenever the weather cooperates, he opens the doors."

By the time we reach the restaurant, we've settled into an easy banter. The restaurant is a shock as Carlo leads me into a tiny foyer. The interior is dark and cramped. How can I possibly work here? There aren't enough tables to produce an income for one chef, much less two, not to mention the owner, the wait staff, and the miscellaneous kitchen staff. Carlo gently nudges me from behind. My feet move forward.

A small L-shaped bar is the focus of the room. It's empty except for one man bending the bartender's ear. His back is to me, but the restlessness of his hands draws my attention. Long, pale fingers with nails a little too long and dirty, systematically twist a shot glass in circles.

I must have stopped again as Carlo gently touches my back and asks if I'm okay. The man's thick neck and bulky shoulders shift in my direction. A brief glimpse of his face reveals dark, beady eyes that look through me. Carlo instinctively senses my unease. He glances at the man, puts his arm around my shoulders, and leads me across the room. He holds a beaded curtain aside and a spacious terrace spreads out in front of me.

White tablecloths gleam against chairs with grass-colored cushions. After so many days of gloom, the brilliant sunlight gives the illusion of tables floating under fire-red umbrellas that tilt lazily in the light afternoon breeze. Clear plastic panels enclose the seating area except in front where the terrace spills into the sea.

"Is this okay?"

"It's beautiful. I had no idea there was a huge deck with outside seating. It's perfect."

Carlo pulls out the chair facing the sea and lightly touches my elbow as he guides me onto the cushioned seat.

"I asked Giorgione for the best table. Practically every special moment in Castello del Mare takes place here: proposals, anniversaries, birthdays, and birth announcements. The entire town comes here to celebrate."

"What are we celebrating?" I smile, delighted with Carlo's explanation.

"What, oh, ah, I didn't mean we're celebrating anything. It's just nice that you'll be working here."

He pauses, trying to collect his thoughts before adding, "But yes, we could celebrate. Yes, of course, we are celebrating," he stutters, trying to salvage the conversation. "You have a new job and a new life in Castello."

He's saved from further explanation by a short rotund man bobbling to our table. He embraces Carlo and turns to me in a full bear-hug stance. When I finally break away, Carlo says, "Cat, this is Signore Giorgio Piestrada, the owner and your soon-to-be boss."

"Call me Giorgione. Big George. I should put an apron on you now and whisk you to the kitchen. I didn't realize we would be so busy."

My clenched jaw betrays me because he laughs and says, "I'm joking. Today you enjoy, but I would like you to come in next week just to show you around. But tell me, why is your hand bandaged?"

I settle back into my chair before saying, "I took a spill which required a few stitches. They're coming out soon. I'm fine, and it won't prevent me from working."

Giorgione's shoulders tensed when I started. As soon as say I'm fine, he relaxes. I can't help but continue, "Although, you might not want me to come in early or ever. I'm a bit of a klutz. I actually tumbled down a cliff while trying to pick wildflowers."

He roars with laughter, his large belly jiggling, "Oh, you'll fit right in. One of us always has a body part bandaged. But what is more important is that you would risk your life for flowers. Can you arrange them? My wife usually does the centerpieces for the restaurant, but she will be visiting our daughter and grandkids over Easter. Could you help out?"

"Of course, I'll come in next week and help with whatever you need."

Carlo chimes in, "Okay, you two, that's enough shop talk. Giorgione, we'd like a carafe of your house white wine and a seafood antipasti. Cat needs to taste the best food in Puglia."

Over a continuous stream of seafood swimming in a lemony, garlicky olive oil, I bring Carlo up to date. His face twists in concern as I explain finding the necklace only for it to be stolen from the villa while I was sleeping. I continue with last night's visit to the police station. I hold back on the horrible scare my first day in town, the subsequent choking scene in the piazza, and the dead bird on the gate. I unknowingly shiver, longing to know who in this town can be trusted.

"What's wrong?" Carlo asks as he reaches across the table, placing his hand on mine.

The gesture startles me. His fingers are cool. His touch gentle. He lightly squeezes my hand before releasing it.

"I'm upset because Lorenzo thinks Gino stole the necklace. Tell me what you think. How long have they worked for you? Do you trust them?"

"They have worked for me for over ten years. Of course, I trust them. There were some minor adjustments when I first hired them, but overall, I'm satisfied. There has never been a complaint from a single guest. And once Stella took up permanent residence, she asked them to stay on. They take care of the villa for her, and they look after my other rentals in town. They're as fiercely loyal to her as they are to me."

"What kind of adjustments are you talking about?"

"Gino has a minor record, nothing to worry about. Initially, there were a couple of times when he mismanaged funds for the villa, but we worked it out. Maria has always been dependable. They both grew up around here and have family scattered in the countryside. I provide them with a bank account so they don't have to ask for money for maintenance and supplies. It works well for all of us."

"Lorenzo thinks they're involved—or at least he's suspicious of Gino," I say as I manipulate a slice of olive-studded bread to mop up the last little bit of garlicky sauce.

"It is strange that the necklace was stolen immediately after you found it. Who knew you had it?"

"Unless someone saw me on the cliff, and I'm not ruling that out, the list is short. Antonio knew, maybe his nurse Sylvia. Although I'm not sure she was in the room when I gave Antonio the necklace. But he could have told her. There's Gino and Maria. If Maria did find the necklace, she would tell Gino. But what would they want with it? The last name on the list is Lorenzo. Antonio told Lorenzo I had the necklace. Any thoughts?"

Carlo scrutinizes me across the table before saying, "It worries me that someone came into the house and stole the necklace while you were sleeping. Why don't I have the locks changed? I'll talk to Gino and Maria although it's hard for me to believe they would steal it."

"Oh, no, please don't talk to them. If they think I don't trust them, it will create issues for all of us and for you. It's better if I smooth this over and go on as usual. They've been great since my arrival. I'm sure it will all be cleared up. It's just that things are a mess right now. I didn't mean to involve you, but I thought you should know."

"Of course, and I would rather hear it from you than Lorenzo. He'll be contacting me, and thanks to you I'll be prepared. What concerns me is your safety. If you are uncomfortable with Maria and Gino, I can replace them. It might take a few days, but."

"No, they're wonderful, and they love Stella. Since I'm Stella's best friend, they wouldn't hurt me. I'm sure they aren't involved. Let's wait and see what happens. I'll be more mindful of my surroundings. If they are involved, maybe they did it for someone else."

We sip our wine and watch the waves lap at the steps to the terrace. The day is gorgeous, the food spectacular, and there's an interesting and handsome guy right next to me. The subject we are discussing doesn't leave room for light conversation. Before I can figure out how to change the subject, Carlo resumes.

"There's always the mafia and the drug connection. In this small town, everyone knew Stella had problems with drugs. Perhaps the necklace was stolen to pay a debt. Do you have reason to think that either Antonio or Lorenzo were involved in Stella's disappearance or perhaps the disappearance of the necklace? Do you think Stella was involved with the mafia? Maybe she knew too much."

Clouds pass over the sun, blotting out light and heat. "What makes you ask these questions?

Carlo hesitates half a second then says, "Antonio has been withdrawn since Stella's disappearance. Maybe you heard that he and Stella had a fight shortly before her disappearance, something to do with drugs. The village gossip says Antonio was her supplier. He's a good doctor and a friend. I hope he isn't involved. But my fear is he may be. Whatever Stella asked him for, he gave her. The only exception to that is if it endangered his practice enough for him to lose his license. If that happened, then I'm not sure what he would be capable of doing. His practice is his life."

After a long pause, he continues, "What I can't figure out is why he didn't keep the necklace? Why did he give it back to you?"

"Why not? It makes perfect sense. He was leaving for Gallipoli for the weekend. He knew Lorenzo would want the necklace right away. When he couldn't reach Lorenzo, he gave the necklace to me for safekeeping until Lorenzo picked it up the next day. It was logical."

Creases pucker across Carlo's forehead as he concentrates, "And Lorenzo? What happened when he discovered you didn't have the necklace?"

"He wasn't pleased. Actually, he was angry, really angry."

"Does Lorenzo think Gino stole the necklace? What did he say after talking to Gino?"

"He wouldn't tell me anything. Why don't you talk to him? Aren't you colleagues and friends?"

"The three of us work together sometimes, but we are more colleagues than friends. You may have noticed last night that Lorenzo and I aren't on the best terms. Stella's disappearance and the ongoing investigation have him on edge. I'm closer to Antonio. I've known him ever since he came to the region. He bought his house from me. That's why I was invited to the wedding. I met Lorenzo at the wedding, the same time I met you."

He smiles, takes another sip of wine and squints as the sun swings higher. "Lorenzo is a no-nonsense kind of guy when it comes to cracking down on crime around here. He's put quite a few behind bars which means he has a lot of enemies. But he also has friends. Breaking up some of the protection rings has given many small business owners breathing room. Giorgione is one of his biggest fans. Lorenzo's first assignment after he came to town was to ensure that the small business owners no longer had to pay the mafia for protection. As a result Giorgione's restaurant has become profitable. If anything is going down, Giorgione would know. He would tell Lorenzo."

"What else do I need to know about the Commissario?"

"Well, he's a bit eccentric."

"Eccentric? In what way?"

"He owns a small villa and citrus grove in Leuca. He doesn't follow soccer, and he loves to cook. Not exactly a standard Italian man."

"Hmmm," is all I say before Giorgione waddles toward our table with another platter.

"*Polpo fritto*," he hums as a grin as wide as his body embraces us.

"*Oh, sono piena*," I whimper.

Carlo laughs, "You can't be full. There are more courses waiting for us."

I surrender to a fragrant stack of delicately fried octopus, tender slivers barely dusted with fine bread crumbs and plunged into shimmering oil for a few seconds. Lightly browned and crispy, the aroma invites me to attack the food as if it's the first I've eaten in days.

A palate-cleansing salad of fennel, orange, and arugula follows. But it's the breathtaking dessert that makes me forget all of the splendid food that came before. A golden orb arrives. It's centered on a pure white plate dusted with cocoa and a sprig of mint.

"What is it?" I ask Carlo.

"It's the speciality of the house, and the best version of tiramisu you'll ever taste. Break it open," he says with a wicked grin.

I push my spoon through the fragile cake shell. Thick globs of pastry cream, caramel and chocolate ooze onto the plate. My spoon collects a portion of cake along with scoops of pastry cream, caramel, and chocolate. All land in my mouth simultaneously.

When I can breathe again, I say, "If I don't do anything else during the time I work here, I'll learn how to make this."

Carlo leans across the table and whispers, "If you do, I'll marry you."

Our laughter slides out to sea as we consume the remains of the tiramisu. Not another word is spoken until our spoons scrap the last bit of goodness off the plate.

CAT & CARLO

Before we leave the restaurant, Giorgione stops by our table, "Come in Friday if you can. I'll show you around and introduce you to the staff."

He laughs warmly. "Now I have to warn you about Chef Sebastian. He's a bit temperamental, but you'll get used to him. He's loud and quick to lose his temper. But his heart is kind and his food is exquisite. Maybe you've noticed?"

"Noticed? It was perfect!. Every single bite tells me he's an exceptional chef. I'm grateful for this opportunity. I won't give him any trouble, and I'll do anything to learn how to create this tiramisu."

"That's something you'll have to discuss with him. It's rare to find an executive chef who is also a skilled pastry chef. Don't let him overstep his authority. He'll try to bully you but give it right back to him."

He hands me a sheet of paper and says, "Here's a rough schedule. You take the lunch shift and the smaller catered events. Sebastian will be in charge of dinner and large events. We'll try this for a few weeks. *Va bene*?"

"Yes, of course. I don't have any obligations. If Sebastian needs help in the evening or for the larger events, I can assist him."

"*A venerdì*," Giorgione says before waddling off to the next table.

A quick espresso for Carlo, then a wave at Giorgione as we leave the terrace. A crowd has gathered in the bar. I search the faces, but the man with the dark, penetrating eyes is not there. Relief follows me out the door.

"Do you still want to go with me to San Cataldo? If you're too tired, we can go another time. Cat, is something wrong? Cat?"

"What? Sorry. What did you say? I was just thinking about that grand lunch and must have drifted off."

We're almost back at the villa. I don't remember the walk or the conversation. The man in the bar was consuming all my thoughts. I'm sure Carlo saw him, but he didn't say anything. The way that man looked at me was evil, as if he had some personal vendetta against me. I shiver.

Carlo takes my hand and faces me, "Look, we don't have to drive to San Cataldo today. You're tired and distracted. Between your party and the late-night visit to the police station, it can wait."

"Oh, no. It's a beautiful day with no rain for the moment. I want to go."

I am exhausted and that man in the bar really frightened me. But I don't want to be alone today. The question is on the tip of my tongue to ask about the man, but the moment passes. Carlo opens the car door. I slide into the seat. The warmth from the sun penetrates the windshield and radiates its energy into my tired body.

"Are you alright?" Carlo asks again.

"Yes, really I am."

"Good. I have a surprise for you."

His face lights up like a kid's at Christmas.

"What?"

He reaches in the back seat and hands me a red bag embossed with gold lettering: *Amedei*.

"Oh my gosh," I exclaim. "Where did you get this?"

I tear into the bag without waiting for an answer. Inside are six bars: Toscano Nut Brown, Toscano Red, Acero 95, Blanco de Criollo, Toscano Black 63, and Porcelana.

"Carlo?"

"*Si*," he says, looking at me with pure pleasure. "As a chocolate connoisseur, you deserve the best."

The deep, rich aroma of cocoa fills the car and saturates my pores. I can't speak. I know how expensive this chocolate is.

"Grazie mille. Thanking you a thousand times isn't enough," I say, smiling with delight.

He touches me lightly on the cheek and says, "A gift from one connoisseur to another."

He puts the car in gear. We leave Castello behind.

CAT & CARLO

SAN CATALDO, ITALY

Forty-five minutes later we are in the foyer of his villa. The elegant surroundings are calm, soothing. The sea gleams emerald, touched with white froth. The view of the Adriatic is reminiscent of Botticelli's *Birth of Venus*. Floor-to-ceiling French doors wrap around three sides, enticing the outside world to come in.

In the late afternoon sun, Carlo's eyes search my face as I survey the luxurious white sofa with pillows in shades of soft greens and blues. The Murano chandelier glows as the sun flicks rainbows across the glass prisms, dangling with tiny starfish.

"Why starfish?" I ask.

Carlo joins me under the chandelier. "It was the designer's idea. I didn't realize at the time how strange and sad that seems now. It has nothing to do with Stella."

"Did she ever see it?"

"No, of course not. Stella and I aren't friends."

When I don't respond, he asks, "Does that sound harsh?"

Instead of answering, I say, "There's a similar but smaller chandelier like this at the villa. Why?"

He pauses for a second before answering, "I owned the villa before Stella bought it. I liked the design. It's in several of my properties. Surely you don't think I was involved with Stella? I didn't know her or socialize with her except when we happened to attend the same functions, which was not that often. I live in Lecce, not Castello. Whenever I take time off, I come to San Cataldo."

"You don't seem smitten with Stella like everyone else is. Why is that?"

"I believe when two people commit to each other, it's permanent. There's no room for experimentation with other partners. It was humiliating for Antonio."

"Did you ever think that Antonio might not have been an ideal partner?"

"Yes, I considered that, but marriage, particularly in Italy, is for a lifetime. You're so loyal to Stella, but she wasn't faithful to Antonio."

He hesitates, his eyes lock on the sea.

"Stella even flirted with me. To her, I would be another conquest —just another publicity stunt. She was angry when I didn't succumb. She was quick to run to Antonio and Lorenzo and tell them lies about me. She did everything to close down our business relationship."

He stops speaking and the silence drags out. Finally, he says, "I'm sorry. It wasn't my intention to tell you any of this, but it's important you understand the situation. Surely you don't approve of her behavior."

We're standing next to an alabaster reproduction of the Roman goddess Diana, the huntress. She's the focal point of the room with her bow and arrow aimed toward the sea. Her haughty expression reminds me of Stella. There's great strength and great sadness.

When I don't respond, Carlo says, "I'm sorry. I know Stella was—is your best friend, but I'm still angry about her accusations. It took great effort on my part to convince Antonio and Lorenzo that she was lying. The camaraderie and trust the three of us had developed was broken and suspicion took root. Our partnership suffered because of her."

"Okay," I shrug, "now I know how you feel about Stella."

He reaches for me and pulls me close. "You need to hear the truth. The Stella you know and the Stella I know are two different people. The drugs created a volatile, unstable personality. The thing is, you're a loyal friend. The friendship you and Stella had—have is unique. Stella is sacred to you."

He releases me, touches my hair lightly and then walks across the room. The white marble fireplace jumps to life when he presses a button and Andrea Bocelli's voice floats across the blue-gray marble floor. The music crescendos in time with the waves crashing against the stone wall below the terrace.

O Mare e Tu—The Sea and You. The words capture the essence of my friendship with Stella.

In your eyes a watery mirror to steer life through the dreams and the pain without even a farewell.

The pain and sorrow of losing Stella haunt me as we stroll on the beach. Carlo senses my mood. He fills in my silence with stories of the area and speaks about the importance of Blue Flag beaches.

As I relax in his presence, I share my story about the red starfish that scuttled across my feet. He speaks about the ocean's ecosystem and the role of the starfish—both predator and prey and the balance necessary for the ocean to prosper.

I weave the magical story of how starfish were created—how one night the sky overflowed with stars. They hung so low that their arms touched the waves. The water felt so remarkable that many of the stars let go of the sky and began a new life in the sea. He smiles. His lips brush against my hair.

When he holds my hand to guide me over some boulders, he doesn't let go. When I don't protest, he tucks my hand in his arm. The rhythm of our bodies synchronizes. We walk without speaking. When we reach the main piazza, he points out the best bars, cafes, and restaurants. Everyone knows him. We are offered espresso, wine, or bitters wherever we go.

"What do you think?" he asks when we return to the villa.

"Carlo, it's wonderful but when do you have a chance to use it?"

"Not as often as I'd like."

He opens a drawer in the early 19th century burled walnut sideboard in the foyer. "Here's a key. I want you to use the villa whenever you want."

"What? No! No! I couldn't."

"Look, Cat. It's impossible for me to get here on a regular basis, maybe I use it one weekend a month. In August I take time off and hang out here, but it's empty the rest of the time. You'd be doing me a favor."

I'm not sure how to respond. I like him. He's easy to be with, but friendship is all I'm looking for. I don't want any complications during this year. I want to be free and on my own without considering anyone else.

"Cat, the place needs to be enjoyed. Restaurant work is hard. You'll need to get away. Keep the key. Think about it."

"Thank you, but my job will keep me too busy to use it."

Longing must be in my eyes because he nods and presses the key in my hand.

"Give me a call anytime you want to come. I'll let the housekeeper know you have a key. I promise it will be your time alone."

On the drive home the sunny day slips into gloomy. Rain follows us all the way back to Castello. Carlo's steady hand on the wheel, soft classical music, and the winding roads fade as I lean against the headrest. A gentle shake to my shoulder wakes me.

"We're here. It's raining pretty hard. Give me your key. I'll unlock the gate and the house. Back in a few minutes with an umbrella," he says, smiling and touching my face.

I gaze into the rain careening off the karstic rocks and tumbling down to the marina. I jump when Carlo's hand touches my arm.

"Gosh, sorry again. I didn't realize you had drifted off."

"It's okay. I'm exhausted."

I stretch and yawn before saying, "Thank you for such a perfect day. Lunch was superb, and your place in San Cataldo is magnificent."

"Cat, it was a beautiful day. Can I see you again, soon?"

I nod as he holds the umbrella over my head. We trudge in unison up the steps. Even in my drowsy state, I count. A fire blazes in the hearth. A bottle of wine and one glass are waiting on the table by the sofa. A pillow and blanket nestle nearby. He tucks me in and pours me a glass of wine.

"Would you like one too?" I ask.

"No, you rest. I'll call tomorrow."

I want to tell him I am petrified. But the moment passes. He tucks the blanket under my chin. The light touch of his kiss lingers on my lips as he softly closes the door.

CARLO

CASTELLO DEL MARE, ITALY

Carlo sat in the car outside of Stella's villa and considered staying another night on the chance he might see her again before he returned to Lecce. There was something about her—something that made him want to hang around. She was fierce and independent and yet so vulnerable, and she was so loyal to Stella. As far as he was concerned, Stella didn't deserve her loyalty.

His thoughts wandered back to those long-ago summers. He had not been included in their crowd. He could not afford to play their games. His family was poor, well below the poverty level. He spent most of his time scratching the land for a living. He had been so envious of the idle days the summer kids had spent playing in the sea. When he wasn't farming, he was fishing to put food on the table.

He shook his head. He didn't have room in his life for Cat—too bad because he felt drawn to her. He had spent years enduring well-meaning family, friends, and colleagues who were intent on forcing the entire female population on him—endless dinners of shy smiles and shallow conversations.

He had only been with Cat a few times but those times had been full of laughter and light. He imagined sitting across the table from her in his villa in San Cataldo. *What would it be like to wake up with that gorgeous wild hair spilling across his pillow?*

His lips curled in derision. No, it didn't matter what he wanted. There was no room in his life for anyone. He had made that decision years ago. The only thing he wanted now was to have the situation with Stella resolved. He wanted some sort of normalcy back in his life. He knew Antonio and Lorenzo did too. Stella's disappearance was creating colossal problems for all of them.

Carlo had first met the summer kids when he was hired to serve at the grand parties the rich families held on the beach. Of course, they wouldn't remember him. He'd left Castello at sixteen, hitched a ride to Bari and found a job as a dishwasher in a small restaurant. He had discarded his father's name and adopted his mother's. All connections to his father's family were cut off. They were all scoundrels, petty thieves, abusers, and pretty much worthless.

He had worked his way through university and law school with help from the restaurant owner. His first big break came when his father died, and he inherited an insignificant piece of property outside of Castello del Mare. Fortunately for him, a bit of the land bordered the sea. A wealthy German family saw the beach from their yacht. They made inquiries about the property and eventually landed on his doorstep with cash in hand. That had been his first land deal. It had been enough to start his property management business in Lecce.

The Germans hooked him up with other friends. His knowledge of the law and real estate gave him a lucrative income. He hung out with the most influential people in Lecce and throughout Puglia.

It was only by chance that he and Antonio had met. It had been one of those must-attend dismal functions. Stella, as an international movie star, had been the draw. Carlo had taken it as an omen that no one from his past recognized him. He made a point of introducing himself as Carlo Rossini, not letting on that he was from Castello. He was ashamed of his poverty-stricken past and didn't want to be reminded of it. He and Antonio found themselves at the bar while everyone else hovered around Stella. Over drinks and conversation, they discovered common ground.

After that chance meeting, whenever Antonio had a conference or meeting in Lecce, he would call Carlo for lunch, a drink, or dinner. When Carlo was in Castello he always connected with Antonio. Over time, they became friends.

He had been invited to the wedding. That was when he had seen the grown-up Cat. From that moment on he had thought of her as *un arcobaleno di colori*—a rainbow of colors. He never thought he would see her again. But now that he had, it was difficult to quit thinking about her.

He had been brutally honest with Cat about Stella. He wondered if that had been the right thing to do. Sure, Stella could charm a cobra, but she had the same deadly venom. He had watched on the sidelines when the relationship between Lorenzo and Antonio disintegrated over her. Stella had tried to throw him into the mix, but he had not succumbed.

Although he has no room for a relationship in his life, he wanted to see Cat again. He called the hotel and reserved a room for another night. Before leaving, he opened the glovebox, and pulled out a pack of cigarettes he kept for whenever he felt the need. He took one from the pack and opened the car door. He hated smoking and the smell of it on his clothes, in his house, or in the car. He rarely smoked although it was an Italian pastime and a nasty habit he'd grown up with. If he smoked now, he'd have his clothes cleaned overnight. He toyed with the cigarette, asking himself why he needed one now. He stood for a long time looking at Stella's villa and wishing he was inside with Cat. He dropped the cigarette and ground it into the sandy soil.

CAT & LORENZO

He watched her sleep, the easy rhythm of her breath, the full curve of her body through the sheets. Her red curls splashed in the moonlight sending sparks of fire across the pillow. He could kill her now. Get it over with. If only she hadn't found the necklace. But she had. Now he had to find out what happened to it. It belonged to him. Eventually she would lead him to it. Too bad she would be destroyed once it was found.

I dream—heavy sluggish dreams full of blackness. Dreams where hands clamp down on my mouth. A body straddles me, pressing my head into water. Struggling, I fight back, pushing and shoving against the powerful force. My bound legs flounder uselessly. A hand fastens around my throat. I howl in pain but no sound emerges from my paralyzed vocal cords. With my last breath, I beat and claw at the arms holding me down. For a second the hands loosen. I gasp for air and scream and scream until I wake myself.

My body quavers as I twist in sheets coated with sweat. It takes time for my mind to turn away from the nightmare. I curl into a shivering fetal position until the fear subsides. A breeze teases the shutters. Fog drifts across the terrace and creeps softly into the room.

I throw back the soggy sheet and slide out of bed. The terracotta floor is cold and damp. To stop the trembling, I stay in the shower a long time—letting my fears seep into the drain.

As I dress, I notice a fresh pile of laundry neatly stacked on the chair. Maria must have done the laundry and tidied up the house yesterday while I was with Carlo. I pull my frizzy curls into a knot on the back of my neck before walking into the kitchen. A box of pastries rests on the kitchen table which means Maria has been here while I was sleeping. Trying to sort through my feelings about them has been difficult.

Do I trust them? Yes, I do, particularly Maria. If I ask for the key back, it would create anger and suspicion and fracture our relationship. Maria trusted me enough to give me Stella's ceramic box. If I'm going to find out anything about Stella, I need them. They know everything and everyone in this town. They will help me. They loved Stella too.

I pour a glass of my favorite orange, lemon, and carrot juice and wander out to the terrace. The fog has thickened, drifting around the table and chairs. A black lump lies on the table. Nothing was on the table when I came home last night. Even if I didn't notice, Carlo would have.

Frowning, I lean over the chair and start to pick it up. I jerk my hand away. A black leather glove lies in the center of the table. The fingers are stiffly curled into a gnarly claw. In its grasp is a single black rose. A smear of red paint across the table spells out *Omertà*. I clutch the back of the chair. Stay calm, don't scream. Think!

The doorbell chimes. My mind is frozen. I automatically release the gate before checking to see who it is. I back away as footsteps trudge up the sixty-eight steps. A strangled cry of relief escapes from my mouth when the top of Lorenzo's head comes into view. He blends into the fog with his dark jeans and a dove gray turtleneck.

Buongiorno, he says. "A messy day, *no*? It will be an hour or so before the fog burns off. Are you up to some coffee and conversation?"

I shake my head, pointing at the table.

His smile disappears, "What the...? When did you find it? Did you touch it?"

"Just before you rang the bell. No, I didn't touch it. What is it? What does it mean?"

Lorenzo moves close enough to touch my arm before saying, "Before I leave, I will arrange for a guard around the clock."

"No, please. I don't want to be incarcerated."

"Would you rather be dead?"

I shake my head.

"I'm not giving you a choice, Cat. Do you understand how serious this is? Someone is threatening you. The same someone who threatened Stella."

"How do you know it's the same person?"

"Stella received the same messages you are now receiving—*Omertà* is the code word the mafia uses. It's telling you to go home or you will be silenced."

"A black rose and a dead bird were left for her too? And, this horrible word—*Omertà*?"

"Yes, then she disappeared. I can't let that happen to you. If I had taken Stella seriously, she would still be alive."

"Are you saying she's dead?"

He takes my arm and gently propels me into the house. "Make some coffee. I'll take care of what's on the table."

In the kitchen I tap in the dark aromatic coffee, pour water into the bottom of the espresso pot, twist on the top, and place it on the back burner. Mindless activities I can accomplish while counting and not thinking. While I wait for the espresso to perk, I pop in a pod and push the button on the cappuccino maker. I count as the steaming purr of rich coffee drips into my cup followed by layers of milky froth, forming creamy waves.

Although it's closer to lunch time, the pastries are here. I pile a plate with lemon, chocolate, and almond-studded *coronetti* and walk back into the living area.

A fire blazes in the hearth. Lorenzo dusts his hands on his jeans as he rises. I put the coffee and *cornetti* on the table. We sink side-by-side onto the sofa.

"Cat, you're not familiar with the way things work here. The mafia still has a stronghold in this area. To them you are a weak link—a nuisance—something that needs to be disposed of once they get what they need from you. There is a long history, actually since the 16th century, of *omertà*. It's a threat—the code of silence. It's used to scare people so they won't cooperate with the authorities. If you are fingered as breaking the code of silence, as Stella was, your life is in jeopardy."

This would be the right time to tell Lorenzo about the ballet slipper, the ceramic box, and the clues, but I don't. My mind is full of words telling me Stella is dead and this new word— *omertà*.

"I'm so sorry Cat. This whole thing with Stella is bizarre. Please tell me what you know, and don't hold anything back from me. You have been, haven't you?"

Warmth creeps up my throat. I'm thankful for the turtleneck pullover. When I don't respond, he continues.

"I've been running some background checks since we last talked. Gino has a record— petty theft, small items, that kind of thing. He's been clean for years. Yet, I'm sure he took the necklace. What I can't figure out is why? Any thoughts?"

"Maybe to protect me. He didn't murder Stella. He wouldn't do that."

"I'm not ruling anyone out."

"But who would gain the most if Stella disappeared? What was she involved in that created this situation in the first place?"

Anger, pain, and sadness flit across Lorenzo's face. He pushes up from the sofa and crosses to the fireplace. He leans his arms on the mantle with his back to me.

"Stella was thrown into the glitzy Hollywood lifestyle when she was too young to make the best choices for herself. A big part of that lifestyle was drugs. Stella was hooked early. It became a huge problem when she turned to the mafia to buy her drugs. When she decided to break her habit, they were unhappy. They tried to recruit her. Initially, she dangled the possibility in front of them that she might. She thought that would give her enough time to collect information and report them. Somehow the mafia discovered what she was doing. That's when she received the *omertà*—just like the one you received."

"Did Stella tell you all this?" I ask.

"Yes."

"Why didn't you protect her?"

"I tried. But, you know Stella. In fact, just like you, she refused my protection. She did tell me that if she went to the police, Antonio would be the one to suffer. His license would be revoked, and he would never practice again. As difficult as Stella could be, she knew if Antonio lost his practice, it would kill him. Her plan was to go through the backdoor, find the ringleaders and concrete evidence before she decided what to do. But these people are killers. They demanded her compliance, more money, and also her necklace. She thought that asking for the necklace was a way to humiliate her and to keep her under control."

"But I found the necklace. What you're saying doesn't make sense."

"Cat, as far as I can figure out, you were not supposed to find the necklace. No one was, but something went wrong. Somehow Stella was able to remove the necklace and discard it. Whoever killed her either didn't see her take it off, or maybe they thought she didn't wear it to the photo shoot. It's hard to say.

"Somehow they found out she knew about the drugs coming into this area, but even I don't know if she actually fingered *il padrone.* That was her goal. Spying on the drug ring made her a huge liability. These people do not fool around. That's why she's dead."

A tear escapes from my eye and rolls down my cheek. It plops on the front of my sweater. Another follows.

Lorenzo walks the short distance to the sofa and drops next to me, his eyes dark with sorrow, "I saw Stella shortly before she disappeared. Although I had pushed her out of my life and she was really angry with me, she told me you were coming to stay with her. She was excited and said you would support her through recovery. That's all I wanted for her. Whatever dreams she and I had about a life together had died. I still love her just as you do, but it's based on the bond we all formed during our childhood summers. Stella was right that she had a chance with you here.

"The second thing she told me was she had enough information and photos. She said she was sending it all to Rome because she no longer trusted me. Then she disappeared."

I don't respond as Lorenzo could easily be the person who killed Stella. What if he thought the information she had implicated him? I'm confused, conflicted, and no closer to discovering who's behind her murder.

Lorenzo's eyes hold mine. The frustration there tells me he'd like to shake out of me whatever information he thinks I'm holding back.

Instead, he says, "You know something, don't you. Your eyes say so. If we're ever going to find out what happened to Stella and if I'm going to keep you safe, you have to trust me. What aren't you telling me?"

"Not much. My trip to Italy was all organized well before Stella called me and asked me to stay with her. She's the only reason I came to Castello to work at La Canzone del Mare. Stella arranged that part of my stay. She said she wanted me here as she needed my help. I wasn't surprised. She had hinted that her drug problem was more involved than she had let on. I knew she was separated from Antonio. Nothing else."

"So you changed your plans for Stella."

"Yes, I did. All my life I've been at her beck and call. She wanted to enter an intensive drug rehabilitation program, and she wanted me to be with her. I rearranged my trip to come here instead of Rome. Of course, Stella had already canceled me from the wait-list for a place in Rome and arranged my life before she told me why."

Lorenzo stares at me for a long time. He reaches for my hand and holds it firmly in his.

"Stella was like that. We all did what she wanted. I changed my plans for her too, until one day I realized it wasn't a healthy relationship. But what happened after you changed your plans for her?"

"Shortly after that last conversation, she stopped calling. I wasn't worried as that's often the case with Stella. There was always an unscheduled photo shoot or an unexpected interview. We had planned to talk before I left, but instead I found that dreadful message from her on my phone."

I pause but he doesn't comment, "That's the message you heard. That's when I called Antonio. You pretty much know the rest. Initially, I wasn't worried. Not until I found the necklace. I couldn't understand why you didn't find the necklace. That's why I went back to search. I left a message, but you didn't return my call. Is that why you're here?"

He stands, "You think I don't know how to do my job?"

"That's not what I think."

"Then tell me."

"Look," I say, slowing my words to appear calm, "I thought I could help. Maybe see or hear something. I couldn't sit around hoping Stella would return, and you haven't been exactly helpful."

"Well, do you think you might be better at investigating than I am? Is that it? Do you realize you could be killed? One bullet to that pretty head of yours while you are snooping around and that would be the end. What in the hell are you playing at?" he says as he turns to me. His face inches from mine. Our breathing patterns synchronize as we lock eyes.

"This isn't a game, Cat. I returned your call—more than once but you were occupied yesterday. I guess being with Carlo is more important to you. More important than finding Stella."

Blood rushes to my face as I say, "You're spying on me? Is that what you did to Stella? What are you worried about, Lorenzo? Was Stella seeing Carlo too?"

His eyes turn from dark blue to black. He abruptly stands knocking over a coffee cup. We both grab for it before he jerks it out of my hand. He fights for control of his emotions before saying, "You could get killed poking around. How in the hell do you think I can do my job? Yes, I'm watching you. I took my eyes off Stella for twenty-four hours and she's dead. Do you want to join her?"

The question is mean and anger boils up in my throat. Screaming comes to mind but Lorenzo might haul me off to an institution.

I take a breath and change the subject, "You think that the mafia killed Stella, don't you?"

"Cat, you are not part of this investigation. Do you understand? The only thing I need from you is any information you have that would help me find Stella or at least find out what happened to her."

I weigh my options and decide to tell him a little of what I know and see how he responds.

"I did find something when I went back to the site early yesterday."

"You what?"

"That's why I called you. I found something."

"And you were going to tell me exactly when?"

"Lorenzo, I don't know whether or not I can trust you or anyone else who might be involved in Stella's disappearance. "

"Save it, Cat. Tell me what you found."

Anger washes across his face, showing lines I hadn't seen before.

"I went back to take photos of the area. Near the edge of the cliff the camera picked up something wedged between the boulders about halfway down the slope. I couldn't reach it, so I zoomed in to capture whatever it was. It could belong to anyone, but I think it's a clue. Let me get my camera."

I start to leave the room, but he grabs my arm.

"What else haven't you told me?"

"What?"

I jerk my arm free. "That's all."

"Are you sure you don't have the necklace? Maybe that's part of your little game too."

"Lorenzo, you are right, it's inappropriate of me to interfere with your investigation. I will give you the photos but there is nothing else."

"Give me your phone."

"Why?"

"Give me your damn phone, Cat. These people have already figured out you're involved and that you are the reason the investigation has become a priority. You're in trouble. In far more trouble than a dead bird and a black rose. They are watching you. I'm putting a guard on the villa 24/7. The reason I want your phone is to list my cell number in your emergency contacts. All you have to do is hit *5 and I will answer. Okay?"

"Whatever you say Commissario," I sneer as I hand him my phone and walk down the hall toward the bedroom for the camera.

CAT & LORENZO

Lorenzo paces back and forth in front of the fireplace. His steps are slow and tired. There's a weariness in his eyes and his body pulls in on itself. I watch fatigue etch his face and wish I could ease his pain. Instead, I glance at the time. It's well past lunchtime and neither of us has touched the pastries. I hand him the camera, pick up our coffee mugs and the plate of cornetti, and return to the kitchen.

The fridge is full of good things. I scrounge until I find enough to fill a platter with salumi, cheese, olives, roasted peppers, and crusty bread. I grab a bottle of Primitivo and two glasses with my free hand. Lorenzo has moved outside to the terrace. He studies the photos, and then calls the station to assign a team of investigators to return to the location. The scowl on his face reveals how furious he is. I can't blame him as it does seem strange that both the necklace and the shoe were missed by the *Guardia*.

We sit apart from each other and gaze at the horizon. My eyes focus on the lone tree. I long to transfer the ache of my grief into its sturdy trunk. Lorenzo scans the marina, always looking for clues. Our thoughts weave a different story.

"Did you kill her?"

"I might as well have. I was responsible for keeping her safe. I failed. It's complicated, and with the ongoing investigation it's sensitive. Here's what I can tell you."

He stretches his legs and shifts in his chair. I want to wrap my arms around him. I look away from his face, weary-with-fatigue and listen to his voice devoid of conviction.

"When Stella left Antonio, she came to me. I wasn't ready. I told her she needed to be on her own a while. She needed to resolve things with Antonio first. Either go back to him or make a clean break. She was shocked and angry. She knew I had always been in love with her, and she believed she could move into my life. It was simple for her, but Antonio was my best friend, and Stella had a drug problem—two huge roadblocks."

He pauses and picks up his empty wine glass. "Would you like a refill?"

I nod. He pours wine into our glasses. Instead of drinking, he swirls the glass and watches the subtle hues change color as the rays from the late afternoon sun brush across the horizon.

"I wanted her, more than anything. I waited years for her. Yet, I wasn't prepared for her to move in or for us to get involved until she had sorted out her life. She said Antonio had given her the drugs. At first, I didn't believe her and that hurt her. I asked for details, and she gave them to me. She swore she would stop the drugs if I would support her. I wanted her to come clean on her own. It's only in retrospect that I realize she wasn't capable. She physically needed me, and I said no."

He stops and stares. I wait, in no hurry to hear the end of Stella's life.

"It's funny when you want someone so badly. I had created a fantasy world for Stella and me to live in. I had never truly believed that it would happen. When it did, I was overwhelmed with my work. I didn't have the time or energy to give to Stella. She needed too much from me."

"What did she need?"

"She wanted all of me. She wanted me to push for a post in Rome. She wanted me to leave Castello and create a new life with her. She wanted me to stay with her through rehab, but I didn't have months to devote exclusively to her.

"If she had come to me a few years earlier, I would have done it. But now, my life is here. I don't want to leave. The day will come when I'm called back to Rome. I plan to say no. But that's another story.

"When I told her I couldn't take time off to help her, she said she would do it without me. That's when she asked you to stay with her. She had a place to live, her work, and Gino and Maria. With you here, I believe she would have made it. She had already put her plan in place and had been clean for a couple of months when she disappeared."

"Is that why she was killed? Because she was trying to break a habit?"

"That could be a small part of the reason. Dealers don't trust you not to talk when you come clean. But Stella had been spying on the smugglers and planned to turn them in. The only thing I could do was offer her protection. She said she would only consider protection if I was the one protecting her. Again, I failed her because I couldn't drop what I was doing to watch her twenty-four hours a day. Things were coming to a head with the SCU. I had no choice but to focus all my energy in that direction. I've done nothing for the past five years but make it a priority to clean up this area. That plan couldn't be jeopardized, not even by Stella.

"The last time I saw her, she was calmer and more centered. She told me she was scheduled for a photo shoot, and it would be the last for a while. She said you would arrive in a few weeks and would help her through rehabilitation. She was rational and reasonable. I truly believed everything was going to work out."

"What do you think happened?"

"I wish I knew. Maybe she pushed back against the mafia, or maybe she needed more drugs to get her through the photo shoot. She told me she was being leaned on. To me that meant her life was in danger, so I put a tail on her. It wasn't anything she would notice, but it was enough to ease my concern about her well-being.

"She told me about the photo shoot, but she didn't have a date, time, or location. In fact, she complained that it was not like Stefano to have his assistant call and make the arrangements. I was stupid not to pick up that something was wrong. But Stella wasn't concerned, so I didn't react. There was something I didn't understand. She told me that after the photo shoot, she wanted to meet with me. She said she had evidence that might interest me. She would not answer any of my questions. When I pushed, she said it could wait, and she would contact me in a few days.

"Things had been quiet with the SCU for a while. I had planned one last stake out before we busted the drug operation wide open. My informant told me something was going down. I needed everyone at the stakeout, so I pulled the two guys who were watching her. I was sure she would be safe for twenty-four hours. The problem was it coincided with the photo shoot. I didn't know that until we searched her house and found her calendar. I didn't realize I'd been set up."

"Were Antonio and Carlo with you at the stakeout?"

"Hell, no. They only assist in collecting information on the logistics and the players. They are never involved in the actual police work."

"Did anyone else know about her photo shoot or her intentions? Carlo maybe? Or what about Antonio? He's the most distraught, barely functioning."

"That is because he loved her the most."

"More than you?"

He moves his eyes over my face before saying, "You helped me be alone with Stella all those summers ago, why?"

"Oh Lorenzo, that was so long ago. It was a time when I still believed in fairy tales. You and Stella were magic. I saw it that day on the beach—the day we first met you and Antonio. He brought you along for extra courage. You and Stella locked eyes, and I knew you belonged together. Stella was my best friend which made it feel like a betrayal when I got a school-girl crush on you. I never told her. It was all a game to Stella, but when she needed my help to slip away with you, I couldn't refuse. Helping you was my childish idea of proving that I loved you both."

Lorenzo drops his head into his hands.

"Cat, I was incredibly naive back then. It's crazy when you fall in love the first time. I knew Stella loved me. I was sure she would choose me over Antonio. She wouldn't commit. When I asked why, she blamed her parents. Said they would worry if she spent too much time with me. They believed she was too young to be serious or to make major life decisions. Then little by little Antonio gained ground. Not with his passion, as he gave all of that to his studies. But with the picture he painted of how life with him would be. She craved attention as much as she craved drugs. Antonio lavished her with flowers, jewelry, first class flights, three-star Michelin restaurants, and his family connection to royalty was something Stella had dreamed about as her life. As beautiful as she was, she had no self-confidence. What Antonio offered her was a substitute. I couldn't offer her any of those things. And I didn't have faith that she would be happy with just a comfortable life."

"What are your reasons for ruling Antonio out as a suspect?"

"I didn't say I had. It's just unlikely. He's not violent. The night Stella stabbed him, she was trying to get a reaction of any kind from him. He could have easily killed her in self-defense and gotten off."

"And Carlo?"

"Carlo, as far as I know, never showed any personal interest in Stella. And you know Stella. That infuriated her. She flirted and suggested, but he never took the bait. Carlo keeps to himself. He rarely shows up anywhere with a date. When he does, he introduces them as friends of the family."

"That's strange. He's a good-looking man. Do you think he's gay?"

"My guess is he's more of a loner than anything else. He's one of a few local boys in Castello that made it big time. That doesn't happen often. Don't you remember him? He's from this area. I recognized him but quickly realized he didn't want to be recognized. Don't blame him. He came from a pretty rough environment. He escaped from his family and has done well. I've never mentioned it to him as I didn't want to embarrass him."

"Hmm, he doesn't look like anyone I remember. That was a long time ago, and there were a lot of kids. All I know about him is he's a property attorney. What does that mean exactly?"

"Ha, in Italy, and particularly in the south, that can mean almost anything. Carlo started small with a bit of family property in Castello. He was the oldest male, so he inherited a crumbling villa and a shrubby bit of land. But Carlo has the gift. People gravitate toward him. He sold the land for an outrageous price. That was his seed money. He knew every person in the surrounding area and began to sniff out families who desperately needed money. He would entice them to sell with dreams of finding work and living in the city for so much cheaper while he took the property off their hands. He would pay the back taxes and liens when necessary. He didn't tell the folks that the cheaper life in the city was a tiny apartment often without electricity and with crooked landlords who raised the rent the day after they moved in.

"When he made enough money, he moved to Lecce—lives in a palazzo in the main piazza and has a stunning villa in San Cataldo."

"Yes, I've seen the villa. He gave me a set of keys to use when I have time off from the restaurant."

Lorenzo glares at me but doesn't respond.

"You don't approve?"

"Who you see does not concern me."

"I'm not seeing him. We just drove to San Cataldo together so he could show me his place."

An icy silence hovers between us until Lorenzo says, "I need to get back to the station. By now, a guard should be stationed outside the gate. I'll check before I leave."

I want to say something to keep him from leaving, but I can't think of anything. He puts the cork back in the wine bottle and picks up our glasses and heads to the kitchen before I can stop him.

His footsteps echo throughout the house, hollow and rigid. We have all suffered because of our love for Stella.

CAT & ANTONIO

My appointment with Antonio was supposed to be a quick check on the wound and removal of the stitches. Sylvia was waiting for me with a smile tightly plastered on her face.

She nodded and said, "Follow me."

Dutifully slinking behind her, I left enough space to make it difficult to have a conversation. I was being childish, but the thought of Sylvia in bed with Antonio and Stella confronting them alone, burned me to the core.

Sylvia stops at an exam room door and stands aside. When I pass by her, she whispers, "I'm sorry."

Or, at least I think she did. But when I look up, the door is already closing. After a few minutes, Antonio enters with Sylvia trailing behind. He's a disheveled mess. Dark circles sag under his dull eyes, his shoulders slump forward. His gaze is vacant and his greeting listless. His face is a swallow tinge of yellowish-green. He checks the incision, declares it healed, and removes the stitches. Once that's accomplished, he dismisses Sylvia.

"How are you settling in? Do you have everything you need?"

"It's a lovely place, and I have everything I need. Thank you."

"When do you start at La Canzone?"

"Friday."

That depletes our small talk. It's so damn hard for me to be quiet. I don't have anything to say to Antonio, but I'm determined to wait him out. Finally, with a sharp intake of breath, he begins to speak, his voice a low droning sound.

He runs his hand through his already standing-on-end hair and shrugs. "Cat, I think you need to leave Castello. Go home. Lorenzo agrees."

Once again Lorenzo is interfering in my business. I'm sure he's behind this you-should-leave movement. I have become a nuisance just like Stella. The heat of my anger floods through my veins. I remain seated on the exam table while I wait for Antonio to continue.

He paces back and forth, his eyes on the floor. "Lorenzo says you are in danger just like Stella was. Neither of us wants to be responsible for something happening to you too."

I start to object but he raises his hand and says, "Let me finish. Stella had a photo shoot scheduled to publicize her latest film. Several days before, she came to the house, opened the door, and walked in as if she still lived there."

I interject, "I'm guessing she still had a key? Was the house off limits for her?"

"Well, no. She should have knocked. But that's not the point. She barged in, pushing right past me. I was entertaining a friend. Stella demanded I give her some pain pills to get her through the photo session. When I said no, she started laughing, then she screamed at me. She said I'd be sorry if I didn't give her the pills and she would report me to the medical board about all the times I had given her drugs."

He stops in front of me, his eyes not meeting mine, and says, "Sylvia was there."

He has the decency to blush and pause before continuing, "Sylvia suggested that we all sit down like civilized humans and discuss the situation. Ha, not Stella. She ignored me, smacked Sylvia, and ran into the kitchen. She grabbed a knife and started slashing at us. I was cut trying to take the knife from her and trying to protect Sylvia. I grabbed Stella's arm and knocked the knife out of her hand."

"Was Stella hurt?"

He looks at me in horror, "You're no better than Stella, Cat. Asking about Stella but not Sylvia. I wish I had hurt Stella, but I didn't. Thankfully, Sylvia's a nurse. She took care of my hand and then iced her face. Stella packs a mean punch. Sylvia had planned to stay the night as we were driving to Gallipoli for the weekend. I told her that until Stella and I straightened out the mess we were in, she needed to stay away."

"That must have hurt her. How did she react?"

Antonio shrugs and releases a long sigh, "She was furious with me but more so with Stella. She said I was a fool to let Stella jerk me around."

I shift on the table and say, "Is that what Stella was doing, Antonio or was she begging for help?"

He drums his finger on the metal tray before saying, "Stella's behavior has been erratic for so long. I couldn't continue my life with her. After the incident, Sylvia gave me an ultimatum. You don't need to say anything about how stupid it is to get involved with a coworker. I know that. My life is this clinic. Now, I hate it. Sylvia's here. I can't fire her. And I don't want to continue our relationship."

"What are you going to do?"

"I don't know. I'm already in trouble because Stella had previously broken into the clinic and stolen drugs. I didn't report it. If I had, the investigation would have led to Stella, and I would be implicated. I'd given her drugs before—first sleeping, then anxiety and finally pain pills. Stella was so unsure of herself. She needed more and more pills to numb her fears. I was complicit when I gave them to her and when I didn't report it. That was bad enough, but Sylvia knows. There's nothing I can do to stop her from reporting it. That's why I'm keeping her on and pretending that once this blows over we'll get back together—another lie."

The cold white clinic walls close in on us.

"When I refused to give Stella the drugs, she turned to the mafia. I signed her death warrant."

My first reaction is to throw those words back in his face by agreeing. But what's the point? Listening to him now, I realize he doesn't need my wrath. I start to slide off the exam table but he keeps talking.

"If I don't tell Lorenzo and he finds out, he has to turn me in. If I do tell him, he has to report it. Either way, I will lose my license. If that happens, I will lose my life. This practice is the only thing that compels me to get up every day."

"You believe Stella is dead?"

"I thought she was alive until you found the necklace. Even when she knew the marriage was over, she still wore it to all her publicity events. It was her identity. It meant far more to her than I did. She would never take the necklace off during a photo session. If for some strange reason she did, she would not have left it behind, unless it was intentional—unless she was hoping the right person would find it."

"But couldn't she still be alive? Suppose no one saw her remove the necklace? Suppose they let her go or maybe they're holding her for ransom. Stella's smart. If she had an opportunity, she would have left some clue. I think the necklace is that clue."

"Cat, a kidnapper would have contacted me right away for money. Maybe Stella did leave the necklace behind on purpose. It certainly identifies that she was there. What I don't understand is what happened to the necklace after you found it. You must have some idea. It's hard for me to believe that you didn't put it in a safe place."

I stare at him waiting for horns to grow out of his head. Does he think that I deliberately took the necklace?

Finally, I say, "You're kidding! You can't seriously think that I have the necklace or that I might know who has it. Are you nuts? What would I have to gain?"

"It's valuable."

"So that's what you think of me. Imagine, all this time I thought you were a saint. I thought you loved Stella even when she wasn't always lovable. I thought you were a decent person. I always defended you when Stella complained that you were too absorbed in your work."

"Wait Cat. I didn't mean to upset you. I'm not accusing you of stealing the necklace. I just thought you might know something."

I stand, abruptly knocking against the table which created a cacophony of metal instruments bumping together.

"You just thought I might know something? You just thought I might withhold information? That's crazy. Anytime you want to search the house, please do. I have nothing to hide from you or anyone else. Lorenzo has already searched it but don't let that stop you from doing the same. You can bring the entire village if you want. I will gladly vacate the premises since my staying in Stella's house seems to be a problem for you."

He drops his head. I storm out the door. He calls my name saying, "Cat, wait—please don't leave. Let me explain."

He runs after me. I glance back. His white coat flaps open and his tie flies over his shoulder. I leave him behind as I jaunt to the car, jump inside, and lock the doors. He hesitates for a second, then walks back to the clinic. Near the door, he leans against the wall and fumbles for a pack of cigarettes. He pulls one out and places it between his lips.

Sylvia's hand reaches from behind him and knocks the cigarette out of his mouth. "Remember, you gave them up."

She grabs his arm and pulls him inside.

CAT

ZINZULUSA CAVES, ITALY

I sit in the car not knowing where to go or what to do next. Anger at Antonio boils in my blood. I'm so tired of this intrigue. Stella continues to rule my every waking moment. All conversations begin and end with her. My thoughts flit back and forth in a jumble. I'm still wondering who can be trusted.

The parking lot is full. The cars are empty except for a black Mercedes. The engine idles, probably someone's ride.

I slump in the driver's seat for a minute before turning the ignition key. The steering wheel is frigid. Still I grip it until my knuckles turn white and ache. Leaving the gear in park, I sort through the conversation with Antonio. He wants me out of the villa, but where will I go? I can't leave now. Stella wanted me to stay there because the clues are somewhere in the villa. I have to find them.

Shifting into first, I spin away from the clinic. Gravel spews in all directions while my mind tries out different scenarios. What about Carlo? I could call him. He offered to find me another place. My cell phone remains in my purse.

Instead of heading home, I turn onto the coastal road. Driving will give me time to organize the kaleidoscopic thoughts galloping in my mind like some b-rated western movie. My anger distracts me.

When the black Mercedes pulls onto the road behind me, my mind is too busy to see it.

The back country road requires all my attention. I lean into the pull of the car as it hugs the winding curves. The jumbled mess in my brain untangles little by little. The cliffs drop away into a rocky coastline. Thick, concrete, gray clouds lower onto the sea. Sheets of foam lick and curl the waves. I drive on until I'm saturated with fatigue.

The tense, hard muscles in my neck and shoulders ease as I loosen my grip on the wheel. A brown attraction sign announces *The Caves of Zinzulusa.*

The name comes from the term *zinzuli*, a regional dialect word meaning rags. It refers to the karst stalactites hanging from the ceiling in rag-like shapes. I shiver at the memory of my first time through them. There was unrelenting darkness, not a warm and cozy darkness, but an evil dank feel-of-terror darkness. The guide tested my bravado over and over by shutting off his lantern without warning. Without light, a hellish fear took control of me. Several times when he turned the torch back on, I was teetering on the edge of a black abyss while he grinned in enjoyment over my distress.

Even after that scary event, I still love the caves. I've spent hours exploring them both as a child and since my return to Castello. There's something ethereal and mystical about them. They overflow with childhood memories.

Easing off the accelerator, I vear off the road and park. A low stone wall surrounds the entrance with an opening down to the caves. As I leave the car, the wind huffs and jerks at my jacket. The zipper catches. I struggle to secure it under my chin while breathing in the mist-laden air. It cleanses my thoughts into some sort of erratic order. I search the coastline before beginning to count—pebbles at my feet and then the waves crashing into the rocks.

Ponderous clouds gather and darken. They move rapidly across the water. Raindrops splatter on the windshield. Walking is not going to happen. As I reach for the door handle, a black Mercedes passes. I barely look up until it slows and pulls off the road. Shivers dance across my spine, stimulating some ancient fight or flight pathway in my brain. I plunge into the car, turn the key, and shift into first gear as the Mercedes makes a u-turn. It gathers speed, hurling toward me.

The thudding of my heart reaches my ears as adrenaline kicks in. I stomp on the gas turning sharply to the right as the Mercedes continues on its trajectory toward me. I shift into second. The tinted windows obscure the occupant until the car is almost parallel with mine. The window on the driver's side is lowered. A gun points in my direction. Behind the gun, steely, black eyes connect with mine for a second before I grind the gears and shift into reverse. Bullets ricochet across the hood. They leave open wounds of paint and metal. I ram the gear into third. The car careens onto the road. Behind me the sickening scrap of metal on stone fills my ears.

Castro Marina, some three kilometers south of the caves, appears like a mirage in the bleakest desert. Speeding into the village, I slam on the brakes, stalling to a stop. Throwing open the door, I run into the nearest bar. Inside I pull out my phone hit *5 and only exhale when Lorenzo picks up.

"Pronto."

"Lorenzo," my voice squeaks but no other words come out.

"Cat, what's wrong?"

"Lorenzo," I stutter, "someone tried to kill me."

"Cat, are you okay? Where are you?"

"Castro Marina."

"I'm leaving now. Tell me you're okay?"

"Yes, I'm fine other than scared stupid. A black Mercedes followed me from the clinic. I stopped at the caves. The driver tried to shoot me."

"Tried to shoot you? Black Mercedes? Did you see the license plate?"

"No, but it's a current model with tinted windows. It happened so quickly, I didn't hang around."

"Are you somewhere safe?"

"I'm at Sottovento."

"I know the owner. Ask him to put you in one of his rooms over the cafe. Where is your car? Never mind. Give him your car keys. Tell him to move it out of sight. *Va bene?* I'm almost there, Cat."

"*Va bene. Fai presto!*" Please hurry!

CAT & LORENZO

C*ASTELLO DEL MARE, ITALY*

The sun nestles into softly draped clouds of peach fuzz. The breeze is clean with scents of sage, mint, and rosemary. It ruffles the winter flowers. I shudder. Lorenzo gathers me in his arms and gently holds me until my trembling settles and sighs into quietness.

"I promise, you're safe," he murmurs into my hair.

But the ra ta ta of the bullets, ricocheting across the car, still hammer inside my skull.

Aldo, owner of the Sottovento, had tucked me away into a back room and spirited my car out of sight. Lorenzo arrived before I had time to sort through the nightmare. A million questions later, he drove me home, poured me a large glass of Amaro, and insisted I lie down. He arranged for my car to be picked up and repaired, and he posted a second watch on the house.

From the terrace, I can see both the guard and the surveillance car. They aren't trying to be discreet. Lorenzo wants to whisk me away to a safe house.

"No," is all I say. He doesn't argue with me.

I push away from his embrace.

"Who was in the Mercedes? Why was I being followed?"

"We don't know. We picked up some shell casings and a few pieces of metal, but the car was long gone. It could have been a hired hit from another region or more likely it was probably stolen. It'll be difficult if not impossible to make a connection with the drug ring here. But we'll try."

"Lorenzo, I've seen that car and driver before."

"Are you sure?"

"How many black Mercedes are there in this area? Can't you trace the car?"

Lorenzo frowns, "The only black Mercedes on our radar was stolen last week from a businessman staying in Tropea. We checked him out. The people who stole the car are professionals, Cat. They are not going to make it easy for us."

"Why am I the target? I don't have the necklace. Surely they know that? Do they think I know where it is?"

Lorenzo leans back in his chair and says, "Cat, we don't know if the person who stole the necklace is the same person or people who have targeted you. But when you found the necklace, it identified the scene of the crime and put Stella's disappearance on the priority list.

"Someone knows that Stella was spying and collecting information. She stashed it somewhere. The odds are it's hidden here in Stella's house or it's somewhere she thought you'd remember and find. Since you're staying here, it automatically puts you on their radar. Every time you return to the scene, you make yourself more vulnerable. You do realize you're being watched? You're making people unhappy, including me. You need to stay out of the investigation."

"Yes, Antonio made it clear that you not only wanted me out of the investigation but you wanted me to go home. He also doesn't want me staying here. Since I have nowhere else to go, I'm asking Carlo to find me another place."

"What? I haven't talked to Antonio. When did you talk to him?"

"When I was at the clinic this morning."

I held up my hand for him to see the long jagged scar.

"Cat, I have not talked to Antonio. You're smarter than that. If I wanted you to leave Stella's house and Castello, I would have told you. Whatever motivated Antonio to ask you to leave has nothing to do with me. I only want you to be safe. Although leaving Stella's house isn't a bad idea."

"Look Lorenzo, I know I'm in the way. But I'm here, and I'm not leaving. I'm sick with fear, but I need to know what happened to Stella. Why can't we work together?"

I don't give him a chance to answer. I just rush on, "Who has a key to the villa? It seems that all of you have keys—Gino, Maria, Antonio, Carlo? And you—although you didn't bother to tell me. Any of you could have stolen the necklace. Maybe it was for personal gain or maybe someone thought it would keep me safe?"

"Me? You think I stole the necklace? You're joking, right? What would I want with Stella's necklace? And what about you? If you want to point fingers, you're actually the only person who had possession of the necklace."

"That's true. But if I wanted to keep it, why would I have taken it to Antonio? I had no idea he would give it back to me. Do you really suspect me of killing Stella? I wasn't even in the country when she disappeared. How would I do that?"

"Cat, you're way ahead of yourself. I know you had nothing to do with Stella's death, but I believe you're not telling me everything you know. Are you protecting someone?"

I roll my eyes. "Sure, I come all the way to Italy thinking Stella is alive, and then I steal her necklace. Then someone steals it from me. Next I choke myself and leave all sorts of threats lying around the house to scare myself. You are so clever, Commissario."

"You are making this difficult, Cat. It's going to take time to work the case. Although Antonio can't kick you out of Stella's house, I recommend you stay somewhere else. Giorgione has an apartment above the restaurant. It would be easier for us to keep you under surveillance there. This villa is too open, too exposed."

"Unless Antonio forces me to leave, I'm staying. If someone wants to hurt or kill me, they'll find me wherever I am. And what if they only want to scare me?"

"Cat, this has gone past scaring you. While I don't think the person who wants the necklace would kill for it, I do think whoever wants the documents would. That's why you are in danger."

His eyes soften as he reaches for my hand. "Let's eat and forget about this for a while. Can we do that? We both have had enough for one day. I've been cooking all afternoon. Are you surprised I can cook?"

"Carlo told me you could. He actually said you should give up your job as commissario and become a chef. So whatever you've prepared had better live up to those standards."

"*Allora*, I was hoping to surprise you with my skills, but like I said, everyone knows everything that goes on around here, and they are happy to spread the word. I hope you won't be disappointed."

He stands and pulls me from the chair into his arms. His heart beats strong against my chest. I don't return his embrace. He abruptly lets go of me.

The meal is splendid, almost as good as the one with Carlo at La Canzone. The first course is *involtini di melanzane*, slices of eggplant, roasted and layered with prosciutto and mozzarella, then rolled up and baked in a marinara sauce until the cheese is gooey. Lorenzo garnishes the plate with shredded basil and grated parmesan. The flavors of garlic, basil, and peppery spices burst in my mouth. I'm quiet except for an occasional *hmmm*.

The next course is grilled *pescespada*—swordfish embellished with hints of mint, garlic, lemon, and rosemary. As I savor the perfectly cooked fish, I ask him if Antonio can kick me out of the villa.

"Cat, he's not serious. He's upset and not thinking straight. I'll talk to him. There's no reason for you to move unless you want to.

"But if Stella's dead, doesn't the property belong to Antonio?"

"Cat, there has to be an inquest before any decisions are made. If there's no evidence that Stella has been murdered, it'll be another ten years before Antonio can begin the paperwork to declare her dead. I'll speak to him. Let's not think about it tonight, okay? You're stressed enough."

He reaches across the table, places his hands on top of mine and says, "Let's enjoy the food and wine. Next course is coming up."

A salad of grilled radicchio, roasted beets, hazelnuts, and parmesan twills is followed by crispy cones of cannoli stuffed with sweetened ricotta, candied fruit, and chocolate bits. The entire meal is superb.

Lorenzo shoos me out of the kitchen to the terrace, hands me a glass of limoncello, and returns to the kitchen to clean up. I prop my feet on the stone baluster and consider the lone tree. Stella must have loved its raw branches, devoid of leaves, and its contorted trunk bending toward the sea—an anchor, something tangible to cling to. The breeze winds its way up the sixty-eight steps. Its tune is sorrowful as it swirls at my feet and sighs, *Stella*.

Lorenzo wanders out to the terrace with a glass of grappa. He sits next to me, takes my hand, and pulls me into the curve of his arm. I long to nestle in his arms, but my mouth opens and words tumble out.

"Lorenzo, if I'm a central player in this mess because of my friendship with Stella, let me help you. Is there anyone connected to the mafia that I could make friends with? I could ask questions, maybe get some information? You could point me in the right direction."

He cuts me off with a snort, "Cat, you're too smart to ask me to involve you in the investigation. Plus, it would take a long time for you to get next to anyone that might help. I only know a few of the minor players myself. I've already asked around. No one's talking. My job is to find the necklace and to continue the investigation of Stella's disappearance. Your job is to stay safe."

He stands and walks to the edge of the terrace and gazes down at the marina. The moon paints a willowy trail of light, stretching from the terrace to the edge of the sea. I move beside him. The night breeze rustles softly through the tangled vines. He snaps off a cluster of tiny white flowers and tucks it into my hair. Sparks shoot in the night, my white dress radiates the heat of my body as his hands slip from my hair to my shoulders. He tenderly guides my body into his. I forget to think about the consequences.

He's gone when I wake up. The flowers droop on the nightstand. In the kitchen, the coffee is ready, and a chocolate-stuffed cornetto languishes on a cloth-covered plate. A note on top says, *Bellissima, I will stop by at the end of the day to check on you. Do not leave the house today, please.*

I'm horrified that I let yesterday's fear consume me to the point of sleeping with Lorenzo. He must feel the same. Our mutual pain and grief of losing Stella binds us together in ways that even we cannot explain or control.

Do I regret it is a question that will take time to answer.

CAT & MARIA

March awakens, pushing aside the last bits of winter. Days whirl by, bringing no answers. Once I start my job at the restaurant there won't be time to snoop. The only good news is Lorenzo smoothed everything over with Antonio. He apologized and practically begged me to stay. He said Stella would be furious if I didn't.

I throw back the duvet and leap out of bed. I have time for a jog and a shower before I meet Giorgione. I'm exhilarated at the prospect of spending the day at the restaurant, but I'm fearful as well. I've reached a blank wall with the clues Stella left me. Maria, Gino, and I have discussed them at length.

Initially, the caves at Zinzulusa seemed right for our special place. We had spent a lot of time exploring them, but nothing in the area looked like an onion or a dome. And so far Caesar's Latin words *veni, vidi, vici* haven't conjured up any answers.

Maria and I continue our daily chats, but there's a tenseness that wasn't there before. When I return from my jog, accompanied by the annoying policeman who jogs with me, I'm surprised to find Maria waiting outside the door with a covered dish proliferating the terrace with delicious aromas.

"Ciao, Caterina. Come stai?"

"Bene, Maria. E tu?"

"Sto bene, can I come in?"

"Of course, Maria," I respond, while unlocking the door. "You could have let yourself in."

"Oh no, not without your permission. Not after what has happened. Lorenzo believes Gino took the necklace. You must be uncomfortable knowing this. I'm here to return the keys. I spoke to Carlo last night. He said it's your decision, but he doesn't want you to worry about anyone entering the house when you are not here or when you are alone."

"Maria, I trust you and Gino. In fact, I feel safer knowing you have a key. You'd be here immediately if something happened. Both of you would help me in any situation. Please keep the key."

"Caterina, Gino is sorry for causing so much trouble."

"What do you mean, trouble?"

"I have said too much. Please understand that we would never do anything to hurt you. We loved Stella like a daughter. She had many problems. Some we knew about and some we didn't. When she didn't come back, we kept hoping she had checked herself into a rehab center far away from here. But after a week or two without hearing anything, we became suspicious.

"Gino says she was murdered. He never tells me how he knows things, but he is rarely wrong. Even if he took the necklace, he would have taken it to protect you, not to harm you."

I start to ask what she means, but she's already headed toward the kitchen. I follow and watch from the doorway as she places the dish on the back of the stove and removes the towel—a still-warm pork stew with soft polenta.

"Oh, that smells amazing," I say, smiling and reaching for a spoon to taste.

"This is delicious, Maria. Would you teach me some of your recipes? Everything you make is wonderful."

She shyly smiles and nods while looking at the floor.

"Maria, I want you and Gino to continue to be part of my daily life. But we have to be honest with each other. You have to tell me what you meant when you said if Gino had taken the necklace, he would have done it to protect me."

Maria turns back to the stove and covers the savory dish before saying, "A nice caprese salad and a glass of Primitivo with the stew will be all you need tonight. It's an easy meal for you after a long day at the restaurant."

There's an extended pause, long enough for me to think she's not going to answer my question. Eventually, she speaks. I shift closer as her voice sinks into a whisper.

"Gino thinks that some of the people who are involved or who are helping with the investigation are perhaps part of the reason Stella is missing. Stella was not always discreet. She talked too much. She made the wrong people nervous. She hinted about what she knew which put her in danger. Stella was always kind to us. We protected her as much as we could, but there are powerful people in this area who are involved with drugs and prostitution. They make a lot of money from illegal activities. If Stella overstepped the boundaries, these people would have taken care of her."

"You mean kill her?"

"Yes, I am sorry to say this, but you need to be careful. The risk is real. When you found the necklace, eyes began to follow you. They want to know what you know. Before I came here today, Gino said you must stop asking questions. Go to the restaurant. Enjoy your time cooking and learning. He says you must not explore anywhere near the place where you found the necklace. He is very concerned you will be harmed."

"Does that mean he doesn't want me to talk to Lorenzo, Antonio, or Carlo?"

"Carlo is okay. Gino says if you need to talk, contact Carlo but no one else. And even then, be careful because we don't know who is involved."

"Who does Gino suspect?"

"He will not say until he finds proof of the killer. When you found the necklace, it was dangerous evidence. The kind that gets you killed. Promise me you'll be careful and that you won't try to find out what happened to Stella or the necklace. Please?"

I nod, but I can tell I'm not convincing Maria.

"Gino knows where the safe deposit box is located. He believes the key in the ceramic box will fit it. But since Stella has not been declared dead, everyone's hands are tied."

"Do you think the clues Stella left for me will lead to the information?"

"Gino says yes. He says the clues are the answers. When you remember the location, he asks that you please let him go in your place. He fears for your safety."

CAT

After much persuasion, Maria agrees to keep the key. Once she leaves, I shower and select well-worn jeans and a pullover with comfortable shoes for my day at the restaurant. I still have an hour, so I remove the ceramic box from its hiding place and take out the two clues: *la cipolla a cupola* and *vieni, vidi, vici*.

My voice echoes across the terra-cotta floor when I say out loud, *a domed onion—I came, I saw, I conquered*. The sun casts streaks of light across the paper creating jagged lines on the floor that lead to the painting over the fireplace. My heart gallops as I leap from the sofa. The pieces of paper float in the air as I grab the painting and lift it from the wall. I search our innocent faces. Nothing. I search for the artist's name but there isn't one. The painting is large and awkward to handle but I flip it over. There! Taped to the back is a small piece of brown paper. I slip my nail under the tape and pry it loose.

Il nostro nascondiglio segreto per la narrazione—our favorite place where we shared our secrets and told our stories.

All the clues fall into place: the domed onion is Villa Sticchi; I came, I saw, I conquered is Julius Caesar and the town is Santa Cesarea Terme; and the last clue about our favorite secret place—the one where we made up childhood stories—is a small cave in Cesarea. Relief floods my body in warm waves as I shout, "I know, I know exactly where to go."

Of course, I have to wait. The walk to La Canzone is short, not nearly enough time to sort through my emotions after finding the last clue.

The who and what ifs land me at the door of the restaurant. I temporarily tuck them away and enter. Giorgione bear hugs me until I am breathless. Over his shoulder, another presence looms. My eyes flicker toward the bar and a shadow. But Giorgione hustles me into the kitchen to check out the prep-stations.

Then he says, "Follow me. Grab that menu on the counter, read it to me, and make changes as I tell you. Bring those napkins too, the red ones for today."

The napkins, menu, and notepad balance precariously as I read aloud and quick-step to catch up.

"Stuffed squash blossoms on a bed of fava beans and chopped tomatoes, monkfish ravioli, wild asparagus, marinated leg of lamb with baby artichokes and roasted potatoes, rabbit stuffed with lemon and wild greens, and for dessert sweet ricotta pie and Colomba.

He nods as I read. When I stop, he asks, "What do you think? It's the Easter menu."

I blurt out with my best killer smile, "Oh, I hope I don't have to work on Easter. I want to reserve the best table for this fabulous meal."

"Ha, of course, you have to work. Don't try to charm me into giving you the day off. The big meal for Easter is always lunch. Both you and Sebastian will work. But there will be plenty of food for the staff. You'll not go home hungry."

"The menu is amazing."

"It's good, but add *insalata mista*, Easter breads, a seafood lasagna, and anise cookies for the little ones."

I write furiously to keep up with his fast-moving words.

"Finish setting up the service in this section," he indicates with a wave of his hand. "Stop by before you leave. Can you start next week? When we agreed on your date, I had forgotten that Easter is early this year. I could really use your help."

My thoughts jump ahead as I calculate how much time I have to find the information Stella has hidden. At this moment it seems possible that I can do both. And having an opportunity to experience preparing a traditional Italian Easter meal is too exciting to turn down.

"Yes," I quickly respond before he changes his mind. "When?"

"Next Tuesday. Can you be here at eight?"

"Of course," I say, realizing I'll have to double down in my search.

We are deep in conversation as we pass through the bar. The shadow moves into my field of vision. A gasp slips from my mouth as Giorgione stops suddenly. He puts his arm protectively around my back and moves me quickly by. But not quickly enough. I catch a glimpse of dark, beady eyes and a smirk before the kitchen door swings shut behind us.

CAT

SANTA CESAREA TERME, ITALY

The next morning Lorenzo stops by. Since our night together, I've locked a steel door around my heart. It's impossibly hard to resist his sweetness, his shy looks, and his soft touches, but I do. The conversation is light, and I want to keep it that way. I don't breathe a word about finding the three clues that Stella left for me. I don't tell him I know where the hiding place is.

After he leaves, I text Maria and ask if she can pick me up to run some errands. Lorenzo seems to think it's okay for me to go out during the day as long as someone is with me. It puzzles me why he thinks that would prevent anything from happening. So far every scary thing that's happened to me has been in daylight.

In my market bag, I place a notebook, a pen, the three clues, bottled water, a hunk of *caciocavallo*, an apple, and a small loaf of olive-studded bread. I grab a sweater and run down the steps as Maria pulls up. The officer on duty approaches Maria's side of the car and asks where we're going. Maria glances at me with a question in her eyes.

"Maria is taking me shopping today. We'll be gone most of the afternoon, but we'll be back before dark."

He smiles, tips his hat, and walks back to his position by the seawall. Maria is silent until we turn the corner.

"Where are we going, Caterina?"

"Maria, I need a really big favor. I'm close to deciphering the clues Stella left. But I want to check out a few more places to be sure. Would you let me borrow your car? Mine's still in the repair shop. It's just for the afternoon. Giorgione wants me to start work next week. After that, I won't have time to search."

"Caterina, you're asking a lot of me. Gino will be furious if he finds out. Someone could follow you. Are you prepared for another shootout?"

"No, of course not. But if we are being followed, wouldn't we know it by now?"

"Humph," is all she says.

"I'm sorry for putting you in a difficult spot. I wouldn't do it, but you and Gino know how important it is for me to find Stella's hide-away. I won't do anything foolish. I promise."

Maria removes her foot from the gas and pulls off the road. "Caterina, I'm doing this because I understand how much you love Stella. You must promise to be back no later than five. If you're not, I will call Lorenzo and tell him you threatened me with bodily harm."

I gasp, then look into Maria's eyes and see the smile.

"Grazie mille, Maria."

The winding coastal road leads me to Santa Cesarea Terme. The drive is far enough to give me time to think about the three clues. By the time Stella and I were twelve, we had learned to drive *l'ape.* We'd sneak away during siesta when all the grownups retreated to their rooms and stayed for hours. Fortunately, we were never caught, and we never revealed our special place to anyone.

Santa Cesarea Terme is an upscale spa town, overrun with tourists until late August when it closes up tight. During our summers, it was a grand place for privacy and picnicking on the rocky beach. Tourists avoided the rough terrain and spent their days being pampered at the spa.

Whenever we could slip away, Stella and I would head to Cesarea. We would spend the day in the pit of a giant rock formation that we called our cave. The super large boulders, over time and weather, created impossible-to-find hideaways. Our special place was fronted by a flat rock that jutted out in terrace-like fashion. We would soak up the sun and pretend we were rich and famous. If the day was windy or rainy, we would retreat into the cave-like depths and munch on cheese and olives and weave our stories. We wrote promises on the walls and tucked small treasured items in the crevices.

From our private space we would pick out one of the gaudy summer homes and make up stories about the families who vacationed there. Throughout the summer our stories changed. When we returned home to the new school year and were given the dreaded assignment of *what I did on my summer vacation*, we would write about the architectural wonder of Palazzo Sticchi. We invented a fictitious family who lived in this Moorish palace with its large onion-shaped dome and with its array of colors worthy of an artist's palette. Our teachers were always mystified how two young girls came up with such unbelievable stories.

Palazzo Sticchi is the *onion dome* clue that Stella left me. My hands tighten on the steering wheel as the town comes into view. The day is warm. Hints of spring flourish in the lush green hedges and in the stretches of white winter crocuses and toadflax dotting the terrain. Since I'm driving Maria's car, I park on a side street. These small towns overlap, and it would put Maria in an awkward position if someone saw her car and asked questions.

I grab the sack out of the back seat, sling it over my shoulder and walk a few streets over. The parking area by the seawall is empty. Nothing stirs except a stray cat or two. They stretch but decide I'm not worth the effort required to move from their sunny perches.

There is no walkway, just a straggly path down to the rocks. In a crouching position, I hop from boulder to boulder as the incoming spray coats my face with salty droplets. My feet slip and slide between the rocks. I stop every few minutes as I search for our place. Several small formations appear, but they're not the right ones. My back muscles burn in the hunched over position, so I stand up and stretch. That's when I see it—giant rocks wedged together with an opening that can only be seen from the sea side.

Stella's squeals of delight, when we discovered the cave-like structure, still cling in the air. We stood on this same outcropping of rock and chanted in our best theatrical voices, *veni, vidi, vici—I came, I saw, I conquered.*

I crouch down and jump onto the flat ledge outside the entrance. I drop the sack in front of the opening and crawl inside our special place. The one that tucked Stella and me away from the entire world.

For an hour, I don't move. I breathe in and out with the tide. Waves break over the rocks, sea birds cry, and an occasional car rumbles through the village. Memories crash over me forcing me to let go. Sometimes I laugh; sometimes I cry. When all my emotions are drained, I poke and probe every crevice in the cave. There's nothing.

I move to the ledge. The warm afternoon sun bathes my face. I nibble on my stash of food and fill my notebook with columns of names, incidents, and time lines until I determine I know very little more than when I started. I line up the three clues, forcing them to tell me Stella's secret.

Who would Stella trust? Not Antonio. Would it be Lorenzo? Carlo? Gino or Maria? If I were to talk to either Antonio or Carlo, the odds are they'll take the conversation back to Lorenzo. And Lorenzo seems to tell the other two everything I share with him. But I need to confide in someone.

Lorenzo, I don't realize I've said his name out loud until the sound of my voice lifts on the breeze. He's everything I want, but he has never gotten over Stella. Antonio lives in the past. That leaves Carlo. Maria and Gino believe Carlo is trustworthy. I like him. He's attentive, never pushy, always the gentlemen, almost too much.

But Lorenzo is the logical choice, and I like logic. I close my notebook and wonder why I don't feel good about telling him. He is intelligent, empathic, and in control. I avoid words like admirable, strikingly handsome, and sensuous, and oh-so-tempting—all words from the heart that can deceive. Objectivity and finding Stella or what happened to her are my only goals.

I gather up the half-empty bottle of water and the remains of my meal and stuff them back into the bag. The sea laps restlessly against the rocks. A cool breeze has me plowing through my sack for a sweater. It's on the bottom, so I dump everything out. In my haste, the pen falls out and rolls into the back of the cave. Scrambling after it, I bang my head against the low-pitched overhang. A stream of small pebbles rains down on me. I crouch with my arms covering my head until the flow stops. When I look up, a plastic edge protrudes from a gap. I reach up and tug. More dirt, twigs, and small rocks plummet. I keep jerking and clawing at the pebbles to free the water-proof folder from its hideaway. I'm ecstatic as I crab-crawl to the opening, clutching my find. I place the folder on the ledge, grab the wayward pen and my sack, and uncoil my body to stand. Voices float toward me. I freeze.

Maybe clandestine lovers or tourists? Words dip then rise on the wind. Small rocks tumble to the sea as footsteps and voices come to rest right over the cave. I stay smushed inside and pray they go away. The folder, snug in its waterproof pouch, is in full view if anyone looks down.

The wind shifts. Garbled words penetrate my space.

"You screwed up."

The wind whirls around the open. Bits and pieces of conversation float into the cave.

"Stella ... necklace ... find ... Cat ... has to go ..."

Seabirds scream above the alcove. My legs cramp. My heart drums against my ribs. I hold my breath until lightheadedness descends and blackness blots out the sun-sparkled sea. Minutes or hours pass. The voices drift off until there is only silence. I take small cautious breaths and tremble with the realization the voices sounded familiar.

Sitting back on my heels, I slide my phone out of my pocket. It's after five. Maria will be frantic. Inch by inch I back out of the cave. I raise up from a squatting position until my eyes clear the top of the boulders. No one is around. In the distance, a car door slams. A blue *Alfa Romeo* pulls out of the parking lot. There's a black Mercedes parked across the street. I duck down and wait. When all is quiet, I raise my head and search the area thoroughly before crawling out of my hiding place. There are other cars parked along the side streets but I don't check them out as I run to Maria's car.

Il padrone adjusts the seat, leans back, and waits. He's not sure what attracts him to her. She's such a snoop and so clumsy in her eagerness to find Stella. But those out-of-control red curls and the big green eyes often pop into his thoughts. He reaches for a cigarette cursing his weakness. He has tried to give them up a hundred times. But always right before something big goes down, he has to have one.

He watches the cluster of rocks, knowing she will soon make her way back to the car. Most days he has others follow her, but today he took over. He hit the jackpot. He smiles when he sees the bobbing red curls top the wall of the parking lot. She is so fierce, yet so vulnerable. He likes that but knows in the end it will kill her.

CAT, GINO & MARIA

C *ASTELLO DEL MARE, ITALY*

"Gino is waiting for us," Maria says when I pull into our agreed-upon meeting place. Her arms are crossed on her chest, lips tight. I trot around to the passenger side. She pushes off from the wall and slides into the driver's seat.

She scowls at me.

"When he noticed the car was gone, I had to tell him. He is furious with both of us."

"Sorry, Maria. I lost track of time. I didn't mean to worry you or Gino. It's okay if he's mad at me but not you. It's my fault. But Maria, I have so much to tell both of you. The clues finally came together. Our special cave is in Cesarea."

Maria takes in my disheveled appearance, "From the looks of you, it seems you might have gone rock climbing while you were trying to find this place. You did not go back to the scene of the crime, did you?"

I brush twigs and grit from my hands and jeans before saying, "No it wasn't necessary. I found everything I needed at the cave."

"What? You found the evidence? You found what Stella left?"

I pat my sack and say, "Yes, it's all here. Give me a chance to shower and change clothes. There's food in the fridge. Do you mind putting a few things together along with a bottle of wine? Then we'll talk. I'm sorry I didn't tell you where I was going today."

"Caterina, you did exactly what I would have done for my best friend," Maria says as she slows down in front of the house.

The same officer who was on watch this afternoon still guards the villa. He gives a half-hearted salute as Maria parks in front. His uniform is rumpled, and his cap is cocked back on his head. It's been a long day for him too.

Maria touches my arm, "I thought you might be late, so dinner is made and in the oven. Please understand that Gino is not mad, but he is scared."

I give Maria a hug. We climb the sixty-eight steps in silence. Gino leans against the railing on the top terrace, his hooded eyes observant as we climb. When we reach the top, Maria rushes off to the kitchen. Gino nods, his hands white from gripping the rail.

"Where were you?"

"Gino, you can't babysit me."

He interrupts, "I know only a small piece of what is going on and that small piece is enough to scare me. Maria and I are still suffering because we lost Stella. It's a heavy burden to know we failed her. I should have been more vigilant. When she asked me to watch the marina with her and follow the vans, I should have said no. I should have stopped her from doing the photo shoot. I'm frightened that you are destined for the same conclusion as Stella if you do not trust me."

"Please understand that you were not Stella's protector. She made her choices. You couldn't have changed her mind or stopped her. But thank you for being there for her. You and Maria meant everything to her."

Misery paints a pasty white over his normal olive complexion.

"Gino, I found the evidence that Stella left. You know more than you're saying. We need to share our information so we can figure out what to do next. We need to be honest with each other. Did you steal the necklace? If you did, please tell me."

He pushes away from the stone railing and walks to the far end of the terrace. He hunches his shoulders and shakes his head.

He straightens, walks back, and says,"Yes. If I had not taken it, you would be dead by now. Some people did not want the necklace to be found. Those people would have done everything to make it disappear again. Then there are other people who want the necklace out of greed or revenge and for their own personal enjoyment and would stop at nothing to get it."

"Who are these people?"

"Some I know, but others I am not sure yet. When you discovered the necklace, the investigation was made a priority. That was an unexpected complication for the people who killed Stella. Before you found the necklace, everyone believed Stella had disappeared as usual and eventually would show up again. Antonio thought she had overdosed. But Stella would not have taken her own life. She was working hard to overcome her addiction. She was making progress.

"Stella confided in Maria and me. She trusted us. Things had been bad between her and Antonio for a long time. She moved into the villa because she wanted a divorce. But Antonio would not consider it. I should say his family told him he could not get a divorce. Stella believed she had a far better chance overcoming her addiction by living on her own. When you agreed to stay with her for a year, she truly thought, with your help, she would be strong enough to quit. We believed her."

I look away from his angry eyes and clenched fists. I shift my weight before asking, "Where is the necklace?"

"When the time comes, it will surface again. For now, it is safe."

"But Lorenzo says you gave it to Franco and that he's mafia."

"Caterina, the mafia encircles all of our lives in various ways. It's been around for hundreds of years."

I start to protest, but Gino silences me, "Wait. Listen. No, I am not a member. Yes, I have used the services, and I have run a few errands when necessary. Franco does a little more than that, and he has a few more contacts."

"Why didn't you give the necklace to Lorenzo? Don't you trust him?"

Before he can respond, Maria returns with wine and a platter loaded with olives, cheese, sun-dried tomatoes, tiny meatballs, and toasted bread. She sets the platter on the table, looks at both of us, and says, "There is not much time before Lorenzo arrives for his evening check on Cat. Should I invite him to stay for dinner?"

"No," says Gino.

"Yes," I say.

We glare at each other until Maria sighs and sits down. She sips her wine and studies my face. "Caterina, we are not sure, but..."

"Hush, Maria. I have already frightened her enough."

"Gino, we have to tell her everything we know."

There's a roaring noise in my ears as blood rushes through my veins. I'm exhausted and confused. I realize I've been in this state since the first day I arrived.

"What do you need to tell me?" I ask, bracing myself for whatever bad news I don't already know about.

Gino and Maria glance at each other. He nods. Maria turns to me and says, "First, take a shower. You need to relax after the difficult day you have had. Then we'll talk."Before I can respond, the bell rings. We freeze as Lorenzo's voice echoes up the steps, "Ciao, Cat. Open the gate."

CAT & LORENZO

We wait in silence as Lorenzo bounds up the steps. He teeters at the top and absorbs our solemn faces before saying, "Well since you are all here, we can talk."

He pulls out a chair and places it next to mine. Maria scurries off and returns with another wine glass. Her pasted-on smile contorts her face, and Gino's dark scowl is enough for Lorenzo to wonder what we've all been up to. I focus on neutrality. I press my lips into a straight line and stare into my glass. I haven't had time to read what Stella left me which leaves me in limbo. I squirreled the folder away in my sack when I left Cesarea, and now it's resting by my foot. Whatever message Stella left, I will read alone before deciding what to do.

Lorenzo's face, as he settles into the chair, is without expression. He appears oblivious to the tension, but I know he's not. Like the good hostess I was brainwashed to be, I invite him to stay for dinner. When I do, Maria and Gino murmur their regrets. They bolt down the steps and out the gate before Lorenzo is halfway out of his chair.

"Well," he says with his eyebrow cocked in a question mark. "What was that about?"

"We're all tired, Lorenzo. Tired of not understanding what's going on and tired of not knowing what happened to Stella. And I'm tired of being cooped up in this house with a guard outside."

"According to Alfonso, you weren't cooped up all day."

Fear tiptoes in like a shroud. I focus on a wine spot on the table and don't respond.

"Do you want to tell me where you went? Don't bother to tell me you were shopping with Maria because she was seen at the market. You were not with her. Do you think I only have one person watching you? Cat, you are making this difficult for me. It would be a shame if I had to take you to the station for questioning. Tell me where you were and what you did today."

"Would you mind if we eat first? I'm tired and hungry, and I'm not willing to talk at the moment. If you think the station is where I need to be, then let's go."

I'm praying he won't call my bluff, but the hardness in his eyes leaves me unsure. He doesn't answer. Instead, he gazes for a long time at the sea. The setting sun waves flags of red, orange, and purple as it blazes into the Adriatic with its defiant end-of-the-day dance.

I pour myself more wine and push back my chair to stand, "Maria left lentil soup along with a skillet of sausages, peppers, and onions. I'll slice some bread and make a salad. I hope you'll stay. Give me a few minutes to shower."

After a quick shower, I busy myself in the kitchen as I sort through my chaotic thoughts. I need to invent a plausible explanation without telling the truth. When I bring the soup into the dining room, the table is set and another bottle of wine is open. Lorenzo lights a small circle of candles while I return to the kitchen to retrieve the platter of sausages, peppers, and onions and the hastily mixed salad of arugula, fennel, and tomatoes.

He smiles wearily while I pick at my food. Several times he places his hand on mine. His touch is gentle and comforting, but my level of fear has ratcheted up another notch.

The conversation drifts. My mind keeps racing back to this afternoon. The bits and pieces of words still echo in my ears. Was it his voice, his car? I long for him to go away so I can discover what Stella left for me.

"What's wrong, Cat? Are you ill? You look pale. Did something happen today?"

He reaches for my hand. I jerk away, knocking over my wine. It puddles across the tablecloth. Trails of blood red wine trickle to the floor. I jump up, knocking my chair over. When I grab for it, a vase of flowers heads towards the edge of the table. I snatch it up seconds before it hits the floor. Without looking at Lorenzo, I dash to the kitchen for a towel to clean up the spilled wine and splashed water. He's right behind me. He grips my arm. I whirl away, but he pulls me back and holds me tight.

"Cat, stop," he demands. "Something has happened. Tell me what's wrong."

"Nothing, I'm just tired. Having someone guard me round the clock makes me jittery. I can't think clearly. I feel like I'm being punished. I haven't committed a crime."

My heart pounds. Heat rises up my neck and into my face. Lorenzo doesn't move or say anything. His lips flatten, his jaws clench, and his eyes stare through me. I shiver but not from pleasure.

"Well, this is quite a change from a couple of nights ago. You were grateful for my protection and for my concern. Actually, you were more than grateful."

He kisses me long and hard. I almost topple over when he suddenly releases me.

"I'm grateful, Lorenzo, but I did not come here to be a prisoner. My sole intention was to be with Stella and to work. After Stella disappeared, all the reasons for my being here no longer exist. I don't want twenty-four-hour police protection. It's not how I choose to live."

"Are you discounting the fact that the necklace was stolen right from under your nose, threats have been left on your doorstep, you have been shot at, and your life is in danger?"

"No, I haven't. But if someone wants to kill me, it will happen with or without your protection. You understand that. Isn't that what happened to Stella? One second you looked away. You removed her protection for a bigger operation."

"You're saying it's my fault she's dead?"

"Yes," I snap, my voice brittle with suppressed tears.

"So that's how it is?"

When I don't respond, he says, "Okay, I guess this is when I leave?"

He turns and walks toward the door.

He's halfway down the steps but stops and climbs back to the top, "Cat, you're right to blame me for Stella's death. But no matter what you think about me, I won't let it happen to you. The guard stays."

His feet trudge down the stone staircase. The gate slams. I move to the terrace and follow him with my eyes. He speaks to the guard. Then he glances to where I'm standing on the terrace. Our eyes lock. I want to call him back, but I don't. My hand automatically rises, but he's already in the car and driving away.

CAT

My dearest Cat, In my best dream you are here in Castello, and we are giggling our insides into helpless mush. Our feet are balanced against the terrace wall, and for the first time I am sharing my misguided life with you. I'll introduce you to the lone tree—the one I gaze on day after day to find the courage and strength I need to live another day without drugs. A couple of months isn't much, but it's a start. And this time as I gaze at my tree and write this letter, I know you will soon be sitting next to me. My survival depends on your help as I continue on the road to recovery. I will die if I don't make my way out of this hell I've created for myself.

My greatest joy would be that you never read this letter. But my greatest fear is that Maria has given you the ceramic box, you've found the clues (you are clever enough to do this easily), and you've remembered our hideaway in Santa Cesarea Terme—all of which leads to this letter.

How did I end up in this mess? It's pointless to

rehash the sad story of my life other than to give you some threads that I pray will lead to my redemption.

Everyone surrounding me has labeled me as an addict, including myself. But a few weeks ago, I added "recovering" to my name. There have been times—six months, sometimes a year—when I was totally clean. Those are the only times I called or asked you to meet me. I was so ashamed of my habit and my life. You had accomplished so much in the face of adversity while I held together a facade of an empty and meaningless life that only appeared glamorous to those who didn't know the truth.

But that is not why I'm writing this or why you're reading it. You'll have heard I've disappeared, maybe checked myself in rehab or more likely I went on a binge and fell off a cliff never to be recovered. I've lived here long enough to know how things are done when you're in the way.

Cat, I don't want to involve you, but if I don't confide in you, a lot of innocent people will be hurt—people like Giorgione, Gino, Maria, little Gino, (help him as much as you can please) and the other small shopkeepers here and in the other villages.

I feel stupid playing this game of intrigue with you, leaving clues and hoping you'll find them. But I don't know what else to do. I don't trust anyone except Gino and Maria. I believe they are the only true friends I have in Castello. They did as much as they could to protect me. They will help you.

There's not much time for me to tell you what little I know. It may not help, but I will give you the names of those connected to the smuggling operation. I could be wrong, and I could be too angry to think clearly, but please find the truth for me.

The pages spread across the bed. Antonio, Carlo, Lorenzo, Riccardo, Sylvia, Gino, Maria, and other names. Some names I recognize and some I don't. Stella's words blur as I scan the pages. Each person's involvement fills my eyes with tears. They slide off my face, landing with soft plops on Stella's neat still-schoolgirl handwriting.

Reading these pages stacked with her words and voice is agonizing. I can't acknowledge she's dead—gone forever. I'll never see her again. Sobs rack my body as I fold into a knot and pull the duvet over my head. When the flow of tears dissipates, I turn on the bedside lamp and reach for the last page.

I'm not optimistic I'll be alive much longer. I know too much. I've threatened the wrong people. These people are the rot in our society. Their greed consumes them. Finding ways to make the rest of us suffer, gives them the greatest satisfaction. Try to stop them but don't risk your life.

Why didn't I call you or leave this place? I tried many times but when I was on drugs, they were more important to me than life. I truly believed there would be time to quit. I was sure I had another chance. I was wrong!

Do you remember when we were kids? You envied me, thinking I was everything you wanted to be. All those years you suffered. I was such a nasty kid. You always forgave me even when I betrayed you with Lorenzo. How I hated myself for that. Now, I can promise you that he no longer loves me.

I was a fool. I'm so sorry for all the times I let you down. I never meant to hurt you. I hope you'll stay and fight in my place. But if you believe your life is in danger, then Go Home Now! Whether you stay or go, live your life fully and beautifully for both of us.

I love you, my forever friend,

Stella

CAT

Sweat drips, saturating my multi-colored headband. I pause from slicing and dicing to swat at my forehead. Sebastian grins, cool and composed as he stuffs and trusses another rabbit.

"So, it's tough for you to be in a kitchen without air conditioning, no?"

He doesn't wait for a reply but continues, "When you finish peeling the potatoes, the artichokes are next. You know what to do with them?"

"Yes, of course I do," I stammer and look away.

Gosh, Giorgione was right. Sebastian's a royal pain. I bite my lip because I'm not in the mood for a kitchen war. The ancient potato peeler rakes across the potato leaving teeth marks.

Next time I'll bring my micro peeler from the villa, along with my chef's knife, and a decent apron. How can the bastard whip up such fabulous meals without tools I consider necessities?

Giorgione pushes through the door, "Cat, come with me. I need help with the table arrangements."

I peel and quarter the last potato and drop it in the massive roasting pan on the back of the stove. Wiping my hands on a less-than-clean apron, I rush after Giorgione. The door swings shut behind me. He's not in the narrow, dimly lit hallway. I wipe away the sweat and straighten my headband while examining the tiny corridor that has to become a collision course when filled with wait staff rushing back and forth during opening hours.

Loud voices stop me from moving down the hall. A fist slams on the bar. The words aren't audible until Giorgione's booming voice ricochets off the soft wood.

"Why do you keep hanging out here, Riccardo? Go away."

"Hey, old man, don't tell me what to do. You think Lorenzo is protecting you? Do you see him here? Busy guy our Lorenzo. He's not concerned about what happens to you. You need me to protect your interests."

"Look Riccardo, you're not welcome here. I'm tired of looking up every few minutes to find you slinking around. Stay away. I owe you nothing. If you mess with the girl, Lorenzo and I will kill you."

"Ha, you will wake up one morning, old man, and Lorenzo won't be around. But I'll still be here to save you and your business. You'll pay then, including all the back pay you owe. If the girl is still here, well."

The swinging door slams into my back. I involuntarily croak. Sebastian's hand steadies me as he sheepishly apologizes.

"Sorry, you'll learn soon enough not to linger outside this door. What are you doing here anyway? I thought Giorgione had summoned you. Better move."

"Hey, what's going on?" Giorgione says as he turns the corner.

Sebastian and I are smashed against the wall. If I weren't so frightened, it would be one of those laughable moments.

"Come on, Cat. I don't have all day. Keep up with me," he says as words trail over his shoulder.

I rush past the bar. The man has withdrawn into the shadows but the smirk is clear. His intense black eyes sweep over me. My skin tingles with fear and the blood drains from my face as I'm almost sure this is the man who shot at me.

Giorgione stops and snarls, "This is Riccardo. He's not welcome here. He's leaving now. Remember his face and stay as far away from him as possible. If he shows up, you call me or Sebastian, *va bene?*"

"You gonna be sorry old man—real sorry," Riccardo responds before dropping the espresso cup on the bar hard enough to shatter it.

We freeze in place until Sebastian arrives with a broom and dustpan.

"I heard a crash. What happened? Riccardo, it's not like you to mess yourself up. Looks like there's a little coffee on your shirt."

Riccardo glances at the brown spot spreading across his once pristine white shirt. He tugs his leather jacket closed, pivots on his heel, and walks out of the bar. Giorgione scowls at me. I want to ask why, but I keep my head down as I wipe coffee off the bar.

Just as I sop up the last bit, Giorgione gently touches my hand, "Don't worry. That despicable creature won't bother you."

Before I can respond, he's halfway down the hall shouting over his shoulder, "Come on, hurry up. Check the flowers I ordered for the centerpieces. Do you remember saying you would arrange them for me since my wife won't be here for Easter?"

He doesn't wait for an answer. I dash after him.

Arranging flowers is therapeutic. There is a peacefulness in the contours of each petal as I weave the ivy and baby's breath among the masses of yellow roses and white lilies. My thoughts ricochet, hell bent on stressing me into hysteria. I count until Riccardo's face disappears. I focus on the flowers but thoughts of Lorenzo sneak in.. He hasn't called or texted. I didn't expect him to, but still. Our angry exchange of words stays lodged in my chest.

Stella will always separate me from Lorenzo. He made that choice. I was foolish to sleep with him. He will always love her. It was our grief for Stella that propelled us into each other's arms. She still has the ability to reach from wherever she is and twist my heart. Still, I will keep searching for her and the truth. She deserves one person on her side. Her sad, confused words lie frozen on the paper she wrote them on. The one sentence that resonates is *Go Home Now*. She is right.

But before I go, Stella's information needs to be passed on. In the meantime, I hid the folder in the secret drawer and stacked the desk high with inconsequential things.

Sebastian yells from the kitchen, "Done with those flowers yet? I need the artichokes now."

I quickly move the large centerpiece to the bar where it will be on display tomorrow. I place the smaller centerpieces for the tables in the large wine cooler. I lean my forehead against the cool glass and count the containers. *Happy Easter*, I wish myself.

CAT & SEBA

Easter Sunday is a blur except for the moment Giorgione sent me to table one, the best table in the house. He said there was a complaint, and I needed to handle it.

With all the work still left in the kitchen, I rush out with red curls flying from my headband, sweat pouring down my face, and a variety of food smeared on my apron.

All three customers turn to face me as I approach the table. The grins on their faces are short lived as rage bubbles up in my eyes and spills over. I bite my lip so I don't blurt out what I'm really thinking. But they see my bloody anger displayed in red splotches on my face and neck.

To calm myself before speaking, I look over their heads and observe the tranquil sea. "Giorgione tells me there is something wrong with the food. Whatever isn't satisfactory will be replaced and your bill will be adjusted."

The grins fade. Carlo finally says, "No, Cat. We just wanted to see you and say hi. We knew Giorgione wouldn't let you out of the kitchen unless we complained. The food is perfect. We wanted to tell you that."

"Thank you, Carlo. If that's all, I still have work to do."

Carlo's face flushes. Antonio stares at his food. Lorenzo gazes out to sea.

I return to the kitchen and to Sebastian's question.

"What's wrong with the food?"

I drag a dish towel across my forehead and go back to preparing the next order.

"Nothing. It seems the table thought it was a joke to get me out of the kitchen."

"Who was at the table Caterina?"

"Since we're going to be working together, would you mind calling me Cat?"

"Only if you call me Seba. Who is at the table?"

"Lorenzo, Antonio, and Carlo."

"Ah."

"What?"

"I think you have a trio of admirers. You're angry. Why?"

"I don't have time for school-boy pranks. We're too busy for that."

"Cat, relax. Have some fun. I know what's been going on. The entire town knows. Being Stella's friend puts you in a difficult position. She caused a lot of trouble. Let's finish up here. We will talk after we close. *Va bene?*"

"Sure, Seba. Thanks."

Seba and I feast on the remains of the Easter meal. The dishwasher, the service staff, and even Giorgione wrap up their chores and go home to celebrate the rest of Easter with their families.

Seba pours more wine in my glass and says, "Tell me about Stella."

Tears leak. He reaches across the table with his napkin and dabs at my eyes and waits.

"You're the first person to ask me that. Did you know Stella?"

"It would be hard not to know her. I moved to Castello about five years ago when she and Antonio were still together. She was beautiful and famous. She ate here often and brought celebrity types with her."

He's quiet as he contemplates what to say next.

"She had this sensual, mysterious quality—the way she moved was like warm liquid gold. She looked straight at me and was interested in what I had to say. I was only a line chef at the time. It was hard not to like her. People talked bad about her, but I never listened. She was nice to me—complimented the food, asked questions about the wine, and even made suggestions about the decorations. Giorgione loved her and lit up like a neon sign whenever she was here. He couldn't do enough for her. But did I really know her? No, I didn't. Tell me about her. Tell me why you are her friend and such a fierce supporter."

The memories flow like a silent film—no words and over-exaggerated movements. I see her parading across campus in her school uniform, playing the role of Juliet in the school play, sharing colas and fries with me at the corner drugstore, splashing in the waves during our Italian summer vacations, riding on the float as queen of the prom, and moving her body sensually on a movie set. All of these images mutely file through my mind. Her radiant smile, her warm embrace, and her breathy way of speaking come at me in waves.

I hold back the tears and begin, "We were born friends—a friend who would desert me one moment and give me everything she had the next. She was as rare as a white Bengal tiger—unique and elegant—and ready to strike if you moved into her space without permission and ready to protect if anyone threatened those she loved."

Seba nodded.

"I simply can't believe she's dead," I sob.

He reaches across the table and pats my hand. I cry until there are no more tears. He leaves and returns with a damp towel. The cool cloth allows me to regain my composure. When I look up, Seba's eyes are misty.

"Are you okay?"

I nod.

"Tell me why you think Stella is dead."

"The necklace, the red starfish—the one she always wore. I found it on the cliffs. Stella would not leave it there if she was alive. I believe somehow in the final moments of her life she was able to remove her necklace. She meant for me to find it. That's how I know she's dead."

CAT

Talking to Seba and listening to his stories about Stella eased my grief. Over our Easter meal, I released some of the pain that had been bottled up for weeks. I returned to the villa lighter and less threatened by the situation.

My phone had been turned off for the entire day. Although I'm exhausted and desperately need a shower, I pour a glass of water, pull out a kitchen chair, and check the messages. I'm not surprised to find Carlo, Antonio, and Lorenzo's names flaring across the screen.

Lorenzo must have been the ringleader today. Antonio isn't capable of joking, and Carlo wouldn't until he felt more comfortable with me. Lorenzo must think the intimacy we shared gave him a special privilege. He is so wrong.

The anger rises, but I can't let it consume me. I put the phone down, open a kitchen drawer and randomly count utensils until I no longer see Lorenzo's handsome, grinning face. I continue the long-practiced method that numbs my mind and restores my balance.

The jangle of the doorbell jolts me. My heart, which had finally settled into a slow, easy rhythm, gears up to horse-race speed. It's late. I'm so weary, and I smell like food. My muscles tighten with fear until I remind myself that a murderer probably wouldn't ring the bell. Plus, the guard is still patrolling unless someone slit his throat.

I press the intercom, and Carlo's deep voice penetrates, "Cat, I'm sorry to come by so late but when I saw your lights, I stopped. I apologize for my behavior today. It was childish and inappropriate. Will you forgive me?"

"Of course, Carlo. Thank you for stopping by."

"I'd like to come in for a few minutes. I have something for you, and I don't want to leave it outside."

"Carlo, I'm too tired. I'm in the same clothes I wore all day at the restaurant. It's not a good time."

"Of course, Cat. What about tomorrow? I'll bring lunch? Say around two?"

I close my eyes tight trying to think of something to say. I don't want to see him or anyone. I want to be quiet in my own space. I want time to think about Stella and what to do next. My lack of response generates a slight cough from Carlo.

"Cat, are you there? I understand. I do. When you are ready, please call me. I want to apologize face to face. I want everything to be okay between us. Look, I'll leave what I have for you right outside the gate. Okay?"

I nod with relief, then realize he can't see the nod. "Thanks Carlo. I'll call you. Buonanotte."

There's a small scraping sound, the crank of an engine, and then silence. I look over the wall but can't see anything. I count the steps as my weary body trudges down. There are still sixty-eight, but I relish the tempo of the count. It wraps around me holding me secure until I reach the bottom.

I slide back the deadbolt. Red roses lie by the gate. When I pick them up, a card falls from the bouquet.

There are only eleven roses. To find the twelfth, look in the mirror. Bellissima Rossa!

Mi dispiace, Carlo

Monday the restaurant is closed. Maria and I chat over laundry and other household chores. She and Gino have seen Stella's letter, photos, and numerous contact lists. Gino filled in more pieces when he explained the midnight vigils with Stella and forays into the countryside tracking drug-laden fish vans. We decide to put the information in the secret drawer until Gino can make a connection with the authorities in Rome.

My phone is silent. I'm grateful. As I place the last stack of twice-counted linens in the closet, Maria pokes her head in the door.

"Gino picked up some fish. If you make a salad, I'll make some seafood pouches with potatoes, onions, tomatoes, capers, olives, and lemon. How does that sound?"

I smile and nod my approval.

Gino moves the table to the edge of the terrace. We have front row seats to watch the burnt orange sun hurl into the sea as Venus rises. The good weather lingers. We celebrate *Pasquetta* by dining outside. All over Italy, Easter Monday is a day of picnicking with friends. It's considered the first day of Spring, regardless of the date. I love the tradition and plan on incorporating it into my event calendar when I return home along with International Women's Day on March 8.

Prosecco is poured. Gino stands and says, "*Alla nostra per sempre amica Stella.*"

We join in, To Stella—our friend forever.

Night whispers on the edge of the terrace as the last ray of light folds into the sea. The lone tree stands ancient and strong, weathering whatever comes its way.

Will I stand strong? Will I stay and fight for Stella, or will I go home?

The scrapping of Gino's chair as he sits down pulls me back to the terrace. Maria has made wild mushroom ravioli for our first course. The pasta is tender and stuffed with freshly picked porcini, spring onions, ricotta cheese, and a pinch of thyme. Once plated, she sprinkles the dish generously with grated Parmesan, adds more sautéed mushrooms and a drizzle of olive oil.

Maria and I listen as Gino weaves stories of the ancient tradition of mushroom gathering. The land where his mushrooms grow is unknown even to Maria. Gino holds the long-standing family secret that is passed from father to child to grandchild.

It's the perfect opening for me to ask Gino and Maria about their family. Stella's letter indicated there was a child or grandchild that needed looking after.

"Are both of your families from Castello del Mare? Do you have children? Grandchildren?"

Gino glances at Maria and bows his head. Maria frowns and then says, "Yes, both our families have lived in this area for many generations. We have only one child—a daughter, Annalisa. She also has only one child, a son Eugenio Francesco. He is our little Gino."

"Tell me about him. How old is he? Can I meet him? Where do they live?"

Gino continues to keep his head down. Maria hesitates.

So I plow on, hoping they'll tell me.

"Is he in school? What grade? Maybe I could help him with his English."

Maria sighs, "He is eight, but he is not in school."

There's another long pause before Maria continues, "He's very sick, sickle cell. We both have the gene and passed it on to our daughter. His father is also a carrier. Little Gino suffers from our genetic failure. His life is painful. He cannot play like the other children."

"He cannot hunt mushrooms with me. I cannot pass my secrets of the land to him."

Gino lowers his head, agony written all over his face.

"I'm so sorry," I mumble, and I am so, so sorry.

Maria picks up when Gino stops, "Stella paid for all the extras: his private tutoring, special foods, and the medical bills not covered by the state. Dr. Moretti was treating him because Stella insisted. We don't know what will happen. Without Stella, we no longer trust him to treat Little Gino."

What can I say? I don't trust Antonio either.

"Is there another doctor in town? What about Lecce or Brindisi? Perhaps there are better doctors in the larger towns."

"Little Gino needs to see someone on a regular basis. Stella always called Antonio ahead, so we didn't have to wait. Now we never know if a doctor will see us. Sometimes we drive back and forth three days in a row because we cannot get in. Appointments are not honored. Without Stella's help we are at the mercy of the system."

"Tell me how I can help."

We talk until the moon is high in the sky and the sound of fishermen returning from the sea reminds us we need to sleep.

CAT & CARLO

Carlo pushes back from the table. He strolls across the terrace, slow deliberate steps, hands in his pockets, shoulders scrunched up. He leans against the baluster and drapes his well-toned upper body over the edge and gazes at the lone tree shrouded in black as the sun sets. The sea has been restless all day, brooding, frothing at the edges.

He rotates in my direction. A frown creases his forehead, his arms are tightly crossed on his chest.

"Are you sure it was Lorenzo's car?"

"No."

"Do you know who the Mercedes belongs to? Did you see anyone?"

"No."

"What made you think you recognized the voices? The words, the tone?"

"It's intangible—it was more the way the words were said, a pattern of speech although the speech was distorted. Does that make sense?"

Carlo shrugs and turns back to the sea.

Last night Maria and Gino suggested I confide in Carlo. He was delighted when I called and invited him over. He said he would bring dinner—an extension of Pasquetta.

The sky glows with a red-gold hue. He returns to the table and pours us another glass of Prosecco and unpacks our picnic supper. He has the gift of making me feel desirable. He's generous, attentive, and a smooth talker with years of calculated practice. But he is not Lorenzo.

Several times during our meal I begin to tell him everything only to find myself pulling back. Antonio and Lorenzo are his friends and colleagues. Whatever I tell one of them, the others will hear about soon enough. For now, Stella's letter and the drug smuggling evidence is a secret.

Carlo is easy to look at. He stretches back in his chair. His navy pullover is taut across his chest. He looks into my eyes without shifting. His stare is full of longing. He pours a splash of Salice Salentino in my glass and then his. When he hands me the glass, his hand lingers, wrapping around mine.

"Cat, you have a couple of days off. Why don't I pick you up in the morning and we'll drive to San Cataldo? I could stay or not. It would be your choice. You need to get away from here. It would be a good change for you."

This is exactly what I didn't want to happen. Anything I say is going to sound like rejection. I hesitate a little too long.

"Not a good idea, huh?"

I glance at the scattered remains of the scrumptious picnic supper: thin slices of lamb, the traditional dyed boiled eggs, tiny wild asparagus dressed with a squeeze of lemon and a drizzle of olive oil, fava beans and paper-thin spirals of prosciutto on a plate with soft pecorino, roasted baby artichokes, and a savory torta Pasqualina filled with ricotta and spinach, all next to a board of cheeses and fruit. And, of course, the Colomba di Pasqua—a traditional dove-shaped Easter bread filled with candied fruits.

The joy of the delicious meal fades as his smile hesitates between scorn and pain.

"Carlo."

He looks across the table and reaches for my hand.

"Cat, it's okay. I was just hoping. When you're ready. I'll be waiting."

Speechlessness is not one of my traits, but no words emerge as I struggle with what to say. Thankfully, Carlo keeps talking.

"You probably wish you hadn't told me about what you overheard and saw. I can understand why. I don't want to think Lorenzo is involved either. But seeing his car is incriminating. I've had my suspicions for some time. As long as no one else mentioned it, I dismissed it. Now, I need more information. What else do you know? Is there anything you're not telling me?"

My face heats up, but I hold his stare. "I can't think of anything. It was Maria and particularly Gino who thought it would be helpful to talk to you. Gino says my life is in danger and you are trustworthy."

"What about you, Cat? Do you trust me?"

What a predicament? I rack my brain for something plausible to say. Of course, I don't trust him. But I'm not going to broadcast that bit of information to him.

"Look, Carlo, I don't know you well enough to say I do or don't trust you. But according to Gino, you're my best bet. That's not exactly a feel-good answer, but it's all I have at the moment. I don't know who's responsible for Stella's disappearance, or I guess I should say her murder. It could be anyone."

I pause, but Carlo seems distracted. His hands are restless as he swirls the wine glass. He doesn't look at me.

I continue, "Both Lorenzo and Antonio are withholding information. Antonio because he gave Stella drugs and Lorenzo because he knew about Stella's drug connection with the mafia. What about you Carlo? What aren't you telling me?"

Carlo stares at me. Tense lines crease his forehead. He pushes up from the table and paces the length of the terrace.

"What do you know about Stella and Lorenzo's relationship?"

Of course he picks the one topic I refuse to discuss.

"What do you mean?"

"They were sleeping together. They thought they were being discreet but in a small village that's impossible."

I shrug and say, "If they were having an affair, then why didn't Lorenzo protect her?

Carlo's stare penetrates my thoughts.

My mind rushes ahead trying to pick a neutral conversation. But Carlo lets me off the hook.

"Maybe all of this is about a love affair and a jealous husband?"

"Maybe, I don't know. Maybe Lorenzo or Antonio thought they would be better off without Stella around. If she talked, it would be trouble for both of them. They each had a reason to get rid of her. And what about you Carlo? What did Stella have on you?"

The question hangs in the air. He sits back down.

"*Allora*, you don't trust me. You think I murdered Stella? Or would you rather not say?"

The question is unexpected.

"Gino and Maria said I could trust you. I trust them. I have to leave it at that."

I hope that sounds genuine. If he could read my mind, he'd see the thin veil of contempt I feel for him and all the others.

Carlo stands up abruptly, hitting the table leg and knocking over his glass of wine. We both stare, watching the crimson stain spread. "I'm sorry, Cat."

"Why?"

"Because I'm not going to do what I want to do."

"Which is?"

"Stay here with you. Protect you. That guard outside your gate is a joke. Half the time he's dozing and the other half he's eating, smoking, or talking to someone who wanders by."

His off-the-wall response surprises me.

"I don't need your protection," I snap.

"I know you can take care of yourself, but you need to be prepared."

"For what?"

"How proficient are you with a gun?"

"Somewhat. When I filed for divorce, my priest suggested I purchase a gun. He was concerned about violent repercussions from my ex. He knew my story, and he saw what happened at the divorce trial. A good friend picked up a Friday night special for me and tried to teach me to shoot it. I wasn't a great student, but I can pull the trigger."

"I'm guessing you don't have a weapon now?"

"Heavens, no. I'm not eligible to carry one in Italy. It would be illegal for me to be armed. What are you suggesting?"

"I'll get one for you. I'm staying in town for a while longer. You have tomorrow and the next day off. I'll pick you up at three thirty."

"What for?"

"For target practice."

I stammer, "What?"

"Target practice. I'll pick you up tomorrow.

"But if it's illegal for me to have a weapon, it means you'd be in big trouble if anyone finds out."

"I won't tell anyone—what about you?"

"No, but I don't want this to backfire on either of us. I think the penalty for me would be prison. And probably a tougher sentence for you.

"Oh, Cat. No one will know. The places we'll practice are remote. And as long as you don't flash the gun around, you'll be fine"

Shit. What the heck is this all about? He's crazy to get a gun for me. I'm crazy to agree to this. But I do want to protect myself and right now he's the only person who's offered.

"Well?"

"Sure. Thanks for not only believing I can take care of myself but also for giving me the tools to do that. That's an unusual characteristic for an Italian man."

He grins back at me and says, "My mother was Sicilian and fiercely independent. She taught me to respect women and to understand their strength and courage. She also taught me to cook and to clean. I'll help you clean up this mess."

After a long lingering kiss, Carlo walked down the steps and out the gate. He wondered what had possessed him to offer to teach Cat to shoot. Somehow in her presence he became an idiot. He'd had a few dumb moments in his life, but this one was the dumbest.

CAT

The joy of being in the kitchen and cooking with Seba makes me less lonely. The restaurant keeps me focused and my mind occupied. Giorgione and Seba make me laugh. The hours fly by. Often I stay after lunch to assist Seba in preparing the dinner menu. He quickly caught on to my scheme to butter him up for his splendid ball-shaped tiramisu recipe.

For the past couple of days, Carlo has picked me up and driven me to target practice. I'm now in possession of a delightfully small Pico that fits snugly in my purse. At first I was nervous about carrying a concealed weapon but with each practice session I gained confidence and my marksmanship improved.

Each time Carlo picks me up, we drive to a different location. When I ask why, he says he doesn't want to draw attention to what we're doing. He says it would be a problem for both of us if we were observed and reported. I don't ask whose property we are using or how he knows all these different people. But wherever we show up, the target practice area has been prepared ahead of our arrival. I also don't ask what will happen to me if I actually shoot someone with Carlo's gun. Normally, knowledge is the most important thing to me, but sometimes, like now, it's not.

Today, as usual, I arrive at the restaurant at six in the morning. Based on our arrangement, I arrive first and leave first. Giorgione comes in a couple of hours after I do, and Seba joins us around one.

Since Carlo picks me up around three most days, I've been putting in longer hours and working with Seba on the evening menu.

Last night Giorgione and Seba surprised me with a birthday cake—a delectable chocolate, caramel concoction. To my delight, it was topped with Seba's special golden orb of tiramisu. Of course, I wept. It's my thirty-eighth birthday—and Stella's. She's not here to celebrate with me. The sense of loss permeates every inch of my body. But still I'm so grateful for the loving gesture from these two men who have completely captured my heart. Our mutual love for food gives us hours and hours of succulent conversations.

The morning is cool for May. I shiver as I search through my purse for the key. It takes a few seconds to open the door as the key always sticks. I keep forgetting to tell Giorgione. I drop my purse on the floor so I can close and lock the door behind me.

As I reach for the light switch, a voice growls, "*Ferma*—Stop!"

"What?" I stammer.

"Move away from the door! Now!"

My hand falls away from the light switch. My keys clatter to the floor.

My voice almost disappears, "What do you want? There's no money here. The owner removes it every evening before closing."

I speak slowly and clearly with a silent prayer that my voice sounds steady while I back away from the door. The person behind the voice moves into a shadowy light, but I can't make out his features. His clothes are dark. A black hat is pulled low on his face and a black scarf covers his nose and mouth.

"Money—ha. I want the folder Stella left you and the necklace."

"What folder?"

The person shifts, hitting the coat rack which bangs into the wall. I grab my purse and duck behind the reception stand. I huddle in fear, grateful the podium is solid wood and bulky. Crouching low, I'm paralyzed until a small part of my brain yells at me to get the gun out of my purse. My trembling fingers fumble until they touch the cold metal barrel. With shaking hands, I pull it out and crawl along the back wall.

"Stand up," the voice snarls. "Now or I'll blow you and this place to bits!"

I whimper—a fragile and weak sound—even to my ears. I throw my purse across the floor away from the voice.

A barrage of shots rings out and then stops. Silence prevails with only the acid bite of gunpowder in the air. After my shooting experiences with Carlo, I know the shooter's gun isn't empty yet. I wait, listening for sounds.

"If you don't come out now, I'm coming in and nothing you say or do will stop me from killing you. You're dumb just like Stella."

Footsteps move in my direction. There's a bottle on the low shelf behind me. I grab it and throw. It hits the wall and ricochets across the room. Gun fire follows its trajectory. I stand on wobbly legs and fire in the direction of the shots until I hear a yelp. I continue pulling the trigger until there are no more bullets. Then I hit the floor.

"Shit. You stupid bitch. You will pay."

Sirens blast through the walls of the restaurant, wailing harmoniously in my ears. The door to the terrace slams against the wall as the sound of running footsteps fades. La Canzone is eerily quiet until the front door is splintered, and police in riot gear push through.

"You are an idiot. You could have been killed. Why do you have a gun?" Comes flooding out of Lorenzo's mouth in one long sentence as he helps me off the floor and jerks the gun out of my hand.

"Stay here! Don't move," he yells as he rushes to the terrace.

I slump against the wall and wonder where the person with the grappa is when you need them. My knees buckle as I slide into a weepy clump on the floor.

CAT & LORENZO

"Why do you have a gun? Did it ever cross your mind that it's illegal for you to have a gun in Italy? I could throw you in jail. Perhaps that's what I'll do to keep you safe and out of my way."

Lorenzo's sullen frown consumes his face as he paces back and forth in front of the fireplace. We are the only two in the villa. Giorgione and Seba have returned to the restaurant. Antonio has patched the scrapes and bruises on my body and left. Maria wrapped me in blankets while Gino built the fire and thankfully provided the shot of grappa I so badly needed. When Lorenzo dismissed them, Maria gave him a stern warning that he was not to upset me. None of them know exactly what happened. Lorenzo had warned me not to open my mouth, and I hadn't.

"Before you arrest me, would you grant me leniency to sleep in my own bed for one more night or at least a short nap?"

"Not funny, Cat. This incident was not only serious, it's the third time someone has tried to kill you. Are you waiting for the fourth and final time? Is that it?"

"No, I'm waiting for the time when there's a slip up—a voice or a face I recognize. I was close today. I'm pretty sure it was the same guy in the Mercedes at Zinzulusa. My mind is a scrambled mess right now, but I believe I can make a positive ID. But please don't drag me down to the station. I've had enough excitement for today. Let me rest, get a good night's sleep and come down to the station tomorrow."

"Cat, you are still in shock. I have to go back to the restaurant to ensure the crime scene isn't compromised. But before I leave, you have to tell me who gave you the gun. Then I have to figure out what to do with it."

"Carlo."

Lorenzo looks both surprised and hurt by my answer. "I don't understand. Why would he do that? Did you ask him?"

"No, of course, I didn't. But after I told him about the two previous attempts on my life, the dead bird, and the black rose, he said I needed to be able to protect myself. He's been teaching me how to shoot."

With every word I utter, Lorenzo shakes his head, "*Sei pazza* —you are crazy. Why would you confide in Carlo? What's going on, Cat? You're forcing me to put guards inside your house. Do you want that? Why are you letting Carlo teach you to shoot? Why?"

"Please, no guards inside the house. I know it's illegal and wrong and you're angry. But so far he's the only person who has offered me a way to protect myself."

"You realize I can haul you to the station and Carlo too. If I do that, you won't have to worry about going home for a long time. Cat, why didn't you ask me?"

"Ha, why would I do that? Would you have given me a gun and offered to teach me?"

"You think you're in control here, but you have no idea the trouble you're in. Go to bed! I have to leave. If you don't promise to stay put until I return, I'll lock you in a cell."

It seems I've pushed him as far as I could, so I change tactics.

"Before you go, do you think I hit him? There were a lot of expletives, so I'm hoping I did."

"Ah, so now you want me to tell you if your training paid off. Yes, there were traces of blood on the terrace. And before you ask, the answer is no. You cannot have the gun back. I'm going to cover for you this one time. But if you ever pull a stunt like this again, I'll be the first to testify against you."

He stands, daring me to say anything.

"I'm doubling the watch. It doesn't matter whether you want me to or not. It's done."

"Thanks Lorenzo. I won't protest."

He starts out the door then turns around and asks, "What did the intruder want?"

The question is unexpected. I hesitate before responding, "I guess he wanted to rob the place."

"Hmmm," is all he says.

His footsteps chime sixty-eight steps. The gate creaks open, then closes with a thud. The silence is replaced by the sound of bullets ricocheting in my mind. I need a long run to make the sounds go away, but when I peek over the wall, two police officers are conferring. I'm sure they won't let me out of my prison.

I turn away, pick up one of Stella's starfish books and fall asleep dreaming about this amazing sea creature that can regenerate its arms.

Later, I take a shower and prepare a simple caprese salad and heat up Maria's leftover cannellini bean soup. A crusty hunk of bread and a large glass of Le Petri, a lush Salento Fiano produced from the Mottura vineyards, is all I need for a feast. All is well with the world as long as I can cook, eat, count and not think too much.

Lorenzo returned in the afternoon with a smile on his face instead of the scowl he left with this morning. When I ask him about the gun, he's evasive.

"It's fine. You're not in trouble."

"Then Carlo's not in trouble either?"

"Of course not. Why would you think that?"

"You were angry with me."

"Yes, angry and worried about you. I'm not sure you've told me everything about this morning's robbery. If the person who broke into the restaurant this morning is connected to Stella, you would tell me, right?"

I don't answer, pretending I don't hear him. Instead, I say, "It's a beautiful day. You've been promising to take me for a boat ride. What about today?"

"Now? Cat, you were nearly killed. I've lost track of how many times I've said that. I guess you are named correctly, but even cats run out of lives at some point. You're headed in that direction. You need to rest, and I need to get back to work."

"Do you have to go back? Could you knock off early just this once? Wouldn't a boat ride be good for both of us?"

He's at the door before he turns around. "Cat, you're impossible. Apprehending the person who is behind all these attempts on your life is my job."

"Lorenzo, you haven't taken any time off since I've been here. Just for a few hours. Please?"

"Cat, are you sure you're up to it?"

"Yes, I desperately need parole from my prison."

He manages a smile before saying, "Grab a jacket. It'll be cool on the water. We can stop on the way to the marina and pick up a bottle of wine and some cheese."

"There is plenty of wine and cheese here. Let me throw a few things together.

Lorenzo follows me to the kitchen. Together we pack olives, a round of Burrata, grapes, a small loaf of olive studded bread, and a bottle of Primitivo.

The spray from the boat's wake covers me in salty mist. The warmth of the down jacket is comforting as clouds dart across the sun. Lorenzo stands at the helm, strong and steady. The wind whips through his hair. There's a partial smile on his face as he guides us out of the harbor into the sea. Once we are clear, I join him on the upper deck.

"Do you mind if we cruise around this area and down to the caves?" I ask.

"Still looking for Stella?"

"Maybe."

"Cat, the tides are too strong and changeable around here. We'll never find her.

"I need to look."

He cuts the engine back. We drift toward the rocks and a small sandy beach.

"Do you remember?" He asks softly.

"Yes, I remember everything about those summers."

His hand caresses the teak helm as he gazes at the shoreline.

"Dreams are our imagination in overdrive. Stella was my dream. I wanted her to remain the same young girl that I fell in love with—the girl from those long-ago summers. I couldn't reconcile the real Stella with that dream. If I had, she would still be alive."

I touch his arm, "Don't Lorenzo. Reliving it won't change anything. We make choices based on who we are and what we know. It's called on-the-job living. We don't always make the right decisions. It's impossible to get through life without regrets."

We gravitate toward each other in our mutual sorrow. He reaches for me, pulls me into his chest, and holds me tight. We stay that way, watching the tide drag our dreams out to sea as the waves shatter our hearts, and our lives beat against the rocks.

CAT

The afternoon on the boat with Lorenzo leaves me sad and restless. We had talked openly as we drifted down the coast. The conversation was far more intimate than the night we had spent together. We shared a glimpse into the people we had grown up to be. When he dropped me off at the door, I asked him to come in. He said he had to get back to the station. He held me tight as his lips brushed my hair, cheek, and lips. He left me without any answers.

Now I pace the terrace, wine glass in hand, as I contemplate the lone tree in the glow of moonlight. Words escape me as I search through my vocabulary in an attempt to describe the dark and light merging into a thousand cracked images. In Italian there's a beautiful word that artists use: *chiaroscuro*—contrasting light and dark, created when light falls unevenly—a texturing and layering of the light and the shadowy shades.

We live in a shadowy world that requires us to abandon our true selves. I'm guilty of that as was Stella. We each, in our own way, desperately needed to fit in. We sought approval from others until the gifts we were born with disappeared. We settled for lives that quietly killed all we were meant to be.

A deep sigh rises from my chest. I long for Stella to be standing beside me. It's an ache that will not relinquish its hold on me. My throat tightens as I focus intently on the tree in an attempt to prevent my backed-up tears from flooding the terrace.

Once I finish the wine, I wash the glass and prepare for bed. I'm not sleepy, so I pull a heavy volume from the bookshelf. I laugh out loud at the title *Starfish: Biology and Ecology of the Asteroidea* by John Lawrence. I laugh because Stella never cracked a book throughout our school years. Yet she liked to impress and a heavy-duty tome like this is exactly what I would find in her house. I can hear her saying, "Oh Cat, who cares whether or not I've read it. Doesn't it look grand on the coffee table?"

The bed beckons. I crawl in and open to the prologue:

Among the most fascinating animals in the world's oceans are the more than 2,000 species of starfish.

Starfish are of interest not only to echinoderm specialists but also to marine biologists and invertebrate zoologists in general and, increasingly, to the medical community. A starfish's ability to regenerate body parts is almost unequaled in the animal world...

I'm captivated by this tiny predator who turns its stomach inside out to capture food and who can break off its arm if captured and regenerate a new one. I want to keep reading, but my eyes droop. My eyes close.

A loud thud startles me awake. I scoot up in bed and listen. A faint click like a latch being lifted drifts into my half awake mind. Then silence and I'm left with my vivid imagination. I put the book on the floor, turn off the light, and snuggle under the duvet.

CAT & CARLO

When Carlo doesn't show by four, I stick my head in the kitchen and tell Seba I'm leaving. He's never been late before. I'd made it clear to Lorenzo that I would tell Carlo in person that our target practice days were over. His not showing up guarantees Lorenzo told him.

I'm more than disappointed. During the time Carlo and I had spent together, I discovered I really liked him. That made it even more important for me to tell him in person. Each time Lorenzo gets close to me, his behavior gives me another reason not to trust him.

Carlo's car is parked in front of the villa but I don't see him. I drop my tote on the ground, brush crumbs from my shirt, and attempt to untangle my hair. As I scan the landscape, I notice that the police are not visible. But Carlo is.

He's leaning against the crumbling wall across the street, the one built centuries earlier. His gaze follows the flight of sea birds. He doesn't seem to notice me.

As usual, including when we were target practicing, he is attired appropriately. Contrasting thoughts cross my mind as I slow my pace to feast on his profile. He's so elegant in dress, speech, and mannerisms, as if he's trying too hard to make a good impression. What little he shared about his childhood was harsh and probably contributes to his need to be in control. Most of us are lost children still trying to make amends for not being the perfect child—years later still wondering why we aren't good enough.

His black blazer pulls tight across his hunched up shoulders. Black slacks outline his slim body against the gray stones of the wall. He turns to face me and the startling whiteness of his shirt against the black makes me blink. I wave and pick up my pace. He doesn't acknowledge me.

"What happened, Carlo? I waited for you."

"Why would I show up? You must have known Lorenzo would contact me. Did it ever occur to you to call? To let me know that someone shot at you? Why didn't you?"

Yikes! He's angry. I stew on what to say as he continues.

"Cat, I'm disappointed. I thought we were friends. I was hoping we'd become more than friends. This little incident shows me just how much you don't trust me. Why is that?"

"Let's go inside, Carlo."

"Why? Do you want to humiliate me further? Do you think I enjoyed having Lorenzo ream me out for giving you a gun, for teaching you to shoot? We had agreed not to tell him, or maybe you forgot?"

"Look, I'm sorry. I had to tell him after I used the gun to shoot the person who broke into the restaurant. But he promised me he would let me tell you. I planned to do that when you picked me up today."

"*Madre di dio*, what's wrong with you? You are like Stella—playing me for a fool!"

"What?" I shutter as words leave me. I stare at him while the anger rises from deep within the pit of my stomach.

"How dare you compare me to Stella. I'm not Stella. I didn't play you for a fool. If you feel like a fool, that's your problem. You can come in and we can discuss this, or you can leave. I don't give a damn."

I fumble with the keys and leave the gate open as I rush up the steps. I'm half way up when a car door slams and the high-pitched whine of an engine roars into life. I trudge back down and watch as he drives away.

After a shower to remove restaurant fumes from my hair and

clothes, I lounge on the terrace. As spring advances, the sunsets are longer, slower, and much showier. This evening an endless exuberance of color plays out its dramatic death of another day—a day which has strayed far from my expectations. Like the sunset, after its first burst of magnificent colors, I wane into shades of darkness.

A message buzzes on my phone. From Lorenzo: *Sorry could not text sooner. Major breakthrough today. Had to contact Carlo about the gun. Heads up. He is angry. See you tomorrow.*

Shit, thanks so much for letting me know too late.

A sliver of moon pokes through the clouds as I contemplate what to fix for dinner. I often bring food home from the restaurant but didn't today. I push myself out of the chair and lean against the baluster. A car without lights moves slowly up the hill. It's a perfect *chiaroscuro* moment when light fades and shadows grow.

The police patrol is still not visible. Lorenzo must have pulled them off to assist with whatever major breakthrough he mentioned. But why wouldn't he let me know when he texted? I debate whether or not to text him, then decide against it. I don't want him rushing here to babysit me.

CAT

Z *INZULUSA CAVES, ITALY*

Rough hands jerk me from bed. My knees buckle and hit the floor. I'm yanked upright. Pain radiates up my arms as they're twisted behind me. Ropes burn into my flesh when I struggle to free myself. The dark room is heavy with sweat—mine and theirs. A low curdling scream erupts from me as something wet smoothers my nose and mouth. A strange, sweet odor curls into my space. A rough shroud is placed over my head as consciousness leaves. A soft, droopy sensation courses through my veins.

Cold water laps at my feet. Blackness and fear surround me. My skin shivers. Drums pound relentlessly against my skull. I retch as waves of nausea buckle my stomach. The vomit backs into my taped mouth. I hold my breath until a shudder bursts, forcing air into my lungs. My back aches from the cold, wet stones. Intense pain flows through my body. I drift into darkness.

Gagging wakes me. The shroud is gone. I gulp in big chunks of air, hungry for life. My hands and feet are still bound. Struggling only tightens the rope's grip. I scream in silence. My mouth rips away from the tape leaving raw flesh in its path.

Bit by bit my eyes adjust. Wet boulders surround me. My throbbing eyes notice and follow the filtered sunlight to a small opening directly above. In a lucid moment, I realize I'm in one of the hundreds of dwarf-size caves close to *Grotta Zinzulusa.*

The thunder of my heartbeat overcomes all other sounds. Darkness descends again.

When I surface, the gloom of the cave surrounds me. The sun has shifted indicating its early evening. The water swishes around my calves. I force my mind to function, to stay awake. I won't be a victim.

These are caves I know. I have explored them many times, first as a child and several times since my return. There are hundreds of hidden nooks and crannies scattered along the coastal road. There's always an opening somewhere; otherwise, I wouldn't be here. I shift my body to the left until I see a minute shaft of light. The wet ropes around my ankles tighten when I move, but the ropes around my hands are dry. I rotate my wrists until draggers of pain stab into my flesh. They don't give.

I rest, letting waves of fatigue and nausea pass. I gulp in more air and begin again. I rock back and forth until the wall becomes a brace, enough to push myself into a standing position. Dizziness slams into my head as it cracks against the serrated boulders—blood trickles down my face.

My mind ricochets to Stella. Is this how she died? Was she bound up and thrown into the sea? Or was she left in one of these caves to drown inch by inch?

My soggy nightclothes cling to my body. The water laps in and out of the cave as the tide ebbs and flows. I press against the wall and try to take a step.

CAT

Hobbling, I inch my way toward the shaft of light. My breath comes in heaving pants. I fall against the cave wall as my muscles cramp. The sluggishness of my body makes progress slow and painful. The light shaft gives way to a small jagged opening. A silhouette stands just outside. A sob hovers in my throat as I push away thoughts of dying.

A whisper enters the cave.

"Cat, are you in there? If you are, make a noise. Don't be afraid. I'm here to help."

I don't breathe or move.

"Cat, it's Gino. Cat, can you hear me?"

My mind, dulled from the drugs, can't process the words.

The figure moves away from the opening.

I frantically search for anything that will make a noise. A small ledge behind my back is lined with stones. I backup and move my tied hands back and forth until they hit and scatter the pebbles.

First a hand and then a body squeezes through the small opening. Relief floods every crevice of my body as Gino steadies me.

"It's going to be okay. Stay in the cave. They are coming for you now, but I will take care of them. Don't make a sound. I'll be back for you as soon as I can. I promise"

I catch a glimpse of the back of his dark jacket, then he's gone. Silence echoes around the chamber. I close my eyes, lean against the ledge, and focus on hope. I will be rescued.

A small rumble of stones gathering and rolling into the sea alerts me that Gino's not alone. Muttering voices start and stop. I drag myself closer to the opening. Gino stands in front of the cave, his back to me.

He says, "Don't come any closer. I will shoot."

The response is harsh, "Move away from the entrance. I don't want to kill you. If I do, your crazy brother will be breathing down my neck and causing trouble. Leave now. Cat is no concern of yours."

"She is my concern. You killed Stella. I won't let you kill Caterina."

"Ha, don't be stupid, Gino. I didn't kill Stella. I don't ever have to pull a trigger."

"True. You don't have that kind of courage. Riccardo did the job for you, but it's the same as if you killed her. We have Riccardo under surveillance. He'll be captured. He'll double-cross you when he's indicted for murder.

"Ha—Riccardo will not be captured. I patched him up myself after that bitch shot him. If you look behind you, you'll see he's here as my backup in case you get any crazy ideas. When this is over, he will simply disappear. There is nothing you can pin on him or me. You see, I know how it all works—both the Guardia and the mafia."

Gino struggles to keep the conversation going as he edges away from the entrance of the cave, "You think you know everything, but you don't. You thought Riccardo was smart enough to kill Stella and take the necklace. You thought Stella wasn't clever enough to catch on, but she did. You haven't been able to find the evidence she collected on you, and you haven't found the necklace. How smart does that make you?"

"Ah, Gino, you're just a petty criminal. In a minute, I'll shoot you. It's your choice. I can kill you or wound you. You still have some usefulness for me, and I don't hold grudges. First, move away from the entrance. Cat will tell me where everything is. She won't have a choice."

Gino glances around as something moves on his left. Riccardo slides out from behind a boulder. He's so close I can see the dark stubble on his face. He points his gun in Gino's face. There is only the cave behind him. If Gino enters, both of us will be killed. There's no escape. But Gino continues to inch away from the entrance.

"Stand still," the voice commands.

Gino freezes in place. From a distance other voices ricochet among the boulders. My heart leaps until I realize it's probably fishermen putting out to sea. Gino sees his chance and leaps to the side. He ducks down as an explosion of bullets pelts the cave's entrance.

I press myself into the wall. The thuds of bullets slamming into the cave and into Gino's body remove all hope. The shots boomerang, leaving me deaf. Through the narrow opening, I catch a glimpse of Gino's body—still and crumpled.

More rocks tumble as footsteps approach the cave.

"You stupid shit. You killed Gino. I wanted him alive."

Riccardo scowls, "I thought he was going to shoot you? What did you want me to do? Let him?"

"You are an idiot. Move away from the entrance."

More shuffling until a voice calls to me. "Cat, are you okay? Stay inside until I make sure it's safe."

The voice is low. My ears still echo with the cacophony of bullets smashing into the rocks. Is it Lorenzo? Did Lorenzo let Riccardo kill Gino?

I shuffle toward the entrance.

"It's safe to come out, Cat."

My gut tells me it's the wrong thing to do. But if I'm going to die, I would rather be outside.

I hobble into the open space and lock eyes with the dark beady stare of Riccardo. His arm is bandaged at the elbow. I shiver with fear. Before I can say anything, Riccardo points the gun at me and motions.

"Drop to your knees and don't move," he snarls.

There were two voices, but only Riccardo stands in front of me with a gun. I take a furtive look around. There's nothing but endless boulders and the sound of waves slapping them. I drop to my knees. The image of my demise, hands and feet tied execution style, consumes me. My silent voice screams—I want to live! I want to go home!

CAT & IL PADRONE

Riccardo moves closer. All his anger focuses on me. The gun points at my chest. His cruel eyes never leave my face.

When he's only a few feet away, he smirks, "You're gonna die for what you did to me. But before I kill you, tell me where I can find the necklace and the folder. Gino said you have them."

He leans in and rips the tape off my mouth. Warm blood mingles with dried vomit and oozes down my chin. He puts the gun against my forehead and shifts it back and forth. Sweat pours down my face and merges with the filth on my chin.

"It's too bad I don't have time to torture you," he says, speaking softly as the gun trails down the side of my face and stops at my throat.

He laughs, a hollow, brittle sound that echoes off the boulders. His crackle becomes an evil staccato tune in the air.

"Please, please don't do this. I have the necklace and the folder. You can have them if you let me go. I won't tell anyone. I swear."

My words sound stupid to my own ears and also to his. He laughs again and kicks me. Whatever is left in my stomach erupts covering his shiny black shoes. He screams at me, "You bitch" as he slams the gun into my head.

"Stop!"

We both look in the direction of the voice. Carlo steps out from behind a large boulder. His gun is leveled at Riccardo's chest.

"Move away from Cat," he shouts. "Throw your gun over here. You've done enough damage. If you want to live, leave now."

Riccardo backs away from me and appears to turn away before swinging wide and leveling his gun at Carlo. He hesitates only a moment before opening fire, but the moment costs him.

I cringe and drop on all fours. Bullets fly around us. Riccardo's mouth opens, a trail of blood oozes down his chin. His knees buckle as he tumbles into a crevice. A low moan escapes his lips as small rocks tumble across the terrain and land on top of him.

I drag myself closer to Gino. A hand touches my shoulder. Through tear-filled eyes, I look up.

Sobbing, I cry out, "Please, help Gino."

Carlo is so close the heat from his body radiates on mine. He's gentle as he turns me away from Gino's body.

"I'm sorry, Cat. Gino is dead. Let me help you."

He squats in front of me and uses the sleeve of his jacket to wipe my face. But he doesn't untie my arms or legs. The gun is still in his hand.

"Cat, I can't let you go. You would ruin my life."

"What do you mean?" I whisper. "Carlo, untie me. Get me out of here."

"I can't, Cat. If you had gone home when you were threatened, none of this would have happened. Now three people are dead. Why didn't you keep out of this? All I want is the folder with the evidence that Stella collected and the necklace. They're mine.

"I don't have them."

He smirks and continues, "Like you, Stella refused. She's dead."

"You? You killed her?"

"Let's just say I made the arrangements. When Stella went back on her word to become a mule, I threatened to expose Antonio. She was shocked as she thought we were friends—good friends. You understand what good friends mean, don't you Cat? Stella was not naive like you are. She knew exactly what she was doing when she slept with me. Or at least she thought she did. It was my plan all along to sleep with her then humiliate her the way she did me."

"What are you saying? Why would you kill Stella? Who are you?"

"There's not enough time to tell you the whole story. If you hadn't told Lorenzo I gave you the gun, none of this would have happened. I really thought you were different. But, like Stella, you're still one of the summer girls. You almost fooled me."

"What are you talking about?"

"I'm talking about Stella. Her addiction. All Stella had to do was turn over the necklace, the money she owed me, and all the information she had collected. She probably didn't tell you she'd agreed to work for me. In return I agreed not to harm Antonio or his practice. It wasn't difficult to bring her around when I told her Antonio would be the price. Stella was smart in many ways but stupid in others. If she'd kept her word, none of this would have happened."

"You're making this Stella's fault? A reason to kill her? Stella would never work for you."

"You don't know Stella as the conniving little bitch she was. At first, she agreed to transport drugs. But you're right, she was lying to me. She was simply buying more time to collect evidence against me."

I struggle to stand up, but the gun nudges me to stay kneeling.

"Don't be foolish, Cat. Who do you think shot Riccardo? Sooner or later, someone would have connected him to Stella's death. Eventually, he would have become a liability. You, I'm sorry to say, are also a liability. Like Riccardo, you are no longer useful and you know too much. I have to kill you."

"What about the information Stella collected? Don't you want it?"

He grunts in annoyance.

"Of course I want it. But I'll get it with or without your help. And if it never surfaces, it won't matter. The information she collected has lost its impact. I've already moved the drop-off point and the storage area for the drugs. My only concern is if she has a photo of me in her file. I rarely made appearances on the dock but occasionally I had to intervene. What she discovered is certainly enough to alert the police. But if there's a photo, it would make it difficult to extricate myself from the smuggling operation. But not impossible. If there isn't a photo, the information she collected will only curtail our activities while the police poke around. That will create a financial loss for me but one I can easily overcome."

"But Stella has witnesses who are willing to testify."

"Ha, I'm not worried about her witnesses. Not one of the fishermen will corroborate her story. They need their jobs. And Gino's record alone would have easily discredited him as a reliable witness."

He smirks as he looks across at Gino's crumbled body.

"Now it doesn't matter since he's dead. And Stella. Stella got what she deserved except for the public humiliation I longed for. That's all I really wanted."

"Why?"

"I've wasted enough time. The story ends here, Cat."

"No, it doesn't. I deserve to know. You're going to kill me. So what difference does it make? I certainly won't be telling anyone."

He touches my hair so softly, and says, "I'm sorry, Cat. I'd hoped we'd become more than friends and that one day you'd understand."

I wanted to scream out *you're a gangster and a lowlife* but I don't.

"It would have been easy to let you go. That is until I saw you with the folder when you left Cesarea. I knew you'd found Stella's hiding place."

"You were there when I found the folder? How did you know I would be in Cesarea?"

"After you found the necklace, I had you tailed."

"Why didn't you kill me in Cesarea? You could have left my body in the hideaway and taken the information. No one knew I was there."

"I didn't know that. I was sure you would have told Gino and

Maria and maybe Lorenzo. Plus, I had no idea you would find the evidence in the cave."

He chuckles before continuing, "I also didn't happen to have my silencer with me. It would be stupid to kill you in a public place. When you left, I followed you back to the villa. It was late, you didn't have time to hand the evidence over to anyone else. That meant you had to hide it in the house, at least overnight. But somehow you managed to tuck it away where I couldn't find it. Your house has been searched. So what did you do with the information and the necklace?"

"If you kill me, you will get neither. I understand why you want the evidence, but why is the necklace so important to you."

He looks at me with sadness before saying, "I spent years digging myself out of the squalor of my ancestors. You don't remember me, do you? Neither did the others. I was one of the poor village boys back during those summers. All of you went out of your way to ignore me —but none more than Stella. She was so beautiful. I tried to talk to her, but she laughed in my face and called me *escremento*."

I shudder. The past and present are intrinsically bound in a web of deceit and lies. How easy it is for one thoughtless word to leave a lasting scar—to push the start button for a slow descent into hell. An unkind act. A slight. An insult. A betrayal. A split second when we choose to close our eyes and our hearts. That exclusion and that one word had crippled Carlo. They'd dug in like a hook and festered for years. He'd lived out each day of his life with intent to harm Stella. Her murder had been the end result of a deformed seed planted so many years ago.

Carlo's eyes smolder with unforgiving anger. This one incident had infected his entire existence. We were only children, yet Carlo had chosen to let our actions and that one word destroy his life.

"I'm sorry. I didn't know."

The gun eases away from my head as he continues."It doesn't matter. I left my despicable childhood and made a home in Bari. One of the local dons noticed me and groomed me for the life I have now. I've created an empire for myself. I'm not about to lose it."

"But Stella didn't deserve to be killed," I wail.

"Stella was the one complication I hadn't counted on. She knew more than anyone else. But she was stupid to try to con me, just as you are. Both of you snooped into my business. She died for that reason and so will you. I'm sorry, Cat. You can only redeem yourself if you tell me where the necklace and the folder are. This is the last time I will ask."

"Stella's attorney has everything with instructions to contact the authorities," I blurt out.

"Ha, you didn't have time to get the folder to Stella's attorney. How would you do that?"

"If you had me followed, then you know I had three visitors at the villa after I found the folder. It wasn't difficult to persuade one of them to hide it. I'm not as stupid as you think."

He laughs with nervousness before saying, "Nor are you as smart as you think. Perhaps you don't know I'm a close friend of Stella's attorney. In fact, you don't need to tell me more. Gino admitted to me that he had put the necklace in Stella's safe deposit box. It will stay there until I retrieve it. All I need is the folder with the evidence and a crooked judge to give me access to the necklace—an easy task for me."

He pushes the gun against my cheek. "If your instructions were to take the folder somewhere different, then this is your last chance to tell me. We are running out of time. Someone may have heard the gunshots."

"Don't do this. Let me go. You can put me on a plane back home. No one has to know."

"Cat I'd really like to do that, but it's no longer possible. You know too much."

I study his face wondering how I had only seen the alluring, gentle side of him. I had totally missed the anger and resentment racing in his eyes.

"Will you at least untie me?" I plead.

"You must think I'm a useless shit to ask that," he says with a grin. "After all, I taught you how to shoot."

"I can't tell you where the folder is. I gave it to Gino, and you've killed him."

With his left hand, he draws a knife out of his pocket. "Cat, you're lying. I am going to kill you. One bullet. You won't feel a thing. Or, slowly. It's your choice."

There's a long pause as he skims the knife across my forehead and the warmth of my own blood flows down my cheeks.

CAT & IL PADRONE

My thoughts blend with the bleakness of the landscape. This magnificent place is now desolate, colorless, and grim. Stella must have endured much the same at this man's hands. Now he will kill me. But I cannot die before he tells me about Stella. I must know. My dearest friend deserves a moment of reflection and gratitude before we are forever lost to each other.

"Carlo, please tell me how Stella died."

"Cat, you don't want to know."

"Even death row inmates get a last request. Tell me. Were you there?"

He shrugs and pulls the knife away from my forehead.

"Stella knew I was on to her so she was careful. Once she discovered the drug smuggling operation, she moved forward with her plans. Lorenzo was providing protection for her although she wasn't aware of that. We both had her followed—he for protection, me for knowledge of her whereabouts.

"The photo shoot was my idea. It was easy to legitimize. Her ego was her weakness. Same with Lorenzo. I arranged a fake drug smuggling operation and leaked it through Riccardo. I knew Lorenzo would pull all his people to the stakeout. Everything was planned for the same evening. Lorenzo had to get his people into position before dark, and Stella would not have done a photo shoot after dark. So it worked."

"You selected the magazine shoot to take place just above the marina where I found the necklace. Is that true?"

"Yes. But Riccardo botched it up. He missed the first shot and Stella was able to send you a message. His job was to find out where she stashed the information she'd been collecting on the drug smuggling operation. Riccardo really screwed up. Revealing who I was and taking her necklace were supposed to have been the last humiliation before he killed her. Stupid idiot took his eyes off her for a moment and she grabbed his gun. They struggled. He gained control of the gun but not his thoughts. He shot and killed her without retrieving the necklace or the information."

"So Stella died fighting for her life?"

"You could say that, but it's a stupid thing to say. Of course, she wasn't bound the way you are. I don't have to worry that you will grab my gun."

Fresh tears pour. Stella fought for her life. I'm grateful to know that small fact. She fought.

"Why did you want to teach me to shoot? You had to know someone would find out. What was the point?"

"There wasn't any. I let my guard down for a minute. Maybe I wanted a normal life with you by my side."

"I would never be by your side. You can do whatever you want. I won't tell you anything."

He smirks, "If you don't tell me where the folder is, your face will be carved into tiny squares. Your forehead first, then your cheeks. I will slit your lips. I will cut off your ears and cut out your eyes."

My knees give out. I crumble in a heap.

A voice rings out across the boulders. "Drop the gun."

"Well," Carlo says as he looks in the direction of the voice. "I'm not surprised to see you. But you might want to put your gun away unless you want a bullet in Cat's head."

Hearing Lorenzo's voice, I struggle to my feet, but Carlo shoves the gun hard against my head. He whispers, "If you move again, you're dead."

A small ray of hope lightens my heart as my eyes sweep across the large expanse of rocks to Lorenzo's face. He doesn't look at me.

He stares at Carlo and says, "You heard me. Drop the gun. You don't want to kill anyone else. You're already in for life."

"Shit, Lorenzo. If I'm in for life, then I have nothing to lose. Your friend here does."

He drags the gun across the cut on my forehead. A tiny cry escapes as the pain goes beyond bearable.

Lorenzo shifts forward.

"Carlo, you only have seconds before the sharpshooter with a bead on you pulls the trigger. Drop the gun now. You'll have your day in court. With your connections as *Il padrone*, you have a chance of staying alive, a chance you didn't give to Stella, Gino, or even Riccardo."

The gun stays firmly pressed against my head. Carlo's legs press into my side as he chuckles.

"Ha! Since when does the Guardia have sharpshooters? Maybe it's one of the lousy guards you posted for Stella and then Cat. With a few euros, they willingly allowed both Riccardo and me access to the villa. Ah, I see you didn't know that."

"The guards may have succumbed to the mafia, but Stella didn't. She found out about you, didn't she? She smelled you a mile away. She told me you were mafia. I have to say you put on a good act, worming your way back into all our lives. If you hadn't let a teenage grudge consume you with hatred, none of this would have happened."

I struggle to stand, but Carlo digs his fingers into my shoulder and jams the gun tighter against my head.

Lorenzo's voice drifts across the boulders, "Don't pull the trigger, Carlo. You might kill Cat, but you will still die. You can't shoot both of us. Shoot me first, and just maybe there'll be time for you to shoot her and get out of here. You have what you want. Stella is dead. I will be dead and so will Cat. There will be no witnesses. It's your only chance."

The wind picks up as night begins a gentle crawl across the horizon. My last sunset on this earth flares and flames with grandeur before sliding away into shades of crimson and violet. I wonder if in another dimension I will remember the beauty of this last moment—this time of light and shadow.

The cold metal presses deeper into my skull forcing me to lose balance. I sink against the rocks and see Gino's crumpled face. My tears flow for him, for Maria, for little Gino, and most of all for Stella.

As my eyes sweep over Gino's motionless body, his hand twitches. I watch in shock as he fumbles for the discarded gun. For a second our eyes lock. Gino raises the gun and fires. A rush of air oozes from me as Carlo's body slams across me and my head careens off the rocks. The sunset fades into darkness.

Voices tell me to hold on. The heavy weight is removed from my body. Gentle hands cut through the ropes that bind me. I'm lifted, moving without wings through the air. Blackness explodes with flashing lights. I wonder if this is the tunnel of death.

If I follow the lights, will they bring me out of the darkness? I close my eyes and wait for my name to be called.

CAT

CASTELLO DEL MARE, ITALY

There are still sixty-eight steps to count. I drag my luggage piece by piece to the gate. The envelope with all the information for the Andrea Bocelli concert goes in the side pocket of my carryon. Another question to consider: Will I go without Stella?

The final check of the villa has me in tears. I'm leaving Stella behind. No matter how hard I wish there was a different ending to this story, there isn't. My heart twists in agony.

Lorenzo will soon be here. We're stopping to see Antonio before he's carted off to Bari for sentencing. Lorenzo and I testified on Antonio's behalf. The sentence will be light—most likely community service and a restricted practice for a few years. He won't lose his license. I'm glad. Although misguided in his personal life, he's a good doctor and has promised to take care of little Gino.

It's an hour's drive to the Brindisi airport—an hour with too much to say to each other and not enough time—or maybe nothing to say and too much time.

Lorenzo stayed by my bedside at the hospital and wouldn't leave until the doctor assured him I was out of danger. Even then, he was reluctant to go. But the doctor said I needed total quiet. Plus, he had to wrap up the investigation.

When I was well enough, the surgeon told me that most of my

body parts were repairing nicely. He said the plastic surgeon had worked miracles on my forehead and in a few months I wouldn't notice the faint lines. Then he hesitated. When he looked at me, his eyes revealed the next news wouldn't be as uplifting.

The scans showed I'd suffered a major concussion when my head smashed into the rocks. He advised me to see a neurologist as soon as I returned home. He mentioned blackouts and gaps in memory, but said he expected I'd have a full recovery. He handed me a file filled with notes and images.

During my recovery, Lorenzo and I had talked briefly about Carlo and Stella and the events leading up to my kidnapping. Lorenzo had overheard the entire conversation between Carlo and me. He knew what I knew. It seemed heartless for either of us to discuss it. The wounds were too recent and too painful.

During my stay in the hospital, Lorenzo brought me up to date on finding a bullet the day I'd taken him to the cliffs. The lab identified it as coming from Riccardo's gun. That bit of information had changed Lorenzo's perspective on the investigation. He began to tail Riccardo who eventually led him to Carlo. Then he'd discovered that Carlo was tailing me. He apologized for not telling me. He said Carlo was so clever that he would have known if I was suspicious of him. Of course, I let Lorenzo know that I'd come close to being killed because I didn't have that bit of information.

Carlo, of course, was *il padrone.* Although Stella hadn't been able to identify him from the photographs she'd taken at the marina, Gino had immediately recognized the Panerai Luminor watch captured in one of the photos. It was peeking out from the sleeve of Carlo's black sweater. It had been a rough discovery for Gino. It had taken him a while to admit to himself that the only person he'd ever seen wearing that watch was Carlo. It had taken him even longer to tell Stella. If she had given the evidence to Lorenzo instead of waiting, she might still be alive. But, that's retrospective again. It buys nothing.

Gino's hardest role had been not telling me that I was the bait. Not something I'm willing to forgive or forget at the moment although Lorenzo assured me that Gino didn't have a choice. I was the only person who could lure Carlo out in the open. Lorenzo thought he'd be a step ahead to protect me. He didn't know two of the guards on the villa the night I was kidnapped were on Carlo's payroll. I'm not in a forgiving mood for him either.

During my hospital stay, Maria scurried back and forth between Gino and me. Gino had been shot in the leg and chest and his recuperation would take longer.

Riccardo, like Gino, was only wounded. While I'm so grateful for Gino's resurrection, I was horrified to learn that Riccardo was still alive. I wasn't told until the doctors thought I could handle the shock. My anxiety levels required a longer stay in the hospital. Now fear crowds every waking thought—fear of the future, fear of being hunted, fear of never knowing. Fear—buried deep inside. No amount of assurances from Lorenzo that Riccardo will be in prison for a long time alleviate the fear. Maybe time will, but I'm doubtful.

When I was released from the hospital, Lorenzo was there to drive me home. He told me that when Riccardo was searched, a newspaper clipping with the photo of Carlo as a waiter at one of our summer parties was still in his pocket.

As we sat by the fire, Lorenzo opened a file folder and showed me the old clipping. It was shocking to see Carlo so young and vulnerable with a sullen, hostile look on his face. Scorn for the summer kids and their parents was etched in his eyes. We had been oblivious to his pain. The photo clearly revealed he was invisible to us. Some small part of me understands his anger toward us, but no part of me can forgive him for Stella's murder. Over and over the tape plays: surely this could have been prevented—what if one of us had been kind to him. But there are no what ifs, no way to undo what had been done. Stella is dead. It weighs heavily on all of us.

Once I was back at the villa, Lorenzo left the station early every day. He cooked fabulous meals for me that I had little interest in eating. He made sure I took the regimen of meds for the required length of time to ensure no infections. A few weeks ago, I shooed him away. Although I insisted I was safe and didn't need it, Lorenzo ignored me and provided round-the-clock protection. He knows the SCU has long arms.

We haven't seen each other since the deposition and final inquest a week ago. The choice is mine. Before the deposition took place, Lorenzo asked me to stay in Castello. His halting words were heart-breaking when he asked me to take a chance with him. The memory of his hand touching my face still burns. I love him. I want to stay, but I can't. The wounds are too deep.

It surprised me I had the strength to turn away from his embrace. No matter his words, it will take time for both of us to heal. Stella still separates us. It's too soon to know if that will lessen, change, or perhaps one day disappear.

Watching the smile slide from his face when I told him I needed time and I wanted to go home was gut wrenching. He nodded in agreement, but the disbelief in his eyes when I said no is the first thing I see when I wake up. He struggled to find ways to make it work for us. He suggested we live part-time in Castello and part-time in South Carolina. Or if that didn't work, I could shuttle back and forth as often as I needed for my business. Still I said no and felt sadness oozing through my body as I questioned my sanity.

I pivot to the mirror and gather my red curls in a cluster. The soft yellow cotton dress cradles my body. The red starfish pendant lies in the hollow of my throat.

Gino was the great surprise and the hero in our story. Forgiveness for him is close. He stole the starfish and placed it in the safe deposit box. After he had worked the surveillance with Stella, she had entrusted him with the extra key. Once the necklace was safe, Gino created the elaborate scheme of leaving it with his brother. He had become increasingly suspicious of Carlo, but he didn't have any evidence that Carlo was part of the mafia. And, Gino, like the others, was not aware that they were part of a parade of people keeping tabs on me—Riccardo, Carlo, Lorenzo, and then Gino. But Gino had remained far enough in the background so the others hadn't noticed.

It was Gino who saved me simply because he decided to check on me one last time the night I was kidnapped. He had immediately noticed that the two policemen who normally patrolled the villa were not in position. He had wedged himself against a boulder across the street from the villa and decided to be my protector until he could find out what had happened to them. Before he could contact Lorenzo, he witnessed me being dragged from the house and placed in the trunk of a black Mercedes.

He raced back to his house, jumped in his car, and pursued the kidnappers to the Caves of Zinzulusa. He stayed far enough behind not to be noticed and waited until they left. He called Lorenzo not knowing if I would be dead or alive or even where they might have stashed me or my body. Unfortunately, while Gino was looking for me among the many caves in the area, Riccardo returned with Carlo. The rest of the drama played out.

I had hidden Stella's folder in the secret drawer in her desk. Although the house was searched, the information wasn't found. Even with Carlo dead, that folder gave the authorities enough evidence to round up the others.

But two loose ends flap incessantly like a diseased heart valve. Riccardo wasn't killed in the shootout. He was patched up and stood trial, but there was no solid proof that he killed Stella. No witnesses were found. The evidence was circumstantial: the photos Stella had taken of him on the dock, the wound in his arm when he broke into the restaurant and threatened me, Gino's statement that Riccardo had admitted killing Stella, and Lorenzo's statement about Riccardo's connection to Carlo. Circumstantial evidence wasn't enough to indict him for murder. Instead he was only indicted for drug trafficking and received a minimum sentence of ten years.

Now I live with the fact that one day he will hunt me down and seek revenge. This fear is so sharp that every breath I take hurts. Compound that with losing Stella, and I have become an open wound. I ooze with fear and sorrow. They are so intricately entwined that I cannot separate them.

When things settled, Lorenzo was called back to Rome for a promotion. He refused and asked to continue as the commissario in Puglia. The case was wrapped up. The authorities informed me I could leave. Actually, they strongly suggested I leave.

I clasp the starfish bracelet on my arm and run my fingers over the clusters of diamonds until they stop at the red starfish. Tears flood my eyes. Stella was always full of surprises. Besides naming me executor of her will and of little Gino's trust fund, she left me the necklace and the bracelet. I will keep the bracelet, but I'll offer the necklace to Antonio when I see him today. For now, the radiant heat of the red starfish burns in the hollow of my neck. Stella lives on in this sea creature. She, like them, understood her role was to remove the evil that brings harm to the world.

Stella's generosity didn't stop with the jewelry. Shortly before she was murdered, she had managed to buy *Casa di Fiori* from Carlo. Although she had warned me to leave Castello, she still left me her entire estate—including the house. Somehow she knew in the end I might want to stay. My initial reaction was shock and then concern that her ownership might be illegal and wouldn't stand up in court. But Carlo's property management business was one of the few things in his life that had been legitimate. Now I'm the owner of this beautiful villa on the Adriatic Sea.

It's too soon for me to make a decision about keeping the villa or selling it. Gino and Maria have agreed to stay on as caretakers. For now it will be a vacation rental until I can decide what to do. The income generated will be enough to take care of Gino and Maria and more than enough to continue little Gino's treatments.

Will I return? I don't know.

Before I answer that question, I'm going home to the South Carolina Lowcountry. I want soft summer days and the smell of jasmine as I walk in the waterfront park. I want to hear southern voices sweet as honey greeting me on every corner of my small town. I want time to grieve for Stella. The intensity of losing her is made more unbearable because Stella's body has never been found.

There is no final goodbye. The ambiguity of not knowing haunts me.

Swinging my purse over my shoulder, I take a last look around before locking the front door. I cross the terrace and gaze at the lone tree, gnarled and bent in supplication, yet not defeated. Its courage and enduring strength challenge me to move on, but Stella's death leaves me stranded on an island of doubt surrounded with ambiguous loss. What will my life be without her?

The wind stirs. A whisper of Stella lingers beside me. I close my eyes and grab her hand. Our childhood laughter is full of magical optimism and faith as hand in hand we splash into the sea free from fear.

Starfish

...while outside the starfish drift through the channel,
With smiles on their starry faces as they head out to deep water,
To the far and boundless sea.
Eleanor Lerman ~ 2005

Author Notes

Aldo Cipullo (1942-1984) was a brilliant Italian jewelry designer. What's included in the book about him is true except he didn't design the bracelet or necklace for Stella. (https://www.1stdibs.com/introspective-magazine/aldo-cipullo/)

Chocolates by Adam Turoni in Savannah/Charleston is my favorite chocolate shop. The owner is one of only ten certified chocolatiers in North America. His creations are not only melt-in-your-mouth delicious but they are beautiful works of art. (Broughton Street and Bull Street in Savannah, GA and King Street in Charleston, SC). http://www.chocolatat.com

Amedei is an artisan chocolate manufacturing company located in the Tuscany region of Italy. It's considered to be one of the finest chocolate producers in the world. https://us.amedei.it/en/

Poetry: There are seven stanzas of Starfish Ballet by Akira Chinen (https://hellopoetry.com/poem/1891383/starfish-ballet/). There are seven chapters about Stella, each start with one of the beautiful stanzas from the poem. This poem inspired me to include stories of the tiny but magnificent starfish/sea star/Asteroidea (www.blueoceansociety.org and www.sciencelearn.org).

Also the full Starfish poem by Eleanor Lerman can be found at (https://poets.org/poem/starfish). Please read the entire poem as it is a life's story. I am grateful for Akira and Eleanor's permission to use these beautiful poems.

Gianluca Proietto, Hair Artist and owner of Parrucchiere Urban CDB Salon, Via Sapri, 26, Marina di Ragusa, Sicily. Gianluca designed my hairstyle in the cover photos for both *Solo in Salento: A Memoir* and *The Red Starfish.* If you're ever in Marina di Ragusa (Sicily). Here's what he has to say, "True luxury is a hairdresser who imagines more for you and knows how to express your uniqueness with tailor-made services! You choose us, we do the rest." https://www.capellimaniagianluca.com

Place: When I was considering location for The Red Starfish, I found that a mixture of places gathered in my mind—a villa in one town, a church in another, a fabulous food experience in another. Out of these, the fictitious town of *Castello del Mare* was born. All parts of it reside in the region of Puglia in the heel of the Italian boot. Place is and will always be a character in my writing. At a very early age, I recognized that I needed a place. Sometimes the place is physical, other times it's mental. Sometimes it's a combination. My heart and mind places are Italy and Beaufort, South Carolina. While a place isn't always perfect, it's always magical if you believe.

As a writer, I'm allowed free rein to intersperse my work with subtopics. In *Solo in Salento*, I wrote about trash and recycling and the impact that occurs when we do not take care of our beautiful but suffering planet.

In the *Red Starfish* the symbolism lies with the tiny starfish who maintain the balance of the ecosystem in the shallow part of the ocean. We, the citizens of the earth, have trashed the ocean with plastic, waste, overfishing, introducing invasive species, and over polluting overlaid with global warming. If each of us is mindful and sorts our trash and places it in proper containers, we do our part in creating a better world for future generations.

Acknowledgments

Dear Readers:

Writing is both a solitary and a community endeavor. The hours spent in solitude embellish with great joy the time spent in community. It is in community that my writing becomes a book. The people I honor in these acknowledgements are those who gave up their personal time and energy to encourage, support, and give validity to my stories.

I'm grateful to Stephanie Larkin (Publisher of Red Penguin Books) who found my stories worthy of publishing and whose knowledge, guidance and friendship is making this writing journey a grand adventure.

Sea Island Spirit Writers: Katherine Brown, June Labyzon, Susan Madison, Ginny Hall-Apicella, Ellen Kelley, and Karen Warner Schueler. These amazing women were the alpha readers for *The Red Starfish*. They listened to the first of many extremely raw drafts and gently critiqued when I would go astray with information dumps and passive voice. My debut memoir *Solo in Salento* reflects their love as does this novel, and I hope many more to come.

My dear friend Gail Greene who lived through every draft of my first book *Solo in Salento: A Memoir*. She has done the same for *The Red Starfish*. In spite of this she still swears she will continue to read every word of all the drafts for my future books. She has never wavered in her belief that I have stories to tell. She corrects my grammar, my dangling participles, and run-on sentences and tells me she loves the characters as they bloom and develop over numerous rewrites. She has read every single revision for both books. Her friendship is a joy and her objective eye reminds me that I have a tendency to overwrite. She is a light that shines in the sometimes dark solitude of writing.

Alexis Bomar is a new beta reader for *The Red Starfish*. Her mind is like a steel trap, grabbing hold of the story immediately. She questioned my characters and pushed me to make them stronger, better, or worse than they were as the story moved from inception to the final manuscript. The reason there is both a red starfish necklace and bracelet is Lex's doing. She said to me, "You can't give a seventeen-year-old an expensive necklace as a pre-engagement gift." Out of that comment came an authentic Italian jewelry designer as well as a more suitable bracelet for the seventeen-year-old Stella and then the grand necklace for a wedding gift. Thank you, Lex, for your scrutiny, your solid suggestions, and your positive energy.

Gloria Mattioni, a new Italian friend and author, read the completed manuscript and corrected my Italian words and provided me with an Italian point of view. You don't want to miss her book *California Sister*.

Jeff Baker who reviewed my first draft through the lens of a camera. His suggestions as a screenplay writer give credence to the scenes the characters live and play in. He pointed out ways to smooth transitions from one stage setting to the next.

Marly Rusoff gave me the gift of reading my story when it was in its final stage. With her years in the literary world she offered a suggestion that changed the course of the story. She said that the main focus was not just about the mysterious disappearance and death of one of the characters. It was also about the friendship of two women and how they maneuvered and triumphed throughout the changes and disruptions of their relationship. Marly and I spoke of ambiguous loss, the pain of not knowing, the sorrow of separation, and the grief that treads on our pathways. We also spoke of enduring friendships that grace us with joy and light throughout our lives.

The Pat Conroy Literary Center is a special place of learning, literacy, support, and great love. In this place abide many people including the executive director, Jonathan Haupt, board members, volunteers and docents. They all remind me that in spite of the many adversities everyone has faced in the past few years, we are still a community. We still share the love and passion that Pat Conroy instilled in all of us through his words.

In *My Reading Life*, Pat writes, "Good writing is the hardest form of thinking. It involves the agony of turning profoundly difficult thoughts into lucid form, then forcing them into the tight-fitting uniform of language, making them visible and clear. If the writing is good, then the result seems effortless and inevitable. But when you want to say something life-changing or ineffable in a single sentence, you face both the limitations of the sentence itself and the extent of your own talent."

Amen is all I can say. Pat lives on through the Literary Center named in his memory and through the love we share and the community we have built to carry on his legacy of GREAT LOVE!

At the end of the rainbow is always my beloved husband, Ray—my warrior, my personal shopper and chef, the photographer who managed in spite of me to take cover photos, my forever friend and companion, the one person who has given me unconditional love for forty years. I am forever grateful.

Wishing readers everywhere Great Joy!

Donna Keel Armer

Beaufort, South Carolina

www.donnaarmer.com

About the Author

Donna Keel Armer is the author of *Solo in Salento: A Memoir* which has been translated into Italian as *Un'americana in Salento.* She recently completed a book tour of Southern Italy. She's a photojournalist and has published magazine and anthology articles with accompanying photographs on travel, food and wine, home and garden and various other topics. When she's on the road, she writes a private travelogue. Contact her at donnakeelarmer@gmail.com to be added to the list. She graduated with honors from Mississippi University for Women with a double major in psychology and social sciences and graduate studies in theology. Her first job during high school was a gofer for a furniture company and her last position before turning to writing was president of the hospitality business owned by Donna and her husband Ray. She's a former board member of Friends of the Library, a member of Sea Island Spirit Writers, and a docent at the Pat Conroy Literary Center. Donna and Ray split their time between their forever home in the South Carolina Lowcountry and their beloved Italy. Follow Donna on https://www.facebook.com/donna.k.armer/ or www.donnaarmer.com.

Printed in the USA
CPSIA information can be obtained
at www.ICGtesting.com
LVHW050740270324
775525LV00001B/56

9 781637 774632